CAIRO

LOUIS ARMAND

☾ ☐ ☉ ✢ ≋

© Louis Armand, 2014

ISBN 978-0-9571213-7-9

Equus Press
Birkbeck College (William Rowe)
43 Gordon Square, London, WC1 H0PD, United Kingdom

Cover, typeset & design by lazarus
Printed in the Czech Republic by PB Tisk

Parts of this book first appeared in *Golden Handcuffs Review*, *nthposition*, *Numéro Cinq*

Set in Joanna, composed by Eric Gill in 1930, with headings in Futura, composed in 1927 by Paul Renner

For he shall live whose name is named.
— **Book of the Dead**

CAIRO

☾ DOME CITY

Everything about it seems fake and yet too-real. More real than any place on Earth.

Standing on a bridge, traffic streaming from the black open-cut of the City, smog radium-tinted. The tower lights fuse in the river's oxidised sheen, slithering down into it beneath a strangely lit sub-surface. The vertigo of their reflection, descending and forever descending, like the image of a city hung upside-down from a night sky carved out of huge geodesics. Luminous. City of God.

The last thing he can remember: lying on a cold slab like the ones in morgues. A ceiling fan slowly turning. Maybe he was dead. That seemed real, too. But what's real mean anymore?

There's a dry, sour taste in his mouth. He tries to spit, but nothing comes out. A pounding in his head that won't go away. And a smell. Ozone. Sulphur. Combustion. Decay. It's the smell that forces him back from the edge, kicks him awake. He struggles with the desire to slip back into the dead zone, lost inside a thought that's on the verge of being erased. Someone else's thought. Then an image in his head, like déjà vu. *I've been here before.* Not knowing how he got there or who he is, but still familiar with the routine. *Exactly this place, at exactly this time.* He can see the words floating behind his eyes, blinking out of the darkness. Time. Place. So abstract, remote. As if they didn't concern him at all. Just bits of smoke and haze circulating behind a mirror.

This's how it seems, that he's woken up inside someone else's body. In a wrong set of coordinates. Like the coordinates of dreams. Except this's nothing like a dream.

Out across the vista, a constellation of taillights drifts through smog and drizzle. Behind it, the City shudders and groans. He can feel the dead weight in his arms, inching its way up. Behind him, someone grunts. The word *move* through clenched teeth. He's gripping the steel railing so hard his knuckles look like they're about to break the skin. That voice again. Familiar. He strains, willing his hands to open. One tendon, one muscle at a time. It seems to take forever.

Then it stops. Something inside unfreezes and the programme takes over. Somewhere actions have been graphed, positions triangulated, cross-sections mapped out against a lower brain immediacy. His hands come free, lashing the air. It's then he sees they're covered in blood. Blood down the front of his shirt too. He doesn't know where it came from. No-one's there. Then the voice again, repeating. *No time.* Coming from behind him whichever way he looks. He stares at the blood on his hands and it starts to come apart then shudder back into focus. Degauss. Like staring at a computer screen with an error in the system. Perhaps he's the error. The system already scanning him out, quarantined in a sub-programme...

No. Time.

He knows he's got to get out of there before it's too late. But too late for what? The programme, call it instinct, guides him. His body feels wrong. He has to think about each of his actions. To consciously put one foot in front of the other. Keep balance. Get a bearing.

Something stirs behind his left eye. A flicker of green numerics. Data. Actions become automatic now. The transition is so swift it leaves him dazed. *No time. No questions.* He moves, faster now, heading east along the Bridge. The drizzle ebbs and flows, making everything gleam. The blood on his shirt gleams too. He tries to focus on the lights up ahead. Already they're receding. In his mind he's running, willing himself to reach them. His thoughts race, too. Indistinct. Half-formed. His body nothing but a blur.

☐ FINE ART

It began as a faint glint on the horizon, coming in low over the estuary. From the Royal Observatory at Greenwich, it appeared as a glimmering speck in the sky above the Thames Barrier. From Canary Warf, it appeared as a black spot transiting the sun. From Tower Bridge, it looked like what it was, a low-flying aircraft bearing straight for central London. Joblard, idling at a red light, watched the plane's shape enlarge on a twenty-foot digital billboard stuck up on the Holborn Viaduct by a genius for creating traffic hazards. Banking out of pixellated haze, the plane swooped down over a redbrick pavilion, Union Jack bunting aflutter. The pavilion clock registering five minutes past ten.

Joblard squinted at the shape on the billboard, trying to make it out. Then he did. A Messerschmitt 109. Battle of Britain vintage. Flames spitting from wing-mounted cannons as it proceeded to strafe the length of a cricket pitch. Men in white flannels diving left and right. It pulled up vertical just short of the sight screen to loop around for a second approach. While the fielding side ran for cover, a lone batsman stood his ground, staring the Jerry pilot dead in the eye. Close-up on the pilot raising a gloved middle finger in salute as the plane steered back into the sun and the billboard filled with Lufthansa blue and white. *We're back! With more direct flights between London and Berlin than ever before!*

The light turned green and Joblard let out the clutch of his BSA Gold Star, swinging left off Farringdon Road between the old *Daily Worker* warehouse and a brutalist semi-highrise courtesy of the 1940 urban renewal project. By the time he made Gray's Inn he'd scoped a dozen CCTV cameras at least. Like being in the movies. Any second now a giant clapper-board would drop out of the sky and a loudhailer would shout cut! Or some dick in a balaclava from

Counter Terrorism would pop up from under a drain cover, in the event you were antisocial enough to run a light with intent. Shit. More traffic. Even on a bike, you'd get wherever you were going faster in Bombay. Only he wasn't in fucking Bombay, was he.

In addition to which, he was now officially late. For a meeting with one of his regular employers. A geezer known in the business as the Undertaker. The Undertaker wasn't an undertaker at all, but a purveyor of what a certain breed of connoisseur would, if pressed on the point, be at pains to insist was *fine art*. The sort of fine art you put a quid into a coinslot to watch in one of those last-resort Soho cubicle-joints with names like *Vaseline Virgins*, *Hello Dolly Buster!*, *XXX-Men*, *Halal Shlake* or *Scary Tentacles*. The RSPCA probably had a file on the man. His filmography was more outré than avant-garde. Regular pornographers wouldn't touch the stuff with a barf bag. But lateness was no more excusable for that.

As far as H.M. Revenue and Customs where concerned, the Undertaker's real name was Bludhorn. It suited him. At least it suited his oxblood brogues. What he lacked in respectability he made up for in dress sense. A columnist for the *Daily Mirror* once described him as an ex-Hackney showboat who in another life might've been Gilbert and George, if he'd been twins. Those prats.

They were meeting because Joblard was in the retail distribution business. Which meant, putting the frighters on anyone who got in the way of cash-flow. Helping them see the light, in a manner of speaking. Though truth be told, Joblard wouldn't've hurt a fly, unless the fly made it strictly unavoidable. Still, you'd never be too sure.

In headier days, before moving up in the world, Joblard had earned his moniker as a stand-up heavyweight who could take a beating and know when to lie down. He notched up the one KO of his short career without landing a single punch. His opponent, a one-time title prospect, having collapsed from exhaustion in the sixth round, a straight points winner if he'd kept his legs. The scorecard alone was a collector's item.

Joblard now supplemented his welfare cheque trawling the docklands for little fish who'd got themselves stuck out of water. The reason he was late this morning. A small matter of tracking down a missing envelope with certain photographs in it, like he was the Royal fucking Mail. Some hopping mad Greenwich-type, going by the name of Johnny Fluoride, having neglected to make delivery, babbling about the end of the world. Adenoids of doom and all that. Or was it *asteroids*? Fire in the sky. Sign of the devil. Three-fifths through his second bottle of Dewers for the morning. No trouble recovering the merchandise. What comes of reading too many books, as his old mum would've said.

⊙ SECTION 400

Old Glory grunted as Lawson swung out of the back Mission road and headed west along the test site perimeter, shortwave blaring. Two or three white-washed galvanised iron roofs started out of the mulga. The remains of the old railhead, where Afghan camel-trains had once set out across a desert half a continent wide. A hundred and fifty years ago this was the last outpost on the route from civilisation into the great silence. The Nullarbor. The unknown. The Never-Never. It still was. From here, the Indian-Pacific began the longest stretch of straight rail on the planet. Nothing out there but flat, waterless expanse. What once was an ancient seabed. Meteorite country.

The newscast crackled over the radio. A storm-front heading north-east from the Bight. Wind warning. Stock market collapse in New York. Boat people. The Yunapingu Man in Beijing. Dix had said it was unnatural, how in Australia there'd never been an armed rebellion by the colonised against the colonisers. *Intifada*. Lawson tried to explain. About Jandamarra and Pemulwuy. About the smallpox blankets. The flour laced with strychnine. The alcohol. The massacres and concentration camps. The stolen generations. Dix registered her disillusionment.

"Times change. History alone," he'd said, "can't be blamed."

Maybe, she thought. First Survival, then Restitution. And then – the words people were using more and more – *autonomous coexistence*. It was for this the Yunapingu Man had gone to Beijing. To seek intercession, the indulgence of the formerly dispossessed and now powerful. To assert ancient tribal claims against the white invader. Dix shook his head. The Chinese, he'd said, weren't sentimentalists, they were only in it for the uranium. But no-one in their right mind would let the tribes own the mining leases outright. It'd be too much of a threat to the status quo. She tried to picture it. Rogue Abos with dirty nukes.

The news petered out. Lawson spun the dial, switched over to FM. A music station from somewhere down south. Or anywhere. Radio wave deflection from the ionosphere, like a desert mirage. She recognised the song. Billy Thorpe and the Aztecs, *Children of the Sun*. Words beamed back from earliest childhood, where memories began. A faded green two-wheel caravan beside a concrete blockhouse. A woman, her mum, squeezed behind chipped zinc-top. Dead eyed. Portable AWA wireless on the windowsill. Rows of empty longnecks. The music drifting in and out. A fly, trapped behind the flywire, buzzing.

But that was the whole memory. Like the words of the song. *A voice from the sky, past the limits of…*

It was just after eleven when Lawson pulled into the checkpoint to Section 400. Maralinga. A dead cockatoo lay on one side of the gate, shredded with birdshot. The radio boomed. *Through the doors — to a world — of another time…* She dialled down the volume. Outside, a faded metal sign creaked in the late morning heat.

DANGER
RADIOACTIVE MATERIAL BURIED
UNAUTHORISED ENTRY PROHIBITED
KEEP OUT

A guard approached and she flashed the security pass Dix had somehow arranged for her, delivered *poste restante*, Broken Hill. The guard waved her through to the next checkpoint. After that, the road wound across to the small township which had grown up alongside the decontamination project. Like the old soap ads. *Cleanliness and godliness*. White man's burden.

15

+ DEGREES OF ZERO

Osborne stared at the morning's headline blazoned in two-inch serif across the front page of The New York Times. METEOR STRIKES GROUND ZERO. A Dominican waitress came and refilled his coffee. Behind the counter, Little Joe was raving to anyone who'd listen about the Yankees Stadium being torn down.

"I ask you," he gesticulated wildly, "what's the world coming to?"

At the back of the diner, some clown in a suit was complaining into a cell phone, making a regular pain-in-the-ass of himself. Osborne folded the paper and tried to concentrate on the funnies. But they weren't, so he tossed it aside. Little Joe called over.

"Hey, you hear the news?"

"What news?"

Through the diner's half-fogged windows, Osborne made out an old negro sitting on a bench across the street. Dirty red duffel coat. Beside him on the bench, a neatly arranged pile of snowballs in the shape of a pyramid, and a sign: KING CHEPHREN'S BLIZZARD BALL SALE. A group of kids in blue school uniforms waiting for a bus. Early morning traffic. People on sidewalks, minding their business, going places.

"There's some genuinely weird shit happening out there, hombre."

"You don't say."

"Check this out. Last night, some guy on a Greyhound bus, in the middle of Sas-katch-ewan, gets his head cut off by this freak who it-just-so-happens is sitting next to him. I mean, this freak cuts the guy's head off with a steak knife. Comprendes? The other passajeros, they don't even figure what's going on, when the freak starts eating the guy. Right there in front of whoever. Just like that."

"They have buses in Saskatchewan?"

"I'm telling you. *Mucho* – weird – shit."

Outside a prowl car drifted across the intersection and pulled up in front of King Chephren's bench. NYPD 34th Precinct. Tinted windows. COURTESY, PROFESSIONALISM, RESPECT. Three tables up, the waitress was giving the clown in the suit the push-off. Osborne glanced back across the counter.

"Joey, you know anything about meteors?"

"Meteor?" Little Joe leant forward, squinting, elbows on the zinc-top. "You mean like stuff falling out of the sky makes pretty pictures at night?"

"Yeah, that's what I mean."

"*Amigo*. Now you mention it. There was a big piece of *something* landed in the downtown this a.m. Now that's some coincidence, hey? You read about it in your paper there. Lots of talk. Sometimes this, sometimes that. How it always is. Aliens. Terrorists. Who the fuck knows? Pardon my Esperanto. You ask me, it's all that global warming they talk about on CNN too much. How the dinosaurs copped out. *Extinguido*."

"Anyone been letting slip about dinosaurs, Joey?"

"As my Jewish customers say, *Mark my words*." Little Joe straightened up, draping a dishtowel across one shoulder. "We don't find a ticket outta here soon, we'll end up the same way."

He stood there with an almost thoughtful expression on his face, lost for a moment in other-worldly visions, then pointed at Osborne's coffee.

"Need me to get you anything with that? Eggs? Bacon? Piña Colada?"

Osborne shook his head and looked back across the street. The patrol car was gone and so was King Chephren. Someone had knocked the old man's sign over. The school kids were already pilfering the snowballs, chasing one another around in circles, the smallest wearing a too-long scarf that dragged on the sidewalk.

Osborne eyed the traffic as it passed close by. The kid looked like he'd wind up under the wheels of a delivery truck just about any second now. There were sounds of a scuffle from the back of the diner. Osborne looked away from the window just as the Dominican waitress hustled the suit out the door. He thought: *Accidents don't just happen. Something makes them happen.*

It was his cue to check the clock behind Little Joe's head, dimly aware of the need to be somewhere. He fished a crumpled piece of paper from his inside coat pocket: date / time / address, scrawled in thin blue ink. *Doctor D. Cedar St. 10:00. D-for-Doom.*

"Appointment with the devil," he muttered.

Little Joe, index finger of his right hand poised just beneath his left nostril, regarded Osborne with a mix of anticipation and uncertainty, unsure if the remark was perhaps meant for him. He was about to complete his gesture when the lights over the counter flickered and died. It was the third blackout since Osborne had come in.

"You should get someone to fix that," said Osborne unsmilingly, glancing up at the dead fixture.

Little Joe picked at the inside of his nostril. Sighed. Inspected the end of his finger.

"They'd need to fix this whole fucked-up nation first."

"Well," Osborne yawned, getting up from his stool. "You know what the man says." He dropped a handful of change on the counter.

"Not me, *padrón*," Little Joe said, wiping his finger across his apron front. "What he says, *el hombre?*"

"He says, electricity ain't just electricity." Osborne winked. "It's *information.*"

The Dominican waitress stalked back past with a breakfast special on a tray, rolling her eyes.

"You wanna tell me what that's supposed to mean?"

Osborne picked up his copy of the *Times* and thrust it in a coat pocket on his way to the door: "Beats the hell out of me." Then: "Twenty bucks says Pittsburgh take the series."

"Pittsburgh are *maricones*. Pinstripes, five-zero! You don't believe me? Pinstripes or nothin'!"

Little Joe stared after Osborne's departing figure as it slipped out the door. The waitress was standing beside him with a tray of dirty plates, clicking her tongue. Little Joe turned to her.

"*Información*. You think I don't know what the guy's talking about?"

"I think you both *loco*," said the waitress, disappearing into the kitchen.

So this, Shinwah thought, *is what the future used to be?*

The idea came at random. She was staring into a wall of polished glass in which her reflection spiralled off into a fractalised distance. Black silicon veneer, air-conditioned, seamless. Piped music hovered in the background above the sound of running water. It vibed retro. Stanley Kubrick, circa 2001. It could've been anywhere. Sydney, Cairo, New York. Maybe it was just that progress was supposed to look the same from wherever you happened to be standing. Like the universe. Or evolution. All those enzymes and molecules in the struggle of the fittest, to end up in the here and now, staring through your reflection in a penthouse suite at the Millennium Plaza Hotel. *Praha-haha*. Prague. The plughole of Europe.

Her job sucked. There'd been a time when she hadn't been as jaded as all that. The first time maybe. Jacking-up in a Beijing lab after the pre-flight. The pre-flight was hell. DNA transfused. Nerve-job. The real business was all rush, a hit straight to the cortex, teeth singing. Better than anything she'd ever known before or since. The comedown only set in later, like jetlag. Lost in the time-shifts, idiolects, stacked mindsets. You tracked the coordinates at high speed. Synapse-to-synapse. Zeroed the target. Went in for the kill watching your back, in a manner of speaking. Then you did it again. And maybe the next time the opposition got in ahead of you, phase-shifted to the next-plus-one degree – snuffed you without you ever knowing: dead brain-meat for the resurrection men.

Placing an immaculately lacquered fingernail beneath her right nostril, Shinwah inhaled long and hard. Then repeated with the left. She felt the ice cut into the septum and seer the back of her throat in delayed action. The chemical rush came on fast. She swore under her breath. *Wô cào. Ho-ly fuck*. Old habits dying slow. Then slumped forward, face against the glass, eyes glazing over. A small jeweller's case, cross-hatched with lines of ice, lay open on the bathroom vanity. White lines repeating in parallel like a geometric progression, right down into lower brain immediacy. Synapse eugenics.

It passed. Shinwah straightened up and stared into the kaleidoscope of her reflection. Everything was sudden deep focus, white light turning hard-edged. She hit four more lines, plateaud, went deeper. She wiped the residue from the case, licked the tip of her finger, teeth barred in an exaggerated grimace. Like someone in pain. The face in the mirror grimaced back at her. Eurasian, porcelain-smooth, painted eyes and lips. An immaculate horror above a latex bodice and crinoline.

"Why do you keep doing this to yourself?" she mouthed.

The mirror said nothing in reply. Only the sound of the tap dripping straight into the plughole. A far-away plopping sound. Very faint. Very far away.

☾ AL-QUAHIRAH

30°1'44.31"N
31°13'51.73"E

The programme points him south-east. Flicker of green numerics. -00:01. Only a moment ago he was on the Bridge, struggling to stay awake. He can't tell how much distance he's covered, but already the City's begun to feel less alien. Crossing back into zones of familiarity. Retracing. *Al-Quahirah.* The voice is in him now. Distances diminishing.

He stays close to the walls. A stray cat darts from an alley, vanishes into the black-out. The place seems abandoned. He stops, listens. From a window he can hear the faint crackle of a radio set to no frequency. He peers in. On the far side of a room, the shape of a man sitting in an alcove smoking a *ghoza.* Faint ember.

He turns into the alley the cat emerged from. There's a rusty water pump. He washes his hands, his face, peels away his shirt. The whiteness of his bare torso has a strange presence in the dark. A foreign body. He wonders vaguely if the body belongs to him, or if he belongs to it. The water stings. *Don't drink it.* It's just the heat, he thinks. *You're too hot. The water's cold.* Ice cold. He can feel the air with his skin, bristling with static. *Keep moving.*

At some point he enters a half-demolished house. There's an unhealthy smell. He searches the rubble, finds a dirty *jilabîya,* puts it on. Finds the former inhabitants lined up in a back room, dead. Shot through the neck. A slogan painted on the wall. *Death to Rats.* He retreats, back onto the street. Hurrying. Breathing hard.

-00:09. A dull glow reflects from the huge ziggurats of scrap running sheer down into the canal. It looks like it must've been a fork of the river once, now cauterised by refuse and landfill. On the far side, an unending stream of traffic surges out of the sprawl on a flyover heading north.

Without being able to tell which direction it's coming from, he can hear the distant droning of heavy machinery. Somewhere, behind the landfill, are the quarried ruins of a place with no name. Co-ordinate zero.

The programme steers him towards it, down across the landfill. A night-train flashes its morse against the city's blacked-out undercarriage, coming from the Maydan, rising over the canal before banking out of sight. High above, he can sense it, the Dome, sending down a constant drizzle. Here and there a spotlight gropes into the darkness enclosing the city's gloom, an artificial night blanking-out the Earth-bound constellations.

Bludhorn was already waiting at the Red Lion caff, parked by the street window with a coffee, coke, and half-chewed pie crust that constituted his daily breakfast. A ratty *News of the World* lay folded to one side.

Joblard swung the BSA up onto the pavement and strode in, helmet dangling from right hand like a wrecking ball. Seven-foot-five in his boots with shaved head, Joblard was as low-key as it was possible for a giant on a vintage bike to be. The waitress ogled him from safely behind the counter. From its size alone, one could be forgiven for mistaking the helmet for a psychic surge-protector. The sheer mass of the cranium. Light winking across polished geodesics. One thought might set in train whole megatonnages of synapse impaction. Perhaps it was the eyes. Like peering unguarded into an atomic core. Blackholes waiting to detonate. Joblard attempted his nicest smile and the waitress shivered.

As usual, Bludhorn was dressed in a grey store-bought polyester suit and tie, with a trilby in silver-and-duck-egg-blue hound's-tooth, brim tipped halfway down his face. The nine-iron he used as a walking cane was propped under folded hands which in turn propped up the man's overbite. The effect was subtle. Few observers would've realised Bludhorn at that moment was deep in REM sleep, among God-only-knew what vistas of stunted odalisques. He'd picked up the nine-iron at auction. It'd once belonged to Jack Nicklaus, before the incident with the plane. In Bludhorn's opinion, Nicklaus had only gotten better – it was the future of the game, they should've made cutting one of your arms off a prerequisite.

Joblard squeezed himself in across the table and ordered coffee, black, from the bug-eyed waitress. The strain on the metal chair was audible. He set his helmet on the table and fingered the menu unenthusiastically. Eggs, mixed grill, bangers and mash, mushy peas. Cholesterol insanity. As his doctor never tired of informing, the stuff'd kill him in five minutes if he so much as sniffed at it. Not an enviable state of affairs in the land of meat-and-three-veg. Something about enzymes, growth hormones. He'd been a giant from day one. Gave his poor old mum no end of pains in the arse birthing him, and she only five foot four. What the doctors called a *detour of regression*, whatever that meant. He'd never clapped eyes on the man responsible, supposedly a secondhand book-hoker from Camberwell who'd made a late discovery of William Blake and, in consequence, elected mid-life to walk the land bollock-naked. Currently residing at Her Majesty's pleasure and taxpayers' expense somewhere in the far wastes north of Hadrian's Wall.

In addition to being only a moderate exploiter of the unemployed classes, Joblard still wasn't sure it was a blessing or not that his East End slumlord was a self-described militant vegan. The rental contract made certain dietary stipulations as a precondition. He supposed it was in the order of things that only a militant vegan would operate in a former meatpacking factory – the original home, if Bludhorn was to be believed, of the UK snuff film industry. The Fridge, as the inhabitants fondly called it, was a bottle's-throw from Limehouse Station, in the shadow of the Docklands Light Rail. The place was lousy with RSA dropouts, meth addicts, religious diet freaks, and a cook from a Rajasthani takeaway who performed dark magic with non-animal proteins augmented with an industrial supply of creatine.

Joblard moved among the other Fridge inhabitants like a hulking ship amongst flotsam. The twittering blonde who sometimes shared his basement pad was so thin he was afraid one day he'd snap her in half by accident. Bird Girl. She rode on the BSA between him and the tank, so she wouldn't just blow away – she seemed so small and light. *As a feather*, he thought. The two of them in tandem made for a memorable sight. But she'd been away again the last few weeks. He never knew where she got to, when she'd be back. As long as she kept her veins clean, he didn't ask and she didn't tell.

The only other patron at the Red Lion caff was busy watching the boxing replay on a tele bolted to the wall over the toilet door. Joblard gave the Undertaker a light poke in the shoulder. An eyelid twitched. A slit of eye-white. The pupils rolled into view. Bludhorn blinked, glanced down into the profound depths of his empty coffee cup, signalled the waitress for a refill, then looked up into Joblard's face.

"Now where were we?"

Joblard shrugged, pushed a manila envelope with the offending photographs across the table. Bludhorn transferring said envelope into the fold of the ratty News of the World.

"Good boy."

The waitress brought the coffee. Wiped up. Bludhorn spilled sugar from the dispenser straight into his cup. Stirred.

"You ever been inside the Freemason's Hall on Great Queen's Street?"

Joblard fingered his cup awkwardly.

"Nah. Someone over there you want me to visit?"

"I'd like us to do some scenes on the premises but, um, permission might be an issue, if you catch my drift."

"Freemasons?"

"We'll head on over tomorrow and see what can be done. Just us and a couple of the girls. In and out, no-one the wiser. I'll handle the camera, you look after any nosey types."

"Asking for trouble, aren't we?"

"Wait till you see it. Whoever designed the place took a serious dose. Every square inch. Pentagrams. Stars of David. Suns and moons. Solomon's temple. Dragons and knights and all-seeing eyes. Walls, floors, ceilings. By a funny little coincidence, it backs right onto the Twilight Club. Off Kingsway. Tarts in their birthday suits? Sort of place you're liable to run into that idiot son of the Phoney Pharaoh."

"Can't say I know it."

"An Armenian I made the acquaintance of in Leicester Square the other week took me on a guided tour. Of the Temple, I mean. Had one of them pinky rings and all. Turned out he was a real fanatic. *You on the square, Brother?* Must've given him the right impression, eh? Told him we were making a documentary. Sympathetic to the cause."

"Right."

"It's a winner, my son. We could make a whole series out of it. *Ladies of the Illuminati.* What d'you reckon? I've got another idea, too. Afterwards, we scoot up the street to the Soane. As in John Soane. Sir John to you. Bet you haven't heard of him, eh? Turned his gaff into a museum. He was a Mason, too, come to think. Architect of the highest order. Joint looks like an orgy in Milo's workshop. Bits of amputated statuary lying around all over the place. The odd Hogarth to set it off with the appropriate moral tone. A sepulchre even, down in the basement, with an Egyptian sarcophagus. Genuine article. Spiral stairway right up the middle like you wouldn't believe. Picture it: nice long tracking shot from underneath, Siamese twins coming down the stairs in a double pair of stilettos, leaving the rest to the imagination. Know what I mean? Splice in a bit of midget lesbo action with the funhouse mirrors. Mirrors everywhere in there, no end of 'em. Get one of the tarts to suck off an Elgin marble. Give it some class. Be an easy enough job for you, I'd've thought."

"How d'you know I'm not one of them?"

"Give over. I was thinking maybe you could join in the action yourself, later on. We'd powder you up like one of them Greek knobs, with a whopping great trident or whatever, and a couple of mermaids. How's that tickle your fancy?"

"Stuff's for the birds, mate."

"Listen, let me tell you something." Bludhorn flicked at the crumbs on the newspaper and poked his finger with a sudden emphaticness at something Joblard wasn't able to read. "In all seriousness."

Joblard couldn't decide whether to take his coffee with regular sugar or the darker stuff and so settled on neither. Skimmed off the foam and sipped at it, the cup somehow diminutive in his hand, little finger upraised like a swish at a cocktail bar.

"You want to see some real action? Last night, some coked-up hedge fund operator in Wapping blows this kid's head off with a twelve-gauge before sodomising the corpse on an exercise bench. Then has a go at blowing his own head off, but only manages half of it. One eye sticking out of his forehead like a jacked-off Cyclops. Now why couldn't I have thought of that?"

⊙ THUNDER FIELD

30°9'31.50"S
131°36'40.07"E

In the '50s, the British army turned Maralinga into a testing range
for A-bombs. It earned its name. In Pitjantjatjara, Maralinga meant
field of thunder. The whole place went off the scale with Plutonium-
239. Half-life: 24,000 years. One Tree, Marcoo, Kite, Breakaway,
Tadje, Biak, Taranaki – codenames etched in memory like ancestor
spirits. They'd had to scrape a thousand square miles of topsoil
and bury it in concrete bunkers. Now, out of sight and out of
mind, the government talked about handing the scorched land
back to its tribal owners. But the Tjarutja people wouldn't set foot
on the place.

The guard at the next checkpoint was more thorough. He took
down Lawson's rego and passed over a small bundle of forms on a
clipboard to fill out. There must've been a dozen of them. It took
half-an-hour in the heat. The guard waited in his air-conditioned
demountable while she cleared the red tape. One of the countless
pests introduced by the British, she reasoned, along with alcohol,
religion, prickly pear, starlings, cane toads and rabbits. She signed
off and checked her fuel gauge.

The guard was watching her through the flyscreen on his
demountable window, expecting her to bring the forms herself.
She tapped the horn and dangled the clipboard out the window.
He didn't move. She revved the engine and inched the ute
forward. It produced a result. The guard slouched back out, sweat
stains showing on his private cop outfit. He took the forms back
and handed her a slip. She heard him mutter *smartarse* under his
breath, but not the *nigger* it implied.

An ancient Golden Fleece petrol sign rose out of the scrub at
the edge of the township. A shop had been slapped together from
whitewashed breezeblock with a couple of antique petrol pumps

standing beside a corrugated iron shed. A dingo lay asleep in the shade of an awning. Lawson swung in between the pumps. A shimmer of molten air and petrol fumes hung over everything. It could easily have been forty degrees in the shade. The clock on the dash said just before midday. She killed the engine and got out.

Behind the screen door, the shop was dead. An open padlock hung on the nearest pump. Lawson walked over to the shop and peered in. No-one. She went back to the ute and hit the horn. The dingo raised its eyelids and looked at her with forlorn dingo eyes. Nothing else stirred.

Standing out in the sun, Lawson was tall and lean. Dark hair fell flat on a high, narrow forehead over blue eyes. *Nefertiti eyes,* Dix called them. People found them disconcerting. It was a colour thing. A pair of well-worn Levis hung low over dusty RMs. A white singlet clung to dark skin damp with sweat. She was what they used to call a half-cast, before the whitefella dreamt up subtler words for the same thing. The *half* used to bother her as a kid. She'd never thought of herself as half-anything before she went to school, where everything they said made her feel like a leftover of something missing. White man's language taught her an existence by ratios. Half-truths. The other half. The lost half. "Lost" meaning *gone astray, fallen,* like in the Bible. Meaning *sinners.* Meaning *savages.*

But the truth was never just black and white. That's what the Mission Man kept telling her anyway. Grey. *The colour of what* truth is, she thought. Only whose? Fact was, grey really meant black, unless it meant white. When history's grey, it's white. When a person's skin colour's grey, it's black. Or they treated you like you were black, but explained how you weren't *really* black. Not black enough and not white enough. A nothing. A lie. Less than nothing. Like you didn't belong anywhere. A ghost in limbo. Ashen. Outcast. Unnameable. That was the message she'd been getting for as long as she could remember.

In the Land of Bastards, she thought, the half-cast is bitch.

Behind blue eyes a quiet anger smouldered, fed by unwritten laws of redemption and justice. Ancient, timeless laws, whose custodians struggled within her like the two sides of an irresolvable argument. She was reminded of those lines from Shakespeare some crazy English woman had tried to teach them at the Mission school.

Why bastard? Wherefore base?
My mind is as generous and my shape as true,
As honest madam's issue? Why brand they us
With base? With baseness? Bastardy? Base, base?
She dug the Bard after that. Who'd've thought?

+ TAXI DRIVE YOU

The cold hit Osborne full in the face the moment he stepped out of Little Joe's diner. He checked his watch to make sure the time on the clock over the bar had been right. Quarter-to-eight, give or take. Early days. He pulled his coat closer and shivered. Across the street, two women in headscarves were sitting on the Blizzard King's bench, talking and laughing. Yellow school buses chugged up the hill. A Domino's Pizza delivery van. The Paterson Express. The subway seemed like a bad idea in blackout weather so instead he zeroed-in on a cab idling on Fort Washington beside an empty newspaper stand. He rapped on the driver's window. The driver's head reared up from sleep like a sea creature.

Inside the atmosphere was tropical. The driver, air-con working overtime, looked like a comedy stand-in on the Raoul Castro Show: mirrored aviators and a loud – check: very loud – Havana shirt. The heat took Osborne's breath away. In the fewest necessary words, he directed the driver south. WTC. Ground Zero. The driver cast a sceptical look over the rims of his lenses, scoping Osborne in the rear-view.

"Maybe drive so far to Port Authority is possible." Heavily accented Amerikanisch. "After, who know. Traffic much bad. Always in Manhattan bad, but today is worst."

Osborne registered the scepticism and stared back.

"Fine. Get me to 42nd and I'll walk."

"In theez weather? Is much, kamarad."

"Suppose you've got a better idea?"

"Yes, very better idea." The driver spat, hitting the ignition. "Go to Rio, my friend." He grinned as he pulled out into the traffic. "You know perhaps joke of Soviet taxi driver?"

"Do I want to?"

32

"No, but I tell it you anyway."

Osborne stared out the window. A garbage truck passed them heading in the opposite direction, towards the Cloisters. As it passed, Osborne noticed a woman in a fur coat walking along the sidewalk, a large styrofoam cup steaming in one hand and something green perched on her shoulder.

"You're not from around here," he said absently.

Well who the hell *was* from around here, except the Ricans? Osborne's gaze followed the coat on the sidewalk. *It's a parrot*, he thought. *A green fucking parrot.* The driver looked up at the rearview, then back at the traffic, edged into the next lane. He laughed.

"Me? Sure, around here! Hehe. What you thinking? I grow up in Far East Side. Hehe. Vladivostok. Like *Wood*stock. Hehe. Other end from Brooklyn Bridge just. Hehe."

The coat with the parrot was lost back behind the traffic now. The cab made the lights at the bus terminal and swung around onto the Westside Highway.

"When I was boy, they say – in Soviet Union, nobody watch television, television watch *you*."

Osborne watched the river go by.

"Same for taxi. In Soviet, *taxi drive you...*"

The driver guffawed and switched on the radio. A woman's voice was running through a news bulletin at top speed. Osborne couldn't make any sense of it.

A minute later Shinwah walked back into the adjoining suite, the jeweller's case hasped in a black Augé shoulder-bag. Wall-to-wall mirrors distorted space along a fluid horizon. Like her, everything in the suite was themed black. It was the one idea that never aged. Jet, ink, ebony, kohl. The absence of light.

The suite was open-plan. A wide dishevelled bed was the centrepiece, beneath a black muslin canopy. It evoked a room in an expensive brothel. Lying on the bed, eyes open and fixed on a point just above the bathroom door, was a man of average height, blonde, and entirely naked. The way his head was positioned against the pillow looked unnatural. He had the appearance, she thought, of a catalogue picture waiting to be animated. Shinwah stood at the foot of the bed and stared at him through the muslin. Blue light flickered across his face. A thin trail of red bisected the gap between nose and lip.

On the bedside table, an LCD radiated a faint aquarium glow. It reminded her of those Japanese waterfall holograms they sold at bazaars. Across it shifted the current trading figures from the Nikei index. The market appeared to be in freefall. Almost unconsciously her eyes passed across the weirdly pixellated surface of code, tiny squares of muslin distorting her vision.

She'd awoken, still punch-drunk, not knowing where she was. A flash of pain. She registered the dead man and grimaced. *I've been fucking a corpse?* It came back to her, in bits and pieces. And then the hotel phone rang. She'd picked up automatically.

"You're late."

The voice was smooth. Too smooth. The kind of voice people were easily unnerved by. "I hope you've been enjoying yourself."

"What time is it?" she groaned. She blinked at the bedside

clock. It read just after two. a.m.

"You have it?"

It was more a statement than a question.

"I'll be in the lobby."

She hung up and reached for her bag. It was gone. She found it lying on the floor. The handset was inside. Its screen flashed mute. De Laurentiis had been calling for the last half-hour. Fuck. Something must've happened.

Out in the bathroom she'd found the dead man's ice. It was the best ice she'd ever had that wasn't synthed in a Chinese lab. Unless it *was* Chinese. It levelled her out. Reset to zero.

Back in the suite she stared at the dead man. She knew nothing about him, except that he was a trader. He wore a shoulder rig with a .38 in it. He was white. Typical *cháng bízi*. No tattoos. No scars. She remembered he'd spoken with an accent. Russian. Novgorod, de Laurentiis had said. No chance to find out what a great personality he had. He was probably a lousy fuck anyway.

De Laurentiis had sourced the tip-off through an in-house contact when the dead man dialled for an escort, billed to the room number. A real sucker move. Corporation name on hotel register: STROJIMPORT. Amex-corroborated. Credit line wide open. De Laurentiis managed the intercept.

Within fifteen minutes Shinwah had arrived at the penthouse suite posing as the escort. The dead man answered the door in open bathrobe, hotel-monogrammed, coked-up to the eyeballs. Totally edgy. He screamed at her. It freaked her out. He wanted to know where the other girl was. He'd ordered a double act. De Laurentiis hadn't said anything about a second girl. She'd had to improvise. He chilled her. She oozed come-on. She made it through the front door and scoped the room. Zero. It looked too easy. Then he grabbed her by the neck and everything became a blur.

Every time she went on a job, she knew the risk. Time-shifting got to her head. In the split-second of having to act she sometimes couldn't remember where she was, or why she was there, or who she was supposed to be. Switching the role-play was meant to be routine, but somewhere in the mix a part of her got lost. It left her in a kind of psychic limbo. She preferred a job to be quick, unemotional. Never did care for preliminaries, looking into the eyes of the dead man who wasn't dead yet. He was grinning the way only insane people grin. In slow-motion it seemed. She didn't wait to see what he was grinning about. Her body twisted with the upward cut of her hand, but the next move didn't come. She felt her body jerked sideways, wrist and elbow pinioned. Before she knew what he was doing, he kicked her, hard in the back. The blow laid her out. Then he kicked her again on the floor, dragged her by the hair over to the bed. He wrenched her up onto the mattress, kidney punched her. Something flared inside her head. *One of them.*

But no. He'd tried to sodomise her, neck in a chokehold. That wasn't how they worked. In their game it was always a race against time. Standard procedure: kill. Take your head apart in a lab afterwards and see what they could find. Compute backwards. Plug the construct into the firewall and see if they could hack-in to the mainframe back in Beijing, or wherever it was. What she knew for sure was, if they ever took her alive, it wouldn't be pretty.

The trader was stronger than he looked. She'd started to pass-out. He had her pinned with the crinoline up over her waist when the sub-programme kicked in, activating the kill-switch buried deep in her brainstem. The rest was unconscious. Body reflex. She'd woken up afterwards, not remembering. One John Doe *iced*.

The dead Russian's clothes lay draped over the back of an armchair. She'd gone through them meticulously. No labels. No ID. No money. Nothing in the wardrobe. No luggage. No toiletries. No briefcase. She logged the jeweller's case. It turned up one glass tube. One mirror. One block of ice, uncut. She cased the

36

suite again. Nothing. Alarm bells started going off in her head.

What's the gimmick? De Laurentiis always had a gimmick. Something he didn't let on. It was like a game. They played each other. It got on her nerves. Like the two-girl call. He'd *known*. She put it out of her mind. There wasn't time. The place looked like a set-up. She'd assumed John Doe had got there ahead of a deal and elected to entertain himself. There wouldn't've been anything obvious lying around for a couple of hustlers to pinch. But the target still had to be on-hand, where the trader could know it was safe.

She flicked open her handset and cold-scanned the body for electronics. Rings, watch, bracelet. The handset flat-lined. Nothing. Then it spiked. A platinum necklace with black pendant. Faux Egyptian. Hieroglyphics. Ibis-head, adder, kneeling scribe. The handset read circuitry. Embedded processors. Heavy encryption. *Bingo.* She logged the rudiments, hit download, *fast*. The log was for insurance, the chip was for de Laurentiis. She tore the necklace off and slipped it in her purse. *Careless*, de Laurentiis would've said. *Fuck de Laurentiis.* Job done.

☾ FUSTAT

30°1'21.83"N
31°13'48.25"E

Khalig al-Misri. The name of what's left of an old canal. Ptolemaic. Cut out from the right bank of the Nile back in ancient history, that once joined the river to the Red Sea. Just south of it, a ruined aqueduct runs east, forming a gateway beyond which lie the slums of Fustat. A district of smashed buildings used as quarries for the ongoing construction in the north. This's where the first intifada against the corporations long ago retreated and died. All that remain of it now are ghosts, rumours, inventions. From time to time the corpses of saboteurs are hung from the walls, but no-one recognises them.

Along the old battlements, mountains of rubbish and junked-out machinery rise above what once were strongholds. They adjoin the remnants of former cemeteries, picked over by sleepless *zabbalin* from the eastern outskirts, where the dome ends, below the Muqattam. These are the informal sectors, beyond the law. Here the outcasts, smugglers and religious brotherhoods subsist under cover of entropy, hidden from the eugenics squads. Beyond is the desert. And somewhere out in the desert lies the City of the Dead.

He knows this intuitively. Or the Stranger tells him. The Stranger is the name he's given to the voice that accompanies him, directs him from somewhere inside his head like an onboard passenger. As familiar now as a shadow. At some point during the journey from the Bridge it'd occurred to him, *I'm the stranger. We're the same.* The idea had persisted and the voice had done nothing to dispel it. But what did it mean?

He listens for the voice to say something. A shadow casts across his eyes. Then everything stops. He's dimly aware of a presence, like someone standing over him. A white light in his retina. Then black. Suddenly he's looking up at a ceiling. The blades of a ceiling fan very slowly turning. Then blackness again. A sound like static in his ears. Then everything jolts. And he's running. Stumbling down an alleyway. Navigating blind. And then the voice. The green flicker of numerics. *Left*, the Stranger says. He cuts left, weaving through dim bombed-out courtyards. He suppresses an urge to vomit. The vertigo returning, ebbing. *Right*.

He pushes back against the fear. Fear of what's happening to him. *If they're out there, whoever they are, they'll be watching. Perhaps they already know everything. Who I am. Why I'm here. What I'm thinking. What my reactions will be. My history. Things I don't know myself...*

A flight of stairs. At the top, a window onto a ruined vista. The whole district, as far as he can see, is nothing but a demolition zone. In the distance, the shadow of the Tower rises up out of the night like a constant menace. He climbs through the window, following the outlines of what remains of rooftops slanted together in tectonic confusion.

He can sense the Stranger knows about this place. He's been here before, but he doesn't know when. An image flashes, of grey figures huddled under ledges. A scan of urban archaeology, wreckage, buckled concrete, a passage between mud walls, doorways hung with shredded tarpaulin. The dull glow of a brazier radiates from deep within the shadows. Hot cooking oil palling the air.

The Stranger's telling him something. His purpose. To find someone. He doesn't understand. The voice repeats, *the Connection*. A word like two halves of a mirror reflected in one another. Like a rumour from somewhere deep in his sub-conscious. Then the voice tells him of the place beyond the Dome. The City of the Dead.

Numerics blink. -00:20.

At the far side of the demolition zone, a wide road cuts a swathe through the darkness, flanked by a high stone wall in various stages of collapse. An army of construction bots congests the perimeter under a barrage of floodlights that periodically short out, the grid teetering under the strain. Somewhere to the north are the vast building sites which the ruins of Fustat supply with raw material. Spectral minarets flanked by giant cranes, like machined hieroglyphs hanging in mid-air. Corporate zones, gradually propagating outwards, consuming everything. At their centre is the Tower. A black monolith pointing heavenward, orchestrating the movements of this artificial cosmos.

From the shelter of a doorway he scans the scene, trying to make sense of the confusion. At first he thinks the confusion's his, but soon realises it's the scene that's confused. Everywhere he looks, machines of all kinds are engaged in hauling shattered masonry that doesn't seem to go anywhere. Like a production line constantly breaking down. It's an illusion of activity. They could've used donkey carts to shift the rubble faster.

Most of what else's going on looks like maintenance, an effort to mask the general disorder. Construction bots repairing breaches in the wall that competing machines are already in process of demolishing. As many machines again sitting idle, waiting to be repaired. Bored technicians observe the spectacle from outside a kiosk, smoking kif, oblivious to the cacophony surrounding them. Only metres away, a hapless transport droid's being dismembered by *zabbalin* for the spare parts trade.

The main entrance to Fustat is a bastioned portal further south in the wall, the square fronting it congested by hawkers, scavengers and junk merchants, middlemen in the tireless cycle of redistribution. The programme homes in on a pair of under-guarded service entrances, evaluating. One of them's in use. The other appears, like everything around it, out-of-order. He waits for the right opportunity, skirting the kiosk, edging closer to the machines. An armoured security van cuts a path through the vaguely human mass spilling from the square. As it comes abreast of him, it slows for a generator convoy. Now. Immediately he moves in behind it, staying there long enough to find a gap in the oncoming traffic.

He gets a fix on the service entrance. There's at least a dozen blind spots. Obscured by mounds of debris that gleam under the constant drizzle, he gets in past the perimeter lights, blends with the crowd. The dead eye of a camera stares right past him. He has no way of knowing if he's been seen. *Act normally*, the voice says. *Normal.* He doesn't bother to ask what it means. Further in, the floodlights taper off into a gloom punctuated only by the glow of lime-burners' kilns and the random searchlights of surveillance drones. Soon the maze of rubble deepens, becoming less populated. Occasional pieces of hermetic iconography mark out territories, borders the fearful refuse to cross. Beyond, the zone of the sects, reaching down beneath the city's foundations.

He moves on in the direction of the zone. *Stop*, the voice breaking in. Numerics flare. Something shudders into close-up. A symbol like a skull and crossbones, sprayed on a lintel in fluoro paint. Data scrolls. Then everything shifts back into a regular depth-of-field. *Continue.* He picks his way through the rubble, navigating on automatic. Time to time the voice intervenes, but he's begun to notice uncertainties creeping in. The programme no longer seems to be guiding him now, but instead responding to each option as it arises, factoring the probabilities. The sense of déjà vu's gone and in its place a palimpsest of images, memory flashes overlaying whatever's in front of him, patched together from a wrong time and place.

He can feel the Stranger's frustration. Each step, more and more tentative. He realises he's entering a space that's precariously structured, impermanent. Whose coordinates and logic are shifting and barely decipherable. In which it might easily be possible to become lost. Or worse. The only thing he's certain of is somewhere inside the randomness, there's supposed to be a Connection. Someone he's never met. Yet who – his only hope of getting out alive – will know him.

This's all the Stranger will say.

No explanations, no answers.

☐ THE ACE

51°32'28.45"N
0°16'40.53"W

The landscape around Old North Circular Road had evolved into the new millennium with cretacean slowness, a backwater in the march of progress, a stagnant pool left behind by the fast eddying currents of the Cool Britannia mainstream. In the midst of which the Ace Café was like an oasis of the bygone, a mirage in the desert of the zeitgeist. At the merchandise counter you could find keychain memorabilia of the Tonne Up Club's lost golden age. It used to be you made the Club by clocking a hundred down the North Circular without killing yourself in the process. Out back was a graveyard of twisted bike frames dredged from the canal, where the unsung heroes of the Motor Age regularly wound up if they didn't wipe out on the viaduct.

Politics on both sides may've turned the nation into the armpit of mediocrity, but here at least, at the Ace, an older order had survived undisturbed. A veritable Galapagos. With picnic benches for leather-jacketed retirees to sun themselves in the North London gloom. Where a man with a Legion patch could still feel the Earth propping him right-side up. And the bikes were British.

Perched like an overgrown gargoyle at the end of one of the café's dozen trestle tables, pint in hand, keeping his nutrition levels balanced, Joblard surveyed the day's prospects. The usual crowd was scattered about the place, watching the drizzle through the front windows. Outside, a row of bikes leant on their side-stands like dominos waiting to tip over, getting a free wash. The vista petered out in shades of yellow and grey. On weekdays, the Ace was Joblard's home-away-from-home. On weekends, the gymkhana crowd with dolled-up café racers took over and he was obliged to retreat for some peace and quiet to his office on Whitechapel Road – the back room at the Blind Beggar, where

Georgie Cornell had once been gormless enough to cop a bullet in the face.

The box in the corner was running another one of those Wozzie Burger commercials. Genetically modified kangaroo with synthed cheese, the works. This week only, you could buy one Wozzie Burger and get a free serving of chips and a pint of sugary bilge-water, free. Why pay for waste-disposal, eh, when there's always a punter somewhere dumb enough to spend their own hard-earned to choke themselves on it. From all indications, Wozzie Burgers were taking over the world. If you blinked you might just wake up in one.

The ad ended with Wozzie-the-Clown's asinine grin, then over to the day's Ashes replay. England were being unceremoniously dismembered by those lanky convict bastards in baggy green caps. The camera was zoomed on one of them now, taking his time at the boundary shining a ball on his flies before loping into a half-mile run-up. *Woosh!* Another delivery over the batsman's head somewhere just short of the sound barrier. The Aussie wicketkeeper, loitering back in the shade of the Bradman Stand, had to dive to catch the ball. It was day one of the fourth test in Adelaide, the series 3-0 and headed for a whitewash. Watching it on TV was slow torture. Like betting on flies crawling up a wall. If you were there at the payoff, you could be congratulated just for having stuck around.

The next delivery was the same as the last, only this time the batsman made a pretence of swatting at the ball as it zapped past his left ear. The commentators paused briefly in their discussion of sock-darning to point out that no-one had actually scored a run since the tea break, with four wickets down. Joblard checked his phone to see if there was anything new in the world. It was lying beside a sodden coaster, recharging, the screen's faint green glow constantly playing in the corner of his eye. Nix. Joblard turned it face-down, a futile gesture. Gulped his ale. Felt the gas extrude down the length of his intestine and rumble softly between prodigious cheeks.

He wondered what the business with the envelope was. Bludhorn, his usual circumspect self, had only mentioned *photographs*, giving the word a very generic inflection. Being Bludhorn, it went without saying *what kind*. No doubt some Tory MP with his pants down and a whip stuck up his behind. The usual extortion job. Dominatrix, two-way mirror, pinhole dildo-cam. Only maybe the nerd with the surveillance rig wanted to spike the price. Or maybe got the bright idea of playing both sides. And he, Joblard, had been sent to collect. He'd handed the stuff to Bludhorn, got to listen to a lot of balmy crap about Freemasonry and the rights of the handicapped to sexual fulfilment, then took his dough and hightailed it to the Spitalfields Market for some faux '70s lampshade he'd promised Bird Girl in case she ever came back. Some froggy name she had. Jacinthe, maybe.

But no sooner had Joblard hit Bank Street than Bludhorn was on the blower again, chewing his ear off. The reason he hadn't got the call sooner was the old bugger was stuck on the Underground – some nutter had done a bunko under a train, closing down the Northern Line. He could hear the service announcement repeating in the background.

"This isn't a bleeding social call, you git," was the welcoming overture Bludhorn screamed down the airwaves at him. "You brought back the wrong fucking pictures. You flaming fucking tit. I didn't ask you to get me photos of a bleedin' dwarf in a spacesuit. I asked you to get..."

Three bleeps and the phone went dead. No battery. *Well that's progress for you.* So now he had to track down that Greenwich pissant all over again. Needless to say, the gent wasn't answering the door when Joblard came knocking, only some hysterical Salvation Army widow rattling a coin-box at him. For the poor dear children of some famine-ravaged housing estate or other.

Which is also when it'd decided to rain.

He sat in the Ace with his Belstaffs dripping onto the concrete, waiting for a weasel-faced stoolie he knew to turn up. One of those retro-Mod wankers goes on trips down to Brighton Beach with his twelve-year-old tart on a moped. Never've been caught dead, or only dead, at a place like the Ace back in the day. *All before your time, my friend.*

It was going on eleven and his second pint was getting cold in his hand. Embossed on the side of the pint glass, just under the rim, some witty bastard had put *Goering.* Then again, halfway down. And at the bottom, *Gone.* It came with a coaster in red, white and blue. *Spitfire Kentish Ale. The Bottle of Britain.*

Joblard was eyeballing the slops at the dead end of his glass when the Weasel pattered in. He had an oversized Airfix kit under one arm and glue-eyes like he'd been up with the araldite since yesterday. He got halfway to the bar before he scoped Joblard and did an abrupt one-eighty.

"Well, well, well. Look what the cat just dragged in..."

The Weasel froze at the sight of Joblard's reflection in the glass doors looming over him. Instinctively he raised his hands, spilling the contents of the Airfix kit on the floor. A fat ziplock of green mulch, hundred grams minimum.

"Whatever it is," the weasel snivelled, glancing forlornly down at his stash, "I dunno nothin' about it..."

⊙ DELILAH

Leaning against the side of the ute, Lawson polished her sunglasses, taking in the silence, waiting. No-one appeared.

"Hey!" she called out. "Anyone here?"

She looked at her watch and let another five minutes pass before deciding to unhook the padlock and work the pump herself. She'd already filled the tank by the time a middle-aged slob in blackened overalls dragged himself out of the garage to stare at her.

"Nice day for it," Lawson said, replacing the petrol cap.

The metre read forty-nine and seventeen cents. Ever since the latest oil crisis, prices had gotten ridiculous. Black gold. And all the talk of doom from the nuclear lobby. The overalls stared at her, hands in pockets, saying nothing. She pulled a fifty from her jeans and waved it at him. His head jerked towards the shop. *Fine*, she thought, brushing past. *We can all play that game.*

The shop was a large dirty room with racks of machine parts collecting dust. The air inside reeked of sump oil. As her eyes adjusted to the gloom, Lawson saw there was a woman sitting behind the counter, hair in rollers, holding a copy of *Women's Weekly* open in front of her. Lawson was sure the woman hadn't been there earlier. The cow stared at her over the magazine the same way as the slob in the overalls had. The way whitey always stared. It was meant to put you in your place. Like the whole fucking country wasn't your place to begin with. *Whatever.* She handed over the note without saying a word, joining in the pantomime. The cash register clanked. The old cow left the change on the counter and eyeballed her back out the door.

When she'd turned sixteen and moved to the city, Lawson found it wasn't much better there than at the Mission. Especially for a half-cast wanting to study at a university. Worse still, a young half-cast woman with notions of one day becoming a geophysicist. It didn't take long to discover, no matter what the law said, she'd never be the same as the other students. All of them male. And all of them white. But since the uni was obliged to let her in, they gave her just enough special consideration to get her back out the revolving door, degree in hand, ASAP. *Compulsory welfare*, Dix called it. The Ministry for Aboriginal Affairs could be counted on to line up a token job somewhere out on a mining lease in the middle of woop-woop. The message came through loud and clear. Like being a speck in the eye of the national conscience. An irritation the powers-that-be tried to ignore as much as possible, waiting for it to go away.

Dix was the exception. A refugee from northeast Sinai, he'd done it the hard way. Though he had two doctorates, he'd still only been a tutor when Lawson met him, and the only non-white on faculty. His subject was meteorology. Before Adelaide, he'd spent a year in the Antarctic as an assistant on a survey, measuring gaps in the Earth's magnetosphere. He worked with computers, modelling weather patterns on fluctuations in solar radiation. No-one at the university took him seriously.

In some ways they were in the same boat, and when Dix took up a research post at Maralinga, Lawson decided she'd had enough of the papermill too. They kept in touch. She never really understood what the Maralinga gig involved, but one day Dix called with some geo-sat coordinates and that was that. Before long, with her knowledge of the back-country and hankering for solitude, she found herself on-again off-again tracking meteorites, like a boundary rider on four wheels. Old Glory. What she called the ute. It'd belonged to one of the fellas at the Mission she grew up on. After her mum died, he let her have it. She'd cared for it ever since, like family.

Her mother had been a Nunga from west of the Flinders, her

47

father a Goonya, a whitefella, called Henry W. Lawson. Some blow-in engineer from the rocket site at Woomera. Her birth cert said he was a Yank. From Staten Island, New York. Born the year TV came Down Under. 1956. The year they did the atomic tests. He left behind a name and half the DNA that made her. And by a sort of miracle she'd escaped the abortionist, the government abductors and the missionaries, to grow into a woman Mr Henry W. Lawson probably never even knew existed, yet bore his name. A Goonya name. *In nomine Patris.* Name of the father.

The people her mother came from, the Ngarinyeri, or what was left of them, had once upon a time called whitefellas *grinkari.* Grinkari was the word for a corpse whose skin had been flayed off. The Kaurna people called whitefellas *kuinyo.* A kuinyo was a dreaded and, to her, comical monster with a bloated gut, whose presence was supposed to foretell illness and death. The Narungga used the word *koonya,* or shit. Like the Kaurna word *kudna.* She could never get it out of her head that Goonya's really were dead-shits after all. Which made *her* what, exactly?

When Lawson got back in the ute, the overalls followed her over and took a gander inside, letting his eyes linger on the shotgun hanging on the grill behind the seats. This one was definitely a *kuinyo*, she thought. He spoke slowly through a heavy drawl, eyes not meeting hers.

"Doin' some shootin' are ya? S'pose ya got a license for that?" indicating the gun.

He hoiked up a gob of phlegm and spat it on the ground, reddened forearms resting against the side window, bloated face shaded by the car's roof, too close for comfort.

"Wouldn't wanna get in any trouble now, sport."

Lawson scrutinised the face impassively.

"Don't call me sport," she said flatly. "And don't touch the fucking ute."

The face jerked back and disappeared as she gunned the engine and fishtailed onto the road, heading west towards the research station.

"Arsehole," she hissed.

Some Goonya tried calling her *sport*, she had half a mind to shoot the patronising bastard. She jammed the radio back on, loud. It was a song about Delilah, a no-bullshit woman with brown skin, fear-inspirin' and beautiful. She stepped on the accelerator, the ute jagging over the deep sandy corrugations. There ought to be songs about Nunga women, too, she thought. *Walking in the sunlight, walking in the shadows...*

✛ DAWN OF THE DEAD

40°42'55.95"N
74°0'33.58"W

The crazy Russian had been right. It was gridlock across the island all points south-east of Port Authority. Osborne's feet ached with the cold. Blackouts had put the south-bound subway off limits. There were crowds blocking the avenues and cross streets, but the scene below Chambers was like nothing he'd witnessed before. There were people everywhere, spilling out into stalled traffic, moving in a type of zombie automatism. It reminded him of a scene from *Dawn of the Dead*, except it wasn't. It'd been different when the Twins burned. There was no panic this time, only a vast spontaneous migration spiralling towards the Zero.

After Chambers, progress became almost impossible. Osborne tried heading towards Cortlandt, but it was the same story. Then quite suddenly he found himself being swept along by the crowd, trapped by competing cross-currents. For a while the transition left him without any sense of orientation. Then, as he entered deeper into it, he became aware of the crowd as a complex entity with its own mind, its own stream of consciousness. Thought-objects knotted together, eddied, spread out. He searched for the flows, the still points, seeking to make headway towards the impact site.

As he drifted east Osborne gradually felt a change in the atmosphere. The crowd grew more diffuse, less of a mob and more like a gathering of the tribes, each with its vaguely defined zone. It reminded him of the park enclosures on Tompkins Square. Winos, punks, hustlers, old guys playing chess.

At Sixth Avenue the peddlers, sniffing a buck, had set up along the sidewalk. The first one he saw was a black woman, hunched under a blanket in a wheelchair, selling bits of Martian rock behind a makeshift stand. A tiny bleached-out version of Old

Glory fluttered at the end of a car aerial taped to the back of her wheelchair and a black-and-white portrait of Buzz Aldrin. It jived weird. Flashback to the old man's blizzard balls on 181st Street. Flash forward to people standing on the roofs of parked cars. Over the sound of whistles and sirens, a stereo was blasting out a retro Public Enemy track. 911's a Joke. Some of the people on car roofs were dancing to it.

Osborne persisted southbound. Three blocks down, a UPS van had been rolled and set on fire. A mob of office clones gathered around it stamping patent-leather shoes against the cold, shouting into cell phones. A prophet of UFO doom ran through the crowd screaming religious nut gobbledegook. In the distance a police loudhailer, rippling with feedback, repeated an order to stand clear. It was impossible to tell where it was coming from. Up above, the black wasp-like silhouette of a helicopter moved silently in and out between the rooftops.

Osborne veered left and found himself in a narrow cross-street, a backwater the human tide had almost passed by. Abandoned lorries blocked most of it. Under a scaffolded overhang, a dozen or so dead souls were gathered in front of a storefront window, transfixed. Osborne edged by. Behind the window, TV screens flared in unison. Images cascaded. A fireball falling through night sky. Helicopter searchlights above a trademark Manhattan skyline. Aerial views. Smoke rising from the impact site. Crowd shots. Hysterical. Car horns blaring. Someone flipping the camera the bird. Talking heads on fast rotation. Then cut to a patched-in view of what looked like some post-apoc excavation site, flooded up to the knees of emergency workers.

The Zero. A mile-wide hole in the ground. It'd been that way since Al-Q kamikazied a pair of 737s into the Twins a decade or so previous. It seemed like ancient history already. Archaeology. Across the bank of TV screens, a team of army engineers in radiation suits were sifting through debris above the water-line.

The remains of a ruined PATH train hung from a wall of exposed girders. Tilting up, the camera revealed the smashed façades of neighbouring monoliths, their windows blown in.

Osborne pushed on again, circling, cutting back, navigating by indirection. Past makeshift barricades. Across St Paul's cemetery. Almost getting within sight of the Fulton Street station before being forced back again by a scrum of Krishnas in yellow bedsheets. Half an hour of shouldering through the peaceniks he found himself at Broadway and Liberty, at the lower end of the Zero. A street preacher was standing in the middle of the intersection howling into a megaphone.

"AND THE ANGEL TOOK THE CENSER, AND FILLED IT WITH FIRE OF THE ALTAR, AND CAST IT INTO THE EARTH. AND THERE WERE VOICES. AND THUNDERINGS. AND LIGHTNINGS. AND AN EARTHQUAKE!"

The crowd-mind had opened a space around the preacher. On one side of the intersection, the riot squad lined up behind striped blue and white barriers. On the other, a procession of flagellants stalked back and forth like the chorus in a Greek tragedy, weirdly menacing. The crowd dug the scene. Bottles flew. Cops stroked truncheons and tear gas canisters, expectant. The preacher ranted. The chorus threw up their arms and writhed.

♒ STARFUCKER

Millennium Plaza was a post-communist horror jutting up from the expanse of water that was now northern Prague, like a floating glass ziggurat. A series of major floods had earned Prague its moniker as the Venice of Inland Europe. The whole north-side, above the old city, had been rezoned into a network of canals and waterways. Barges, cruise boats and gondolas crowded the quays. Nightlights glimmered everywhere on black water.

Leaving the dead man's suite, Shinwah retraced her steps to the elevator, clutching her bag under-arm. Further along the hallway a late-night party was in progress. A door opened and music spilled out at top volume. She recognised an old Rolling Stones number. *Starfucker*. Like an artefact from bygone days when music wasn't synthed by computer programmes. Some studio geeks staggered out with call girls in tow. *Someone's doing a roaring trade tonight.* One of the geeks waved a video-cam. Shinwah shied. The elevator arrived just in time.

The suites at the Plaza were stacked in tiers that faced inwards onto a multi-story atrium. Like a puzzle cube tipped on its side. The elevator shaft ran diagonally, the atrium opening out as you descended. The descent was fast. A vast enclosed artificial space rushing up out of freefall. Terrace restaurants, cocktail bars, a casino with electric palm trees arranged around an Olympic swimming pool like an eastern oasis.

From below, the tiered lights gave the upper half of the atrium a dusky appearance, evoking late Martian sunsets. The whole place, Shinwah decided, was someone's idea of what a transit lounge in a spaceport might've looked like in an age of pharaonic gigantism. Reality palled.

At zero the elevator went subterranean and re-emerged in a

vault of titanium and black marble. The doors slid open onto warm air-conditioned night air. Shinwah breathed-in the scent of lotus blooms. It relaxed her. She paused and checked her reflection in the polished marble. She felt her face stiffen again, the features harden, eyes narrow. The job, she knew, was only the first move. The opening gambit, de Laurentiis called it. What mattered was how the opposition responded, whoever they were. If something was going to go wrong, it would go wrong now.

Shinwah headed for the lobby, stilettos ringing on polished slate. She entered a low peristyle hall surrounding a tropical garden in a glass terrarium. To one side, a cocktail bar with red upholstered lounge chairs. A bartender with his back turned, polishing glasses. To the other, a long reception desk that took up one full side of the lobby, like the ticket booths at Beijing Zhàn Station. A pair of suits were talking in loud drunken voices, arguing with a girl behind the desk. They wanted their rooms changed. A bellhop was pushing a luggage cart. On the far side, a red carpeted stairway ascended from the entrance to street-level. De Laurentiis was nowhere to be seen. She waited on the blind side of the terrarium, keeping both approaches in view. Ghost orchids like wisps of pale light among the dark foliage.

"You're becoming careless." His voice in her ear.

Shinwah spun around. De Laurentiis was standing, overly casual, with one hand in the pocket of a blue velvet dinner jacket. His other hand held up an unlit cigar. Her own coat, she saw, was draped over the crook of his arm. He reminded her vaguely of a Dirk Bogarde double in a bad Taiwanese cloner film.

"This place gives me the creeps," she hissed, taking her coat from him. Patent lab-grown black leather.

"We're only waiting for you, my dear," de Laurentiis purred.

Shinwah glanced around as they crossed the lobby, trying to sense the next move. She'd missed de Laurentiis. She'd misjudged the dead Russian. Maybe he was right. Maybe she *was* losing her edge. She felt her pulse begin to race again. The ice working in delayed action, giving her a second rush. She'd need to time the comedown. Be sure it didn't take her unawares.

A pair of doormen in livery ushered them through sliding glass. A red surveillance eye scanned them, unseeing. She stared back at it. De Laurentiis had taken care of that, too. They circulated ghost-like, warping machine-reality, a bio-mass glitch in time-space. Anyone watching the security monitors would've seen only the pantomime of the doormen and the doors opening for no apparent reason.

Outside, a line of water-taxis idled under a marquee. An usher directed them to the head of the queue. They climbed aboard. As they did, another taxi pulled in. A very short man, almost a dwarf, stepped onto the quay, briefcase in hand. He was immediately followed by another man, tall and thin with misshapen face. Shinwah stared at them as they crossed to the hotel entrance, just as the studio boys with their escorts weaved out. She turned her back and settled against the taxi's window. De Laurentiis gave the driver instructions in a language she didn't understand. The driver nodded and eased the boat out into the canal, then powered-up. On the landward side, office towers glimmered against an orange-grey night sky.

Moments later they were out on the river, snaking northwards between green and red navigation lights. Dark silhouettes of an industrial zone loomed in the distance.

They continued northward, past river traffic heading in the opposite direction, their wake phosphorescing and fading. Downstream the low arches of a bridge hung just above the tide mark. Engine sounds echoed and then faded again as they rode beneath it. On the farther side, rows of barges, river tugs and houseboats, moored together haphazardly. Lanterns hung out over the water. The arc of a searchlight.

Shinwah shivered inside her coat. Memory flash. Chang Jiang.

Pre-flight sickness. Something moved in her peripheral vision. She clenched her teeth. Images locking and unlocking behind her eyes. She blanked them out. Voices. De Laurentiis was giving the driver more instructions. She heard the engine slow and the taxi arc around to the right. They were weaving back through submerged docklands. Skeleton trees sticking up from the water. It'd begun to snow. Faint specks of grey dissolving into black.

☾ TESSERAE

It's -00:50 already. Fatigue eating away at him. He's just crossed into a region that's virtually deserted. A hole, punched through a high mud-brick wall, leads into a circular courtyard open to the night. It's like standing at the bottom of a well. From all appearances he's walking through what remains of a demolished monastery, the columns of a vanished cloister pointing up out of the rubble like broken fingers.

From here, shielded against the glow of city lights, it's just possible to make out parts of the dome's geodesics, etched into the artificial sky. Up above, tireless nanotech machines reconstitute the city's inner shell, working against the equally tireless processes of erosion and sabotage. On the outside, acidic desert sands constantly seek to wear-away or bury the outer shell, while within the superstructure of the dome itself, between the outer shell and the visible ceiling, there live bands of *zabbalin* who for decades have withered away the connecting struts and ventilators and filled the space full of junk. One day, if the robots stop working fast enough, the whole dome will cave-in under the wait of accumulated detritus.

In the courtyard he hesitates. A thin drizzle of condensation filters through air thick with humidity onto a floor of cracked tesserae. Up ahead, something moves in the shadows. He waits and it moves again, just enough that he can see it. A beckoning gesture, almost, towards a gap on the opposite side. Without thinking he cuts down a passageway to his right, away from the movement, immediately realising his mistake. Someone closes in behind him. It's a dead end, a trap. Straightaway a sub-programme kicks in. Almost without awareness, his body contorts, flattens against the wall as something diffuse and metallic cuts close to his face, wrapping the air.

Then everything becomes a blur. He's hunched low and twists. There's a hard object in his right hand, a rock. He swings upwards and then back into a moving shadow and keeps swinging until the rock sticks there. A groan as body mass falls to ground. Then a blade of light. He twists, smashing into something behind him. Something convulses, slumps. He braces for the next blow, but it doesn't come. Silence. Nothing moves. He breathes deeply. As suddenly as it began, it ends.

Adjusting his vision, he can see now the two androids and the steel net that'd almost caught him. Eugenics squad. Life's cheap here. One of them, its head reduced to a pulp of silicon and artificial brain matter, lies with one arm outstretched holding a subsonic handgun. The other has a hole in its chest the size of a fist where it copped the slug. *Nice shooting, cowboy.*

He palms the droid's weapon. Edges his way back to the courtyard, nerves raw from adrenaline. Instinct prompts him to put as much distance as possible between himself and the stiffs, get out of there before someone cops wise. He threads his way back through the cloisters, estimating his position, the route to the other side. But something's still wrong. The programme's repeating itself now, like a beacon that's been left to flash its morse in the darkness of his mind, warped by interference. A garbled message from nowhere. He's afraid of going around in circles. All the paths look vaguely the same. All he knows is there's someone he's supposed to find. Who can get him to the outside. And that there has to be a reason for all this.

-01:01. Bits and pieces of graffiti start out of the gloom, signposting a route too familiar to be accidental. He tries to get some sort of bearing, having no idea what his destination's supposed to be inside this labyrinth. How he'll know when or, increasingly, if he ever gets there. Up ahead, there's the spot again where the two droids jumped him. He can see their crumpled shapes still outlined against the wall. Shit. He tries a different direction, losing himself in the dark. There's a long tunnel ahead of him now. At least it seems like a tunnel. But as he moves towards the light at the end he feels himself starting to black-out. *Is this how it happened the last time?*

He braces himself. Feels the wall slipping away. The green numerics start blurring out. The light at the end breaking-up into code. He's slipping down into a dark wet place. A dull throbbing at the back of his head. And then nothing.

☐ MILGRAM

Bludhorn's last big-screen extravaganza had been a take on Stanley Milgram's infamous obedience-to-authority experiments from the 1960s. These were designed to test how long someone, under instruction from a labcoated scientist, would keep administering electric shocks to a test subject even after the subject had fallen unconscious. It was a classic interrogation room scenario, to which Bludhorn added a personal touch, of electrodes applied to flagrantly exposed genitalia. In the film, the test subjects were members of an erotic circus – human freaks endowed with every known physical affliction, some which tested even the credulity of Bludhorn die-hards.

In reality, these were all actors from Bludhorn's regular stable. The suckers with their fingers on the electric buzzer were volunteers, white middle-class male predominantly. The clean-shaven type who answer newspaper "wanted" adverts for role-play in university psych experiments, thinking beneath their doughboy exteriors there're dark depths of psychic complexity even their mammies don't suspect. They'd sit at a desk and push a button while, on the other side of a two-way mirror, a drooling eunuch strapped to a padded chair would writhe in simulated agony, smoke spiralling from an array of alligator clips. Doughboy would break into a sweat.

"Gee, doc, sure this's alright? I mean, it looks kinda painful."

"You're doing swell kid, just keep up the good work. Like the coach says, *no pain, no gain.* And don't worry, we'll make sure to send a glowing report to the folks. A-plus. Now fry that geisha right where it counts! Attaboy!"

Joblard always knew when the kid was about to puke. The other side of the two-way partition would be nothing but smoke while a vent Bludhorn had secretly installed wafted the smell of t-bone sizzling on a grill. The kid's face would turn the pallor of herring gut and he'd let spray at the console. It worked every time. Would never want so much as to sniff at a side of steak for the remainder of his days.

Just like with the Weasel. Joblard knew he only had to hold the skinny bastard down long enough to get a jumper lead on the end of a sparkplug and the little runt would spill his guts. Though he hadn't expected the Weasel to actually puke all over his front tyre. As a thank you for being so cooperative, Joblard fed the dazed stoolie half his stash of weed and used the rest to wipe down the re-tread on his second-hand Pirelli. The Weasel gagged, eyes coming frantically back into focus.

"I don't advocate the stuff personally," Joblard deadpanned, "but it beats bangers and mash for cholesterol. And that's got to be a plus, wouldn't you say?"

"Canvey," the Weasel sputtered, grass in his teeth, hands worrying the boot that was even then exerting a slight downward pressure on the hollow of his diaphragm. "The Lobster Smack. Down by the jetty. Jesus, I can't breathe!"

"Why the fuck should I believe you?"

"UFO."

The Weasel was shivering, lying in a puddle of oil-slick and his own vomit, a fine drizzle giving his face a glassy look, like a beaded pint glass on a hot day. Goering, Goering, Gone…

"I can't hear you. What'd you say?"

"UFO! He said there was a UFO. Gone right bonkers. Says they're after him."

"Who?"

"You're choking me!"

"Who?" Easing off with the boot.

"Shit, how the hell should I know? Martians. Whoever. The bastard's flipped. You find him, ask him yourself. Fucking

61

psychopath. And tell your boss I ain't doing him no more favours, neither."

"I just might do that. This, my friend, could very well be your lucky day."

☉ ARCHIPELAGO

Past the old army compound a straight tract of red dirt cut out between wire fences. To the left an airstrip built by the British. To the right, a row of aluminium Quonsets camouflaged in the scrub. The research station was adjacent to the strip, a complex of prefab bungalows bristling with antennae. The sign above the main door said CSIRO CLIMATE-MODELLING UNIT. *Sure*, she thought. *You set up at an atomic test site to study climate change, right?* She waved her pass at a security camera and someone came and led her through. A foyer opened onto several corridors with offices branching off. The foyer itself had the obligatory rubber trees collecting dust in plant pots, maps framed on the walls, and a vitrine containing the Maralinga Meteorite. Someone had discovered it back in the '70s. It took the local eggheads almost twenty years to figure out what it was. A small carbonaceous Mars rock.

Lawson suspected it was this that gave Dix the idea of hunting meteorite falls. He was interested in some sort of correlation between the falls and long-term weather patterns, and the Nullarbor was like a magnet for space junk. It surprised her at first just how few observed falls ever resulted in a recovery. Most meteorites were found by prospectors after they'd been lying around for thousands of years, in places like Antarctica and the Nullarbor Plain. You looked for meteorites where there weren't people. But they weren't the only ones looking.

Dix had what her mother used to call itchy fingers. They were always up to something. Leave him in front of a computer and you never knew what he'd get into. One night he'd managed to hack the missile tracking base at Pine Gap. No mean feat. What he found was a programme designed for ICBMs but which could just as readily be used for pinpointing the landfall coordinates of extraterrestrial objects, such as meteorites. The programme triangulated and set up an alert on any likely collision-course while Dix routed the numbers straight to Lawson by sat-nav. She'd do the rest, keeping ahead of any spotter planes, to collect the score before the competition even had time to get confirmation on an impact.

It all made for a profitable sideline selling Mars rocks to collectors. They ran samples through a lab in case any contained what Dix half-jokingly referred to as the missing link. Martian archaea. Biologists called them the third domain — microbes able to survive in deep space. Dix had a theory that meteors belonged to a vast evolutionary system. Each one was like a taxi, transporting colonies of microbes around the solar system. It made her think of the land-bridge her ancestors crossed eighty thousand years ago. Or the archipelagos of the Polynesians, island-hopping across the Pacific. Currents of randomness feeding into megacycles of probability. Systole and diastole.

The end of the dinosaur age, Dix theorised, was just such a migration. Meteors impacting the Earth's atmosphere at a cataclysmic rate. The rainbow serpent, the Dreaming, when the sky reached down to touch the Earth with fire and made stones speak. Lawson knew her Nunga ancestors considered the stones sacred. She tried to reason it out. Keep a clear conscience.

It didn't always work.

+ THE DOCTOR

"Do you believe in a soul that lives on after death?"

The man Osborne called the Doctor was standing on the other side of a wide sea of herringbone parquet, hands clasped behind his back. He was addressing Osborne and gazing at a large painting on the wall at the same time. The painting was vaguely geometrical, different shades of red that could've depicted anything.

The Doctor abruptly turned and looked straight at him.

"Bodily death, I mean. Of the flesh."

His left eyebrow raised itself into a question mark.

"Do you, let's say, for the sake of discussion, believe in a higher plane of being? In reincarnation? The transmigration of souls? A cosmic mind?"

"I don't believe in anything," Osborne replied, shifting his weight nervously in the low armchair he was sitting in. It was one of those chairs, he thought, intentionally designed to make you feel ill at ease.

"You believe *you* exist, don't you?"

The Doctor took several paces towards a floor-to-ceiling window that faced down Cedar Street fifty floors below, cut across by the brown smear of the Zero.

"I've never been all that sure," Osborne replied. "I distrust certainty."

He watched the other man's features dissolve into silhouette against the white backdrop of the sky.

"There's more than one type of certainty, my friend."

The Doctor's name, Osborne reminded himself, was Suliman. It was an apt name.

"I have a job for you," the Doctor said, turning abruptly, a faintly sardonic smile creasing his lips.

"What makes you think I need one?"

"Come, come, my friend. Every man needs to be used well. Besides, it'll be no trouble for you." He gestured vaguely in the direction of the Zero. "You see what's going on out there? That's *Armageddon Live*. THE END looped in an endless re-run. They're waiting for some reality TV Messiah. Their *Mahdi*. Proffering revelation of the big Universal Picture they all dream of starring in."

The Doctor had his back to Osborne again, looking down at the spectacle below. He stood there in silhouette, against a raw expanse of sky, cut by a faint trail of smoke from where the Twin Towers once stood – a pair of phantom limbs, more present now than they'd ever been. Above the Zero, a pale mist of needle-fine snow had begun to fall. *Like ash*, Osborne thought. Ash falling like snow and children's amazed faraway faces. He remembered a picture somewhere. A newsreel, from before he was born. Children on an island, playing in the fallout.

The Doctor's office was at the far end of Cedar Street in a tall narrow building that looked, from the outside, like a strip of blackened celluloid. The letters on the office door read: AROD SULIMAN, M.D., D.Litt., C.P.P., and a string of other letters besides. *Doctor Doom*, Osborne called him. Like some cartoon mastermind fidgeting with the infinity switch in a corporate highrise. A secret lab hidden behind a fake wall-panel. All the usual modcons. Mind manipulation machines, giant test tubes with vegetating brains, foetal jars, naked women dissolving in vats, a cloned midget lab-technician fiddling the dials...

In a kind of vestibule, doubling as a waiting room, a bloodless brunette sat at one end of a wide reception desk, a large ceramic *macramé* swan poised at other. Minimalist oriental kitsch on the walls. White on white. Talcum on blonde. It vibed subliminals and psychic antimatter. An enamelled steel door beside the brunette's desk led to the Doctor's sanctum sanctorum. To Osborne's disappointment, there wasn't a labcoated midget in sight.

"You've heard, I presume, what they're saying about it?"

"I read the *Times*."

Suliman turned away from the window and faced him. Osborne detected the shadow of a smile playing across the professional doomsayer's face.

"Incredible, isn't it?"

Without waiting for any kind of response on Osborne's part, the Doctor strode across the room to a large mahogany desk.

"Something falls from the sky. We make an oracle of it. A fetish. An object of hope and fear."

The Doctor emitted a dry chuckle. Outside, a helicopter swept low between buildings.

"What likelihood is there, would you say, of an object from outer-space landing at *exactly* that place? What they call Ground Zero. Why there and not some *other place?*" He gave the last two words particular emphasis.

Osborne shrugged, watching the chopper drop out of view.

"About as likely as falling anywhere, I suppose."

"You disbelieve in things that can't be explained by standard deviations, I suppose?"

Osborne blinked and picked at his left earlobe. He assumed the question was rhetorical.

"Now," the Doctor tapped his fingers on the edge of the mahogany desk, "what if I were to tell you," he said in his very best Doom-laden voice, "that what has fallen to Earth so providentially in this particular location, isn't a meteorite at all?"

"Should I care?"

Suliman lost his smile.

"Perhaps you should."

"If you say so."

Osborne felt his eyelids begin to droop slightly in anticipation of another of the Doctor's monologues. Cosmic improbabilities.

Meteor trains tubing their cold way through space.

"But I don't see what it has to do with me."

"Ah," the Doctor said, mouth creasing into an expression Osborne could only describe as ambiguous. "It may have everything to do with you."

As if by some invisible summons, the Doctor's secretary appeared at the door with a silver serving tray. She crossed the room quietly to place it on Suliman's desk and then departed, her thin figure pivoting in a tight black skirt like a mechanical ballerina on a music box. Osborne was familiar with the routine. On the tray, as always, was an ivory box. Suliman's long delicate fingers withdrew from inside it a glass phial and tipped out some powder onto the polished mahogany. Then, with an antique letter-opener, he divided the dirty, khaki-coloured powder into thin lines. With surprising dexterity he scooped some of the powder onto the point of the blade and, raising it to his nose, inhaled first with the right and then the left nostril.

"Won't you join me?"

Osborne declined. He took the opportunity to extract himself from the deep armchair in which he'd been sitting and crossed to the window. Through the glass, the already overcast sky had begun to darken under a pall of smoke. Sirens echoed up from the street. He felt the Doctor cross the room silently and stand beside him.

"Perhaps in the future," the Doctor said, almost whispering, "there'll be other worlds, and all of this, all of human history and its many pre-histories, will seem trivial, remote from our true destiny. Just as, today, the chimpanzee seems remote from us. The merest evolutionary step. It doesn't matter that people might've suffered. Man evolved to suffer. It's the one thing that binds us to the future, that ensures us a future. Without suffering, we're nothing."

"You mentioned a job…?"

Suliman turned to him and looked into his eyes. So close that Osborne could trace the patterns in the Doctor's irises. Grey verging on mauve. His voice was low, almost a whisper. Osborne had to strain to hear him.

"Don't you ever ask yourself what your business is with existing? What it is that really concerns you here?"

"Isn't that what everyone wants to know?"

"No," the Doctor hissed emphatically. "It's what everyone does not want to know."

The water-taxi pulled up beside an old barge moored below the dry docks. Dark figures moved along the deck. The driver grappled the taxi in close. Torchlight arced downwards, pinpointing a line of metal rungs welded to the barge's hull. The engine cut out into silence. Shinwah scanned the perimeter. As her ears adjusted, the silence gave way to a low moaning. Except for the narrow channel they'd navigated by, the inlet was ice-locked. It was the sound of the water moving under the ice.

She felt de Laurentiis touch her face. Turned and looked at him.

"Give me the processor," he said.

Shinwah felt inside her shoulder bag for the dead man's pendant and held it up. De Laurentiis fingered the platinum chain. The scarab spun slowly, catching the light.

"Good," he said, slipping it into his jacket pocket. "You've earned your keep."

He lent in close, his face brushing hers. Involuntarily her lips parted. She closed her eyes, breath halting. He held her chin in his right hand, running his thumb across her bottom teeth. She tried to picture his face. The expression in his eyes. To guess what he was thinking. His thumb withdrew and the pressure of his hand relaxed.

"Wait here," de Laurentiis said. And then he was gone.

She could hear his shoes on the metal rungs. The side of the taxi butted against the hull of the barge. The ice groaned. *You're a fool*, she thought, sinking back into her seat.

De Laurentiis was her control. Her *dûchà*. He kept her on a leash, like a dog. Master and dog. Everything depended on the protocols. Their relationship, whatever that amounted to, was strictly business. Pleasure also was business. Her work was 3R: remote recovery and resolution. Resolution was committee-speak for snuff. Recovery meant *anachronism*: technology smuggled across time-frames, violating the embargo. Pirates, hackers, rogue intelligence, mafia. Hijackers and corporate saboteurs. That was the glamorous life she'd been sold into. It was that or twelve years in Daxing for running dope out of Hong Kong. The choice was a no-brainer. After the debrief, they'd gone to work on her in the lab. Implanted chipsets into her motor cortex. A jungle of microelectrodes translating signal commands into brain pattern. Sub-programmes. Gateway to the computer-biomass nexus.

She wondered about the dead man. Scenes replayed in her head. Six hours earlier, they'd come in at an old Metro terminus. Teleportation. Moscow-Prague. Quantum voodoo. The network was mobile. Sleeper units cross-continent. She never knew where the terminals were at any given time. All she knew was that somewhere in the *future*, in a Beijing lab, her double, her doppelgänger, was wired into a machine. Like a vegetable on life-support. And up there, hidden, the eye-in-the-sky, watching her. Watching all of them.

The idea kept her awake at night. One day, she supposed, something would happen and the future wouldn't exist any more and *she* wouldn't exist anymore. Someone will've fucked with the embargo good and proper. Permanent erasure. Blackhole metaphysics.

Shinwah put her feet up on the seat opposite, coat falling open across her thighs. The driver was smoking a cigarette, killing time. She dipped into her bag for the jeweller's case. Unhasped it. Hesitated. *What the hell*, she thought. She put her head down and scooped a fingernail of ice up each nostril. It kicked lower this time, right down in the diaphragm, eyes black with dilation. An aurora swept across the sky. Tides of white noise. Her body arched against the window, mind blank, floating. Then somebody was shaking her awake. She jerked back.

"Change of plans."

It was de Laurentiis, his voice unusually tense.

"Put this on," he snapped.

He tossed a black jumpsuit at her. She noticed he was already wearing the same. He dropped a pair of boots on the seat.

"Give me the skirt. And the shoes. You won't be needing them."

She kicked the shoes onto the floor and wrenched off the crinoline. De Laurentiis bent to pick them up. She watched him, his shoulder grazing her thigh.

"What're you waiting for? Get dressed."

She shrugged out of her coat and dragged on the jumpsuit. It was loose. She slipped the coat back over it. The shoulder bag fit inside. Velcroed the boots. They were her size. She wondered how much forethought had gone into that detail. Outside she heard the splash of her shoes being thrown into the channel. The crinoline lay on the water like an exhausted bouquet.

Topside, De Laurentiis pushed her ahead of him up the metal rungs that made a ladder up the side of the barge. As soon as they were clear, the driver hit the throttle and the water taxi pulled off into the dark. When Shinwah reached the last rung a hand came down and pulled her up onto the deck. She was staring into a pair of eyes without a face. Then she realised the man was black. De Laurentiis came up beside her. Another pair of eyes appeared. Her own eyes were so dilated as to be nearly invisible.

De Laurentiis shouldered past and headed to stern. Out of the shadow of the wheelhouse, the man beside her became a clear silhouette. More silhouettes were moving between freight containers. At the far end of the barge, a black shape was evolving against the sky. They stopped short and waited. No-one spoke. Gradually she made sense of what was going on. The men she'd seen were unwrapping a large tarpaulin from something perched over the bows.

There were whispers. De Laurentiis had disappeared. Something was up. The black man had also disappeared. She edged through the shadows towards the activity. The tarpaulin was gone now. She stopped. Her hands traced the zip at the front of the jumpsuit. Checked the bag was in place. She felt something touch her elbow.

"We're clear." De Laurentiis.

He guided her across the deck, keeping low. A gyro whined overhead, animating an unseen presence. Someone stepped in front of them. More whispers, louder this time.

Shinwah could see the cockpit lights come on. It was an MD520. She recognised it as the type of helicopter smugglers once used. Black. Low noise. De Laurentiis signalled her to climb in. A door closed behind her. The flight controls radiated a faint green. De Laurentiis strapped himself into the pilot's seat. A flight helmet concealed the top half of his face. He said something. She couldn't hear it. She tried reading his lips.

"This should be quite a ride," he shouted.

Everything shook. The drug kicked back in with the uplift, flooding her synapses. They wheeled about fast, cutting back over tree-level, the dark scar of the island dropping away. The lights of Prague shimmered like radium.

☾ THRESHOLD

The Stranger's trying to tell him something. But it's as if he's stuck inside a dream. He can hear, but not understand. He can see, but he can't move. And all he sees is the same thing. The shadow of the fan slowly turning against the ceiling.

Where he is, he doesn't know. He can think, yet there's nothing he can seem to remember. Nothing that can place him, that can centre his thoughts in himself. The blades of the fan turn, casting long distended shadows. Light, coming from an angle. Red neon. The fan makes no noise, yet there's a buzzing in the room. It comes closer. It could be a machine. Or it could be a fly. The fan, it suddenly occurs to him, is turning clockwise. Probably all fans turn clockwise. *Ventilating time*, he thinks.

The fly lands somewhere on his forehead. He can feel it. Crawling. Down his nose. Onto his left eye. Its silhouette against the ceiling. Rubbing its hind legs together. He wants to blink but he can't. The fly sits there, in the corner of his eye. Perhaps watching him. Perhaps seeing him in there watching it. He tells himself it's a dream. That somewhere he's dreaming he's lying in a room, staring at a ceiling. That when he's not dreaming of the room, he dreams about the other place. Al Fustat. And that these are perhaps versions of the same dream. That in order to escape the dream about the room, he has to find the key to the other dream. The Connection.

He thinks about the Stranger. *What if in this dream, he's me. And in the other dream, I'm him? Is that what he's trying to tell me? We're the same, because something got crossed. A threshold somewhere.* Were these his thoughts? The fly stalks around the periphery of his eye. Then buzzes away. He tries to remember what happened before he woke up. Here. In the room. A dull throbbing spreads out from the back of his head. The fan turns, his head throbs. There's no pain, only something like vertigo. His body feels sick with anticipation of the switch, begins to plunge. The fan turns faster. And the faster it turns, the closer it gets. Until the centre of its spiral is like an eye into which everything is being swallowed.

☐ UFO

51°30'40.03"N
0°33'10.48"E

The proverbial Unidentified Flying Object wasn't something Joblard had strongly formed opinions about. The world was indeed a strange place and who knew what funny goings-on happened out there. But coming from the Weasel, it sounded just kooky enough to be true. After a couple of phone calls to check on facts, Joblard kicked his bike into gear and headed due east out of the Ace and under the viaduct. Towards the docklands and the mythical Thames Delta. Home of the petrodollar blues. Not a Messerschmitt in sight.

You'd never know it to look at it now, but in its hayday Canvey Island was the fastest-growing seaside resort in Britain. Till most of it got washed away by the North Sea flood of '53. After that, the deckchairs and changing cabins made way for a concrete seawall, and the amusement arcades got swapped for an oil refinery. Joblard made his approach along the A13, taking the right-hand turn-off at Mulligan's Tyre Repair, past London City Airport. From which, he noted, Lufthansa no longer had any direct flights to anywhere. If the fuckers had ever tried to invade, Canvey would've been among their first ports of call. A nice welcome it would've made, too. Ack-ack guns poking out the front windows of the Monico Club. Nice day for it, Fritzy!

The Lobster Smack was at the western end of the island. A quaint old bit of Dickens, white clapboard in the lee of the flood wall. Not at all where Joblard would've expected to find Johnny Fluoride on the lamb from flying saucers. But seeing as how Mr Fluoride led a double life as a tour guide for obscure '70s pub band groupies, there could've been less likely places. Joblard's contact at the Big Issue was to be thanked for handing him that little gem. He'd owe him the inside spiel on Bludhorn's next venture. He only hoped he wouldn't find himself in it.

Under a dozen different names, Nicky Cohn wrote most of the *Big Issue*'s music reviews. When Joblard had called he was in the middle of firing one off on the forthcoming comeback tour by Ozrock might've-been, Bruce Wellie. As serendipity would have it, Wellie's first gig was scheduled for that very night, at the Labworth Café, on Canvey. Joblard considered dropping by if all went well and Johnny Fluoride didn't play too hard to get. Nicky Cohn had only good things to say.

"The band's great, if you like things low key. I mean, Wellie's so bloody low key, he's not even under the radar. He's under a fucking rock. But it's some rock, chum."

As for the sightseeing tours, Joblard couldn't make it out. Nicky Cohn filled him in.

"They come all the way from Belgrade, Perth, Singapore, just to breathe the same air. Dr Feelgood groupies. Like it's hallowed ground. All these leather jacket types. Old guys. You had to've lived it, to know what it means."

Yeah, right. Like Canvey was ever the centre of anything, unless it was a V2 falling short of its target. Not that you'd hold it against them. He was sure the people there were very nice people.

Joblard wheeled up to the Lobster Smack in time for the lunchtime special. *Pilchards with Shepherd's Pie.* It came, the chalkboard in the window said, with chips, salad, or cooked vegetables. The connotations of the word *cooked* boggled the mind. Inside the place was mostly empty. There was the usual briny smell of beer-soaked carpet that signalled to the uninitiated that this was indeed an establishment in which a drop spilled was not a drop wasted.

The barman was busy sharing a yarn with a punter on a stool, whose attention was divided between an empty whiskey glass and a bowl of nuts, probably left out free by the management so the patrons didn't starve to death between rounds. The punter's army surplus anorak looked familiar. Unsurprising considering half of London wore them. But this one was especially familiar. Joblard moved in beside its wearer and waited for the barman to wrap up his spiel.

"See, there was this Irish, owned a hardware shop over by Benfleet. Hilty's. Specialised in nails. Business was no good 'cause of the recession. One night he comes in here drowning his sorrows and there's this Channel Four type sitting at the bar wants to start a conversation. So Hilty lays it out for him, the whole sob story from start to finish. The TV knob laps it up. Tells Hilty how it's his lucky day, him being an untold marketing whiz-kid and all. And right there and then he offers to run up an ad campaign for Hilty's Nails that'll really put the old man on the map. Guaranteed. Or it's free."

The barman paused. Gave Joblard a sly wink.

"With you in a second there son."

Then he went on with his yarn.

"Your Irish of course didn't think any more about it. The whiz-kid was just another lush on a barstool and the banks had him by the short-and-curlies. Just a matter of time before the repo men started knocking at the door. Well," lowering his voice for dramatic effect, leaning in closer to the punter in the anorak, "Hilty's up watching tele with the missus a few nights later and what does he see? The ad break comes up and there's Jesus Christ himself being put on the cross. Crown of thorns and all. Baking in the sun, eyes turned up to heaven. A couple of Romans down below congratulating themselves on superior workmanship. Up comes the sales pitch. USE HILTY'S NAILS!"

The barman looked over at Joblard again.

"Pint is it?"

Joblard nodded. The punter in the anorak kept shtim, fidgeting with his glass. The barman set down an ale and Joblard shuffled some change across the counter. The punter in the anorak stared morosely at the full pint as if it represented seven years bad luck. Or worse luck. He wasn't far wrong. The stuff tasted like degreaser someone had already put to good use. The brand on the tap was something unpronounceable.

That's the problem with this country, he thought. You can't get an honest pint the way you used to. Give me a Fullers any day...

"Well Hilty was in a real fix," the barman cut in, polishing the taps with a dish rag. "Gets straight on the blower to the whiz-kid. Mary and Joseph! He screams. You've ruined me! I'm done for! May as well go hang myself now, as wait for the lynch mob to come and do it for me. The whiz-kid meanwhile's already had himself another brainwave. Listen, he says, take it easy. We'll fix it. Promise. We'll get another ad up by tomorrow. Right as rain. Never fear. Old Hilty's beside himself. The missus tries to calm him down. Can't hurt to try, she says. Always the pragmatist. A rock in the storm-tossed sea."

Anorak took a dry sip from his empty tumbler. Winced. Set the tumbler down in defeat. Both elbows on the bar, head sagging between shoulder blades. Chin barely an inch above the rim of his glass. Joblard shook his head. It was a sorry sight to see a hard working man like Johnny Fluoride so down in the dumps. He'll cheer up pretty smartish once he realises who he's got for company, hehe. Joblard cast a glance around the rest of the bar. No sign of aliens. Just the odd escapee from the local bingo parlour warming themselves over thimbles of sherry.

"So there's Hilty next evening," says the barman, "over at the Admiral watching the tri-nations on the box, when they stop for a commercial break. The poor old bastard can't believe his eyes. Up there on the screen is Jesus Christ in person running down the hillside at Calvary with a mob of angry locals hot on his heels. And in big letters where everyone can see: THEY SHOULD'VE USED HILTY'S NAILS!"

⊙ THE GAP

Dix's real name was Izz ad-Din al-Mutanabe. An ancient Philistine name is what he'd said. And despite herself Lawson immediately thought of Ali Baba and the Forty Thieves, though had sense enough not to say so. Probably the reason he called himself Dix. As in Mason-Dixon. *'Cause somewhere you've gotta draw the line, right?*

The CSIRO CLIMATE MODELLING UNIT, Lawson registered with a vague sense of irony, had a completely schizophrenic microclimate, veering from arctic to subtropical depending on which wing of the complex you found yourself in. Dix's office, whose air-con seemed to've been set to permanent overdrive, was located at the end of a long corridor, facing south through a heavily tinted strip of double-glazed perspex onto a wall of 40-gallon diesel drums.

The office itself looked like a bomb had gone off in it. At first glance, no-one would've guessed the highly structured and precise nature of its chaos. Dix worked within his own system of core probabilities, what to anyone else seemed pure irrationality. His colleagues left him undisturbed to do his work, amazed it produced the kinds of results it did. They suspected the intervention of unnatural forces. Computer geek voodoo. Providence. Sheer luck. They riffed on his Palestine connection. He played up to it. Jokes about Christmas in East Jerusalem. Santa Claus and mistletoe on the Gaza Strip.

"What's new?" Lawson said, arms crossed, shivering slightly in the open doorway.

Dix raised his eyes, grinning up at her from behind a barricade of high-tech rubble. Cables snaked out everywhere. A smell like soured milk and solder hung in the air.

"We hit the jackpot this time, girlie," he said, speaking over the din of the air-con unit and a dozen hard-drives. He stood up, gesturing for her to come in. "Close the door," pulling out a chair for her. "Want some coffee?"

Lawson eyed the coffee pot Dix had installed in the guts of an old mainframe. Obsolete technology. She shrugged her shoulders.

"I guess it won't kill me."

"Don't bet on it," he said, pouring the sinister black liquid into a paper cup and handing it to her. "Put hairs on your chest, that will."

"As if I haven't heard that one before."

Dix barred his teeth in a broad smile.

"You mean I'm not the man of your dreams?"

Lawson rolled her eyes and took a sip of the coffee. She gagged, almost spilling it.

"Jesus, Dix, this could kill a horse."

"What'd I say? Better than Dexedrine."

She took another sip, the bitterness cauterising her mouth.

"I haven't slept all night. Drove straight across."

"It doesn't show."

"Stop flirting with me." She downed the rest of the coffee and tossed the paper cup onto an overflowing pile of trash. "Doesn't anyone ever clean this dump?"

"Sure," he said, settling himself back down in front of a bank of computer monitors. "Once a week they send around a spy to sift through my garbage. I always leave something that'll keep them busy. I've rigged up a line to the windsock on the air strip. Nice pseudo-random data. I let them try to figure out what it is. They think I'm tracking ozone depletion."

Lawson sat down beside him and watched him key-in a series of commands. Alien symbols flickered across the screen. Topographics. Trig functions.

"I picked up something interesting from the Gap's computers last night. You listen to the news?"

"Not really. Only local stuff. There's a storm coming across the Bight. They reckon it might rain."

"Rain? That's one mother of a low pressure system down there, girlie. It'll more than rain."

"I can't believe you got me up here to gab about the weather, Dix." She pointed at the screen in front of him. "What's all this?"

"This, habibi, is a small C-type asteroid I've been keeping an eye on. It was projected to pass close enough to involve an element of uncertainty. Earth's gravity pulled it in. Right into collision course with a satellite in high orbit."

"You're kidding?"

Dix pulled up some graphics. Ellipses and tangents. Satellite coordinates.

"Here's the network of comsats at low orbit. Here're the military birds at high orbit. This is the MIR-III space station. And here's our little friend."

"This is the asteroid?" Lawson lent in over Dix's arm and pointed.

"That's right," he said. "And this's its anticipated trajectory, here."

Lawson followed the lines on the screen. She wanted to know where Dix was heading.

"This was yesterday." He stroked the keyboard and the image on the screen transformed. "And this was last night."

Lawson stared. Moving into a direct line with the asteroid was a satellite that hadn't been there before.

"Interesting, wouldn't you say? That satellite just came out of nowhere. It's moving fast, too."

Dix advanced the image through a dozen time-frames.

"Now this is the collision. After that, the asteroid broke up about fifty kilometres above the east coast of America and fell to Earth as a meteor shower. A couple of sightings were reported by ships on the Atlantic. The only reported impact, you'll be interested to know, was in New York City."

"No joke? When did it happen?"

"About four a.m. local. Which would've been about eight o'clock last night in this part of the world. Needless to say, the yanks have gone completely off the beam about it."

He lent back in his chair and flipped a remote control. A screen came to life above the adjoining desk. A live CNN newsfeed. It looked like 9/11 all over again.

"You mean…?" Lawson said.

"Yep. Bullseye. You couldn't make it up."

They both stared at the news-feed. Smoke rising from a crater in the middle of the New York financial district. Chaos. People screaming at the camera. Meteor mania. Alien attack. National Guards on the streets. The President caught speechless on prime-time breakfast TV.

"Unbelievable," Lawson said. "What about the satellite?"

"Well…" Dix muted the newsfeed and switched back to his console. "That's a very good question. It certainly hasn't made any headlines. Which kinda got me wondering…"

He jumped screens. Pulled up more graphics.

"I tried the NASA directory. Zilch. Same with the European Space Agency. It's not Russian and it's not Chinese. But I did manage to work a trace on an impact. Seems the bulk of our satellite must've spun off from the collision and made re-entry somewhere over the Indian Ocean. And would you believe this – the Gap picked up something coming down in our own backyard, about twenty minutes afterwards. I'm thinking, maybe a piece of our mystery satellite? If it was a satellite. Worth a look-see, eh?"

"What do you mean, if it was a satellite?"

"I mean, this is all kinda guesswork, but I'm figuring it wasn't aliens, it's not Hubble, and it's too small to be a space station. But it's still good to keep an open mind, right? Not everything they put up there gets on the register. Maybe it was a North Korean missile. Who knows. Though I have my doubts about that particular angle."

"So you want me to go and check it out, whatever it is?"

"You're not just pretty, *habibi*."

"If it's like you say, won't there be people already looking?"

"All depends. One thing's for certain, whatever it is, it sure as hell wasn't put up there by any *Australian* government. Which gives us, I suppose, a nominal logistical advantage over whoever else might be interested in a quick recovery job. Wouldn't you reckon?"

"Maybe. What's the coordinate?"

"Lake Eyre south."

A live topographic view came up on the screen.

"I've been running everything through half-a-dozen programmes all day. They've zeroed-in on a patch just north of the Oodnadatta Track. Right about here," he pointed at a narrow peninsula jutting into a salt flat. "But we don't have much time."

He pulled back on the topographic. Dix's finger hovered over a white mass covering most of the Bight.

"There's your most immediate competition. If that storm there keeps heading northwest, you'll have maybe a couple of hours. The chances don't look great, but it's the only opportunity we've got. I have a very reliable friend who's ready to fly you up there, right as we speak. The lake's supposed to be dry as a bone, so you shouldn't have any trouble finding a spot to land."

He turned to face her, mouth stretched into a wide grin.

"As they say in the classics, *good luck*. And, uh, *bon voyage*."

+ MOMO

Six months previous, Osborne had been one of a small army of census workers trawling Manhattan from Marble Hill to Battery Park, delivering, then a day later collecting, duck-egg-blue census forms door-to-door. According to the statistical office, the population of New York County had been in more or less steady decline since circa 1910, when it peaked at just over 2 mil., and only now was trending back on an upswing. Approximately 6% growth in the last decade, up from -9.4.

By an ironic twist of fate, Osborne himself wouldn't be counted among them. His wife had just given him the boot from their Lower East Side apartment. What she called his obsessional problems had got him fired from every other job he'd had, but the Census Bureau had a certain sympathy for obsessionals. His wife, soon to be ex-, no longer did, and for the last week he'd been sleeping rough under the West Side Line with a free view of the New York Department of Sanitation, thinking a change in cardinal points might be in order for a man long set in his ways.

It was there, one morning around 14th Street, that Osborne first noticed the fluorescent orange paint on the sidewalk as he slouched in the direction of the Census Bureau at Hudson and West Houston. The paint ran in a fine trail that appeared purposeful yet erratic, like an unravelled ball of twine a cat had been chasing. The possibility that it led somewhere couldn't be ignored, though none of his fellow pedestrians even seemed aware of it. He alone had been singled out. How long had it been there, waiting for him?

Right there and then Osborne determined to embark upon a quest, to discover where the orange paint would lead – whether it take ten minutes, ten hours, or ten days. Time, he decided, wasn't a factor. He'd follow the orange paint wherever it led, for however long it took. Till, like the man who slew the minotaur, he found his way through the labyrinth.

The trail began auspiciously below the EZ Pawn Shop (watches, jewelry, electronics) and the Great Wall Laundry Cleaning Inc. Next came Luz's Shoe Repair. Charlie's Smoke Shop followed. Then in order: a barber's with red-white-blue candy striped barber-pole, the Dirty Bird To-Go Café (RESTAURANT FOR RENT. Prudential Douglas Elliman 212-692-6182), the Local 237 Teamsters, Woody McHale's Bar & Grill, Discount Liquors, and The Istanbul Grill.

Between 8th and 9th a man with handle-bar moustache and black leather kilt walked past eyeing him. Osborne, mind focused on the miraculated unfolding of the secret trail, blanked him. Sidewalk splotches of chewing gum and tyre tread. Our Lady of Guadalupe on the right. Then down into the meatpacking district. A boutique desert of red brick and window-drape velour.

At several points the trail faded out, got lost between squares of re-laid concrete, cut diagonally across intersections only to be buried under tarmac. Serendipity brought him to Hudson Street. Blue uniformed coworkers stomping by with clipboards and satchel bags. *Hey Osborne, not looking your usual self today. Hey man, can I borrow your ballpoint?*

A pack of stray dogs followed him from the Gansevourt Street basketball court. *Wuff-wuff.* Speed Limit 30. Crossing Jane Street. Black breezeblock parking stations. Trail running cold at West 12th. Doubled back. Greenwich Avenue, the Village Den, St Vincent's. Skateboarders doing monkey tricks on a concrete ramp. Seventh Avenue. Past the Village Vanguard, the Pleasure Chest, the all-night grocery. Christopher Street. Village Cigars. Lost it again. Bleeker. Caught up with it on the east side of 7th. Central Parking Systems, Open 24 Hours. Morton Street. Disappeared for half a block under fresh pavement. Reappeared. Gone again at Bedford.

A yellow cab slowed down and cruised alongside. Osborne, eyes downcast, navigated by pure intuition, east-south-east, the ghost-line all the while accompanying him.

Who put it there? What was its purpose? At the intersection of Clarkson and Carmine, Seventh Avenue became Varick Street and the trail of orange paint jagged left onto West Houston. From there it tended south, weaving the sidewalk along McDougal, diverging again at Prince. Osborne continued south, watching for the trail to reappear. Finally it did, at the foot of a blue hoarding round a vacant lot. Slipped beneath a wire gate and continued on, past eight-foot high chainlink, to disappear once more beneath weeds and trash. Osborne traced an invisible line with his eye till it came to rest outside Sleepy's, the Mattress Professionals. As he knew it must be, the trail was waiting there for him, beckoning him on.

A casual observer might've been reminded of someone wandering about with those glasses, all the rage once upon a time, that turned everything upside down. Groping through the sky on a vapour trail. Do it long enough the world upends itself and sticks there in your head that way. Just as, in a manner of speaking, Osborne's head at that very moment. The flourishing monomania of a man set out upon a course after dwelling in the wilderness. He'd follow the path and dedicate himself to whatever it led to. Bearer of its revelation. *Hosanna! Hosanna!* The word writ in the City's fabric, upon which, day after day, untold thousands trod. From subway grating to the detritus of vacant lots. The great census of the unsaved.

The line once again slithered off into no-man's-land. Rusty barrels, hummocks of green tarpaulin and sotweed south of Spring Street. Slithering back outside the Sixth Ave Car Wash, tyre-blackened on overscarred pavement. Osborne pulling up suddenly at the sight of an enormous negro with face half eaten-away by white plague sores. Grimaced. Talismanic forehead drawn down over eyes distaining to see. Fixed his gaze on the backed-up traffic down West Broadway, navigating it like a man at sea, tossed by furious waves. Reeling himself in, one step at a time. The orange line showing itself in renewed splendour on the south side of Grand Street. More parking lots. The cars of Babel, towering everywhere. By the Greene Street intersection the line was nothing more than a sublimated texture, riddling the black steel gratings beneath which the beast roared, the leviathan shook its tail, the belly of the subway belched its stream. It was there again and gone by Mercer Street.

A sixth sense told him to head north. Broadway. Past the fashion houses and retro Brooks Brothers suits. And sure as night follows day there it was, reappearing in front of a row of 99¢ hotdog and pretzel stands, junk jewellery stalls, sunglasses and hats, discount tribal wear. Then smack into Houston, the border line where East-side meets West. The continuous cross-flow. Telluric force-field patterns in constant flux. A Calvin Klein billboard towered over the Lafayette intersection – a blonde colossus in a red bathing suit.

From there the trail made its precarious way north of Bleecker, winding hither-and-yon, slaloming round streetlamps, coming-and-going between ad hoc strata of urban renewal, erosion, agglutination, deletion. The pattern repeated. Vanishing for half a block at Great Jones Street, resurfacing at East 4th. Buried under freshly laid concrete at Waverley. Turning east at Astor Place. And there it was again, like some imp of the perverse, waiting for him at Cooper Square. Old guy in a wheel chair keeping guard over some undefined territory. A bum passed-out on the sidewalk three feet away wearing a cardboard sign, plastic cup in hand for change, *Why lie? I need a drink.*

Weaving south along Bowery. North again on Third Avenue. East on Stuyvesant. Lost at 9th Street only to be re-found on Second Avenue. Past Sonny's Florist at 6th. Curling left at East 4th in a bold line now barely interrupted. Past the Bank of America.

Doubling itself in parallel paint splotches, swerving off the sidewalk and onto the street halfway down the block from the W.R. Laundromat. Drop Off and Self Service.

What or who was W.R.? Osborne wondered.

Back onto the sidewalk at the First Avenue intersection. Then north past the housing estate at number 80. Stumbling over a patchwork of old and new concrete, like Chinese checkers. It made no sense. Right turn on 10th Street. The Church of Christ. Body Evolution. Russian and Turkish Baths Health Club est. 1892. The Boys Club of NYC at Ave A. Tompkins Square, rats and homeless in cardboard boxes under the trees. Right again at Ave B, then south. The lime green awning of Zee's Pet Shop and Supply, Free Delivery.

Osborne, mouth parched, sweat pouring from his brow, feet burning, pushed on. South now into Alphabet City. The trail feeding itself out, the reel running to an end. It couldn't be long now. He was almost there. Slouching into the sun. *Knowledge is Power!* writ large on a brick wall. PS64. Then at 4th Street, two identical lines crossed. One heading south on Avenue B, the other continuing East. Osborne, figuring the odds, chose East. Through the estates, all the way to Avenue D. Then right, left. Between the red brick towers of Sunshine Gardens, under maple trees with squirrels and blackbirds. *Et in Arcadia ego?* A green pedestrian overpass and the FDR flowing south like the proverbial waters below. Down the East River Promenade tending Williamsburg Bridge-wise. Coming to a sudden anticlimax in a wide splotch of orange household acrylic. As if to say, *Here everything comes to pass.*

Birds twittered in the trees. A ferry tooted on the river. Smoke spiralled from the chimney of the Domino Sugar Refinery into a blue sky growing darker by the minute. Osborne stood rooted to the spot. He'd travelled all this way and now what? The melancholia of the pilgrim began slowly to descend upon him as he contemplated the meaning of it all. The given sign. The strict path. Its gaps and omissions. Its windings and diversions. The route chosen and that declined. Had he erred? Was all this merely the beginning of a ritual to be performed like an ablution from that day hence? Osborne stared at the orange splotch on the pavement. Bits of chewing gum and leaves and loose gravel had become embedded in it over time. Like a general accretion of garbled sense little by little blotting-out The Original Message transmitted down the cosmic line countless eons ago.

And right there in the middle of it, as if by chance, lay the tattered remains of a business card, semi-adhesed in the August heat. *Do you seek guidance?* it said. *Doctor A. Suliman is here to help YOU. Call the Good Doctor now. 212-SULI-MAN. Find yourself!*

♒ COSMIC RAIN

The flight from Prague took them directly across the Alps, tracking low through sheer gorges of grey-black-white. As they travelled south the sky cleared. Moonlight fell radiant on seemingly vast tracts of snow. De Laurentiis chose a point just north of Trieste to ditch the chopper, setting it to autopilot on a heading out into the Adriatic. The fuel gauge was already in the red. In the pre-dawn Shinwah watched the taillight dip down over the Friulian hills, then disappear. The diversion seemed purposeless to her. Another one of de Laurentiis's theatre pieces, played out for an audience she half-suspected didn't exist.

She wondered about the dead trader back in Prague. About the amulet he'd been wearing. The scan in her handset. The block of ice. Later she'd lay out the lines, three open, three whole. Synapse I-Ching. Divine the dead man's spirit. The destiny of the pendent they'd stolen. What it was. What it meant. See if, as she always hoped, death lay in de Laurentiis's path. Or her own.

Perhaps he knew what she was thinking. Watching in the cold beneath the olive trees. She was never for a moment out of his sight. And now, with the fatigue starting to gnaw at her, all she could think of was the yin-yang of the dead man's ice. To bring her back to that plateau of effortless clarity. But he wouldn't give her the opportunity. She wondered how he managed to go without needing sleep. Maybe he wasn't human at all. Even when she went to relieve herself, she could feel his eyes on her. It presumably gave him pleasure, this game he was always playing. Reminding her of the fact that, for all intents and purposes, she belonged to him.

Shinwah remembered the first time he'd taken her. She'd been asleep. A damp foam mattress on a basement floor. She'd awoken, screaming, in pitch darkness with her wrists and ankles cuffed and something sticking inside her. It seemed to penetrate her entire body. The pain was so excruciating she passed out. She never learned what it was. A fine red tracery remained from the cuffs and her abdomen hurt for days. She knew it was de Laurentiis from his smell. The next time, he made her put the handcuffs on herself. It was never fucking in any straightforward sense. It wasn't about that. Only about the power.

The sick part was how she'd grown to want it. As if it was the only thing that could balance everything else out. Anchor her. The real her and not the virtual one. Time-shifting was a bitch. All of reality splintered into a mosaic of nanosecond calibrations. She was afraid she'd wake up one day and it'd all be a dream. Or that she'd only dream she'd woken up. That in reality she'd be one of those half-life floaters inside the cryogenic vats. Zombies of a future she was inhabiting, now, in the past... *Stuck here*, she thought, *because something's gone wrong. Only he's not telling me.*

She'd tried to keep her mind focused on getting through to the next phase in this new game, whatever it was. Not to be taken unawares. De Laurentiis had remained silent the entire time. Later there'd been a rendezvous. A black four-wheel-drive van. Men who looked like partisans from an old war movie. Money had changed hands. Then they were driving without headlights through the foothills towards the sea. After nearly an hour, a farmhouse loomed out of the darkness. The van stopped. There were voices. She couldn't understand what they were saying, only the sense of urgency, confusion. De Laurentiis told her to wait inside the farmhouse. Someone led her inside. It was small. Tables and workbenches were littered with bits of machinery. Monitors. Hard drives. Motherboards. A shortwave radio hissed somewhere in the background. Whispers out of the ether. Cosmic rain.

A young boy handed her a cup of coffee and then went back to work with a soldering iron. From time to time he glanced up, but said nothing. On the radio, fragments of news about an explosion in New York. She drank the coffee, but it didn't effect her at all. Residual ice deadening the synapses. The radio warping in and out. Asteroid. Ground Zero. War of the Worlds. She stared at the mess of equipment spread around the kitchen. The boy was busy repairing or building a circuit board. Diodes and transistors lay spread out on a red and white tablecloth. The scene was unreal. She had no time to make any sense of it before de Laurentiis called through the doorway. They were on the move again, changing vehicles. Radio voices echoing in her ears.

(ACCESS CODE

"Give me a name."

The voice is hard, interrogatory. A woman's voice. He's staring into a blackness without contours. Somewhere, not far away, the ratcheting of a surveillance drone. It sounds strange, like he's hearing it underwater. He's not even sure he's awake, he only knows his eyes are open and he can't see anything. Then a sharp ringing in his ears. It passes, but the sound of the drone's still there. He tries to get up, but his body's locked into a cramp. He breathes, in, out, slowly. Then he feels something pressed hard to his forehead.

"Don't try to move," the voice says.

It's the same voice as before. Not the Stranger's voice, the woman's. It's coming from directly in front of him. The drone's red eye flashes across the courtyard. A beam of red light pokes into shadows, searching for life forms. The sensor whirs, machine-lethal. And for a moment he registers the figure crouching at the base of the wall. Pale skin. Paler hair. Flashback. A pair of eugenics droids.

But if she's a droid I'd be dead already. He feels for the handgun but it's gone. Perhaps it's what's pushing into his forehead. The drone veers away, spotlighting a tower of rubble further off, then dips out of sight. In the silence he can hear the woman breathing He tries to figure out the situation, but the programme's not working. Numerics frozen, fading-out. Crashed. No sign of the Stranger. *What the fuck do I do now?*

"You've got three seconds."

Her voice is like ice. He feels the gun press harder. Emphatic.

"Connection. Looking for the Connection."

"Who?"

"No name."

"Where?"

"Necropolis. Need to get there."

"Who're you?"

"Don't know."

The muzzle of the gun makes the veins in his temples bulge.

"Like I said, I don't know."

Again the flicker of searchlights. He can see his questioner more clearly this time. Pale, short blonde hair, red expressionless eyes like an albino.

"How'd you get here?"

"Don't know."

"Lot of things you don't know, aren't there? Maybe I should shoot you right now, or maybe I'll let the droids have you. Which will it be, Mr I-Don't-Know?"

"I crossed a bridge. There was an island. The programme told me where to go. I came here."

"What programme?"

"In my head. It's like. Hard to explain."

"Try me."

"It's like I've been here before. Only I can't remember. But I do. See?"

"No, I don't see. But thanks to you, there'll be an army of fucking drones down here any minute. They have a thing about retribution. Ever seen someone who's been tortured by those eugenics freaks? Not pretty."

"It was a trap. They tried to kill me."

"No shit?"

"Got to find the Connection."

"No connection here, bigshot. Only ghosts. You come here looking for ghosts? Or you don't know that either?"

He can feel her scrutinising him, but he can't think. The programme's completely dead. His eyes hurt trying to see in the

95

dark, straining too hard. He needs to get things into focus, start thinking for himself. Somewhere in his head, a voice far-off straining to get through. An echo. Repeating itself. He tries to concentrate, but the more he thinks, the less clear everything becomes. He closes his eyes, all the while aware of the woman's presence. Close to him. Gun ready. *Why doesn't she just shoot?*

So far everything he's done's been by remote control. At least, that's what it seems. Call it instinct. As if somewhere, inside, he already knows. He can hear the hammer click back on the gun pointing at his forehead and opens his eyes. The word's in his mouth before he can even think.

"Momo."

There's silence. He says it again.

"Momo."

He doesn't know what it means. It could be anything. A glitch in the programme. Like him. Momo. But he hadn't spoken it by accident, something made him say it. But what difference would it make if the Connection was dead? Or not dead, a ghost. Like the Stranger? An echo, haunting the circuit. Maybe. He tries to make out the shape of the woman with the gun. She should've pulled the trigger by now. But she isn't there, he can't feel the gun any more. For a moment he experiences panic. Then a voice comes from close behind him.

"You're lucky I didn't blow your fucking head off."

All of a sudden it's very bright, the drone seems to be right inside the courtyard now.

"Get up," she says. "Quick. Let's go."

He tells himself to move, but he can't. *Like trying to lift a stone with your mind.* Then he feels himself being dragged to his feet.

"Move!" she hisses, pushing him ahead of her through a gap in the rubble, plunging him back into darkness.

Straightaway he's lost in a confusion of turnings and descents. A dull green halo outlines unreadable numerics, like the after-image of lost time. The albino directs him onwards invisibly. There's only the sound of their footsteps and a dull throbbing at the back of his head that gets louder and louder the further they descend.

Without warning the floor shudders and he feels the walls move on either side, dirt sifting down through the cracks. His legs give out. The albino crouches almost on top of him, so close he can hear her breathing above the dull rumble that echoes through the walls.

"Just like I said. Retribution time."

☐ CON

"You're not a very smart boy, are you Johnny?"

"Listen. I swear on my mother's grave…"

"You what? Give the old bird some credit, eh? Think she gave birth to you and raised you and gave you the best bleedin' years of her life just so you could abuse her memory like some cheap punk trying to get himself off the hook? You should be ashamed, defaming your old mum like that."

"Eh?"

"Now what's this I've been hearing about UFOs, Johnny? Been sniffing the glue again, have we?"

As far as scam artists went, Johnny Fluoride was small fry. How Bludhorn got involved with him in the first place would always remain a mystery to Joblard. He didn't for a moment believe the man presently hanging by the ankles over the side of the jetty was capable of zipping his own flies, let alone pulling a con.

The look on Johnny Fluoride's face at the bar had said it all. Two beady glass eyes peering over the collar of his army surplus, confused by the punchline to the barman's joke – a little too much like rocket science. Then fixing on Joblard. Eyes not glassy anymore. Almost falling off his stool in his haste to get away. Making a pathetic attempt at a runner, hardly able even to find the door, taking a wrong turn and falling over himself trying to scramble up the embankment. *Like a chicken with its head cut off.* And now, in addition, the shithead had gone and pissed himself.

"UFOs, Johnny. Dwarves in spacesuits, is what I'm told. That wasn't my employer's expectation, Johnny. Dwarves in spacesuits. Was it?"

"Not a spacesuit…"

"What's that, Johnny?"

"Raincoat. It was a raincoat."

"…?"

"One of them was wearing a raincoat."

"Who you talking about, Johnny?"

"With this eye thing. And the other one had no face."

"You're not making sense, Johnny."

"They came outta nowhere. Everything was set up like I promised your boss. But they saw me. They knew I was there. They'll kill me too."

"Slow down, Johnny."

"And there's nothing you can do about it!"

"Who'd they kill?"

Johnny Fluoride's scream split the air. The Weasel was right, Joblard thought. *Complete nutter*. But the sudden violence of Johnny Fluoride's convulsions caught him unprepared, writhing like a thing possessed.

Joblard, aware now of a tour group coming his way along the floodwall, decided it'd be a good idea to get the situation back under control. He hoist the screaming Fluoride up by the feet, only to find himself clutching an empty pair of Doc Martens boots with their laces snapped.

Joblard stared at the empty boots like they were something from another planet. Down below the tide was churning. No sign of Johnny Fluoride. Joblard, an uneasy feeling slowly taking hold, turned and crossed to the other side of the jetty, peering downstream through the drizzle towards London. A vague lump of a thing that might've been a man was fast drifting away.

"Well I'll be fucked."

Joblard blinked down at the boots in his hands. He felt silly standing there, holding them like that.

Up on the floodwall, the tourists were busy taking pictures of the jetty and Joblard on it. Though one in particular wasn't taking pictures. A scarecrow draped in overcoat and felt hat, whose face looked like it'd been spatulaed with zinc cream.

Joblard shuffled. Hands behind back, boots in hand. Like a schoolboy caught puffing a splif behind the lavs. And grinned sheepishly up at the cameras.

⊙ WANABI

The single-prop Cessna banked left. Below, the huge tailings ponds from the processing plant at Olympic Dam, like an abstract painting on the desert. This was uranium country. The mines pumped acid down bore holes to dissolve ore and then up another hole to extract the uranium. The wash turned the ponds technicolour. Lawson gazed at them through the cockpit window. Her mother had told her stories. About Wanabi, the mysterious water serpent of the Dreaming, creator of the waterholes. Her ancestors had painted the stories on tree bark, using clay. Red ochre, yellow ochre, white. They knew the secrets of water, appearing and disappearing like the serpent, through underground channels. The knowledge sustained them. Whitefellas knew nothing of this place. Only what their science told them. Uranium ore. Yellowcake. Arsenic. Gold. They took from the land. They poisoned it. The way they poisoned its people.

Lake Eyre was still half-an-hour north. The last remnant of the inland sea that once covered much of the continent. It was this sea that'd first sustained her mother's people. The cradle of their civilisation, their culture. What whitey called their *savage habits*, their *low depraved life*. She remembered the shock of reading that at school. In history books. Then learning about *terra nullius*. Goonya law. It decreed the land was empty, uninhabited. That Nungas didn't exist. It made her bitter sometimes, thinking about it. The one part of her denying the other part.

Lawson glanced at the GPS. Dix's computer was feeding it coordinates. He'd worked the target zone down to a square kilometre, one out of ten thousand. Small enough to compare satellite close-ups for signs of impact. The pilot looked over at her, nodded out the window. Lawson followed her eyes. They were flying low. The Cessna's shadow hovering just below the wingtip. Further off, a black weather balloon was trailing along the ground, a flock of emus keeping pace with it, weaving back and forth across the low scrub. The pilot's voice crackled in the headset above the engine noise.

"We'll end up flying straight back into that, if we're not lucky."

As they banked, Lawson could make out a haze low on the horizon. Red Nullarbor dust. Thousands of tonnes of it ripped up into the atmosphere. With the storm blowing in right behind them, they'd had to cut cross-state and try to out-flank it. She knew it'd catch them eventually, they only needed enough time to set down and locate the impact site before everything was covered over in sand and bulldust. She was starting to think it might be too much of a long shot.

The pilot had been waiting at the bottom of the airstrip, watching the sky. Everything had been too still. It was the lull, Lawson guessed, before the storm. The Cessna Skyhawk was fuelled and ready to go. She'd dumped her equipment across the back seats. A rucksack and flare gun. The rucksack contained a Geiger counter, metal detector, ration pack, the works, just in case. The flare gun was for anything. She'd fried an angry snake with it once. Desert taipan, deadliest things on Earth. Or almost.

It took Lawson a while to figure out the pilot was a woman. Her name, when Lawson asked, was Kath. She was tough, had a man's bones. Deep tanned and black-eyed. They barely spoke. Lawson knew the other woman thought they were wasting their time and running an unnecessary risk. Dix must've done some smooth talking. It quietly amazed her the way Dix got things done. He had an instinct for improbability.

She dialled down the GPS interface on the sat-phone and called him up. Out the window, the landscape had turned dull, monotonous, bleached-out. Lawson loved this country, but she could never get used to the way things distorted from the air. It was like looking at a wall and reading the cracks in it. From time to time you found a window, some shattered masonry, the scars of destruction and abandonment. The horizon suffocated her.

"Hey, girlie!"

Dix's grinning avatar came up on the screen. Lawson pushed the headset back and slipped the earphone in place, dialling up the volume.

"I've got you on the radar," Dix said. "Watch that storm. She's coming up real fast."

"Did you get the coordinates?"

"As good as. I'm sending them now. Listen, I've got a scrambler running, just in case. Looks like my little venture with the Gap's computers may have attracted some attention."

"Shit."

"Hey, I grew up with the Israelis. They taught me a lot. First thing, never get paranoid. Someone's *always* watching you, hehe."

"Dix, be careful."

"It's okay. I'm going out to get a breath of air right now. The coordinates should be spot on. When you're done, meet me at the crossing. Don't worry, I'll take good care of your baby."

"Dix?"

The screen blanked. A green light flashed in the corner. She switched over to GPS. Target: 29°18'43.62"S, 137°27'22.50"E. Flight time: two and a half hours.

Meet me at the crossing... Someone was onto him and he was getting out, that much was clear. Lawson stashed the earpiece and stared at the sat-phone. *Be careful, Dix.* Why'd everything always have to happen so suddenly? Funny, she thought, how much she'd come to rely on Dix being there. And yet how often did they actually get to see each other? She'd always preferred being alone, not depending on anyone. But right then she'd've given almost anything to see Dix's face on the screen again. For the first time in a long time, since the night the cops had come around to her mum's caravan and taken her away, she felt afraid. *Don't leave me, Dix. I need you.*

Lawson felt Kath's hand touch her arm. It startled her. She pulled the headset back on.

"Are you alright?"

Lawson nodded.

"You look like you could do with a rest. Catch some zeds. I'll let you know when the action starts."

Kath showed her the faintest of grins then turned back to the controls. She'd have to tell Kath eventually. That they couldn't go back to Maralinga now. They'd have no choice but to continue on for as long as the fuel held out. There'd be an airstrip out there somewhere. But if the Gap's security was onto Dix, it was just a matter of time before they were onto the plane. And then what? *Just how serious, Dix, is the shit you've gotten us into?*

Lawson stared off at the edge of the world. A blue haze dipping down from space, fringed with reddish brown. Thinking how they'd put men in space and even dogs, but they'd never put one of her people up there. Or one of Dix's.

The horizon just seemed to sit there, unshifting. Like the rainbow serpent with its tail wrapped around the sky. The longer she looked at it, the emptier she felt. Dix's coffee was wearing off, time dilating. The long overnight run, interstate from Broken Hill, iron ore country. She wondered if she knew what she was searching for. Not now, but in general. What her life was for. Why she did what she did.

She'd always told herself the world was lacking in real alternatives. But it wasn't true. She could've left, the way Dix had left Palestine. *Different circumstances.* Besides, this was her people's country. *Her people? What people? You don't have any people,* she thought. And it was true. After her mum died, she'd never gone back. Her kinship ended with Old Glory, her past blacked-out by the kind of taboo that forbids naming the dead. It came back to her in dreams, song-lines, involuntary memories. Spirit reckoning.

Lawson began drifting into half-consciousness. The sound of the engine bored into her mind, long hours of sleeplessness waiting in ambush. A green caravan in the middle of a red desert. Faces glowing out of the sky. *Nganyintja*…

About fifty kilometres out from their target the Cessna started hitting turbulence. Lawson's head butted the side window. She straightened up, eyes bleary. The headset crackled.

"Tighten your seatbelt, love. This is where the fun part begins."

+ KINEZOLOGY

An intersection at the west end of Canal Street. Night. Traffic backed-up out of Holland Tunnel, jamming the river, the distant lights of Battery Park Annex oozing down into it. Wind and rain. Osborne huddled against a lamppost in a worn, brown leather trench coat, upturned collar, peering through fogged wristwatch glass at ancient analogue, right-angled hour and minute hands faintly luminescent. Nine o'clock, post meridiem. Time to do what he'd come to do.

The address the Doctor had given was an industrial storage facility that looked like it hadn't functioned in decades. Above the street entrance a sign with white lettering, streaked with shadows: KINEZOLOGY. ONE MIND INSTITUTE. Osborne stared. It meant nothing to him. All he could think was *two heads are better than one*, like his mother maybe used to say, when he was a kid and couldn't figure something out. Which was most of the time. It conjured freakshow monsters, brains in jars, water monkeys. You could get them mail order, with cut-out coupons from the back page of comic magazines. Somewhere they had a warehouse full of them, some old guy in grey overalls processing the orders, pensive-like, to the circadian rhythms of the pre-automated working life.

He double-checked the address. The numbers tallied, but the place looked dead. No lights on in the One Mind Institute, hehe. Something about it gave him the shivers. The jars, maybe, with brains in them. Like the Doc's secret lab. It was enough just to *think* they existed. Mind-waves from the mothership slipping their frequencies, putting weird ideas in his head. He began to regret his decision to take the job. But then, as always with the Doctor, he hadn't felt there was much of a choice. *Who the fuck are these people?*

"Think of them as *friends*," the Doctor had said.

"What kind of friends?"

"Let's just say," he'd purred, in that impending doom voice of his, standing over the chair in which Osborne had been sitting – especially designed, Osborne remembered thinking, to put you at a disadvantage – "the kind of friends better to be thought well of."

So much for straight answers. And these were people he was supposed to trust with a bag full of cash? He tested the weight of the stainless steel case he was carrying. It made him feel conspicuous. Like someone in a film, engaged in activities of an undoubtedly dubious nature, with God only knew how many government agencies, Census Bureau included, at that very moment watching from the rooftops. It's a frame-up! Nothing the Doctor had told him was any use now in allaying his doubts. Instead of details, he'd talked philosophy.

"That of which we do not know, we cannot speak," he'd said.

And what'd it mean, that the Ground Zero meteorite wasn't really a meteorite? Suliman had offered only high-sounding riddles. About having seen retribution in many things.

"Man is too often concerned," he'd said, "with stating the obvious, yet unable to see what's directly in front of his face. The world," sweeping his arms back to convey some sense of worldliness, "is that it is, and not according to what we know of it."

The sole effect of the Doctor's talk had been to set him on edge. Ever since his Tenth Avenue epiphany, Osborne had felt a suspicion things weren't at all what they seemed. Elements from what could only be a parallel dimension kept showing through. He clung on with his mind to that Ariadne's thread that'd lead him through the labyrinth. The Manhattan grid, streets east-west, avenues north-south. Unassailable constants in a fragmented, ever-changing landscape. But retribution? For what?

"The most important thing," the Doctor had told him, "is to act like everything around you is perfectly normal. And what's normal anyway? Remember, there're crazy people in this world.

You're not crazy, but there're other people who *are* crazy. When the time comes, you'll know what to do. Trust me."

And Osborne had trusted him. The Doctor had picked him off the street, fixed him up, found him an apartment up in Washington Heights. And gave him odd jobs – as a courier of sorts. The kind of jobs that left him plenty of thinking time and the chance to move around the City. See things with his own eyes. No strings attached. So he'd thought. He'd figured he was one of the Doctor's charity cases.

For six months, everything had gone smoothly. To plan. But recently there'd been evidence something was about to slip. A renewed perturbation in the outward appearances of things. Like a face you never suspected was really a mask, behind it could be anything, the awaited revelation. *When the time comes.* And had it come? He'd kept his eyes open for a sign, dispelling the usual aberration of events. It'd happened all of a sudden. The blackouts. Ground Zero. And now this.

Osborne switched the case to his left hand and started across the street, breath streaming ghostlike from his mouth. A ramp and a set of stairs led up to the front of the building, past the collapsed, sodden outlines of cardboard boxes, newspaper bundles and assorted junk. The entrance was a delivery bay. He pressed the only button visible below an intercom set into the wall, camouflaged by graffiti. Every building in the neighbourhood had been systematically wrecked. It looked too deliberate. Someone's idea of a war zone, a ghost city within the city. It vibed 1980s Mondo New York. Devaluation. The hidden hand of the redevelopment lobby. Eminent Domain. Secret deals whose fine print left scars across the landscape, like an insatiable beast alive inside the subway catacombs. Invisible. Unsuspected.

As the Doctor said, "The true government is the one its citizens don't even know exists…"

Osborne pressed the button again, holding it down this time, counting ten. A mechanical whine sounded from the other side of a wide steel door. Then the sound of a lock mechanism thudding open. Osborne found himself, against his better judgement, stepping into a very large elevator. Immediately he was overwhelmed by the stench. Urine and presumably human faeces. The door closed behind him. He was plunged into darkness. Automatically he began backing away from an invisible menace. There was a distant whirr and echo of steal cables straining under weight. Time slowed, minutes seemed to pass. As the elevator broke floor-level, a large brightly-lit industrial loft came into view. A moment later the lift shuddered to a halt. He waited for something to happen, but nothing did.

Osborne stepped out of the elevator. He breathed vapour. The air in the loft was even colder than it'd been outside. His footsteps made dull echoes. The loft extended all the way to the back of the building. A barrage of floodlights arced down from the ceiling at the far end, casting weird shadows. He raised a hand to shield his eyes from the glare. It made him think of a theatre, where the audience remains completely hidden from the actors behind the glare of stage lights. All the windows on the street-side had been bricked-up. The back of the loft was curtained in shadow. Between him and it was a network of beams, rafters, metal scaffolds holding the walls and ceiling in place. The whole place appeared on the verge of collapse.

Halfway across the brightly lit forestage was a trestle table, the kind they used in hospitals. Something indistinct was lying on it. Beside the tables was a high-backed metal chair. Apart from the scaffolding, these were the only objects visible. Like props, waiting for the actors who'll bring them to life. Automatically Osborne took several steps forward then stopped. Behind him, a sound of glass breaking. He looked back into the lift. Nothing. Rats. Wind groaning in the lift shaft.

〰 GOD MACHINE

Shinwah awoke shivering. Grey light through broken skylights, dust sifting down through planking loosened by the wind. She was lying on a foam slab in the remains of an overseer's office, in a disused warehouse. Crates of mouldering routing sheets stacked around the walls. Smell of salt water, engine grease, rodent excrement. She flexed her hands at her side. Her right hand was stiff, bruised across the heal. Flashback to the dead Russian. And then what? Her neck ached. A dull throbbing across her forehead. The come-down had been hard. She tasted gunmetal. Groaned.

The warehouse must've belonged to a coffee import business. Empty hessian sacks hung from overhead beams, stencilled with place of origin. East Africa. Kenya. Tanzania. Ethiopia. The faded paintwork above the warehouse doors read FRATELLI COSULICH. A driver in a grey delivery van had brought them here at dawn. De Laurentiis had told her to wait till he called. She checked her handset. It'd been three hours. She'd tried to sleep, but sleep came only fitfully, the drug wearing off slow. She'd dreamt of a room in Beijing. A body, hers, floating in a cryogenic vat. Hooked into the God machine. That's what she called it. It contained her thoughts, projecting her through time-space, quantum weirdness.

"God doesn't exist," de Laurentiis had said, in that high-minded way he had of turning everything to bullshit. "Only entropy exists. A programme seized with feedback. Crash and reboot. Space, time, are nothing but states in flux."

Except the one state, she thought. That room in Beijing. The centre of the universe. The still point. The question was, how to make that point coincide with where she was. That's why they were here. Because something had gone wrong.

Outside the wind heaved in off the sea. The walls groaned.

The warehouse was part of an old shipping terminal that looked like an anachronism washed-up on the edge of the city. It had all the appearance of an ancient shipwreck time had struggled and failed to redeem. The rest of the city just looked like a dump. They'd taken a circuitous route to arrive there, the driver all the while speaking some impenetrable dialect of what she supposed was Italian. De Laurentiis did nothing to enlighten her. She'd grasped enough, though, to piece together a picture. She was pretty certain, for example, that right now de Laurentiis was off somewhere cooking up a deal to get a boat across the water. The ultimate destination could be anywhere.

Shinwah found her shoulder bag lying on a dusty table beside the office door. Laurentiis had done nothing to conceal the fact he'd been through it. The contents had been tipped out on the table. There were streaks in the dust from where he'd examined only the more personal items. The dead man's ice had elicited no apparent interest. She picked the jeweller's case out of the mess, unhasped the two halves and scraped together a line from the residue on the mirror. The instant she snorted it, the pain dissolved. Warmth spread down her neck and spine into her groin. Memory. Her face to the cubicle wall. De Laurentiis behind her. His hand in her jumpsuit, down between her legs. She felt the wetness come again. Gritted her teeth. Echo of his laughter as his fingers withdrew. Footsteps. His voice across the empty warehouse.

"Be good while I'm away…"

She wiped the last trace of crystal from the mirror and licked her finger. Her reflection looked up at her. Face a mess. She felt dirty. She needed to fix herself up. Wash off the smell of the dead man. And de Laurentiis. The way he made her want it despite herself. Longed for it. Hating him. Some conditioned animal response they'd granted into her unconscious. The humiliation reflex. Back in the lab. Knowing he was her only ticket out of there. Knowing it was only a matter of time before she killed him regardless. Or died trying. She lay back and stared at the rafters caked in pigeon shit.

"How the fuck did I ever get into this mess?" she said aloud – to herself, to no-one.

"Best of all possible alternatives, I'd say."

Shinwah jagged upright. A woman in Hilfiger anorak and white chinos stood in the doorway, an amused look playing across her face. Blonde, well tanned. Grey-blue eyes. Shinwah glanced towards the doorway, holding the fight instinct in check. *Careless again*, she thought.

"Margarita," the woman said, with an accent that sounded acquired. "I've brought you some clothes." She indicated a sports bag lying at her feet. "And food. There's a hand-pump out back. You can clean up there. It's salt water. But then, this isn't exactly the Savoy, is it?"

"I didn't hear you come in."

"You weren't supposed to."

The woman who called herself Margarita stood there with her hands in the pockets of her anorak, loose-stanced, completely at ease. She looked like a woman used to being in control.

"Who sent you?" Shinwah asked.

"Who do you think?"

"I don't."

"That's too bad," Margarita said, eyes narrowing with a kind of predatory intent. "When you're ready, I'm supposed to take you to the marina."

She toed the sports bag across the threshold of the doorway. Blue and white plimsolls. As if, Shinwah thought, she'd just stepped out of an advertisement for an island cruise.

The woman called Margarita observed Shinwah closely as she flexed and stood up off the mattress, her jumpsuit slipping down. Shinwah stared back, trying to size up the situation. The other woman was taller than she was. Chisel-jawed. The cruel mouth of young girls' romance literature. A slight smirk played across the woman's lips. She brushed the hair back from her eyes and let her gaze move slowly down Shinwah's body. The latex bodice and the V of exposed flesh where the jumpsuit hung open.

"We can take our time," Margarita said. "The tide doesn't come in for a couple of hours yet."

I'm the Stranger. We're the same...

The words spiral in the darkness as he feels himself sink down. This time the dream's full of fear, strange knowledge. As if he's passed some kind of barrier, entering deeper into it. The room. The fan. He recognises himself, the way a dreamer does. That he exists in a parasite-relation to the dream, evolving through lifecycles. Dream-cycles. A foreign body exchanging psychic DNA with something that isn't even real. The avatar of some sort of programme. The dream itself, a kind of host.

At first, there'd been nothing. Panic and incomprehension. Everything was pure reflex. Abstraction. He knew nothing about him, the Stranger. Who or what he was. What he was doing *there*. Why he'd been sent to find the Connection. But something's begun to change. The voice, fading out. Getting lost in the ether. But as the Stranger becomes less present in his mind, he feels him becoming more present in his body. A tacit awareness. Fear sharpening the senses. Opening a door previously locked. An insight for which there're no words. As if, in the absence of a clear way forward, they're merging, becoming one. Observer and observed...

When he comes to, there's a weight on top of him. The air's clotted with dust. At first he tries to move but a hand closes over the back of his head, holding him down.

"Don't move."

It's the albino. *I'm still here*, he thinks.

"Percussion grenades. The shock-waves radiate down the tunnels. Move and they'll crush you. Stay still, you'll only end up with a bad headache."

The rumbling gets closer. Dirt and masonry pour down from

the ceiling. The air's unbreathable. Then the pulse hits. It's like being driven over by a freight train. The throbbing in his head's unbearable. Everything goes dead again. Red light strobing through fan blades. Then everything's black. He hears himself coughing. A moment later another wave hits, coming from the opposite direction. Less powerful than the first. He hears the albino cough.

"Still here, baby, don't you worry."

"Where am I?"

He wants to get up but his body's refusing instructions. He feels her get a grip under his arm, hoist him off the ground. She's strong.

"You're bleeding," she says. "Bad."

"How d'you know," he braces himself, trying to keep balance. It's pitch black.

"Hand's covered in your blood, is how I know. Can see you clear as day, so don't get any ideas."

"What ideas? I can barely move."

"You'd better try harder. That was only the warm up."

☐ MERIDIAN

Whatever they were looking for, they hadn't found it. There was no place the carnage stopped. They'd torn up every available square inch. Drawers upended, scabby Y-fronts and ventilated socks scattered about, a busted film enlarger. Mattress stuffing. Camera bags. Shredded paperbacks. Reams of Agfa paper. Uprooted plant pots. Developer trays. Chemical jars. Toothpaste. A dozen empty Dewers bottles. Tinned carnation milk past its sell-by. A reeking toxic slurry of indeterminate origin. Etc., etc.

Joblard stood in the doorway of Johnny Fluoride's bedsit, admiring the handiwork. *Very subtle.* A red and white Salvation Army sticker was half-peeled from the doorpost, as though they'd tried looking under there too. He was idly picking at it with a fingernail when the widow came down the stairs, sans coinbox, to admonish him.

"A right bleedin' mess, that is. Who's going to fix it all up? Who's going to pay for it?"

"It's not safe to go about in your own house nowadays," put in a grizzle-haired Bomber Harris type in third-hand greasy tweed coat and dungarees.

"You could get yourself in trouble sneaking up on people like that," Joblard to Harris. "You didn't do it," jerking a thumb back at the wreckage, "so who did?"

"Eh?" Harris poked the blackened stub of a finger in his left ear, in evidence of a pre-miniaturised hearing aid. *Bastard's stone deaf,* Joblard thought. *Could've slept through the fucking Blitz. Let alone a room getting tossed...*

"How about you?" Joblard eyeballed the widow.

The old biddy, hands on hips, pulled a face like something in the process of being degaussed.

"Well I never!"

Jesus, here we go... Joblard took a last look around and, turning back, gently as he could, to faint protests, guided the two odd-bods from his path. He thought of his dear mum in Lambeth, getting on in years. Meals-on-wheels every Tuesday and Thursday. Could pick them coming five blocks away, her hearing was that good. Not like these two. Roof might've fallen in and they'd only have noticed in passing. Giving him the evil eye now, like it was his doing. Better, Joblard thought, not to stick around in case the neighbourhood watch types got busy on the phone.

Outside a couple of punks were taking a keen interest in the BSA, as if they couldn't decide whether to rip it off or just stand there and gawk. The Gold Star had gone out of production before either them or their mothers had likely been born. Probably weren't even sure what the hell it was. Seeing Joblard coming down the steps, they hightailed it on the double. He had that effect on people.

With his bike helmet and goggles on, Joblard looked for all the world like a Robocop killing machine that'd gone to seed somewhat. Opted-out of the programme. Let the fleshy side of things get the upper hand, while still maintaining a certain impending-doom quality to his general and otherwise peaceable demeanour. It'd been like this, he recalled, since he was fourteen and made a prop on the local men's rugby league squad. He was the slowest thing on the field, but what he lacked in sprightliness he made up for in determination. Setting up a tackle on him was a daunting proposition for even the most sanguine of fullbacks. His record, for which he duly received a little trophy his mum kept on her mantelpiece, was taking six defenders with him over the tryline before going down.

Right now, though, Joblard was feeling more like someone wandering around in the deadball zone. He'd have to call Bludhorn eventually, give him the bad news. Nicky Cohn, in the meantime, had promised to keep an ear out for any floaters that turned up. Contact down at the Met. It tickled the silly bastard pink. Evidently had a bit of spite when it came to Johnny Fluoride's personal hygiene. *Bet it's the first wash he's had in weeks, hehe. Notice the stink that follows him around? Rubs himself in tiger balm to keep out the cold. Got a morbid fear of taking a bath. Opens up the pores, he reckons. Lets all the bacteria in.* Joblard didn't think much of the idea of Johnny Flouride turning up anywhere but inside next season's oyster crop. Army surplus included. It was ticking boxes, was all. Tying the loose threads.

Riding back across the edge-lands he'd had time to reflect on the pointlessness of the day's activities so far. Though any excuse to give the bike a run, take in some unfamiliar scenery. Greenwich twice in the same afternoon. The weird sense of mirror world *déjà vu*, crossing the meridian, spacetime coordinates folding in on themselves like macramé. Labyrinths beneath every loose paving stone, expecting any moment now white rabbits and Jabberwocks. The Millennium Dome like a half-sunk zero, skyhooked and pixellated in the unfailing drizzle.

Joblard caught his reflection in the BSA's mottled side mirror. Gloves pulled on. Foot poised on the kick-start. Goggle-eyed. *And what d'you think you're looking at, eh?* Grinned. Yellow teeth sticking out. Slightly mismatched. Overlapping at the front. Gave the mirror a wipe, smearing it.

⊙ GHAN

The darkness began closing in from all sides without warning. It hit just as Lake Eyre came into view. A vast expanse of salt-pan spreading north to the horizon. Ten thousand square kilometres of it. This was the mythical inland sea men had dreamed of and died searching for. Bone dry. The catchment spread over a sixth of the continent. During the northern monsoons, flood waters from the Diamantina could spend weeks bleeding across the desert before trickling out onto the lake bed, only to evaporate in a matter of days. The temperature out there averaged above 40 this time of year. In the day. At night, you just might freeze to death. But as far as Lawson knew, there hadn't been a lake in anything but name for decades.

The storm came-on Old Testament-like. Weird shapes billowing out of the air. Sand whipped across the cockpit window. The propeller whined, fine red dust choking the air-filters, flooding the engine. The Cessna lurched. They lost altitude. This wasn't what she'd envisaged twenty-four hours ago, when Dix's message came up on the sat-phone. *You take your chances*, she thought. *That's what you're in it for.*

Once, prospecting in Western Australia, she'd been shot at by kangaroo poachers. Rednecks from one of the mining towns. The shell lodged in the back of the ute. It was from a three-oh-three. Guns as old as the Afghan camel trains that worked the Oodnadatta Track. Pre-Federation. Boer War. Back before the railhead opened up the interior as a viable transport route. Nothing left now but mud brick and spinifex and a couple of wrecked sidings sticking up out of the sand...

Guns they used to hunt Nungas with.

You take your chances.

She imagined bullets from antique rifles boring holes through time. A hundred years in a muzzle flash. History. Perhaps, in a parallel universe, the poacher's bullet was forever travelling towards its target. The sum total of all possible trajectories, down through strata of extinction and obsolescence, evolving towards some unknown end. From camel train to locomotive, satellites spiralling through the cosmos. And the aftershock, the recoil, firing backwards into the vortex, the eye of the storm. Collapsing time meridians. Back to the Dreaming. The rainbow serpent. The Big Bang.

An LED flashed on the bakelite handset beside the flight controls. The GPS locking-in on Dix's coordinates. Lawson squinted through the swirling dust. Somewhere down there lay the target. The pale salt crust of the lake hovering ghostlike behind a veil of red. Flat sandy scrubland tunnelling towards zero visibility. The GPS gave out a high pitched whine that was almost lost in the general cacophony. Kath swore.

"We've got to land," Lawson shouted into the intercom.

"No shit, Sherlock," Kath shouted back.

The Cessna dipped suddenly. The GPS flew up, ricocheted against the cockpit window. Lawson grabbed for it. Her head slammed into the door. The cockpit blurred. She braced herself, glanced across at Kath gritting her teeth so hard the muscles in her jaw stood out. Lawson read the determination in her face, trying to fly back into the wind. Knuckles white, fighting the controls. Sweat beading down her arms.

The sheer enormity of the storm was incredible. Sheets of red dust spiralling out of the atmosphere. The altimeter raced. Windshear. The whole plane shook. This is it, she thought. The Cessna skewed around in the air, side-on. Kath looked grim. No end to the turbulence now.

"Hold on," Kath yelled. "We're going in."

Lawson braced herself. The Cessna banked. Dipped. Landing

gear skimming salt bush and spinifex. Climbed. Dipped again. The Cessna slammed into the ground. Bounded. Skidded into a long fishtail. Almost flipped. Somehow didn't. The nose lurched. Visibility zero. The engine cut out. They pitched forward. The Cessna stopped dead.

All around them wind howled, rivets groaned.

+ CASH 4 SCRAP

It looked like something old but unborn. Like a foetus, dead in the womb. Part of a machine that'd been smashed to pieces before it had a chance to take a recognisable form or assume an identifiable function. It lay on the trestle table under interrogation lights, a piece of scarred alloy baked in polymer resin, the size of a large grenade.

Osborne stared at it, a line of perspiration forming across his brow. The stainless steel case felt heavier in his hand. He was shivering. With an effort that seemed out of all proportion to the task, he laid the case on the table beside the thing, whatever it was, and scanned the loft. Something didn't seem right. He glanced restlessly at his watch. Nine-fifteen. And felt suddenly out of his depth, drumming his fingers on the edge of the case. The Doctor had made it sound easy, a routine deal. Cash for scrap.

The scrap was something the Doctor had described with occult concision, though Osborne retained only the vaguest impression of what it actually was. Intimations of Stonehenge, Nebuchadnezzar, the cult of Isis, spectral doom. From the Doctor's office he'd looked out at the Zero, wondering what the hell was really down there. Too coincidental by far. Perturbations in the Force, maybe. Dowsing rods of the coming apocalypse tuned-in like a cosmic homing beacon for radio-controlled asteroids, rogue spy-sats on re-entry collision course, million-year-old Martian escape pods, Quatermass meets War of the Worlds, seeds of superstition in plague proportions poised to germinate...

Osborne figured the Doctor for an antique freak fed some inside jive on the Ground Zero meteor. Or whatever it was. He eyeing the baked polymer thing lying beside Suliman's case. It vibed conspiracy theory weirdness. Black-Ops. Hackers in deep cyberspace jamming the System. Screen-grab of the Oval Office console: *Dud orbital nuke sent off course! Nightmare-chic Chinese stealth birds launching the next phase in the cultural revolution, point-blank. Zombies in Skylab cryogenics breakout. Blade Runner stuff.* Meaning primetime national security issues, right? How the hell could they keep the lid on something like that? Or how about this: some sort of heist deal worked out in the confusion, down in the hole – corporation vaults – Central Intelligence archives – Bruce Willis in radiation suit lighting a cigarette butt with a blow torch...

Just another instalment in Osborne's on-going Doctor Doom fantasy. He tried to picture them quarantining the island. Like that was ever going to happen. One-point-six mill. Bad enough when the grid went down. Just getting over to Canal Street was a hardcore operation. In the space of a couple of hours, the tide around the Zero had increased by magnitudes of bodily density. No subways north or south. Unless you had a helicopter, the easiest way out was swim. Little wonder the Doctor had called him in. A quick job on the side. Quick being the operative word. No strings. Easy. Sure, easy as pie. But if he was lucky, the hard part was already behind him. He'd hand over the cash and get some piece of melted down Buick in return and the Doc would frame it on his wall and be happy as Larry. Osborne would head up to Little Joe's and treat himself to a pastrami sandwich. Watch the highlights of the Yankees game. Take it easy for the night. But something about the deal was giving him the creeps. For one, *where the fuck was the dealer?*

As if triggered by his thoughts, a voice crackled suddenly out of the darkness, edged with static.

"Good evening, Mr Osborne." Osborne froze. "Please show us what you have brought."

Osborne glanced at the case.

"How do I know who you are?"

It was possible, he thought, that there was in fact no-one in the loft. The voice sounded machine-generated. A course-grained transmission that could've originated anywhere. They must've been watching him through cameras, whoever they were supposed to be. Kinezology? He eyed the mouth of the service elevator. Mapped the distance between the table and the curtain of shadows. The mind games seemed out of place. It was supposed to be straight up. The terms pre-arranged. Pre-agreed. All he was supposed to do was make the trade.

The Doctor had been vague about what he was supposed to be trading for. The suitcase, he assumed, was cash-equivalent. He'd been given a code. Numbers he'd had to memorise. Basic instructions. That was all. This wasn't what he'd expected.

The voice crackled again.

"Now if you please, Mr Osborne."

He weighed his options. Walking away just didn't seem on the cards, somehow. He counted the seconds. Decided the best course of action was to play along. And picked up the case. He held it out flat in front of him, for whoever was there to see. Clicked it open.

"Here," he said. "You want to check it?"

There was a long silence during which a new thought crossed his mind. How'd they know his name?

"Thank you Mr Osborne. We don't expect that will be necessary."

The voice, vaguely British, gave Osborne an unpleasant feeling.

"You may close the case now."

He closed it.

"Please lay it on the floor and slide it away from you."

Osborne lay the case on its side and slid it forward. It spun slightly, making a scuffing noise that echoed through the loft. The suitcase came to rest just inside the lit square. As he watched, something in the shadows reached out towards it and the case disappeared. Something shapeless, abhuman.

The hair on Osborne's neck prickled. Scenes from old B-films replayed in his head. *Cat People. The Body Snatchers. Tutankhamen's*

Curse. The Mechanical voice interrupted his reverie.

"You will now please open the cartouche."

Osborne refocused, edged back to the trestle table. His eyes dropped to the object lying there. The pod. The *cartouche*, he guessed. *Cartouche?* He lifted it cautiously in both hands. It was much heavier than it appeared. He felt along the rim and found a catch. It was stiff. He forced it. He felt something release. Twisted. The top began to give way. He turned it and a segment of casing unthreaded from a central core. He slid the casing off and placed it on the table. Inside the core was a transparent cylinder studded with circuitry. It radiated a low warmth. It pulsed red.

"Very carefully remove the incubator."

Incubator?

Osborne's hands trembled. He steadied them. Did as instructed. The wiring bristled under his touch as though it were alive.

"What is this?" he said. "The deal was, I hand over the case and collect. No funny stuff."

"You will find everything quite in order, Mr Osborne," the voice crackled. "Now please open the incubator."

Osborne breathed deeply. He wasn't good at this type of thing. It happened when people tried to get all cute about the census forms. Like it was him they were gonna con. *Ain't got nothin' to do with me, pal. Sell your story to Uncle Sam. Just give me the goddamn form.*

"How do I open it?"

"Enter the code in the keypad."

Osborne turned the cylinder in his hand. Among the embedded circuitry was a miniature LCD like a shrunken strip of tickertape. He pulled a biro from his coat pocket and used the dead ballpoint to type in the ten-digit code the Doctor had given him. Again he felt something move. The cylinder cracked open along its side. The top half folded back. A thin vapour oozed out. Osborne stared.

Inside lay a figurine. A tiny human form no more than an inch long. Like a delicately facetted piece of obsidian. It lay there with large empty eyes. The vapour eddied. Osborne wrinkled his nose. There was a smell of boiled aspic. He thought about what Little Joe had said that morning. *Mucho – weird – shit.* And wasn't that the truth. What would the *Times* have to say about this, if they ever heard about it? Hell, if Tar Baby here came down in the meteor that bullseyed the Zero...

His voice, when he spoke, was barely audible.

"You *sure* this is what was agreed?"

"Look closer, Mr Osborne. You will see that everything is indeed as it should be."

As delicately as he could, Osborne lifted the statuette from its bed. It felt weightless. He very carefully turned it around until it was facing him again, amazed at its detail. *An exact scaled replica*, he thought, *of a real person. Incredible.* As he studied at it, the figurine appeared to hover between his fingertips, absorbing whatever light fell on it. He brought it closer so that he could see it. But as he did, its features became even dimmer and threatened to disappear entirely. Then he felt it move and began to be afraid of dropping it. It moved again and seemed to float out from between his fingers like a disturbance in the air, flowing towards him.

I'm hallucinating, he thought. The figurine, he could've sworn, was crawling through the air, hand-over-hand, like someone crawling up a long tunnel. Then a pain shot through his left eye. Something stabbing, piercing him, gouging through the dilated pupil into the retina. A spiral of light. Electricity. And suddenly it was gone.

Osborne groped at his face.

"Fuck!"

He reeled.

"Is anything the matter, Mr Osborne?"

"I can't see! That thing. It fucking blinded me!"

"Please don't be alarmed, Mr Osborne. The effects you are experiencing are merely temporary. You will soon adjust to your new situation."

Osborne fell to his knees. His mind faltered. The lights in the room dimmed and flickered, and then went out. He struggled to breathe, body jack-knifing onto the floor. There, not three feet away, like a hovering mirage, the dull glow of the incubator. Empty now. A luminous vapour trailed out of it. Osborne gasped. Strained towards it through the pain as the space around him collapsed. And then he was falling.

He barely heard the voice speaking to him.

"Thank you, Mr Osborne. You have provided us with an invaluable service. We look forward to conducting business with you again, in the future."

It wasn't machines that bothered her. It was people. After so many runs, she'd begun to doubt there was any such thing as logical behaviour. Like now. She didn't for one moment believe the woman called Margarita wanted to make love to her. It was a power thing. Like with de Laurentiis. Creating an aura of dependency. But dependency on de Laurentiis began and ended with the fact that he was her only ticket out of there. Back to that room in Beijing. To the possibility, remote as it might be, that when all this was over she'd get her life back.

People, she reasoned, were unpredictable, irrational, random. They were programmable to a point. Beyond that, they might do anything, become anything. Like animals in an experiment. You could only pair the response to the stimulus for so long, before a kind of psychosis kicked in. It bothered her that she'd been one of them. A collection of molecules assuming form in a struggle against itself. Mind and body. The eternal contraries…

Maybe it was just the dead Russian's ice talking. Or the time-shift. It could catch up on you if you weren't careful. They'd never gone in for more than a couple of days at a stretch. Time was always a risk factor. It wasn't just the chance of being caught by the other side. It was more that the longer you spent in, the less able you were to assimilate and the more detached you became. From the world, yourself. And from people. With Margarita somehow it'd been different. She was more like one of them. Like her. They didn't actually touch, before now. In the warehouse, while Shinwah washed and dressed, Margarita's gaze never once left her. But that was all the other woman had needed, to possess her entirely.

The clothes in the sports bag had been plain black, no labels. A turtleneck and slacks. A black nylon bomber jacket. Somehow the combination worked.

"Fetching," Margarita had smirked. She imagined what de Laurentiis would've said. *Like the cat that got the canary.*

Right now Shinwah was pressed close against Margarita's back on a Vespa heading east through a narrow maze of Triestine streets. Cold wind in her hair. *Travelling in style.* The sports bag, with Shinwah's jumpsuit, was in a recycle bin behind an amphitheatre. Roman, Margarita had said. Piles of rubble heaped around in a circle, like the mouth of a stone-age missile silo. She hadn't said where they were heading. It hardly seemed to matter. The Vespa wove through the traffic, its engine quaking under the seat.

Keeping her grip around Margarita's waist, Shinwah let herself drift, the ice feeding a synaptic aura that glowed just beneath the visible surface of things. Like sea-born phosphorescence. It reminded her of that faint aquarium glow the monitors gave off constantly in the Beijing lab. Cold and warm at the same time. The cold warmth of an artificial life-source.

And as it always did when she thought about it too long, a sense of helplessness crept in. Born of the knowledge, held at the back of her mind, that time-shifting was only possible when you're dead. Or half-dead. *The big chill*, de Laurentiis called it. Wired up to the Machine, avatar zapped off to wherever. Matter and antimatter fading back into the mix the instant you do.

Only, if you got chilled time-shifting, that was it. Game over. The eternal bye-bye.

☾ PASSENGER

At first it's like crawling down a long narrow tunnel, hand-over-hand. Then it's like falling. Down through echoes, depth-soundings.

A red light radiates through sifting dust, illuminating a rust-coloured panel with cross-bones sprayed on it. He knows they're being watched, but not how. The albino speaks into an intercom in a dialect he doesn't understand and a moment later part of a wall slides back into hidden recesses. It looks like a service elevator. A steel cage in a concrete shaft with cables hanging down. The albino pushes him in and the door slides back.

For a long time he can't tell if they're descending or ascending, but he supposes they're descending. Something whirrs. The back of his head's wet and when he touches the place behind his right ear it doesn't feel right. The elevator light's dim, but he can see his hands covered with blood. There's blood down the front of his *jilabîya* as well. The albino's leaning against the opposite wall, holding the gun on him. Or just holding it, not pointing it at anything. She keeps slipping out of focus. Then he's lost her.

He's back in the room. Only this time there's no fan. No red light. The ceilings all scummed tiles, chipped, broken away. Resin-coloured fluorescents leeching the static. He's lying on something cold. He can't feel the back of his head. There's a groaning sound. It's coming from his mouth.

"Still with us?"

The albino leans over him, her face all dark angles.

"Looks like you copped something in the back of your head. I've put in a couple of stitches," she says, holding what looks like a bloodied sewing kit. No gun. "It should hold till we get to the outside."

She's wearing black combat fatigues. She stuffs the kit in a hip pocket. Business-like.

"Where are we?"

"An abandoned subway extension. About half-a-mile down. It was supposed to connect Giza to Salah Salem, before the intifada screwed that plan. People used to live here, till the droids got too close for comfort. Keep heading west, and you run straight into the perimeter. After that and you're in Necropolis."

"Necropolis?"

"Where all the dead people live. Think you can stand up?"

Somehow he does. He can see now that they're on a train platform. Where the tracks would've been is overflowing with all kinds of junk. Layers of graffiti cover every inch of wall. He sniffs the air. The smell's indescribable, but bad. A rat with too many legs scuttles from behind a steel girder, hisses, scuttles back. He thinks he can see blood stains on the ground amongst the detritus. He remembers the blood on his shirt, on the bridge. Not his. Whose? He feels for the Stranger but he's not there. The Albino's right in front of him, scrutinising his face under the lights.

"Tell me why I shouldn't've left you up there with the droids?"

"I need your help."

"No shit. What d'you know about Momo?"

"Nothing. I don't know. There're things in my head. I don't know where they come from."

"Likely story."

"It's the only one I've got."

"We'll see about that. Stand still."

She takes out something black, holds it up. A handset. The screen casting a green glow across her face.

"I'm going to scan you, in case you're carrying."

"Carrying what?"

"Bugs."

"Bugs?"

"Parasites, whatever."

He watches her trace a slow arc with the handset, then down, without taking her eyes off him. Red. He thinks, if he moves, she just might kill him after all. Waste of surgery. He still can't feel his head. Something beeps. The albino thumbs some keys on the handset. A sound like scrambled electronics.

"Like I thought," she says. "You've got a passenger on board. Defunct."

"The Stranger."

"Who?"

"It's a voice I can hear sometimes. Telling me what to do."

"You serious?"

"How I got here."

"Scan says it's dead. How'd it get there?"

"I don't know. I can't remember anything. Only bits and pieces. Something happened. I had to run. There was blood."

"Human?"

"Maybe."

"Any bodies?"

"No."

"Where."

"There was a bridge."

"How far?"

"Other side of the Wall. Wrecked houses. A canal. Tower in the distance."

"Al-Gami'ah."

The albino pockets the handset. Reaches up, taking his head between her hands. Peers into his left eye like she doesn't believe he's really there. He can see his reflection, the pattern of her iris, like eddies of red smoke pierced by a black shaft.

"Hold still."

His eyelids part under pressure from her thumbs. He tries to blink. But it isn't him. Just a reflex.

"Almost looks real," she says. "Can you see with it?"

"Yes."

"You sure?"

He closes his right eye. The picture goes dim. The albino's not there anymore. But something's there.

☐ ORGASMATRON

He was past the Royal Observatory when Joblard spotted the tail. A couple of goons in a two-tone grey-and-white smartcar. Not your orthodox, but anyway. He kicked the BSA into high gear and cut up-river on the A200, all the way to Bankside. Past the *Britain at War* exhibition. The London Dungeon. Left on Southwark, losing the tail in the traffic and general gloom. All things being equal, he saw no reason to beat around the bush, unless you had the fuzz on your case. Nothing like riding straight to bamboozle the opposition. He wondered who the smartcar belonged to. If it had anything to do with present business. Or if it was something else.

Joblard made a right at the ubiquitous Golden W. That statue of the Iron Duke munching a Wozzie Burger before serving Napoleon his arse on a plate. Then across Waterloo Bridge, Covent Garden, Seven Dials. Soho pretty quiet for that time of the afternoon. Frith Street all but deserted. He parked down the block from the Dog and Duck, Johnny Fluoride's Doc Martens strapped to the back in a Sainsbury's bag one of the friendly folk on Canvey had lent him.

He'd never been what you'd call photogenic, but the Aussie tourists down by the jetty at the Lobster Smack had taken to him in a big way, begging his address to send copies of their prize snapshots. Turned out to be a busload of hardcore Bruce Wellie fans, story being that Wellie once sat in with the Feelgoods back in the day. Reason he was kicking-off the comeback on Canvey. It gave Joblard a pang of regret to have to blow the gig, but Johnny Fluoride's unscheduled dip in the Thames kind of put a spanner in the works. Manner of speaking.

The publican at the Lobster Smack wasn't the type, thankfully, to be bothered by a scuzzy little runt like Johnny Fluoride getting the clamp put on him, long as it was kept off the premises. He was giving the BSA a squint when Joblard led the tourists down the embankment, recommending they sample the establishment's lunch special. *Authentic Feelgoods landmark,* or some crap like that he'd spieled at them. Shaking hands and wishing all the usual etceteras, begging off on a drink, 'cause he had a job to go to, didn't he. The whole lot of them waving him goodbye. And the publican getting in a line about how he used to ride a Matchless himself and wasn't it a terrible thing, all the great British names gone bust, only that Japanese crap nowadays, the odd Moto Gutless, cops riding that Jerry shite. *Where's our national pride, gone, eh?* Sort of geezer probably kept a Leyland double-decker in his backyard with a plastic bulldog on the dash. For the annual show.

Joblard put a chain on the bike and rang the bell outside a numberless red door with one of those fake bronze knockers that're supposed to give you the idea that what's behind it isn't in the same league as your average Friday night wanker out on the piss. Across the street a wistful looking cockerspaniel was about to crap in the middle of a doorstep. No owner in sight. *Cheeky little bugger, eh?*

Half the shops still had their shutters down. Joblard tried to remember if it was a bank holiday. Maybe things'd liven up later on, when the office crowd knocked off and came down to slum it for a few drinks. The kind of bums that propped up the walls at the French House between six and eight. Ad execs. Theatre critics. Cricket commentators from Sky Sport. He wondered what the latest was on the test. But then it was night down there, wasn't it? A voice came over the intercom and asked him what he wanted.

"Delivery," he said. "For Mister Bludhorn."

A buzzer clicked.

Bludhorn, patron of the spurned, was holding court downstairs in a private booth. Joblard gave the place the once-over. It looked like he'd just descended into one of those Kray brothers cross-dress clubs with too much chintz and velour. Members only. A couple of gaffers with '80s Duran Duran hair were rigging lights behind the bar. Bludhorn's private table was partitioned by a soundboard. Entirely superfluous, Joblard reasoned, on account of all Bludhorn's productions were over-dubbed anyway. He was rounding the soundboard when something flashed and Joblard found himself gazing into the camera eye of a giggling four-foot-something's cellphone. It was all she was wearing apart from the stilettos.

"Mmm. Me like," in faux orientalese. "So big! Me very horny. Love you long time…"

Bludhorn was surrounded by the usual retinue of circus freaks.

"Ah, Joblard!"

Joblard dropped the Sainsbury bag, with Johnny Fluoride's boots in it, on the table.

"The fish got away."

Bludhorn pursed his lips. Poked at the bag with his nine iron. As if on cue, the retinue faded. The pint-sized Miss Saigon blew Joblard a kiss, tottering across the room in those outsized heels. Bludhorn motioned for him to take a seat. A straight-backed wood chair with reddish-pink velvet upholstery. Bludhorn, he noticed, was holding a glass of something bright green in his left hand, the ubiquitous nine-iron tapping the floor in his right. He could imagine how this would get on someone's nerves. Though not his. He didn't give a fuck what Bludhorn did with his right hand.

Bludhorn levelled what Joblard once heard described as a withering stare at him. Blue eyes. Supposed to've been a real ladykiller in his day. Though they never got the charges to stick, hehe. Bludhorn's eyebrows twitched.

"I'm all ears."

Joblard spieled it out in shorthand. The jetty. The bedsit. Bludhorn's trilby nodded.

"It's unfortunate, my son. Terribly unfortunate."

A gaffer slouched past with an industrial pack of Kleenex.

"How were the pilchards, by the way?"

The back of the gaffer's t-shirt had ORGASMATRON printed on it in heavymetal typeface, silver on black.

"I can't eat fish."

"Don't know what you're missing out on, son."

Joblard shrugged.

"That's the name of the film?"

"Quality, isn't it? Think *Flash Gordon* meets *Barbarella* on molly, the uncut version. There's a part in it for you, if you like."

"Unfinished business, Bludhorn."

"Quite right. Here... You want to try this?" indicating the cocktail glass with the green concoction in it.

Joblard peered at something floating inside it. A type of blob twisted on the end of a bit of wire. Like, he thought, *the idea making his stomach turn, an aborted foetus*. Bludhorn groped inside his coat pocket, eventually pulling out the same buff envelope Joblard had handed to him that morning at the Red Lion caff. *Eh?* he thought. *It's a blue fucking octopus!* He was sure he saw one of its tentacles twitch.

"Is that thing alive?"

"Give it a try. You know what they say. Only live once..."

"Thanks. I'll pass."

"Your loss. Now... Feast your eyes on these."

Bludhorn shuffled the photographs out of the envelope and fanned them in front of him like a card dealer fixing you for a sleight of hand. Joblard reached across and picked one at random. *Or did it only seem like it was random?*

"Assuming you haven't seen them already, that is."

Joblard shook his head, handling the postcard-sized print with all the awkwardness of someone trying very diligently to keep from smearing their fingerprints on it. And stared. The picture made no sense.

"What is it?"

"Your guess, my son, is as good as mine."

⊙ STORM EYE

There were voices everywhere. Chanting. Ancient voices. Calling. Telling her to wake up. Lawson didn't want the sleep to end. She was sinking down through an oceanic depth. And then she came out of it, staring at the darkness, wind beating in her ears. First she couldn't remember where she was. Then something flashed. A green light that filled the cockpit like night-vision. The sat-phone's GPS. She looked at it, uncomprehending. Numbers flickered on the LCD. Coordinates. It all came back to her. The storm. The crash landing. They must've been caught right in the middle of it.

Kath was already out of the plane. They'd come down, by something akin to a miracle, tail to the storm. It arched over them like a wave, the air thick with red dust. When she opened the cockpit door, the wind almost tore it off the hinges. She fought to stay on her feet. Kath was on the other side of the plane, struggling to anchor the wingtip. Lawson held a hand over her mouth and staggered across to help with the ropes. The landing gear, she could see, was completely bogged down in the lakebed. The propeller was smashed. *We're fucked*, she thought.

Kath worked with a self-sufficiency Lawson admired. Powerful arms straining against the ropes. Kath shouted at her.

"Go and do what you bloody well came for."

No anger. Just matter-of-fact. Meaning there was no time. If she didn't move fast, they'd've risked everything for nothing.

Lawson dragged the rucksack out of the back of the plane. Jammed the flare gun in Kath's rig, in case. Palmed the sat-phone. She took a reading from the GPS. They were close. South-west. Time: 3:09 p.m. She logged the plane's coordinates.

Kath was already working a tarp over the plane's engine housing. Lawson crossed over to her, helped anchor the line. Kath shouted through the wind at her.

"We'll have this baby fixed up in no time. Get out of here."

"If you don't hear from me by morning, call Dix."

Kath shook her head.

"No fear. You'll be back."

It gave Lawson faith she didn't feel was rightfully hers. She re-checked the GPS, orientated herself towards the fading light. Then, head down, she struck out into the swirling dust, the darkness closing fast around her till she could see and hear nothing but the shape of the storm and the voices chanting.

+ FUTURE-PRIMITIVE

40°43'20.60"N
74°0'21.76"W

The spiral swelled and pulsed and spread out before him. Something hovered inside the lights. A solid form of pain. Something he almost recognised. A city. A tower of light.

The blackout was the last thing Osborne remembered. And then the visions. There had been blackouts before, the power grids going down across the five boroughs. But this had been different. First the lights had gone out and then he'd gone out, as if someone had switched off the juice to his head. But the visions that followed were like nothing he'd ever known.

Slowly and painfully he opened his eyes. The streetlights had come back on. He found himself huddled in a doorway, mouth open, trying to scream. His throat was hoarse, nothing came out. He raised himself on his elbows. His surroundings blurred into sudden focus. Like vertigo. He leaned forward and threw up.

Voices in the distance. Osborne tried to gauge them. Pieces of nightmare fading in and out. He couldn't remember how he'd gotten there. He huddled. Time passed. He tried to get up. Pain behind his eyes. He pulled his coat around him and struggled to his feet. Retched. A sheet of newspaper blew up the stairs and wrapped around his boots. He staggered. He pulled the newspaper away. It stuck to his hands. He stared at it. Something stood out in the light of the streetlamp. Flicker of memory. *What day is this?* The paper slipped from his fingers. He looked at them. They were trembling. Or shivering. Or both.

Osborne, hand out in front of his face like a man unwilling to admit his predicament, weaved down the stairs onto the sidewalk. Wind coursed off the Atlantic between dead façades, faintly moaning. An icy, needle-like rain whipped him across the eyes. Away from the river, human shapes moved against headlights, hunching into the gale. The traffic shunted forward, moving at least. He tried to think.

Turning east, Osborne stumbled off in search of a subway station. Footsteps. He spun around, keeping his guard up, like a disorientated fielder trying to catch a fly-ball, shapes pealing out of peripheral vision, mind gripped by an unusual fear. The moment passed, there was nothing there. He stumbled on. Five blocks. He recognised the Tribeca Interchange up ahead, traffic crawling towards the north-side turnoff. Two figures hunched in *jilabîyas*, arguing in front of a sidewalk *bichra* stand. Behind the counter, black light illuminated a refrigerator with plastic sacks hung from coat-hangers like saline solution in a clinic. Things, suspended in green fluid, moved inside them. The vendor leered through a pair of dead monitors. Osborne stared back.

The scene blurred. A flash of pixellated light behind his eyes. Then something switched. The two *jilabîyas* were gone. Where the vendor had been was now a regular newsstand. A yellow cab idled beside it, mirrored aviators through a fogged window. Osborne came closer. Headlines stood out from the newspaper racks. CHAOS ON WALL STREET. RIOT SQUADS ON ALERT. *Sports Week* was the only voice of sanity among them. WINTER WORLD SERIES. Yankees at home to Pittsburgh. 1-0. Four games to go.

Osborne put down a five dollar bill for quarters and a two-pack of aspirin. It was all they had. The guy behind the partition pushed the change at him without looking up from his magazine. Osborne stuffed the quarters in his coat pocket and dry-swallowed the aspirin. He stood on the curb-side watching the traffic. Drifts of half-melted snow lay banked against the lampposts, pockmarked from the rain. An old black guy in snow boots and duffel coat trudged past. Osborne followed him across the intersection, trying to keep his footing.

Mid-way down the next block he found an old AT&T booth. His cell phone had died. He needed to call the Doctor. It took an age to feed the coins into the slot, his hands shook so much. Eventually there was an answering tone. He made the connection. It was a pre-recorded message. A woman's voice. Osborne hung up. He tried the only other number he could remember. His ex-wife. She picked up. She listened. She told him to come over.

Osborne breathed deeply. Coughed. It was cold, sub-zero, but his skin felt hot. A sky heavy with black clouds swept low over the city, frozen ash and rain spiralling out of it. Something was happening, but he didn't know what it was. Like talismans to ward off the fear, he clutched the loose coins inside his coat. The blackout was the last thing he was certain of. Before that, only vague recollections of traversing a kind of labyrinth. The labyrinth of the city and the labyrinth inside his head. Momo-ology.

He remembered the crowds ringing Ground Zero. The sense that getting out had been more difficult than getting in. Blacked-out streets choked with campfire smoke, tear gas. Like a sprawling refugee camp. Tents and barricades along the canyons. Checkpoints. Helicopter floodlights. They'd been airlifting in and out of the Zero all afternoon. He'd watched it unfold from the Doctor's office. Then the Doctor had told him about the job. Cash for scrap. Easy.

The long-tailed macaque crouched by a pond eyeing its prize, the scales of a golden koi glinting in the sunlight. The monkey cupped the fish in its long-fingered hands, gazing wide-eyed. But just below the surface of the pond an even more brilliant prize glittered. Greedily the macaque snatched at it, but caught only the dazzling water...

Even to a child the moral of the story was obvious. How the macaque was left empty-handed while both fish got away. It was a story in a book. A woman Shinwah supposed was her mother used to read it to her. There was a picture of a silver-haired monkey gazing sadly into the water. Lines of calligraphy like tendrilled vines framing the picture, conveying the lesson of right reason applied to judgement. *Be prudent*, the woman who might've been her mother said.

The set-up was so smooth Shinwah couldn't even be sure when it began. They'd arrived at the marina and Margarita had pointed out a single-masted yacht moored alongside a floating dock at the end of the quay. De Laurentiis was already aboard, waiting. She saw him standing there behind the taffrail, in his blue velvet dinner jacket, waving. Impervious to the cold. A strong breeze blew in off the sea, upsetting his designer hair. The rigging snapped against the masts. A tricoloured pennant flapped violently at stern. The *bora*, Margarita had called it. Winds that were the stuff of legend, coming down from the Karst highlands every winter to batter the coast. Thinking it was typical de Laurentiis would choose to set sail in that.

Margarita was behind her when she began walking across the quay, head still buzzing, lulled by the cross-town ride. The cold wind brought everything juddering back into a sudden clear focus. The white overcast sky. Seagulls. The hulls of the ferries rocked by the tide. She wondered where Margarita's people where. A boy with dark eyes was already working the yacht's mooring ropes, ready to cast-off. *Always in a hurry*, she thought. Behind her, Margarita's footsteps slowed. If she'd looked back, she would've missed the play. The black Audi parked behind the boat trailer to her left. The three goons in mismatched leather coats converging from the right.

Everything happened very slowly and then very fast. The first one waited too long to pull his gun. Shinwah snapped his neck with a roundhouse kick. Dropped for the gun. Austrian. A Glock with a fourteen-round clip. Pivoted in time to see goon number two take aim at Margarita. An uzi this time. From the corner of her eye she caught goon three pull another handgun from inside his coat. Fourteen rounds, she thought, was already thirteen too many. Unless one of the goons missed. But they didn't look like they'd miss. *So this is it, then. The kiss-off.*

"It's no use, Shinwah."

It was de Laurentiis. *That sonofabitch.* Margarita looked at her. Or past her. It was a look that conveyed an intention. Shinwah guessed what it meant. Saw the goon's finger tighten on the uzi's trigger. Heard the first goon groan. Number two began circling around behind her. She kept uzi boy in her sights.

"I had to make a trade, my dear." De Laurentiis again. "You for the boat. It seems fair don't you think? There's really quite a price on your head. Don't worry about your friend. It's not her they're interested in. Besides, there's something I didn't tell you. You can't go back. May as well make the best of it. You never know, there could be a bright new future ahead of you."

She would've given anything just then to be able to see his face. Just before killing him. But her eyes were locked on the uzi now. Calculating how many more steps the other goon would have to take before he got behind her. And in a more or less direct firing line with uzi boy. *You can't go back.* What was that supposed to mean?

She sighted the Glock at a point just below uzi boy's right shoulder. That way at least, when the bullet hit him, he'd spin back, away from Margarita. And he'd let spray. With any luck, right at de Laurentiis. She'd just have time to hit the ground. Maybe the Glock's recoil would be enough to give her body the torque she'd need to get a shot at goon two. If she wasn't already dead by then. It sounded nice in theory.

"Put the gun down, Shinwah. You know what they say. Time and tide wait for no man. Nor woman, neither."

"I hope you rot in hell."

"Oh come-come. You know as well as I do, there's no such thing."

Shinwah very slightly relaxed her grip. She could tell Margarita was about to make a play for it. And if so, that'd be that. As competent as Margarita looked, Shinwah doubted it would turn out any other way than bad. Unless there was something she didn't know. But that was just the kind of constant she'd never want to bet on.

The simple thing would've been to do as de Laurentiis said. Put the gun down. Give up. Play along with the game. The assumption being they'd want her in one piece, or they would've just offed her at the start. If she let it ride now, there might be a better opportunity later. Then she'd track that fucker de Laurentiis down and give him what he'd had coming for a long time. But playing dumb wasn't in her nature.

Right now the two goons were playing it safe. But as soon as they had her immobilised, she'd be driven to a room somewhere and they'd torture whatever they wanted out of her. Then terminate. Or maybe fit her out like a suicide bomb for some shit enterprise, dangling a time-delay like the proverbial carrot. Or use her to hack back into the system. Hell, the possibilities just went on. *Your bright future's just around the corner, sweetheart.*

Shinwah gritted her teeth. All she could see was a window of opportunity steadily narrowing. *You only get to play the sucker once in this life*, she thought. *And you've already played it.* Visions of a cell in Daxing. No other option than to take the long odds. Go out blazing. If she went for goon two, Margarita just might stand a chance, for what it was worth. She felt the wind buffeting her jacket. The ice simmering behind her eyes. She relaxed her grip on the Glock and breathed out.

And for the smallest fraction of a second she saw a silver-haired monkey crouching beside a pond, a brightly-coloured goldfish cupped in its hands.

And pulled the trigger.

What it is, he can't say. A grid overlaid on swirling contours. A diagram. A map. A meshing of cogs like some antiquated mechanism. Time. He wills the green numerics to blink back at him out of the dimness. Perhaps, if he concentrates hard enough, it'll work. The circuit will stimulate back into life. The programme. The Stranger.

"Walk," the albino says. *Keep moving.* And he remembers something. Stumbling, through a dense undergrowth of tangled wires. The subway station echoing with a distant wind. Something booming in his ears. Lights blinking out. Descending onto the tracks. A ladder. Keeping his balance. Weaving through the refuse. The way, as a child. Yes. Crawling along a creek bed. Razor grass and thorn bushes. Fallen logs along the muddy bank. A crack between. Watching. Dark figures moving on the other side. Approaching. And then the shots ringing out. Running. Keeping low. A voice. In his head. It might've been his father's. Telling him a moving target's harder to hit. Not knowing why they were shooting at him. Where he was running. If he'd ever be able to go back.

The stench of the tunnel is overwhelming. As if something had died down there. A festering, dead stench. She pulls him into an alcove. A sound of metal against metal. Un-oiled hinges. Through a doorway now. Concrete. Steel rungs. *Places like this,* he thinks, *don't really exist.* Like being plugged into a game consol. Some pre-loaded scenario. Moving down the levels. Subterra. Collecting points. But the stench's real. The pain. The blank wall in his mind. The room. And now, a first fragment of memory. Something from *before.* His? Or someone else's? Another scenario? Another game?

He listens to the albino talk. He wonders why she's doing this.

What risks she's taking. The sound of her voice in the shifting dark. They're travelling deeper underground. Under the perimeter of the dome. A place. City of the Dead. *Necropolis*. Momo. *Who's Momo?* He struggles to stay with her, but she seems determined not to leave him behind. She's telling him about the past. *Intifada*, she says. It was the intifada that created all this. The ruins. Babylon. Things he already knows somehow. Has seen. Construction bots at work on the Wall. Demolition crews. The *zabbalin*. The eugenics squads.

Whispers from a programme still running in his sub-mind.

☐ ANALOGUE

It might've been one of those Jack-the-Ripper crime scenes. Slashes of black and white. There were about twenty photos in all. They started out ordinary enough. A room. Nothing special. Only what was in the room might've been of interest to someone. In the first picture, there was a man. Naked. Sitting in a chair. The kind of oversized bit of wood furniture you'd expect in the Tower of London, or some place like that. High-backed. Ornate carvings and plush upholstery. The room itself was more austere. Nothing much to distinguish it from an empty room you might come across anywhere.

"Who's the geezer?"

Bludhorn sipped at his cocktail.

"No-one you know."

Almost half of the pictures were the same, the only difference being that in some it was possible to see a second figure. More silhouette than anything else. And the blur of something lashing across the frame. The man in the chair moving his head. Left. Right. Up. Down. On closer inspection, Joblard saw that the man's hands were tied to the chair arms. A black strip of something across his mouth. A gag maybe. But the picture was too grainy to be certain of anything. Who the man was. What the images were supposed to mean. Though Joblard had been pretty sure he could guess. One of Bludhorn's regular types who like to pay to be tied up and whipped by some cold blooded *femme fatale* in thigh-high vinyl boots. But the rest of the photos were something else again.

"Jesus Christ."

Suddenly the man's head was gone. In one frame there was a flare of white and in the next, the head was gone. Like it'd spontaneously combusted. A flash and *boom!* The wall behind the chair was streaked with what could only have been the man's blood, embedded with bits and pieces of skull and brain presumably. The dead man's torso, cross-hatched with grey lines, had sunk down into itself. To the left of the chair, a stunted black shape had materialised out of nowhere. The remaining pictures where versions of the same, the shape gradually metamorphosing till in the last one it was fully turned to face the camera. It looked, just as Johnny Fluoride had said, like a dwarf in a raincoat. The sort of black gutta-percha fishermen out on trawlers used to wear.

"What about this dwarf character?"

"That's what I'd like to find out. Think you can manage it?"

Joblard shrugged. He'd faced worse prospects. He held the photo of the headless man up to the light and gave it a closer squint. Blurred as the picture was, he was pretty sure there was a mirror in the background, between the miraculously appearing dwarf and the exploded head of the punter Bludhorn seemed determined not to put a name to. And when Joblard turned the picture just so, he was pretty sure he could see reflected in the mirror a second mirror. The one behind which he figured Johnny Fluoride's camera must've been stashed. Two mirrors reflecting each other on both sides of the room. The head of the dwarf and the non-head of the punter receding into a grainy abyss into which Joblard, too, felt himself being pulled...

"If you find the bastard, call me," Bludhorn said. "There's a couple of people I need to see after we wrap up here. Business to attend to. Can't let one little mishap upset us, can we, my son. No rest for the wicked. If you don't call, I'll expect you at the usual. Same time. I might have something else for you by then."

Joblard looked back at the picture he was holding. In one eye, the dwarf had what seemed to Joblard like some heavy-duty optics. As if he'd screwed a telephoto lens into the socket. And it was staring straight out of the picture at him. No wonder, he thought, Johnny Fluoride flaked out. Bludhorn must've taken one look at the dwarf with the eyepiece and figured he'd been taken for a ride. Only stands to reason.

He wondered if Johnny Fluoride had actually been there at the time, behind some two-way mirror winding the film on, or if the camera had been set to automatic and he'd come by afterwards, back entrance, to pick up the film. Old school analogue. Darkroom rigged-up in his bedsit. Enlargers. Developer trays. Wet prints hanging from lengths of clothesline. Unable quite to believe his eyes about what's there on the contact sheet. Blowing the frames up. Ogling each one with a magnifying glass. Hitting the Dewers. Figuring pretty fast that if anyone ever found out about the pics, it wasn't going to be pretty. Said they'd seen him. Knew he was there. But what to do about Bludhorn? He must've still been trying to get his head around that little quandary when Joblard came knocking.

Well, Joblard thought, nothing to worry about now, Johnny. Is there?

☉ KATI THANDA

29°18'43.62"S
137°27'22.50"E

Once upon a time white men believed in an inland sea. They crossed the unmapped interior with sailing boats in search of it and found only deserts. Some went blind. Their mythical real-estate paradise waited till 1840 to be discovered by an English and named Lake Eyre. That was the story Lawson had been taught at school. Her ancestors had lived on its shores for eighty thousand years. Kati Thanda, they called it.

In the days when the world was wide, the mulga still grew thick around the lake and out across the plains. Before the invaders came and cut everything down for grazing. Red earth stretched as far as the eye could see, sewn with patches of yellow spinifex. And beyond that, the slow agony of scrubland. Cooper's Creek, the Diamantina, Birdsville. Bare earth giving way to gibber plains. East was Burke and Wills country, white men who'd died by their own stupidity. They'd made it from Port Philip to the Gulf and nearly back again, before they'd starved. Burke, disdainful of natives, refused to beg. The Irish in him blacker than he could bear to admit. He preferred to die the sort of death Kippling might've admired, propped under a mallee tree, briny upper lip. Refusing to bend to something as debasing as necessity.

Then, as now, the country had been in drought. Lawson had never known anything but. The last time it'd rained north of the Flinders, she'd been a kid. There'd been floods alright, but the rain that brought them fell hundreds of miles away. Now it was coming down in sheets, so heavy it almost knocked her down. That and the wind. She was up past her ankles in water and sinking deeper. The wind, which first blew hot, had dropped to freezing. The suddenness of it took her breath away. In another half-hour, it'd be like searching for sunken treasure. She'd need sonar, not a GPS.

And that's when the hail began. Ice the size of golf balls, the air streaked white. The first one to hit her cut her arm. And then they were pounding her. Dozens of them. She got the rucksack over her head and huddled. The dark water boiled, churned into a muddy froth. Sky green-black, the dust tamped down by the rain. She could just make out the front moving north-east across the lake, backlit by lightning-flash advancing from the south. She'd seen things like this in movies. End-of-the-world catastrophe scenarios. Meteors. Crashed satellites. Freak weather. Some white American guy always ended up saving the planet, leading the rest of the survivors off to begin a new life, genetically pure. The long walk to the Promised Land.

It was night by the time the storm passed. Starlight glittered over the lake. The only way Lawson could stay warm was to keep moving. She navigated by torchlight, sweeping the beam back and forth across the water. The sat-phone took a direct hit from the hail. The screen was cracked, omitting a sick green glow shattered into moiré. Its co-ordinates were impossible to read, but by trial and error she got it onto audio, like a homing beacon warped by doppler-effect. She was lucky the damn thing was waterproof or it wouldn't've be working at all.

Which it may as well not've been. Hours had passed and she felt like she was going round in circles. Though it was possibly just the constellations turning in the sky as night slowly faded to pre-dawn and the torch flickered out, batteries dead. The coordinates seemed locked into some sort of logarithmic game of next-plus-one, each step bringing her only a fraction of the way closer across a whole distance that existed only as an hypothesis. Whatever the GPS was pointing at seemed to warp space. A coordinate that didn't belong on any map.

Day was already approaching when the shrill cry of the GPS peaked. According to Dix's programme, this was where the impact had occurred. Give or take a margin of error that at this point in the game could just about be anything. Lawson didn't even know what she was looking for, and any telltale signs of an impact were by now a foot under water. She fished in the rucksack for the metal detector, relieved to find it still in working condition once she'd got the parts assembled. A Bounty Hunter she'd picked up cheap from the Broken Hill Radio Shack to go fossicking with around Woomera. Looking for evidence of her missing half.

Lawson skimmed the Bounty Hunter's dish a couple of inches above water level, sweeping it in a slow arc back and forth evenly. She adjusted the readout. Using the rucksack as a marker, she estimated a hundred-metre grid, paced-out to the cardinal points. If nothing turned up, she'd mark-out a wider grid. Work in a roughly concentric pattern, systematically, till the detector locked onto something. And just hope it was the prize.

✛ KARNAK

Above the Varick Street subway entrance someone had strung up a naked mannequin with a broken papier mâché head. Beside it, a dead surveillance eye swung from a pole by a noose of exposed wires. The belching machine-flares of the Tribeca Reconstruction Zone lit the distance. Osborne descended, weaving his way past sleeping figures huddled inside stripped packing cases. A line of naked fluorescents led down into cloying underground humidity. The passageway was narrow and became narrower as it approached the concrete security barriers that'd grown up after 9/11, blackened with graffiti. Fatigue was gaining on him. He wasn't sure he could make it across town, but the alternative didn't bear considering.

On the other side of the barriers, the scavengers had been at work. A single naked light bulb flickered above the skeletons of what had once been a pair of escalators. Collapsed hoardings filled the gap with makeshift terraces oozing menace and a reek of animal decay. No trains had stopped here in years. Further on, an extension tunnel threaded its way north-east across town towards the Bowery. Airless, dripping with condensation. Vague silhouettes shifted in peripheral vision. At Broadway the tunnel opened out into a half-lit thoroughfare as crowded as a North African soukh. Dime stalls, junk sellers, prosthetics hawkers. Dealers in the city's entropy. From somewhere far off, the throbbing of power generators structured the cacophony into a weird rhythmic music that enveloped everything.

Immediately the crowd swallowed him up, bore him along first north-east and then north, and then, just as precipitously, it spat him out. He came to a stop at the head of an overpass, groping at the wall for support. A billboard cartoon with a set of dentures grinned out at him.

KARNAK CENTER COMPREHENSIVE DENTAL CARE. SOMETHING TO SMILE ABOUT!

Osborne didn't see the blow coming. Blood rang in his ears as he crashed through the billboard into nothingness. *Zap! Kapow!* Then the ground rushed up and hit him. He'd landed on his side on a subway platform. A few feet away a filthy red-on-white sign read CAUTION RODENTICIDE. Something brushed his face. He lay there with his eyes open, immobile, watching a rat sniff the air on its hind legs then scuttle off. In his peripheral vision, a midget in a yellow plastic coat sat huddled over a brazier prodding a couple of blackened chestnuts. The midget paid no attention to him.

Osborne grunted and drew his legs under him into a foetal position, pain burning up and down his ribcage. Except for the rats and the midget, the platform was deserted. Up above he could still hear the crowd. Like the sound of the sea in a shell, he thought, close, yet infinitely far off. *Imaginary.* He screwed his eyes closed then opened them again. Three feet away, lying on the concrete, was a folded newspaper, the day's headline above a picture of Ground Zero. He stared at it as recognition did its work. Wincing, he stretched his right hand towards it. But before he could reach the newspaper, a leather boot came down on his fingers. Pain hissed between his teeth.

"You ought to watch your step, Jack."

The voice was right in his ear. It was vaguely familiar, but he couldn't place it. A gloved hand picked up the newspaper and held it a couple of inches from his face, like the prologue to a parlour trick.

"Interesting, isn't it. I bet you're wondering what it's all about?"

"How the hell should I know?"

"Tut-tut, Jack."

The newspaper slapped him in the face and fluttered onto the platform behind him.

"We know all about your little memory lapses, Jack. We've got something that might help you."

Osborne felt a sting in the side of his neck. He clenched his teeth.

"What the fuck are you doing?"

"Just a little injection, Jack, to unscramble whatever's been scrambled up in your sick head. Maybe you should find yourself a new doctor."

He heard laughter. The clatter of a syringe being thrown onto the tracks. His face twitched.

"Someone's been confusing you, Jack. Confusion's dangerous. You know something, but you don't know that you know it. And now you're going to find out what it is. And when you do, you'll be a free man again, Jack. Free," the gloves paused for effect, "from all of... this."

"What d'you want?"

"What does anybody want, Jack?"

As the man with the gloves spoke, the midget he'd registered earlier waddled across the platform like something with flippers instead of feet and stopped just inside Osborne's field of vision. The midget squatted and began laying out a jeweller's cloth on the platform. An array of chromed instruments on black velvet. Osborne watched with a mixture of horror and intrigue as the midget screwed a jeweller's loup into one eye. The gloved hand reached down and took hold of his face. He felt the lids of his left eye being pulled apart. A dull, anaesthetised feeling. The midget's face came closer. He could smell the PVC of the raincoat, the roast chestnuts, and something else he couldn't place. A metallic, chemical smell. The gloved hand twisted Osborne's head around to the light. The weirdly magnified pupil of an eye stared into him through the loup.

The midget grunted and sweated as he worked. Osborne could make no sense of what was happening. His mind raced, firing blanks. It was no use. Nothing would cohere. He tried to flex his neck, clenched his teeth. The boot pressed harder. His face had gone numb. The rest of his body ached. He could feel the cold of the platform working up through his chest. Time passed. Eventually the midget unscrewed the loup from his eye. Folded away the jeweller's cloth. Nodded. Saying nothing. Features expressionless. Osborne watched the midget turn and waddle away across the platform, disappearing from view behind the pylons. He waited for the punch line.

"The suspense is killing me."

He felt a sudden confused desire to laugh. His own words sounded ridiculous to him. Like words in a film.

"There's someone," the gloves said, "who'd like to discuss something with you."

Osborne felt himself being dragged upright. Stabbing pain down his left side. Nothing seemed funny anymore. Behind him, improbably, the sound of an approaching train.

"Take my advice," the gloves hissed, "don't try anything dumb."

The sound in the tunnel got louder. Then it became a wail. The station lights dimmed. Osborne staggered as a wall of humid air slammed into him. Scraps of newspaper, cigarette butts, crushed Styrofoam spiralled out of the darkness. The platform shuddered. A moment later he felt himself being pushed towards a pair opening train doors. Like the jaws, he thought, of some furious beast.

The boy with dark eyes was looking down at Shinwah intently. At first she took him for a ghost. *Giû*. That she'd woken in hell. *Dìyù*. The underworld. Her mind was a labyrinth of tunnels and catacombs. Braziers flaring through the dark with hell money offerings to the Jade Emperor of a child's nightmares. Lord of hell. *Yanluo*. Unlike de Laurentiis, she was in no doubt that hell existed. She'd been there. It was the first thing she remembered. The fires. The prison underground. Strangers. Clinging to the woman who might've been her mother. Who read stories to her from a book. Before the rats...

But then she recognised him. It was the boy from the safe house. Who'd given her coffee. His clothes gave off a faint smell of solder as he leant over her, mingling with the smell of what must've been the sea. She was lying on her back somewhere. A dull pain throbbed down her left side. Her head rocked.

"Where am I?" she managed.

The boy mouthed something she couldn't hear. Gestured with his hands. *Mute*, she thought. He seemed to be telling her to lie still. She nodded. It produced a smile that made the boy look much younger than she suspected he really was. He touched his fingers to his mouth then pointed up at the wood-panelled ceiling. Shinwah's gaze drifted around the room. She guessed from what she could make out that it was a ship's cabin. Or not a ship, but a yacht. She was lying in one of two berths. A blanket was covering her. Its coarse weave pricked her skin.

Like something she might've dreamed and only possessed a residual memory of, the scene with de Laurentiis came back to her by facets. The standoff on the quay. The look on Margarita's face when she'd pulled the trigger. Then nothing. Blackness. A sick feeling in her gut. Like nodding-out on a high. Only terminal. O.D. A vague sense of panic crept into her. *Am I still here,* she thought, *or back in the other place again and only dreaming this?*

She glanced again at the boy, afraid she might've imagined him. He was still there, holding a glass of water now, his eyes making questions at her. She nodded again and he brought the glass to her lips so she could drink, his free hand tilting her head up from the pillow. Like in the detox clinic in Beijing, when she thought she'd die. The first time. Raw. And the feeling of helplessness. Strapped to a bed. Unable even to move. As now. *What's wrong with me?* she thought.

The cold water wet her lips. Her tongue felt swollen. A taste of metal in her throat. It hurt to swallow. Everything went white. A white hiss. Then slowly the cabin shifted back into focus. Only the boy wasn't there anymore.

If I'm not dead, she thought, *then where am I?*

She tried to prop herself up but her body wouldn't respond. The cabin blurred. Her breathing became erratic. Then Margarita was there, looking down at her. Holding a wet cloth to her forehead. It felt cold and then hot.

"Shhhh," Margarita said, "you're still in shock. I'm giving you an injection. You're going to be fine. Just a couple of scratches. Nothing you can't live with. Now try to sleep. We'll talk later."

"Where are we?" she managed.

"Aboard the *Volta*," Margarita said, flicking the syringe. "Just off Corfu. By tomorrow, if the wind holds and the sea isn't too rough, we should be in Santorini. Not the best time of year to visit, but then we're not going for the scenery."

Shinwah concentrated on the hypodermic in Margarita's hand. Light glinted on the needle as it retracted from the glass ampoule. Like amber with a bluish halo. Shinwah watched the eye of the needle come towards her. Felt a prick in her arm. And somewhere at the back of her head, an echo. De Laurentiis. Warping and

160

fading like the sound of wind or water against the bulkheads. She felt the cabin sway. What'd he mean, *you can't go back?*

An image flashed through her mind. The quay. De Laurentiis's blue velvet dinner jacket. Everything seemed to spin. And then darkness, telescoping. A long tunnel of black like a rifled gun barrel, with de Laurentiis standing at the end of it. His mouth open. As if he was trying to tell her something. But it was too late. There was only a pinprick of light, centred on his mouth. Then nothing. The darkness had her completely.

☾ INTIFADA

The space they're moving through is becoming narrower and narrower. There're cracks in the walls. The floor. Subsidence. For his benefit, the albino shines a dim torch. Her shape in front of him. He's tried to count the steps from one turning to the next. There's no pattern. At some point the passage levels out, assumes a type of neutrality. It's impossible for him to retain any kind of map of their journey. Even his sense of time's completely lost. There's only an abstract momentum. A feeling of being propelled, in slow-motion, through the dark. And somewhere ahead, in some unspecified time-frame, the destination. As if the entire journey was just that – a means of arriving at a point in time. That point and no other point. Space nothing but archaeology now, time stratified. And the catastrophe, which'd brought all the different strata into collision. The *anachronism*.

The way the albino says the word gives it an almost mystical resonance. He doesn't know why she's telling him this. Something to do with the name. Momo. The Connection. To what? An outside perhaps. Where they were going. Outside the Dome. It may as well be outside the universe. Something in him afraid of being stuck here, the way the Stranger was stuck in his head, or he was stuck in someone else's head. The person in the room. The boy in the memory. *The wrong place at the wrong time.* Was that really him?

"They built labour camps," she says.

"Who?"

"The corporations. Began as enclaves. High-rise wage ghettos. In the end, people couldn't leave. Debt-bound. Nowhere to leave to. Outside the Dome, nothing survives for long. Unless it's underground. Or up in space. But the Dome economy was always virtual. Nothing but an oversize bubble waiting to burst. Only the

Dome itself, what you see when you're up there instead of the sky, *that's* real. Like an abscess on the brain. You can't fight something that doesn't exist, so the intifada targeted infrastructure. No Dome, no corporations. Now the corporations are stuck up there, praying to their machine God. The one they created. Got so they even started believing in it themselves."

"You want to destroy the Dome?"

"No need. It's destroying itself. The corporations liked everyone to believe they could survive in a vacuum, breathing nothing but pure profit. They took the existing infrastructure and sucked the life out of it. Only a matter of time before the whole thing started crumbling under them. The intifada just sped things up. Nothing the corporations would like more than to turn back the clock. And keep it there."

☐ REARVIEW

The black-and-grey smartcar was parked directly across the street. It gave Joblard a bad feeling, even if the short-arse in it looked like the butt of a practical joke. Head barely showing over the side window, giving him the beady eye. He couldn't be sure, but something told him it was the same smartcar he'd picked up in Greenwich. Which meant it'd followed him at least since Johnny Fluoride's. Maybe the demolition job on the bedsit was the dwarf's handiwork? Tossed the place over, then sat and waited to see who'd show. Unlikely.

But there'd been two of them in the car that'd followed him. At least it'd showed all the signs of following him. Which must've been some sort of cue, because right then Joblard almost ran smack into the second one coming down the footpath from where the BSA was chained up. *Well if it isn't Ol' Pasty.* The scarecrow with zinc smeared all over his face, who he'd spotted on the floodwall back at Canvey. Same felt hat and coat. Brushing past in a hurry, it seemed, muttering something Joblard didn't quite catch. *That,* he thought, *is sure as shit no coincidence.*

Joblard turned and eyeballed the back of Ol' Pasty's head, thinking now might be a good time to collar the skinny bastard and find out what the gag was. The scarecrow pulled up outside the red door from which Joblard had just emerged and gave it a close inspection. Then, casting a dirty look back at Joblard, crossed the street in a hurry to the smartcar and got in beside short-arse. The car sputtered to life and pulled away, making a sharp left at the intersection, a pair of dark eyes scoping him in the rearview.

Joblard stood on the pavement staring after them. *Maybe it was Bludhorn they were looking for. Couple of circus freaks bearing a grudge.* The sort of kinky shit Bludhorn got up to was bound to find a few detractors in the community. But it was him they'd been following. And he'd lost them, too. He was sure of that. How the hell did they find him again in Soho? Maybe the two things were just a coincidence. But Ol' Pasty on Canvey? Uh-uh. As far as coincidences were concerned, Canvey just didn't cut ice. *And wasn't that a dwarf behind the steering wheel...?*

Pensively Joblard unlocked his bike and wrapped the chain over his shoulder. He was staring into his helmet when the connections started forming in his head. *Canvey. Johnny Fluoride.* A dwarf in a raincoat, is what he'd said, before taking the long swim. Joblard hadn't noticed if the dwarf in the smartcar had been wearing a raincoat or not. And there hadn't been much in the photo to make a positive I.D. Besides, sorry as he was to say it, all dwarfs looked pretty much the same to him.

But that was only half of it. *One of them,* Johnny Fluoride had said. *One of them* was wearing a raincoat. Which meant there had to've been something missing from those pictures in the envelope. Two dwarfs? It sounded far fetched. Or maybe, a scarecrow in a felt hat? Ol' Pasty? The second one, he'd said, *didn't have a face.* His exact words. Which possibly was the sort of effect the scarecrow might have on a fragile psychology like Johnny Fluoride's, under the circumstances. And they'd *seen* him, he'd said. Knew he was *there.* Were out to *get* him. But how'd they *know?* How'd Johnny Fluoride know? And if the scuzzy git was just paranoid, why were there two goons in a smartcar following him?

Joblard began to feel unwell. *Too many questions,* he thought. *Christ, and what about the trollop with the whip?* Did she get her brains blown out too? Why wasn't it in the news? Had someone gone in and cleaned up the mess, buried the whole thing? Who'd be in a position to do something like that? Dodgy was hardly the word. What did Bludhorn know about it that he wasn't saying? Who was the headless punter? Where was the room? What was the fucking angle supposed to be?

⊙ BLACK BOX

What it was, was a helicopter moving low on the horizon. It was too small to have much of a range, so Lawson figured it was local. But something about it wasn't right. She'd heard the beating of the rotors long before she spotted it, instinct making her get as low down as she could in the water. The way the chopper moved suggested purpose. When the second one came into view, she new it was bad. What was worse, they were bearing straight for where Kath had landed the plane...

It was almost dawn when Lawson found the first bit of wreckage, north-east of where she'd started and about two hundred metres out. Her third go round. Exhaustion had just about gotten the better of her. Hands numb from the cold. No more sign of the storm. It'd passed as suddenly as it'd arrived. Up above, a clear sky showed the first faint traces of approaching sunrise. The scene was nothing she could've imagined. The lake like a sheet of mirrored glass laid flat, horizon to horizon. A lone pelican drifted across opalescent water, blown off-course, a thousand miles from the sea.

Most of the wreckage was small, pieces no bigger than Lawson's fist. Shattered remains of something metallic, sheered on impact. They were embedded in clay two feet under water. Keeping her gear dry was a bitch. Metal detector perched atop rucksack like some exotic bird. The real prize almost escaped her. It was stuck deep down, but when it came away in her hand, she knew she'd scored. In the pre-dawn, it didn't looked like much. A dirty mustard-coloured film cartridge. Only bigger. Bits of charred tape hanging from it. There was a canister moulded at one end and a box at the other, the rest was flat. *I hope to fuck this was worth it, Dix.* The markings it bore weren't anything Lawson recognised.

She wrapped it carefully inside the rucksack and kept scouring the area for more wreckage till the lake had gone through a dozen shades of blue-pink-red and the temperature had risen enough to make her sweat. And to bring out the flies. But somehow she knew the cartridge was it, the proof of Dix's mystery satellite.

By the time the sun poked over the horizon, the air was alive with insect-noise. And with the heat and noise came renewed fatigue. The rucksack weighed a tonne. Her boots dragged. Gauging east by the sun, Lawson made a bearing towards where she hoped the plane was. Immediately she found herself in deeper water and backtracked. With the GPS busted, her directional sense was being tested to the max. Thinking wryly how whitefellas would expect a Nunga to know instinctively which way to go. Like how to dig up witchetty grubs or find water in a desert. Stand on one leg with knee up, spear in hand, surveying the distance for a sign. Lawson raised a hand to shade her eyes. The horizon offered no clues. *Well girlie*, she thought, *your guess is as good as mine.*

She hoped Kath'd have enough presence of mind to send up a flare if she didn't make it back by the time she said she would. Which was pretty much now. Though if the prop was still buggered they wouldn't be going anywhere soon either way. Or Kath might've got it fixed only for the plane to've sunk in the mud, which'd be just their luck. Or everything'd be rosy and Kath'd be sitting on a dune having a smoke waiting for her to get her sorry arse across the lake. But it'd never be rosy enough with those two helicopters on the scene...

Unless her instincts were very wrong, the choppers didn't belong to any kind of rescue party. If it was the authorities, they could always just play dumb, say they'd lost radio contact and been forced down in the storm. But something about the look of the choppers told her it wasn't cops. Not ordinary cops, anyhow. The way they were zeroing in.

With every passing moment the lake grew wider, Lawson's

position more exposed. There was no cover in sight, the shore a vague haze of landform in a distance towards which she was groping like a witless animal in the crosshairs of a hunter's scope. The silhouettes of the helicopters grew larger against the glare of the lake. Lawson prayed they wouldn't spot the plane. Wouldn't spot her. But praying had always struck her as white man's superstition. Like their God, it didn't belong here but somewhere far away, on a mountain in Egypt.

The beat of the rotors echoed in unison across the water, the choppers' movements now a synchronised dance like dragonflies in a courtship ritual. A sense of foreboding began to overtake her, exhaustion gone, adrenaline driving her now as she struggled not to panic. Then something else caught her eye, rising out of the heat-shimmer. A white birdlike shape, becoming airborne and banking immediately towards the low-lying sun.

The effect on the choppers was instantaneous. Now like angry hornets they swung around in pursuit. The Cessna dipped and weaved, unable to gain altitude. Lawson pictured Kath at the controls, teeth clenched, gauging the true nature of the situation, ready to put up a fight. But that wasn't going to happen. Lawson watched helplessly as the choppers closed-in. There was a flash. Smoke billowed from the rear of the Cessna. And then it went up in flames, coming apart in mid-air. *No Kath! Not like this...*

Lawson's first instinct was to run, but the choppers were already swinging back around, heading straight towards her. She went cold. Her only hope was they hadn't spotted her yet. Then her blood froze. Frantically she grabbed for the sat-phone, tearing at the bakelite to get the chip out of it. Drown it. Shit. How dumb could she be? If they'd tracked Dix, they could track where his computer sent the coordinates. And what those coordinates were. Scrambler or no scrambler.

But it was too late for all that now. She felt like a sitting duck, no matter how low she crouched in the water. The choppers were still far enough away for her to hope, but that was all. The beating of the rotors was getting louder. And somewhere in amongst the beating, a high pitched whine. It, too, seemed to be getting closer, but from behind. Lawson turned her head, expecting to see a spotter plane sweeping low over the lake. Flocks of startled birds rose up off the water. Lawson stared. As if things weren't crazy enough already, a powerboat was cutting a wide arc in her direction. In its wake, two figures danced about on the water. It took her mind some moments to assimilate this new information.

"I'll be fucked," Lawson said.

The choppers, no longer approaching, had split up, circling higher. The skiers circled, weaving back away. Lawson wondered if the skiers had seen anything. The wake from the powerboat washed over her. In synchronicity the choppers began to move in again, lower, hovering. She could hear the powerboat coming around for another run. Closer this time. A couple of meshbacks at the wheel. Behind, two sheilas in bikinis, each riding single-ski. Lawson could hear their shouts over the revving of the motor. The choppers backed-up again, the shapes of the pilots clearly visible. It was weird, like a standoff in a film with too many witnesses. She toyed with the idea of flagging down the boat, but kept her nerve. *You'd be kidding yourself anyway*, she thought. *What whitefella would stop for a Nunga in the middle of Lake Eyre?*

The wake hit harder this time. Lawson stayed under, counting to a hundred. Had almost made it when the burning in her lungs forced her up for air. Gasping, she scanned the lake. The choppers were like two specs moving south. The whine of the powerboat rose and fell at intervals as the joyriders, oblivious to everything, slalomed their way back from whence they came.

+ CIRCLE LINE

It was one of those old trains that'd mostly been decommissioned, with long blue moulded benches facing one another across the aisle. Expired CIRCLE LINE adverts. Osborne staggered. Something hard was thrust into the small of his back. He collided with a pole and spun around. Facing him was a man with yellow eyes and a heavily pockmarked face under a grey fedora. The man was pointing a gun at him.

"Who are you?"

"Don't you recognise an old pal, Jack? It's been a while. Don't you remember?"

"No."

"The bridge."

"What bridge?"

"You don't remember the bridge?"

"I don't know what the fuck you're talking about."

"You certain about that, Jack?"

"Told you, I don't know anything."

"Just can't help yourself, can you? People. Always deny knowing anything. Like idiots. You're not an idiot, are you Jack?"

Osborne stared into the black hole of the gun barrel. An irrational thought entered his head. And then a seemingly rational one. *He isn't going to kill me. He wants something from me*

"Don't tell me. You *are* an idiot."

The doors of the carriage rattled closed. A warped machine voice came from the overhead speakers. NEXT STOP. FRANKLIN. STAND CLEAR OF THE CLOSING DOORS. Pockmarked face grinned. *Don't think*, Osborne told himself. *They know what you're thinking.*

He backed away down the carriage. The face matched him step

for step like a mime. Skin greasepaint-white. It seemed to have been eroded by some sort of disease. Osborne backed into another pole, gripped hold of it. Then the train lurched. For an instant the face lost his balance. And that's when the irrational thought came back and stuck in Osborne's head.

He turned and ran, pain searing up his left side. The train lurched again, sending Osborne careening through the connecting doors into the next carriage. Momentum alone carried him. He could hear the face cursing behind him, caught in the connecting doors. Outside the platform disappeared. Then everything went black. The train banked and Osborne found himself sprawled across a row of seats, head-first, sliding. The train tilted back and he rebounded off invisible poles. Struggled through the next set of doors, lights flickering in a carriage up ahead. He could hear his pursuer gaining. His lungs heaved.

Somehow Osborne got to the back of the carriage and through the last set of doors. It was the end of the train. He looked back. Pockmarked face was right behind him now, smirking through the glass window of the connecting door. Osborne staggered backwards. The door slid aside and the face came slowly towards him, gun levelled at his chest.

"What'd I say about being dumb?"

Osborne blinked. Now you're fucked, he thought. The train rattled and heaved. The face said nothing.

Behind him Osborne heard a dry rasp of laughter. It froze him. The laughter had the sound of autumn leaves blown by the wind down a dead-end street. Ancient laughter.

The face wasn't grinning anymore.

"Turn around."

Osborne gritted his teeth. The pain up his side made breathing difficult. He expected that once he turned around, that'd be the end. But it's the end already, he thought. He could feel the fear mounting inside him. Pointless fear. There was no way out. He tried to resign himself. He remembered the room on Canal Street. The powerlessness.

He turned around.

It wasn't what he expected.

In front of him, standing in the middle of the carriage where it hadn't been before, was a figure completely covered in black cloth. Like it was trick-or-treat. There was a black grill where the mouth should've been.

Osborne swayed on his feet. The goon with the pockmarked face pressed close behind him.

The sound of dry leaves.

"I don't wish to harm you."

Osborne realised the apparition was speaking to him. The voice seemed to come from nowhere. Behind the black grill there could've been anything. Or nothing. It radiated only absence. Looking at it made his eyes hurt.

"Approach."

It was command, not an invitation. Osborne felt the gun in his back, nudging him forward. He took two steps before he was pushed to his knees, lost his balance and found himself face-down on the floor a gun pressing against his neck. In this position, he could only make out the lower half of the black figure. It seemed to float above the floor, like a bed-sheet on a string. Without appearing to move it came closer.

That sound again. The voice. Not like leaves, but static, Osborne thought. White noise.

"You will know me," the voice hissed, "only when your eyes are truly open."

Osborne strained to look up. A hand, covered in a fine tracery of tattooist's ink, reached out to him from the folds of black drapery, unfurling like an exotic flower coming into bloom. Déjà vu. In its open palm lay a tiny black manikin. It caught the light like black obsidian.

Osborne flinched. The gun pressed harder.

"This," the voice said, "belongs to me. It was stolen from me. You have perceived it. It exists somewhere in your mind. Men of evil intent have hidden it there. You must find it and return it to me."

The voice paused, switched register. It reminded Osborne of the dead witch's voice in The Wizard of Oz. The voice of the insane. Leaves rustled.

"Can you even begin to imagine what it is?" The rustling came closer. "It is something more precious than a million souls." Laughter rose and died out. "Could it be possible for a mere mortal to comprehend such a thing?"

Osborne stared at the manikin as if his eyes were magnetised by it. He pictured his own reflection in its eyes, and the reflection becoming tinier and tinier, sucked into a vortex. As if something inside it was collapsing, till there was nothing left of it but a black hole. A soul that lives-on after death. Suliman. And that picture coming back to him again, of children playing in the snow, which wasn't snow. Their faces. All of them smiling…

The tattooed hand closed into a fist. Turned sideways. Grey ash trickled out of it and dissolved into air. Like a magician's trick.

"A million souls," the voice rasped. Fainter now. As the black manikin, too, receded from his gaze. And then was gone.

Osborne struggled to breathe. These people, he thought, are completely nuts. But though he knew in his mind that nothing that'd just happened made the slightest bit of sense, his body was unable to hold-out against the facts. The pain behind his eye seared. The train's screech split his ears. Waves of peristalsis overcame him. Osborne retched. He could barely keep his head off the floor. He retched again and again, barely feeling the blow to his neck as the last wave spilled over.

At one end of the laboratory, two girls are sitting, side by side, on a metal bench, holding hands. Two identical twins. Naked. A cell division. An accident within the evolutionary process. They wait there, impassive. Dead kohl-rimmed eyes staring. Alabaster-pale. Two Nefertiti heads surmounting long graceful necks, sculpted from the one stone. Necks intertwined like the necks of swans.

The laboratory in which they're sitting is a large, windowless space. White. Like a piece of over-exposed film traversed by silhouettes standing out of it in relief. To one side of the twins, a row of computer consoles, monitors, scanners. To the other, a washbasin, a trestle table littered with surgical instruments, speculae, probes, latex gloves. A transfusion catheter runs from the left arm of one of the twins to the right arm of the other. Their skin, like the room, is perfectly white. The ambient hum of overhead lights is punctuated only by the sound of an oscilloscope, its green wave-patterns rising and falling with hypnotic persistence...

When Shinwah woke, there was a stabbing pain in her head like the pain in her body, but the dream stayed vivid in her mind. So vivid it was as if it hadn't been a dream at all, but something else. *They were me*, she thought. *Both of us...* Morphine working the neural pathways. Taking her back to the place she couldn't get to. How long had it been? She'd completely lost track of time since the episode on the quay. Everything was fragments. Adrift on a sea. Margarita had explained everything to her, very slowly, but still she couldn't remember. Only that somehow they'd made it. Ghost trigonometries, making the impossible possible.

The second goon's bullet had caught her just below the shoulder. Small calibre, or she wouldn't've had any shoulder left at all. She couldn't recover a memory of hitting her mark. But she must have. Right between the eyes, Margarita said. Dead centre.

Shinwah dragged herself up from the berth, trying to keep balance one-armed, making her way with nauseating slowness out to the galley. She put her head in the sink and turned the tap. It helped. Her face in the mirror was a mess. Grey with dull matted hair framing it. Black around the eyes. She wrung the water from her hair as best she could. Felt it run down her back and legs, pooling around bare feet. The bandages across her left shoulder were stained with old blood, darkened almost to black. Someone had tied her arm across her abdomen in a sling, keeping it immobile. The bullet must've struck as she was turning. Any lower, she thought…

Back in the cabin, Shinwah found her old clothes folded in a cupboard. Minus the turtle neck. Gritting her teeth, she managed the slacks and a black singlet. Doused herself in deodorant spray. When it came to the boots, she found herself begrudgingly thankful that de Laurentiis had given her ones with Velcro tabs. Blood had stiffened the fabric of the bomber jacket around a hole the size of her index finger. The bullet had exited through the seam, where the back of the sleeve joined. Nothing fancy, then. Regular shells. Designed for precision, not a Jackson Pollock paint-job. What'd that tell her?

Her shoulder bag was stashed with the clothes. She spat on her thumb and wiped the dry blood from the patent leather strap. The jeweller's case was still zipped in the inside pocket. She sat back on the bunk, unhasped the case, dipped the long nail of her little finger and snorted twice. Her nail needed lacquering. Like it mattered. Almost instantly the drug transformed the pain in her body into a warm glow. The rising-falling motion of the cabin melded into waves of something very much akin to pleasure. She slipped back against the pillows. The strangeness of her dream returned to her in a sudden rush of images that multiplied but went nowhere. Two

Nefertiti heads. Necks entwined. Dead eyes. Naked.

It seemed like an age, but it was probably only a matter of seconds. The white ice oblivion. Then clarity. Everything in heightened focus, more real than the real. Shinwah searched the bag for her handset, to check-in, get her coordinates. But the handset wasn't there. She tried to think, but her thoughts wouldn't gel. She'd had the handset with her when they left the warehouse. Which meant she had it when the shit went down. Someone must've gone through her bag while she was unconscious. Margarita. She'd've done the same in her position. Even so...

Shinwah wrapped the bomber jacket around her and retraced her steps to the galley. Still no sign of whoever was aboard. They were probably up on deck. How many people anyway, she wondered, did it take to sail a yacht that size? The hatchway was forward of the galley. No sooner did she reach the top of the steps than the wind whipped her hair back in her eyes. The boom was directly above. A triangle of white sailcloth sliced across a blue nowhere on any chromatic scale. The jib billowed. Seagulls streaked overhead.

Shinwah's eyes, dazzled in the light, traced the oblique line of the mainsail down to where Margarita was standing behind the wheel, tossed blonde hair backlit against the water. Hilfiger anorak and a pair of Milanese sunglasses like she'd just materialised from a 1980s cigarette commercial. Merit Ultra Lights. Time-weirdness creeping back in.

"This is where they kept the mainframes."

They're standing in one of those cavernous spaces he imagines being like the inside of a ship, dry-docked, mid-construction. Some old ocean liner. He must've seen a picture once. An ark with enormous steel struts, curving up like a dinosaur's ribcage, tangled in a mess of girders, plastic corrugate, electrical wiring palimpsested like a vast dissolved circuit board. The pervasive smell is battery acid and cordite. The albino is telling him it used to be a kind of bunker, torchlight tracing the outlines of debris-encrusted silicon stalactites and stalagmites. Banks of shattered monitors. Consoles with their guts hanging out. Industrial-sized air conditioning units that'd since been used for target practice by something with an artillery calibre.

"The corporations moved all their hardware down here before they built the Dome, is how the story goes. Something they did to the atmosphere. Ozone depletion. Who knows. Cosmic rain fritzing the System's memory banks beyond repair. So they had to rebuild underground. Type of Year Zero thing, before the Dome went up."

He pictures cosmic-ray traces running like scars through silicon labyrinths. Exotic digital landscapes dissolving into white noise. Ravines of antimatter and randomness. Death from the sky. Flashback to the chaos at the East Wall. Like a mind issuing a dozen conflicting simultaneous commands. Synapse implosion.

Across a concrete barrier, someone's sprayed a skull and cross-bones sign, with DEATH TO MACHINES. Only it's not a skull. And they're not bones. Something else.

"Joke is, this place was supposed to be impregnable. You know, A-bombs and all that. Like the Titanic, kind of."

"What's that?"

"A ship they said couldn't sink. Back in the day. Hit an iceberg and went down on its maiden voyage. Same with the System. They said it couldn't be hacked, but it was the first thing the *intifada* took down. The only reason there's anything left here at all is the machines can't bring themselves to blow it up. Like they believe this's where they came from. The motherboard, right? As if it's sacred or something. Their Babylon. Cradle of machine civilization. Because by then, machines had become *intelligent*. Weird intelligent. Before they pulled the plug on the A.I.s and tried to make machines stupid again, the way they make people."

"What're A.I.s?"

"Artificial intelligence. It was the big thing pre-Dome. Machines that can think. Someone figured this was where they kept all the memories. Like a collective unconscious or something. Ghost memes. Ever heard of a superstitious machine?"

"Why would anyone want to make a machine that can think?"

"Because they can."

"It's hard enough to think for myself."

"You can think alright, only you're too used to listening to whatever crap's inside your head."

"And what's inside your head?"

"Not a fucking machine, for starters."

He wonders what a human meme machine might look like. And if somewhere there was one that contained his memories. Or was it already inside him? Or him inside it? Not just bits of code, but real memories, in all their analogue glory. Ghost vectors in a circuit that lives and breathes.

"Just like we do," he hears himself say.

The albino shines the torch in his face.

"Like we do what?"

He puts his hand up to shield his eyes.

"Pray," he says, not knowing where the words are coming

from. "To some God of the machines. Of the ultimate programme."

Woman and man it created them, he thinks. *To rise up and uncreate it again*. The albino points the torch away from him. He can see her eyes. The way she's watching him. Strangely.

☐ FLOATER

51°31'11.49"N
0°3'25.42"W

Nicky Cohn's answering machine wasn't giving much away. He must've been one of the last people in London who refused to be suckered into owning a mobile telephone. Very strictly old school, Nicky Cohn did all his research by landline, calling-in stories from one of the ever-diminishing number of red boxes still scattered about the city, mostly for the tourist trade. Mention the internet and he'd spit on the floor, throw you the sign of the cross, toss a pinch of salt over his shoulder.

Joblard left a message, then waited for the cut-off. There was a click and the line went dead, while at the other end Joblard knew a magnetic cassette tape with Nicky Cohn's voiceprint would be rewinding, spool-to-spool, ready to play back again on the next call. He was half-tempted to try to catch it mid-process, just for badness. The engaged signal's whir and click. His recorded message, meanwhile, cued on a separate tape which Nicky Cohn, if the mood took him, could remote-access by calling his own number then dialling an additional three-digit code. And when it came to Nicky Cohn, chances were the phone he'd be using really would have a dial.

What Nicky Cohn and Johnny Fluoride had in common was an abiding faith in all things pre-digital. Even Nicky Cohn's handwriting belonged to a previous age, half Saxon rune, half Egyptian hieroglyph. If there was anyone with the vaguest inkling what Johnny Fluoride had been up to the other night, it was a fair enough bet it'd be Nicky Cohn. Bludhorn wasn't making the job any easier playing cute with the details. Someone had to've missed the headless geezer by now. And with any luck, Nicky Cohn might even be persuaded to get the lowdown about any stand-up duos touring around in a smartcar. Joblard still owed him the dope on *Orgasmatron*, but the man was always good for a favour.

It was after eight when he got the call-back. Nicky Cohn's voice sounded like it was coming from half a mile away, looped in copper wire time-delay, somewhere in the city as yet untouched by optic fibre, wireless, or any other post-war amenity. Joblard was parked at the Blind Beggar with a plate of mushy peas and a pint of Bombardier. He'd been considering swinging by the Hindu takeaway later for some vindaloo and a bottle of Jacob's Creek for Bird Girl, in case she was back at the Fridge. Maybe kick on a video and enjoy a quiet evening together at home, let Bludhorn's mystery dwarf entertain someone else for a while.

"Looks like I've got news for you, old chum."

Joblard dropped his fork in his peas, took a gulp from his pint and wiped his lip as Nicky Cohn gave him the narrative.

"Seems a floater just got pulled out of the river at Canary Wharf earlier this evening. Sans head. You didn't say anything about our Johnny not having a head when you dropped him in the drink."

"Maybe a fish ate it. Or he took a fancy to someone's outboard."

"Uh-uh. My mate over at the Yard says more like a double-barrell twelve-gauge in the mouth. Blew his lid clear off. Said you could see what he had for breakfast."

"No mystery in that. He was pickled in the stuff."

"Eh?"

"Dewers is what it said on the bottle."

But already Joblard was getting a bad feeling about all this. The headless geezer in the photos. And now Johnny Fluoride washing up, with a serious case of over-stimulated imagination. The barman gave him a curious look. Joblard lowered his voice.

"You're not pulling my leg, about the head I mean?"

"Uh-uh. I'm on my way to the coroner's myself to have a look-see, in case you want to tag along. Something like this, it's too good to miss."

How'd they get to him, Joblard wondered, *in the middle of the fucking Thames and all? Shit. Even a drowning man wasn't safe in London these days.*

"He didn't say anything about a dwarf, did he?"

"Who?"

"Your mate at Scotland Yard."

"No, why?"

"Nothing. Just a funny idea I had."

⊙ WOOMERA

29°9'40.97"S
137°42'44.31"E

Lawson never knew her father, though sometimes she felt him. A kind of residual presence inside her, half-genie, half-genetics. He'd been an engineer at Woomera, listed among the personal at DSS-41. DSS for Deep Space Station. Fancy name for a tracking base at the edge of Island Lagoon. It played a part in the first moon landing. But when the Yanks left in the mid-seventies, they dismantled the facilities and sent DSS-41 back to America in crates. All that was left now was a grid of weed-infested tarmac and brick foundations, the odd rocket motor sticking out of the overgrowth. The lagoon was just dirt. They named the place Woomera after the spear-thrower, used to increase range, speed, accuracy. Nunga technology from eighty thousand years ago. The Romans and Greeks had nothing like it. She'd gone there, to Woomera, on a tour operated by the Defence Department after they opened the base to the public back in the '80s, before she enrolled at uni. Looking for clues to who she was. The missing half...

By the time Lawson reached the eastern shore, the sun was directly overhead, the humidity stifling. If she didn't keep walking, she was afraid she'd just lie down. That'd just be funny as hell, drowning in the middle of the desert. She could've been walking in circles for all she knew. The heat-shimmer like molten glass, eyes playing tricks. She half expected to look down and see the water start boiling for real all around her in the heat. There was no way of telling whereabouts exactly she was. All day she'd scanned the horizon, expecting any moment to see the choppers return. Black specs coming out of nowhere. Hunting her. She'd followed, as best she could, the direction of the skiers, thinking there had to be a road they'd come in on. Kath had said they were only a hundred clicks to the airstrip at Muloorina. From there she could try her luck hitching a ride. South. To the Oodnadatta Track. To Woomera...

The only picture she'd ever found of her father was a black-and-white group photo at the museum in Missile Park. The caption didn't say what name belonged to who, so she'd had to try and guess which of them H.W. Lawson was. None of their faces looked like hers. But somehow she thought she recognised the eyes. Left of centre, tall in a civilian shirt, grinning at whoever was behind the camera. She'd tried to see the blue in the grey. Her black in place of the straight blond hair, falling down over a high forehead. She wrote a letter to the USAF but never got a reply...

The sun burned. The whole lake was like one great shimmering strip of celluloid. It must've been pushing forty-five. Her body ached. Arms bruised from the hail. Like a residual bad dream. One bad dream after another. The moment she got clear of the choppers, she'd ditched the inessentials. Only the rucksack with the canister, water, ration pack. First she skirted the lake shore, hunting for tyre tracks, watching the sky. As soon as the sun dipped, she'd be able to get a clear bearing. Head east, then south. Find a way to the rendezvous. If not to herself, she owed it to Kath, to stay alive. And Dix. She only hoped he made it out. That he'd be there at the crossing. Like he said he would...

For years the question had gnawed at the back of Lawson's mind. About her father, who he was, what he knew about her people, their land, their history. Impossible for her to believe a whitefella could be innocent of all that. Clean hands. Besides, they'd done the same over there. Put the Indians in camps. Shot, raped, poisoned. Stole their land, destroyed their culture. Only the Americans had made laws and treaties to keep it all civilised somehow. The destruction of her people began on 28 December 1836 without even a mention of their existence. Men who'd never set eyes on the land signed a bit of paper in London, declaring it *waste and unoccupied*. Terra nullius, they called it. The lie on which a nation was founded. Whitefellas with all the righteousness of law on their side brought dogs, guns, smallpox, to decimate the tribes. The Adynyamathanha, Bungandidj, Dirari, Erawirung, Guyani, Erawirung, Marawara, Ngarinyeri, Pitjantjatjara, Raminyeri, Tanganalun, Wotjobaluk, Yaraldi...

From the shore, a broad, shallow sheet of grey water with dead trees standing out of it, stretched off towards the horizon. In a couple of days, she thought, there'd just be saltpan and fissured mud out there, with cockatoos scrounging about for the last of the groundwater. The rivers up north might still bring floods, but those would soon be reduced to a string of brackish waterholes. Only yesterday there'd been no water at all. Then the storm came. Fifteen years of drought and then a moment of rain. One day nothing, the next, an inland sea. And still everything was dead...

Lawson's father had been stationed at Woomera when they put the first whitefella on the moon. DSS-41. Built on land where the white man had tried, and only just failed, to make her people extinct. The great evolutionary leap. And by sharing his chromosomes with a Nunga woman, her father had become part of all that. The contradiction. The paradox...

The land, too, was deceptive like that. Maybe it was the vengeance of ancestor spirits upon Goonya avarice. The white man had brought sheep and cattle to this alien place. Cut down the trees for boundary posts. Stripped the land till there was nothing but dust. Put chains around the necks of her ancestors. Flogged and starved them. Hanged them. No grazing anymore. No natives. Just Goonyas on water skis. Death from the sky. Madness.

+ FUTURE-PRIMITIVE

A blind army of centipedes writhed beneath the Manhattan grid, tunnelling through subterranean night. Osborne could hear them out there in the blackout. Tireless. Directed by some future-primitive force. Out of the darkness an overhead light stammered on and the train began moving again, gathering speed. Osborne kept his eyes down away from the glare. The floor was littered with debris. There was no-one else in the carriage, only a metallic voice coming from time to time over the intercom in a hiss of static and feedback. They were somewhere south of Chambers on diversion. Ghost stations flickered between pylons where no train ever stopped.

At Fulton Street some late night commuters got on, dead-eyed, non-descript. Something clicked in Osborne's head and he got out. Stairs. A long tunnel. Navigating on autopilot. Subway zombie. Another platform. He waited for the Brooklyn-bound J. When it arrived he got aboard. As the train pulled out of the station one of the connecting doors opened and a blonde in a tight denim miniskirt staggered in. So messed up she could hardly stand.

"You got any change, mister?"

Osborne stared through her as if she wasn't there. Another ghost.

"Hey mister, I'm hungry, you got any change?"

The blonde gave up, staggered the length of the carriage and then staggered back. Slid down onto the seat opposite, beneath an advertisement for VIAJES SOUL-MATE TOURS. CHILDREN OF THE SUN! COME TO RIO DE JANEIRO. Osborne watched her pull a blue paisley carry-bag onto her knees and begin counting out pocketfuls of money on top of it. All dollar bills and change.

"Hey," the blonde said jerking her face towards him suddenly. "Don't I know you?"

She looked bloodless. Pale, translucent skin. There were needle tracks on her neck.

"Yeah," she went on, "I saw you before, at that place. You know, *the place.*"

She's a nut, Osborne thought. The city was full of them. Junkies, bums, outpatients from God-knows-what loony bin.

"Don't you remember?"

"You never saw me," Osborne said, edging himself off the seat.

The moment he stood, pain shot up his side. He clenched his teeth, groped under his arm like a man fumbling for a gun. Memory flash. His hand recoiled. He stared at it, seeing red. Blood. But there was nothing. Only the screech of the train as it bore its way towards Canal Street. Back where he'd started from, but east this time. Two more stops. He staggered to a seat further down the carriage. The girl followed him with dead eyes. Muttered something. Then turned her attention back to the money spread out on her bag, like a fortune teller appraising her cards.

At Delancy Osborne got out. The sleet had turned to rain and was coming down heavier, soaking the shoulders of his coat as, breathless, he climbed the narrow stairs to street-level. A black van cruised past. Red taillights blinking back at him. He glanced nervously around. A couple of hookers were huddled under an umbrella at the Lewis Street intersection, stamping knee-high boots to keep warm. Stray headlights swept over them. Even before he could see the pimp he could sense him, leaning in the blacked-out doorway of Famous Ray's Pizza, pimp sunglasses.

"Yo slick, how you like you liddle fuck face? Over-easy or sunny side up?"

The pizza joint was blacked out and the chairs stacked. A piece of paper stuck up inside the window said CLOSED BY ORDER OF PUBLIC HEALTH INSPECTOR. Osborne backed away. It didn't make sense. A meteor had whacked into the Zero. Half the city was shut down. And the fucking health inspector chooses this of all days to hit-up a pizza joint?

"Yo white man, check it out."

Osborne veered into the rain. He stumbled against a trashcan rounding the corner onto Lewis, keeping one eye on the pimp. Winced. A cold wind blew weird shapes out of the shadows cast by the streetlights. He pushed on through the projects, hallucinations creeping up on him at every step. Scenes leaked out of one another like planes of celluloid dissolving and reforming.

He had no idea how long he'd been resting his forehead against the glass door of his ex-wife's apartment building before the pain behind his eyes became bearable again. Then the questions started. A voice inside his head. Asking why they'd let him go. The manikin in the box was. The midget with the needle. The Halloween spook on the train.

The symmetry of events was all wrong. If the pain hadn't been so real, Osborne would've been convinced he finally lost it. Worse than the time on Tenth Avenue, his mind collapsing around that Ariadne's thread as it unwound through the labyrinth, bringing him to his saviour. The Doctor. Who, Osborne thought, was probably madder than he was.

With cold-stiffened fingers he punched the access code and weaved inside. A sound like a punctured lung sucking-in air as the door shut behind, the vestibule echoing his footsteps. The elevator that took him to the fifth floor stank of rat bait. A fisheye camera stared unblinking. Then a corridor, telescoping. Lights dimmed, brightened. Just another couple of steps and he'd be there at last.

"Tell me he suffered."

But he hadn't suffered and that was what galled Shinwah the most. She'd like to've seen him chopped into bits. Would've preferred to've done the chopping herself. But she'd had to go and get herself shot. And Margarita's people had traded him back to the same people he'd traded her to. The problem was, she knew they wouldn't kill him, that they'd want him very much alive. And as long as de Laurentiis was alive, she could rely on him to come after her. Which meant she had to get back to Beijing before he did. Except that, de Laurentiis was her dûchà, her controller. He had her coordinates. It didn't matter where she went, he'd find her. It'd be simpler just to pull the plug, but with him it'd be personal. A power thing. He'd want to look into her eyes while he was doing it and know she could see him while he was killing her.

So now she had enemies on both sides.

"You've got nothing to worry about," Margarita said, clasping Shinwah's hands between hers. They were sitting in the galley in a padded booth, like the booths in diners, facing one another across the table. The dark-eyed boy was making coffee on the stove. There was someone else on the yacht too, who Margarita called Paladino and who Shinwah also recognised from the farmhouse. At that moment he was manning the wheel. Margarita looked hard into Shinwah's eyes.

"Right now," she said, "this is the safest place in the world for you to be."

Shinwah shook her head.

"You wouldn't understand."

"Oh?" Margarita's left eyebrow rose almost imperceptibly.

"I'm not what I look."

"Well, from where I'm sitting…"

"It'd be hard to explain. But there's… A computer. In Beijing. It keeps tabs on me. De Laurentiis was my… Control. If they can't pull me in, they'll pull the plug."

"You know," Margarita grinned, "if you'd said that to anyone else, they might decide you're crazy."

Shinwah shut her eyes. *What the hell are you doing?* The words had come out of her mouth without her thinking. Margarita was right. It sounded crazy.

"What I meant…"

"I know what you meant. We're in the same business. Only not for the same reasons. That's why you're still here. But you may as well know now, whatever they showed you on that slab in Beijing wasn't you. They lied. Like they lied to all of us. There aren't any avatars. The teleports are real. All of it. You go in, you come out. You just rely on them to get it right. And so far, they've been pretty good at that."

"Then what about…"

"What loverboy didn't bother to say is the comsat that used to feed the coordinates back to your Head Office got taken down. We don't know how. The signal went dead two days ago. Something crashed in New York. Ground Zero. Maybe that was part of it. The Americans are pretending it was an asteroid. But then they would, wouldn't they?"

"Ground zero?"

The lines at the corner of Margarita's eyes deepened when she smiled. It made her look older. Shinwah wondered how old she actually was. Like that meant something.

"Ever been to New York?"

Shinwah shook her head. She'd seen pictures, films. It'd never seemed real. Just a bunch of programmer's code patched-in behind action sequences to provide a famous backdrop. Empire

State. Brooklyn Bridge. All that.

"Well," Margarita said, "when it went down, the bird took all the coordinates with it. Yours and everyone else's, too. No more protocols, honey. Not for now at least. Call it a relativity effect. Time maps aren't like ordinary maps. You lose the connection, it's not like you just try dialing the number again later. The whole grid gets changed. All they can do is try to recalibrate it. Put up a new satellite. Turn back the clock. Pin a locale on you. In the meantime you're stuck here."

Change of plans was all de Laurentiis had said. Sonofabitch.

"What about... the opposition?"

"No such luck."

"So they're still out there?"

"Ah-huh. Except the narrative's been screwed up. There're factors no-one anticipated."

"I don't follow."

"You will."

"De Laurentiis knew?"

"That's why he wanted to be on this boat. We've been waiting for him. When he showed up on the radar, we sent out a signal and he came right to us. He's nobody's fool, de Laurentiis. He built a network in every time-zone. Sleeper cells. In case something ever happened and he needed an out. I bet you're wondering how I know that. You see, loverboy and I, we go way back. Further than you can imagine."

The dark-eyed boy brought a tray with three cups on it and a stained metal coffee pot. Margarita let go of Shinwah's hands and sat back against the padded upholstery. Shinwah scrutinized her face while the boy poured the coffee. The coffee was thick and dark and aromatic. The boy handed Shinwah a cup and she thanked him in Italian. He pulled up a stool and squatted at the end of the table, stirring what seemed to Shinwah like an unfeasible amount of sugar into his cup. His name, Margarita had told her, was Momo. He was mute, courtesy of a couple of New York cops who'd worked him over with truncheons for spray painting subway cars. He was supposed to be a computer genius. And she thought, if he was such a genius, maybe he could get her out of this mess. But what the mess was, exactly, she wasn't sure.

"I didn't realize you knew each other," Shinwah said, scrutinising the older woman's face. Only it was impossible to tell how old. Was that why Margarita had helped her? Because of de Laurentiis? Or was there something else?

"It's a long story," Margarita replied. "Some other time." She took a sip of her coffee. "Right now, what matters is the only way loverboy has of ever finding us, is the transmitter they wired you up with. Same with the boys in Beijing. Unfortunately, the transmitter's in your head. Fortunately, there's a way of getting rid of it. You can try digging it out yourself, or finding a doctor who'll do it for you, if you don't mind a bit of serious brain damage. But the only way of doing the job clean is if you have a cartouche. And the only place you'll find one, is Cairo."

"Cairo?"

"Heard of Egypt?"

"Yeah."

"That Cairo."

"I was there once. It's a big city."

"One of the biggest."

"And what do we do when we get there?"

Margarita pulled the dead man's pendant from the pocket of her anorak. The black silicon turned slowly at the end of its silver chain, hieroglyphics catching the light from the porthole window.

"Find whoever loverboy wanted to sell this to…"

☾ QUARANTINE

The way you stop a sickness spreading is by quarantine. Which is why they built the Dome. To keep death out. And why the intifada blocked every tunnel past the periphery. To keep the entropy in. Once upon a time they holed things up in quarantine for forty days and nights. Now it's forever, or as close as they can get. Unless the sickness beats them at their own game. The albino explains this to him at the beginning of the ascent. Directly above, is the old necropolis, where they used to bury the dead. Though people have lived there also, since before records were kept. The fringe-dwellers, tending the graves, inhabiting the between-world. A ghost tribe, exercising the sacred duties of the Pariahs.

The ascent is long and arduous. A vertical tunnel entered by way of sealed hatch hidden behind a wall of junk. Steel rungs lead up to the next hatch. Then the same again, each hatch at an interval of approximately fifty rungs. Though when he tries to count them, he keeps losing track. Unable to move his hands and feet in unison, each movement requires its own thought. The darkness, absolute. The throbbing in his head, like a faulty connection at work. Afterimages flare and fade behind his eye.

While he climbs, he speaks to himself in an effort to summon forth the voice. He misses the Stranger's presence. Though his guide remains merely several rungs ahead of him, he feels alone in some profound way he's unable to describe. Like discovering while speaking to himself that there isn't in fact anyone to hear him. That his other half has somehow ceased to exist. That possibly it never existed. This thought evokes a kind of vertigo, and he's all of a sudden acutely aware that beneath him is a hole as deep in all probability as the Dome is high. A depth from which he's separated only by something that, in the dark, has an existence in his mind more virtual and yet more real than any actual thing ever could.

The albino tells him to keep moving. At a certain point he can no longer trust his hands to grip the rungs on their own. He can't feel his feet. They must've been climbing for hours by now. Perhaps it only seems like that. The more they climb, the more the distance beneath them opens a chasm in his mind. He uses his teeth, biting a-hold of the rung directly in front. To steady himself while his hands grope for the one above. Then his feet. Then both hands together pulling him up. Legs pushing. Then on to the next. Slower and slower. The desire to give up gaining on him inch-by-inch.

At some stage, he knows, his body will cease entirely to obey commands. His mind will refuse to issue them. He'll contract into a knot of flesh, clamped like a mollusc to the tunnel wall. He's about to succumb when a light comes on. The albino peers down at him through an open hatch. She might even be grinning, but he can't be sure. Perhaps it's just that he feels ridiculous, now that he's aware of her watching him. If the Stranger was here, he wouldn't have to think like this. He wouldn't have to think at all.

"Put this on," the albino says, handing him a dark cloth sack as soon as he gets to his feet.

He feels like someone who's just climbed out of the ocean onto a life-raft. There's a light overhead. A naked bulb inside a mesh cage. They're standing in a narrow chamber. At the end of it, a concrete stairwell leads to a door laid horizontally across the top of it. While he examines the sack she's just handed him, the albino secures the hatch. The sack appears to be some sort of hood, with a mesh grill for the eyes. He hesitates. The albino takes an identical sack and pulls it over her head. Unfolded, it extends all the way down her body. She gathers the cloth around her arms, keeping her hands covered. He follows suit. Immediately he's enveloped by a sense of claustrophobia.

"Breathe slowly," she says. "Be silent. Don't trip. Stay as close to me as you can."

☐ MORTUARY

The East Ham Mortuary off Barking Road was a squat cube of dark brick, a set of blue doors at the entrance. Nicky Cohn was waiting under a yellow sign with a picture of a security camera on it, collar up, fag drooping from the corner of his mouth and somehow still alight in the drizzle, when Joblard wheeled up riding the clutch. A naked fluorescent blinked over the doorway, lending the journalist's features a decidedly funereal cast. The light glistened on the wet chrome of the BSA's petrol tank, catching the steam as it hissed up from the single cylinder. Then it didn't. Then it did.

"You're looking bright and chirpy," Nicky Cohn said as Joblard yanked off his helmet, face a blur behind frozen breath.

"Nice night for it," Joblard said. "Though to be honest, I'd rather be in the back lounge getting intimate with a pint. Paid your respects yet?"

"Nah, just got here. Thought I'd have a quick puff before trying to blague my way past the Homicide and Serious Crime boys. I recognised two of them when I peeked in through the door. They can be right cunts when it suits them."

Joblard stuffed his gloves inside his bellstaf jacket, helmet under one arm.

"That's good, I could fancy a couple of cunts on a night like this."

"Not like these you wouldn't. Speaking of which, what's your boss up to these days?"

"You on the square brother?"

"Eh?"

"Freemasons. Grand Lodge. He's got a hard-on about poking a camera into the holy of holies. *Ladies of the Illuminati.*"

"The what?"

"Yeah, I reckon our mate Johnny Fluoride might've been getting him some of the more candid stuff. Kind of spank-and-tell exposé of the secret handshake brigade."

"Tell me about it after," Nicky Cohn said, tossing the unsmoked half of his cigarette on the ground. "I'm freezing my balls off out here."

Behind the blue doors was a corridor and an office with a little window where Nicky Cohn showed his press credentials and signed in. Joblard took in the atmosphere. A couple of plods eyeballed him from where they were sitting beside a pair of swing-doors, like they were on stakeout duty waiting for a corpse to show up and trying to outguess each other about whose it might be. Joblard grinned at them. It was a rule he had with cops: you never break eye contact and always smile, drives the fuckers nuts. Nicky finished with the forms and they waited for a technician in a blue smock to come and give them the grand tour. He was tall and skinny, with a straggly goatee and hair down past his collar and acne on his neck. Student-type. Taking full advantage of the opportunities society had on offer.

"This way gentlemen," he said, taking a chit from the receptionist behind the window. "My name's Zack and I'm your guide for this evening. The main attraction's just through here and on the left."

They ran the gauntlet of the two Homicide boys, busy giving Joblard the business with their cop stares, tongues working the backs of their teeth, but not making any more than a show of it.

Joblard jerked his thumb over his shoulder at the swing-doors, behind them now as their guide steered left along an underlit tunnel of half-tone green.

"What's with the local entertainment, Zack?"

"One of our residents has attracted special attention."

"Zack," Nicky said, "I have a confession to make. That's who we're here to see."

The technician stopped and scrutinised the chit he was holding. Joblard, trying to get a peek at it over Zack's shoulder, found himself with an unobstructed view of a dandruff condition on the verge of spiralling out of control. Greenish flakes of dead scalp layered the back and shoulders of Zack-the-mortuary-technician's smock, sifting down between greasy cords of dyed black hair.

Joblard edged back to maintain a safe interpersonal distance. Dandruff always made him think of leprosy. It was an association he'd had ever since boyhood and the smell of antidandruff shampoo in the locker rooms. Afraid he'd catch the stuff. At least they'd had the decency to wash. Some people, he thought, ogling the back of Zack's head, lacked the very basics of self-respect.

"You're not here to see 856?"

"No."

"We're supposed to report anyone who wants to visit the new guy."

Nicky slipped a freshly minted portrait of Queen Liz into the pocket of the technician's smock.

"Put this towards your scholarship fund, Zack. No-one ever need know. You just got the numbers mixed up, that's all."

Zack glanced at the bill, which in the light of the corridor was the brown of a freshly minted turd.

"She looks kind of lonely, don't you think? Got another one of those to keep her company?"

Nicky slipped the technician another royal likeness. The kid grinned.

"Right through here then, gents," Zack chirped, leading the way...

Once, when he'd been KO'd in the ring by the southpaw Mickey "the Hammer" Mulligan, Joblard had woken on the floor staring at a light thinking he'd died already and was stretched out on one of those mortuary slabs they have in movies, and any minute some geezer in a white labcoat was going to come in and poke a scalpel in his brain and pronounce the cause of death. Telling himself how "Hammer" wasn't a name Mulligan earned in the ring but operating a protection racket off Brick Lane. But the room Zack-the-technician ushered them into wasn't like anything in a film, more like a wholesaler's stockroom. The far wall was lined with time-warped refrigerator doors you'd expect to find racks of frozen meat behind. Sides of beef, lamb, pork. A whole raffle bonanza.

Zack went straight to the third door along and yanked it open. Behind it were three square hatches, one above another, old paint a dozen hues of off-white cracked and flaking. Like a Japanese coffin hotel in need of a re-fit. Johnny Fluoride had taken up residence behind the hatch at the top. Zack trundled out the slab. Joblard shivered. Johnny Fluoride's body, sans head, was wrapped in semi-opaque plastic. The swim hadn't done him any kindnesses. Even with the plastic on he looked terrible, like he'd been force-fed through the proverbial wringer. But whatever took his head off, that sure as hell hadn't beaten around the bush.

"Jesus!"

The corpse, Joblard duly noted, had bare feet. Eventually, he supposed, the Coroner's Office might wonder how it came to be that Johnny here had gone paddling without his boots on. Getting a head start, so to speak. The violent crime boys hadn't made a positive ID yet. Their floater had washed up not only sans head but sans anything in his pockets. According to Nicky's mate at the Yard, Johnny Fluoride's body had still been zipped into his army surplus when they found him. Which was how he knew it was Johnny Fluoride. The anorak had somehow kept him afloat, otherwise he mightn't've turned up at all till next week. Or never.

Still, Joblard supposed, it'd only be a matter of time now before the Homicide boys rang the old widow's doorbell over in Greenwich and got themselves an earful. And then from

Greenwich to Canvey, which was all they'd need to put him on the spot. A knock on the door in the middle of the night. But at that moment, all Joblard could really think was how the fuck...?

The three of them stared at the corpse for a while in silence. Nicky flicked at the chipped paint on the freezer door. The room, it seemed to Joblard, had grown noticeably colder. A type of mist seeped from the hatch. Nicky pulled a splinter of old paint from under a fingernail and held it up to the light.

"You know," he said, breaking the silence, "they reckon lead paint's accountable for half the violent crime on the planet. God's truth. But just try telling that to the Homicide boys. And the responsible parties? Why, only the honest-living folk at Innospec, up on the Manchester Ship Canal, flogging tetraethyl lead wherever it hasn't been banned yet. Fun places like Burma, Iraq, Afghanistan, North Korea. The fact it's illegal to peddle the shite in good old Blighty doesn't mean they can't manufacture and export the stuff. Now if it was anthrax..."

"Somehow I don't think it was lead paint did that," Joblard said, pointing at the mess where Johnny Fluoride's head formerly resided. "Or anthrax."

"The interesting thing," Zack said, fingering the tag affixed to the big toe of Johnny Fluoride's right foot, "is they found river water in your man's stomach, but not in the lungs. Whoever blew his head off gave him a soaking first. Must've had something they wanted. That's my guess. Held his head under till he talked. Then pop. No further use. Seen it before. The Albanian they found in a suitcase last year? He'd swallowed half a gallon of Thames water too, and not from any tap. Except they used a saw on him instead of a canon. Never found the head, either. Your mate involved in any funny business, then?"

"Nah," Nicky said. "He ran nostalgia tours for old pub-rock fans. Didn't know shit from clay. Probably a case of mistaken identity." Turning to Joblard: "What do you reckon?"

"Yeah, mistaken identity," Joblard echoed. "Poor sod."

"Did he have a name?"

"Mmm," Nicky said. "Can't remember." To Joblard: "D'you remember his name?"

"Don't rightly think he ever told us."

"Too bad," Zack said. "Too bad."

⊙ WANDJINA

29°31'16.16"S
137°56'39.06"E

The track wound south-east among low stands of mallee and gidgee trees, apostle birds slouching ghostlike among the branches, haunting the roadside, greyblue avatars of the hidden ones. The ruins of an old railway siding loomed out of the haze, a mirage of some remote, mythological time, a crashed higher world like a piece of space debris sticking up out of the landscape, alien and tawdry. Lawson estimated she was about forty miles shy of Marree with half an hour of daylight still left. She'd taken the land option after all. If she'd headed north, she'd've been in Birdsville by now…

Luck, Lawson decided, must've been on her side after all. The joyriders had set up camp not more than a kilometre from where she'd come ashore, materialising out of the heat-shimmer. A boat-trailer was backed down to the shore, hitched to a Range Rover. All the joyriders' gear was in the car. Clothes, a couple of eskies of West End, cellphones, binoculars. Keys in the ignition. Only thing lacking was an invitation stuck to the windscreen. Well, here she was, living up to expectations, blackfella nicking a white man's 4x4, leaving him to the mercy of the cruel elements.

Now that's what I call injustice, Lawson told herself, as she hit the ignition and pulled away, leaving the trailer, the joyriders' kit and the eskies of warm beer behind in the dust. Wouldn't want to be accused of letting anyone perish of thirst out in that heat. Though of course, she grinned, catching her reflection in the rearview, every whitefella knew how to find water in a lake, right?

As soon as she'd put some distance behind her, Lawson tried Dix's number on one of the joyriders' cellphones. He wasn't picking up. Maybe he didn't trust the number. Maybe they had his phone and where already tracking her call. Shit. What didn't have a tracking device in it nowadays? If it'd been like that in the past, every Nunga in the state would've had a tag stapled to his arse. Wildlife management, they'd've probably called it. Environmental preservation. Figured into their sustainability flowcharts.

With her knees bracing the steering wheel, Lawson pulled the back off the cell and stripped out the SIM, then jacked the cigarette lighter by the gearbox. The SIM turned grey-green when it came into contact, giving off a smell of molten plastics. Lawson powered down the side window and tossed out the fried remains.

"Keep Australia Beautiful!"

Hell, they stole the land, ripped every cent-worth they could out of it, shot whatever moved, cut down the rest, then flogged the leftovers to China – and all the nation cared about was the litter problem. *Well*, Lawson thought, *they get a big enough broom one of these days, maybe someone could sweep the whole country clean. Sweep them Gunyas right back where they came from.*

"You too, baby," she told her reflection. "Maybe time you took a fancy holiday yourself, eh? Go visit that Staten Island in New York. Look up the old man. See if the Land of the Free's all it's cracked up to be. As if."

After deciphering the Range Rover's control panels, Lawson switched on the radio in case there was any news. A report of a plane going down, maybe. Or someone's car being jacked at Lake Eyre, description of said vehicle, fugitive considered dangerous. Crap to that effect. Like it mattered. The radio crackled through a hiss of white noise, out of broadcast range. There were supposed to be UHF repeaters every hundred clicks along the Oodnadatta Track, but she wasn't there yet. Lawson fiddled the dial, but there was still nothing. Voices fading in and out, ghosts raving at one another through the ether.

Dix had a theory about all that, too. Where the voices went. Like the ancestor spirits, whose songlines still echoed somewhere in the general interference pattern, bled off into space, borne on solar winds. Perhaps aliens would eventually decipher them. Trace the signal back to its origin. Wandjina men coming down from the sky. And if they did, what would they learn that they didn't already know? If the whole world wasn't already extinct by then. As once before, long ago, during the Dreamtime. Coming like the rain. The spacemen in cave paintings. Eyes but no mouths. White ghosts. Only to find everything undone. The ancient law...

The way Dix had tried explaining about electromagnetic fields and the poles switching every so-many hundred thousand years. North made south. Sending all the limbic brain navigation coordinates off. Re-setting the prehistoric migration paths. Global entropy spiral. It sounded crazy. The sort of thing they put in films because the real-life catastrophe of the world wasn't photogenic enough. But the way Dix told it, it *was* real. It'd happened before. It was supposed to've happened again already, only it seemed to be waiting. For a catalyst.

How the Dreaming began. The ceremony of order re-emerging from chaos. *A voice from the sky...*

Lawson tried to get her head around the idea of all the directions turning inside-out. Like spinning in circles then trying to walk in a straight line. She pictured birds flying backwards, fish swimming upside-down never finding the surface again, preservation instincts turned lethal. The whole planet in schizo-mode, everything reversed, re-set. As if one day it woke with the hemispheres of its brain switched, Nungas suddenly running the show. Now that was something she'd want to stick around to see.

+ MONKEYSPEAK

40°43'0.09"N
73°58'34.75"W

The black security eye stared at Osborne as he rang the doorbell to apartment 5C. He kept ringing. He knocked. There was no answer. He fumbled around the doorframe for the key. Fatima, his ex-wife by six months, always kept a spare, in case of emergency. Eventually he found it but the lock was stiff. He inspected the key. It fit but wouldn't turn. Eventually he tried the other way and got it right.

A cacophony of animal noises greeted him when he opened the door. For a moment he thought he was hallucinating, before reminding himself that his ex-wife kept an (ever-expanding it seemed) menagerie of animals at home. Crows, mice, African cichlid fish, and a monkey who at that very moment was sitting at the kitchen table making a mess of some Chinese takeaway. The monkey said something too fast and high-pitched for Osborne to make out, grinned, then turned its attention back to eating. Osborne shut the front door behind him and lurched down the hall to the bathroom. He was still doubled over the bathroom sink when Fatima came in.

"You don't look so well, lover. What's up?"

Osborne glanced at Fatima's mottled reflection in the bathroom mirror. Water was dripping from his coat onto the floor and forming a pool around his boots.

"I fell down some stairs. I think I broke a couple of ribs."

Osborne grimaced straightened up. Wiped his face with his hands. Exhaled, as though he'd been holding his breath the whole time, face pale.

"Here, take your coat off," Fatima directed him.

Osborne shrugged out of his coat and let it slide to the floor. Fatima bent and picked it up. She threw it over the edge of the bathtub and took him by the arm.

"Sit down, let me look at you."

Osborne sat down beside his coat. She handed him a towel. He took it in his hands and held it.

"You're drenched."

"It's raining."

"That's one hell of an observation, lover. Open your shirt."

Osborne looked at her blankly without moving.

"For God's sake," Fatima shook her head, squatting in front of him, elbows against his knees. She was, he noticed, wearing something vaguely oriental over a pair of Levis. "This is typical. You come around in the middle of the night. I haven't heard from you in months. We're not even married anymore. And you sit there waiting for me to undress you. Tell me I'm a fool for doing this."

"I'm sorry."

"You're *sorry?*"

"I'm sorry."

Fatima reached up and unbuttoned his shirt. The fabric was soaked through.

"You're freezing. It must be Arctic out there. What's gotten into you?"

She pulled the front of his shirt open and stared. A patchwork of bruises blackened his left side.

"Ouch. So you fell down some stairs?"

"Maybe I missed the stairs."

Osborne winced when she pressed her fingers against his ribcage. Her brow creased in thought, then she stood and riffled the medicine cabinet behind the mirror.

"These might help with the pain, but you really should see a doctor."

"I thought *you* were a doctor."

"I'm an animal doctor."

"Same difference."

Fatima handed him some tablets and a glass of water. He took them. It was difficult to swallow. He handed the glass back. She looked him in the eyes.

"Where did it happen?"

"Downtown. I don't know. The weirdest things have been happening."

"What do you mean? What kind of weird things?"

"Look Fay, do you mind if I stay here for a while?"

She gave Osborne the kind of sceptical look he'd grown used to over the years.

"Exactly what kind of trouble are you in this time?"

"Not the kind you think."

"Try me."

"There's people. I think they're following me."

Aware he probably wasn't making much sense, Osborne tried to slow down his words.

"Look, I don't know how to explain. You probably wouldn't believe me anyway."

"Thanks for the vote of confidence."

"I'm sorry, Fay. I'm sorry."

Fatima leaned her hip against the sink, arms folded.

"So make it good."

"How about a drink first?"

Fatima shrugged.

"I'll put on some coffee."

Osborne stared at the ornamental carp pattern on her tunic as she turned and went across the hall. Then clutching his side, he got up and followed her, feeling short of breath all of a sudden. Maybe it was the painkillers. It felt strange being there, in the old apartment. Like time travel. He'd made himself promise he wouldn't go back. Even when he'd had nowhere else to go. Sleeping rough under the West Side Line. Believing he'd be able to start again. On his own.

Fatima was in the kitchen, busying herself with a kettle on the stove. Osborne leant against the doorjamb, letting his gaze wander aimlessly about the kitchen. Nothing had changed. There were still those white magnets on the refrigerator door, with bits of words printed on them, jumbled up into nonsense haiku. He watched Fatima empty a packet of gluten-free pretzels into a bowl. They'd got married, as far as he could remember, for all the wrong reasons. He'd found her sympathetic, she'd found him touching. Like one of her pets. Only, after four years, he still wasn't house trained she'd said.

Another of those pets was right now sitting at the kitchen table. Osborne was sure it was grinning at him.

"Fay," Osborne said, trying not to sound irrational, "there's a monkey in the kitchen. Eating egg noodles."

Fatima kept doing whatever it was she was doing.

"They're rice noodles," she said, as if addressing the cupboard. "And he isn't a monkey, his name's Kye and he's a bonobo."

Fatima took down a jar of instant coffee and fixed two cups. The bonobo started talking again at high speed, a now empty bowl of Mr Chow's in front of it.

"Not for you," Fatima said, patting the bonobo's head. She caught the expression on Osborne's face. "Coffee gives him nightmares."

"Jesus, Fay, you're still bringing your experiments home from the lab?"

"Stop feeling so threatened."

"Fay, I *am* threatened."

"You're *paranoid*. Bonobos never hurt anybody. Besides, you don't live here anymore, sweetheart. Or have you forgotten that already?"

"I don't know where else to go, Fay. I'm worried."

Fatima turned and faced him squarely, hands on narrow hips.

"*You're* worried? I'm worried. We're all goddamn worried! The world's going to hell, Osborne, and your paranoia isn't what I need in my life just now."

Fatima stormed past him, voice trailing down the hallway.

"I'm not paranoid," Osborne said, though he barely heard himself say it.

He glanced at the towel he was still holding in his hands. A white towel with a hospital laundry mark. Columbia. Fay worked there. She did experiments with animals. She had a monkey in her kitchen.

The overhead light dimmed and came on again. Osborne glanced up from his hands. The bonobo was grinning again, bits of noodle stuck between its teeth.

"It's not me," Osborne said quietly to himself. "It's not me who's paranoid."

Suddenly aware of someone's presence behind him, Osborne jerked his head around, causing pain to shoot up his side. But it was only Fatima, standing there holding a bathrobe, lips pursed. She only ever pursed her lips when she was unhappy. He hoped she wasn't unhappy now.

"Put this on, you can't stand around half-naked."

"I'm sorry…"

"And stop apologising."

Osborne blinked without making any move to take the bathrobe from her, till in exasperation Fatima flung it across his shoulders and pushed past into the kitchen. Osborne grimaced. Glanced down at the towel still in his hand as if unsure what to do with it. Decided to do nothing.

"What're you waiting for?" Fatima said. "Sit down."

Doubtfully Osborne eyed the chair opposite the grinning bonobo, but said nothing. He edged across the kitchen and pulled the chair as far back from the table as space in the tiny kitchen would allow, then eased himself down sideways, gritting his teeth. He bunched the towel up in front of him as a sort of protective barrier, just in case the monkey tried anything. Fatima handed him an over-filled cup of coffee. He took it shakily in both hands, slopping the black liquid over his thumbs. He could see the steam coming off and had to bite his tongue.

The bonobo smacked its lips at him, zapped a stream of highspeed monkeyspeak in his direction, then climbed down from the table and waddled off down the hallway. For a moment Osborne thought he heard it laugh.

"Okay," Fatima said, in a voice that was nothing if not matter-of-fact, taking the monkey's place at the table. "I'm listening."

♒ ANACHRONISM

30°2'19.58"N
31°13'47.31"E

Cairo was what de Laurentiis called an anachronism waiting to happen, from the day they laid the first stone. By the time she got to see it, there wasn't much resemblance left between the real-life city under the dome and the pictures she'd seen in books when she was a kid. The pyramids at Gizah. The Great Sphinx. Everything not inside the dome had slowly been eaten away by the atmosphere, just like the dome itself was slowly being eaten away, under constant repair by nanotech construction bots. The only pyramids on view were holograms projected above the slums, honeycombed labyrinths of human garbage that'd collected around the quarry sites. You could watch an electric sun go down over the ruins hourly from the terraces of the more expensive hotels along the Nile. Highrise Babylons for the visiting elite.

This future Cairo was a corporate oasis on the verge of being overrun, with its own artificial atmosphere, protected from the corrosive desert sands by geodesics of heavy duty alloy, designed in a more optimistic era to support colonies on Titan. Only there'd never been any colonies on Titan, because no-one had ever been able to survive the journey, except the robots. Besides, the hydrocarbon seas the corporations dreamt of exploiting there were a hundred miles beneath ice. And at those temperatures, even if it was possible to go that deep, the drills wouldn't've worked anyway, no matter what alloys they were made of. So the robots just sat there disassembling and reassembling useless machinery, till their batteries ran flat...

In Shinwah's business, Cairo was the closest thing on Earth to a black hole. The embargo simply didn't apply there. It was a hotbed of traders, thieves, assassins, smugglers, spies, hustlers, scumbags from all rungs of the money ladder, dealing in anything you could put a price on. It was an information nexus, linked into every conceivable economy.

They called it the Cradle of Technology. The New Silicon Valley. Sand of Black Gold. More volume traded per nanosecond there than on any stock exchange anywhere, and most of it never saw the light of day. Everyone wanted a piece of the action. Beijing, Moscow, London, New York. The desert beyond the dome was studded with radar towers, drone bases, rendition centres, covert sigint intercept stations. On the fringes of the dome, black markets thrived. In the shanties, provocateurs in the employ of competing commercial interests fed a general state of emergency, which in turn kept the whole power structure operating.

In the background there'd been rumblings of dissent, talk of an intifada, a word Shinwah had needed de Laurentiis to explain to her. A word from the past. From now, she thought. But in the future it meant a type of hack. Cyber-guerrillas raiding the networks in fly-by-night combat formations. Anonymous. With no stable modus operandi. The only real opposition had been literally driven underground years before. Just another myth, like the old gods, dead and buried.

Going in, she remembered, had been like crossing an event-horizon. The City had a reputation for swallowing things up. She'd counted her blessings they'd ever got back out. Time-shifting gained you no advantage in Cairo, but lumped you with all the usual liabilities and more. Everywhere you looked, there was evidence of infiltration from futures remote even from anything she'd been wired in to. Things way beyond the mapped temporal horizon, where even the very existence of the world as she knew it may well've been cancelled-out by incompatible probabilities. De Laurentiis had called it the palimpsest. All the possible worlds that'd never come to fruition, overlaid in a kind of schizophrenic mesh, in which only contradictions survived.

It'd given Shinwah the creeps. In the first ten minutes she'd seen enough never to want to return. The job had taken three hours. Waiting on a bridge for a contact who was supposed to lead them to the target – only de Laurentiis had shot the contact in the head. Said it was a set-up. It was the longest three hours she'd ever spent outside the lab. Who the actual target was, she never found out. Strictly need-to-know. And as usual, de Laurentiis had let her get closer to the action than was strictly necessary. Just like the last job. And all the other jobs she could remember.

Now she was supposed to be going back to Cairo to find a way of breaking the connection for good. But not the same Cairo. Not *that* Cairo. That was still the future. Out of reach. But if Margarita was right, they could hack the System by a back door. The Cartouche. And if it worked, her coordinates would simply vanish. No more signal.

And if you stick around long enough, Shinwah thought, you might even get the chance to meet yourself, there, in that future which's already the past. And de Laurentiis. She'd just need to be there at the rendezvous one step ahead. And if she hadn't already done it before then, she'd give him exactly what he had coming. *Sure, sweetheart. And then none of this will ever have happened.*

That was the paradox. She knew the rules. Being in two places at the same time was a cinch, but you could never be in the same place at the same time. Not if there were two of you.

☾ NECROPOLIS

30°0'29.99"N
31°15'19.08"E

There's no way of knowing if this's where he's supposed to be. Necropolis. The City of the Dead. It looks like a giant tip. Shanties of corrugated iron, cardboard, plastic, mud brick. What once were mausoleums have long ago morphed into multi-storied warrens, windowless labyrinths teetering over the catacombs. Behind them, the Dome bulges up out of the desert like a great ulcerated stomach. In the opposite direction, between teetering minarets and barely visible in the smog, the Muqattam Hills with surveillance drones hovering over them, like flies over meat…

The Albino leads them along a dusty path between walls of compacted amalgam. Through the body-sack's dark grill he can just make out the shapes of people darting in and out of shadows. Dark eyes watching behind curtains.

She explains in whispers how the sun's rays are deadly. How those who live above ground are mostly refugees, from the Dome or anywhere. Palestine, Somalia, Libya. Fugitives, too. Anything he can imagine. Pimps, pushers, junkies, cripples, pan-handlers, body-parts traders, Bedouin, Tuaregs. The placeless. The exiled. Tomb-dwellers. Only the zabbalin and the insane went about in daytime. Their life expectancy, already short, cut increasingly shorter.

The City of the Dead has many zones, she tells him, divided between the sects, the cartels, the brotherhoods. Rival flags surmount the minarets of junk that spout up everywhere, made grey in the heat.

The Stranger's been silent for hours now. He can't tell how many. It's difficult even to think, he's grown so tired. His body aches, but not as much as it should. His head feels like nothing at all. The albino keeps having to slow down for him, he's afraid she might leave him behind. But something tells him he's become important to her somehow. Valuable. That having come this far she's not prepared to give him up. He wonders how long he can go on not thinking for himself. Or if the Stranger will ever come back. Or if he's gone for good. And if he's gone, where to?

"Salafists," the albino hisses, pulling him to the roadside.

Up ahead he sees black flags strung above the path. Black figures hunch beneath covered head to foot, like them, in black sacking. Unlike them, hung with ammunition belts. The glint of a scimitar.

"This way," she says, hustling him through a doorway hidden behind a tarpaulin.

As the door opens, a waft of something. Citrus, he thinks, grasping at the word though unsure of its meaning. Bitter, maybe. An old woman is cooking Bichra over a primus stove. Brown-faced. Wrinkled. The room's barely wide enough for them to slip past into a passage built of styrofoam cartons and bits of improvised plumbing. Bundled cabling snakes overhead. Daylight filters through slabs of corrugated plastic. They pass through a series of interconnected courtyards draped with camouflage netting.

His bearings are lost within seconds. The further they proceed the more crowded the way becomes. Urchins scrabbling about barefoot. Chickens, goats, an ass covered in welts. Skin-and-bone men flapping soiled and unravelled turbans. Toothless. Dead-eyed. Beggars, pox-cratered, eyes dissolving in their sockets, groping through the half-light. Denizens of hell.

He can smell death everywhere. It grows more and more intense the further they continue through the labyrinth, as if it was the smell that was leading them, directing them towards their destination. It seems like hours have passed by the time they come to a halt outside a tannery. He can barely breath. The smell only seems to be getting worse and he has to struggle not to throw up.

From the outside the tannery is little more than a chipped adobe façade with a sign painted on it. The circle and the cross. MOHMED MOMSEN-MOMSEN, LEATHER GOODS. There's a gate, set in a recess, angling away from a pair of rusty hinges. A child in indigo rags is squatting against one of the doorposts picking at the scabs on its knees. The albino speaks to a grill in a language he can't understand and the gate opens. A man, the lower part of his face wrapped in a keffiyeh, ushers them inside. The child, brought suddenly to life, scoots between the man's legs. The man shouts and runs off in pursuit.

Through the grill's moiré it's difficult for him to make out the details of their surroundings. They seem to be standing in an atrium which opens, almost at their feet, onto a sea of dying vats arranged in tiers. Red, blue, orange, yellow, white. There are strips of bleached hide mounded up on walls, dripping into rivers of grey mud through which the tanners trudge back and forth, grey up to their loincloths.

The stench is by now unbearable. He can taste the bile in his mouth. His eyes water. The albino walks ahead, a pixellated blur through the grill covering his face, slipping in and out of the frame with each turn. Descending now, a flight of crumbling concrete stairs, then along a wooden gangplank between charred gibbets, lime-kilned catacombs, serried racks of cured leather. On all sides, scummed whitewash teeters inwards as if upon an abyss.

☐ REMIX

A wedge of lemon floated in the glass of water Nicky Cohn was holding up to the light, eyeballing the citrus bits drifting around in it. He'd watched the waitress closely while she filled the glass straight from the tap.

"That stuff comes direct from the river, you realise?" Joblard said, trying on the tone of voice of someone attempting to be helpful. "Courtesy of Thames Water. If you're lucky, there might even be a couple of particles of Johnny Fluoride in there. Not to mention all the other crap they dump in it. London's Pride."

Nicky Cohn snorted and set the glass down in front of him. The bar they'd retreated to from the East Ham Mortuary was slowly filling up for the evening with what looked like a regular crowd. Joblard counted at least a dozen different types of Adidas tracksuit. The only beer they had on tap wasn't beer at all but some foreign crap called Carlsberg, so he'd settled for a cup of tea instead. The publican had given him one of those looks. The de rigueur TV in the corner was running the day's Ashes highlights. Depressing viewing. They'd've done better switching to one of the disaster channels. BSkyB or whatever. Rapping out the lowdown on why the world was going to shit. Global warming conspiracy nuts. The latest candidates for nuclear meltdown.

On cue the box cut from the cricket roundup to the news desk. Some joker in a flash suit talking to himself in a studio with lots of high-tech graphics making up the décor. Lip-syncing to a soundtrack that'd been swapped for the usual pub banter in competition with some sort of Kylie Minogue remix. Text scrolled across the bottom of the screen. Then cut to footage of what looked very much like riots on Wall Street. Archive material of the Twin Towers going down. Joblard registered crowd shots and helicopters. Something brewing on the other side of the pond, he figured. Nicky Cohn was still eyeing his glass in a manner you might describe as pensive.

"Gone to a better place, if you believe that stuff," Joblard offered, thinking condolences of some sort might be in order.

Though exactly what Nicky Cohn's connection with Johnny Fluoride was, he couldn't say. Nicky Cohn looked up from his glass at the bulge Joblard's gloves made inside his jacket.

"Your tea's getting cold."

"Don't really fancy it anyhow."

"My mum used to say cold tea's good for piles."

"That right?"

"She made my old man drink the stuff till the day he died. Sure enough, never did get piles. Fucked his liver good and proper though."

"Eh?"

"Used to slip rum in the tea to make the stuff drinkable, when the old girl wasn't watching. She'd keep a pot cooling on the windowsill for all occasions. Earl Gray. By the time he finished his third cup of an evening, the poor bugger could hardly stay on his perch. Which the old girl attributed to the tea's potent medicinal effect."

Joblard sniffed his cup then set it back down on its saucer.

"Just regular tea, this. Probably doesn't work."

Nicky squinted up at him.

"They put out a call for witnesses, I heard. A couple of those lugs might want to have a talk with you if they get wise to what went down at Canvey jetty. Just how many people saw you and our Johnny together?"

"Only the barman. And maybe this scarecrow character, had some sort of skin disease on his face."

"Mmm. Barmen usually mind their own business, unless the rozzers make a point of it. Who's the scarecrow?"

"Dunno. Followed me, though."

"Followed you?"

"Yeah, him and a dwarf. They both followed me when I went over to Johnny Fluoride's gaff. After the shithead decided to take a swim. That's the bit I can't figure out."

"Dwarf?"

"Former associate of our headless friend, I do believe. Seems Johnny accidentally snapped a pic of him and he didn't like it. Kind of in *flagrante delicto* as they say."

"You're not making much sense, old chum. Care to fill in the blanks?"

Joblard, against his better judgement, took a sip of the tea. Grimaced. Resisted the urge to spit it back out.

"Disgusting."

"Like I said."

Joblard wiped his mouth on his sleeve, pushed the cup and saucer aside and folded his arms.

"Bludhorn paid Johhny Fluoride to take some candids. Some geezer getting his jollies being tickled with a riding crop. High class stuff. In the middle of which, this dwarf turns up and blows the geezer's head off, no preliminaries."

"Kosher?"

"One hundred percent."

"So Johnny was tied up with Bludhorn, eh? And that's why you went out to Canvey? To put the hand on him? Because of these photos?"

"Except I never knew what was in the photos till after."

"I suppose your boss has them safely under lock and key?"

"Curious are you?"

"Curious, old chum, is hardly the word."

"Doesn't look like you're the only one."

"You think whoever nixed Johnny is after the candids?"

"Stands to reason, doesn't it? Besides, I spotted scarecrow and his half-pint mate loitering around Bludhorn's crib in Soho."

"Maybe we should give the old bugger a call."

"Maybe."

"Got anything better to do for the next five minutes?"

Joblard creased his brow like someone trying hard to think, glanced sidelong at his teacup, then fished his mobile out of his inside pocket. Nicky Cohn looked at him in disgust.

"Knowing how you hate these things…"

"You're begging for cancer of the brain, you realise?"

Joblard grinned, fingered the keypad, stared at the screen. The background noise covered the dial tone, but a little icon on the screen indicated that the phone at the other end, Bludhorn's, was at that moment ringing. In theory, that was. Joblard had barely counted to three when the icon was replaced by a message saying his call had been interrupted and please try again later.

"Not picking up?"

"Nope."

"Mmm. You know, this could be one hell of a scoop."

"Could be. Could also just be a coincidence."

"Come off it. Why the heck'd anyone go to the trouble of saving a clown like Johnny Fluoride from drowning just to blow his head off?"

"Beats me. Maybe he got bored with splashing about, pulled a magic shotgun out of his arse and blew his own head off, just for the change of scenery. Or maybe he got sucked into another dimension. Dr *Who* stuff. And his head's still on the other side, mashed into the vortex."

Nicky Cohn tutted. Joblard stuck his right index finger into his right ear and stirred some wax around experimentally.

"One thing I do know," he said, "Johnny boy was scared shitless of *somebody*. Said *they* were out to get him. Said it was because of something he wasn't supposed to *see*, only somehow they put the finger on him. Or maybe they just wanted to send a *message* further up the line. Join the dots, you know, so whoever arranged to take the pictures in the first place'd get the connection. So they'd know not to fuck with it. Masonic conspiracy stuff, maybe."

"Is that what your Mr Undertaker says?"

"Bludhorn knows who the geezer is, but he's not saying. In the photos you can't really make out the face. There's just this geezer tied to a chair getting whipped. Stiff upper-lip type. Then there's a big flash. Next thing the dwarf appears out of nowhere and the geezer's head's gone. Just like that."

"Too bad."

"Hey, did you hear about that coke-dealer, blasted some kid's nut clear off in Wapping last night?"

"Twelve gauge? Yeah. Sodomised the corpse. Made a real mess of himself afterwards, too. You don't think there's a connection?"

"Never know."

"Nah. It's too crazy. The lunatic shot himself in the head."

"What if it only looked that way and someone else shot him in the head?"

"Nah. You're pulling my leg."

"It's possible."

"That makes four, you realise? Four headless fucking corpses in one day. One of whom we don't know anything about. Nah. It's too much."

"Don't forget the tart with the whip. If she copped the same treatment, that'd be five."

"Five? Nah nah nah. I don't buy it."

"Why not ask your mate over at the Yard to run through the register. See if anyone else's checked into a morgue lately without their head attached."

"Those bodies could've ended up anywhere. In a bleedin' meat factory, for all we know. Fed into a mincer. Bzzzz. Like the way horse DNA keeps turning up in beef paddies. What if it was headless Tory DNA instead? *Soylent Green* stuff. Kid munching on quarter-pounder spits out thumbnail. Not the sort of thing you'd want to see on the six o'clock news. Picture it. Wozzie the Cannibal Clown! Bad for business, is what that is."

"I'll stick to being vegetarian."

"You could do far worse, chum. Say, what're the chances you can actually find this dwarf character?"

"Dunno. All look the fucking same to me. I was figuring he'd have to show up eventually anyway. Unfinished business. You realise Bludhorn's got this thing about midgets?"

Nicky Cohn nodded sagely.

"Size."

"Eh?"

"It's all about size. Midgets. Small."

"I know what a fucking midget is."

"Same reason they go for the oriental girls. Little hands."

"What're you talking about?"

"Nothing, chum. Over your head."

"There's a nutjob running around blowing people's heads off and you're on about some slanty tart's manicure?"

"A dwarf. Blowing people's heads off. Apparently connected in some way to your Mr Undertaker. Capische?"

"What's that mean, then?"

"What's what mean?"

"Capische?"

"Don't you watch films?"

"Not those sort of fucking films I don't. You want to have a conversation with fucking subtitles, go to fucking Poland."

"Maybe the dwarf's fucking Polish, ever consider that?"

Joblard blinked, looked thoughtful, creased his brow. Nicky Cohn shook his head, muttering to himself. He sniffed at his glass of water, took a sip.

"Oh, and I forgot to mention," Joblard broke in, "they were

driving a smartcar."

Nicky Cohn peered over the rim of his glass, set it carefully back on the table while picking a sliver of lemon seed from his lip.

"What?"

"You know," Joblard said, "one of those poxy little two-stroke jobs, like a golf buggy with an M.O.T...."

Nicky Cohn made a sucking sound with his teeth. Poked his tongue up under his lip.

"I'll tell you something, chum," Nicky Cohn said, straightening his mouth out. "If I hadn't just seen Johnny Fluoride's headless corpse with my own eyes, I'd swear you're flaming nuts."

⊙ ROAD GAMES

The rail line ran direct from Section 400 through the WPA where it met the Stuart Highway and continued south and east. *The crossing*, as Dix called it. From there to the Woomera township was a short stretch of blacktop. If you were on the run from the type of people who shoot down civilian planes, it'd be the last place you might be expected to go. Like Maralinga, the Woomera Rocket Range was a prohibited area, but there weren't any checks on the public visiting the township. The tourist trade was practically all that was keeping the place alive. Nowadays the only permanent residents were a couple of dozen army personnel. The Yanks hadn't staffed the base there in donkey's years.

From Woomera, if you didn't have a permit, there was a choice. You could head north-west on the highway to Coober Pedy. Or south, to Port Augusta. Or backtrack on the India-Pacific, all the way to Perth. Or fly to wherever, if you could find a plane to take you. To look at it you'd never guess, but back in the fifties Woomera was like a second Cape Canaveral. The only thing getting airborne on any regular basis now, though, were the pink corellas that flocked around the boreholes.

Lawson had been thinking about what Dix told her, about hacking into the Gap's computers. The helicopters back at the lake had been too small to've come far. Short-range. Probably why they hadn't hung around for long. Even Woomera seemed like a stretch. As the crow files it'd still be a couple of hundred clicks each way, over the middle of Lake Torrens. Where the fuck else would they station choppers like those in the desert? The time-frame and the geography didn't add up, even if they'd made a fuel stop, there was nowhere south that made sense. *Except* Woomera. Some kind of atavism at work.

It was a fair guess there'd be people by now out on the lake sifting the debris, hunting for the blackbox. Or her. But for all she knew, they could've been looking straight down at her from up in a satellite, like in the movies. *Sure,* Lawson sneered at herself in the rearview, *it's your big fifteen minutes.* But nothing was ever like it was in the movies. Call it fugitive-paranoia. The cop she half-expected to find in the backseat each time she glanced over her shoulder. The cop in the side window. The cop over the next rise.

The reason, in the end, she'd elected to steer clear of Muloorina. You just never knew. The only town on the map between her and Dix was Marree. There was a cutting just north of it which'd get her onto the Oodnadatta Track, if she didn't miss the turn-off. And if it hadn't been washed out by the rain. There were still another four hours before she'd make the crossing at Pimba. If nothing went wrong. No checkpoints. No white kangaroos. It almost seemed possible to convince herself she stood a fighting chance. Almost.

Being on the run should've been in her blood. Like the old fellas. Going bush. Back in the day. Lawson told herself she'd feel safer after dark. The sound of the tyres on bitumen enlarged the sense of being over-exposed. Flatness stretching for miles and miles. The white of the 4x4 against the red of the earth. She kept one eye on the rearview and the other on the sky. Seeing in her mind over and over again the Cessna banking away, erupting into flame. Holding back the emotion welling up inside.

Had Dix made it out? That look in his eyes back at the CSIRO, with his computer toys and his itchy fingers, getting up to mischief. Like an overgrown kid. *What the fuck have you got us into, you mad bastard?* Did Dix know what happened to Kath's plane? Sunlight glinting off the wings as it banked and rose. And then...

Lawson blinked at the rearview. A pair of bloodshot eyes stared crazily back at her. She struggled not to close them again, for fear they'd stay that way. She'd've given anything for a shot of Dix's coffee. It'd been...? Her mind got stuck the moment she tried to count the hours. Like she'd fallen into a different time. Or a parallel universe where arbitrary things happened. Crashed satellites. Inland seas. Killer helicopters. Maybe, before the day was out, the very ground beneath her would swallow her up like a sinkhole appearing out of nowhere. Or someone would push a magic button, which'd probably amount to the same thing.

The radio, when she switched it back on to hear if there was a signal yet, produced only static. Lawson stared at the dials and LCD, trying to figure what she was doing wrong. It was a dead straight road with nothing coming the other way, so she let the Range Rover drive itself while she fiddled with the settings. Each time, though, it pulled to the left. Bastards had probably gone cheap on the wheel alignment. But somewhere in the back of her head Lawson had the nagging suspicion these particular cheap bastards wouldn't be worrying about wheel alignment from now on. In the movies, people who owned killer helicopters never let a witness just walk away.

Lawson tried to shut the thought out. She pictured eskies of warm beer. A pair of sheilas on skis. A lost pelican. Somewhere there'd be others picturing her. By now they'd know almost everything there was to know about her. It was all there, on the CSIRO security pass. The rest... But maybe it was the rest, the stuff they couldn't know, that just might save her. She readjusted the frequency on the radio. A voice blared from the static speaking Chinese. Or what sounded Chinese. She pressed buttons, but the voice only got louder. The Range Rover jagged across a rut, her hand slapped the control panel. More static. She spun the tuning dial as far as it'd go, the voice came back, multiplied by reverb. Lawson swore. With one eye on the road she tried to re-set everything. The Chinese only got more distorted, like a roomful of people speaking at once in a language she couldn't understand. She beat the radio with the side of her fist until the LCD went black. Blood pumping in her ears. Tears starting in her eyes.

And then she screamed till her breath gave out and she was left in the silence. Shaking. Hands gripping the wheel the way Kath's had gripped the flight control, careening into the storm. And she saw that look of determination on Kath's face. And she told herself to cut the bullshit and pull herself together. Wiped her eyes. Jammed down on the accelerator. *Think straight. Or don't think. But keep going. Till it's safe.* But when would it ever be safe? It hadn't been safe for two hundred years.

Lawson made the turn-off onto the cutting half-an-hour later, just as dusk was fading out and the constellations rose in the sky. A falling star streaked across the horizon. Sign of good luck, that was supposed to be. Lucky knowing you weren't right under it. *Well,* she thought, *you make a wish, there's always next time.* And right then the engine died. Lawson pumped the accelerator, but nothing happened. Eased in the clutch and rolled to a stop. She turned the ignition, but it was no use. Jerked the gearstick into first and tried again, the starter coughing itself out. *Shit.* It dawned on her slowly. Pressing the palms of her hands against her eyes, she swore at herself for being such an idiot.

Elbows on the steering wheel she dragged her hands through her hair, thick with sweat and dust, and stared into the weird glow of a dashboard that looked like the instrument panel of a 747. The fuel gauge was in the red. The crazy idea occurred to her that if Dix'd been there with her, he'd be able to hack into the Range Rover's on-board computer and re-calibrate. Summon the spent diesel back by cybernetic voodoo.

Outside, the dirt road seemed to float in the headlights, corrugated with shadows. Everything was suddenly very still. Only the ticking of the Range Rover's engine as it cooled. Lawson sat there trying to think what to do next. But the only thought that came to mind was that if Dix *had* been there, she wouldn't've got into such an idiotic predicament to begin with, would she?

Dix, as he liked to tell the story, had grown up in Rafah, northeast Sinai. A tunnel rat. Smuggling flour, tuna, bags of cement through one of the hundreds of tunnels that ran under the border to the Gaza Strip. It paid for his education in Cairo, after the first Intifada closed most of the tunnels down. Smuggling taught him, he said, the value of impermanence. Underground economies. Escape routes. The geopolitical flux as butterfly-effect. That a transaction under the Egyptian border involving tinned food might one day cause the Twin Towers to collapse. *The ways of this world, habibi, are most strange indeed...*

Out in the periphery of the headlights, away from the road to the right, Lawson could just make out a latticed silhouette rising high off the ground. She got out of the Land Rover and saw that it belonged to a derelict drive-in cinema. Wondered what sort of film anyone would come all the way out there for. Panel vans loaded with cases of VB. *Razorback.* Some shit like that. *Road Games. Mad Max...* Then she did what she should've done to begin with. The spare jerrycan was right were it was suppose to be, clamped beside the spare wheel at the back, under half an inch of bulldust. Not such cheap bastards after all. When she got the cap off, the fumes from the tank made her head swim. She emptied the jerrycan into the tank, trying and failing not to spill diesel on her boots. The RMs were caked with mud anyway, the leather sodden with lake water. She screwed the cap back on and wandered away from the track to take a piss, squatting down.

Afterwards, facing the horizon, the sky dark blue fading to black, Lawson drank in the night air listening to desert sounds, watching the stars come into view. Just how many eyes-in-the-sky had whitey put up there, watching, factoring all the coordinates? If she had her bearings right, Lawson guessed she was about ten miles east of where ten years ago some genius with a tractor and a GPS had laid down the world's largest petroglyph. A two-mile Pitjantjatjara man holding a woomera. She'd never been there, but she'd seen pictures of it. It bordered the WPA. People called it Marree Man. From the ground it was supposed to look like just a half-finished plough job. The only way you could see what it really was, was from up in the air. Or outer-space.

+ L. RON

"The *what* Institute?"

Osborne did his best to meet Fatima's gaze. Her eyes reflected his look questioningly. Osborne hung his head. He breathed deep. Exhaled.

"Kinezology. That's what it said. The One Mind Institute."

"It isn't one of those L. Ron franchises?"

"I don't know. Maybe it was just an old sign…"

"And that's all?"

"No," he shook his head. "That's not all."

Fatima put her hand on his shoulder.

"Take your time. I'll make some more coffee."

While she refilled the kettle, Osborne related, as best he could, the afternoon's events.

"I was going to meet some people. A courier job."

"This sounds bad already."

"The Doctor set it up."

"What doctor?"

"Suliman. He's like a… kind of guidance counsellor. He's been helping me. You know, since I left."

Fatima looked at him thoughtfully.

"I see," she said. "And where's this *doctor's* Mind Institute?"

"Canal Street. Right near the tunnel."

"Wait a minute."

Fatima cleared a space amongst the debris of Chinese take-away and set a fresh cup of coffee beside the one Osborne still hadn't touched, wisps of steam rising from it. Clutching her own cup in one hand she took a small handset from her jeans pocket with the other and began thumbing the screen while somehow also wedging herself in behind the table where the monkey had been sitting before. Osborne couldn't help but admire his ex-wife's talent for multitasking. Nothing, he'd discovered long ago, could ever be too simple for a multiple approach.

"Kinezology is what you said, isn't it?" Her eyes didn't leave the screen. "Nothing on Canal Street. Mmm. You sure you don't mean kinetology?" She took a gulp from her coffee. "The phonetics of human movement...? Or there's Kinesiology here. Sort of new age homeopathy." Her thumb made strange signs in the air. "Nothing under One Mind Institute." She glanced up from the handset and looked at him, half-expectantly. "That's what you said, right?"

"It was dark..."

Fatima shrugged, put the handset down on the table and leant with her back against the window, coffee resting in both hands against her sternum. Any minute now she'd start tapping the sides of the cup with her fingernails. Osborne new the signs.

"Okay. So what else?"

"I don't know," he said, opening his hands palm up to show he really didn't. It was a reflex, but the gesture made him suddenly more self-conscious than he already was. He found himself wondering if monkeys did the same thing when they wanted to convince a sceptical female member of the species there was something they didn't know. "It wasn't supposed to be anything complicated."

"But I'm assuming not entirely legal, either."

The corner of Fatima's mouth twitched. It was enough to make her entire expression seem sarcastic.

Osborne grunted.

"It was connected somehow with the thing at Ground Zero."

His ex-wife gave him a blank look. It made him uneasy.

"You haven't seen the news?"

"No."

"You haven't heard of the meteor? Fay, half of Manhattan's

shut down. The blackouts? Jesus! You think my head's in the clouds. Turn on CNN…"

"It's okay," she said, reaching across to touch his hand. "I believe you. It's just I've been in bed the last couple of days. You know how my period gets. We watched the whole series of Twin Peaks, twice. I just got up when you called, right when the murderer turns up, thank you very much. Then we ordered some Mr Chows because Kye was hungry. As you can see, I've been a very busy girl. No time for CNN."

"You said you weren't going to watch Twin Peaks again. Remember the last time?"

"I couldn't help it. The cramps were bad. If it was something funny I'd end up laughing my guts all over the sheets."

Damn, Osborne thought. Why'd she always have to make him feel like that? Like he'd just said the dumbest thing imaginable?

"Fay…"

"And you know I never laugh where Kyle MacLachlan's involved. That FBI shtick. It's a killer, though."

"You could've chosen a wildlife documentary."

"Kye hates them. He prefers suspense."

Fatima's handset blinked. Osborne glanced across at it.

"Look, Fay. If it's not convenient…"

The handset stopped blinking. Fatima went back to cradling her coffee. Her expression settled back into its previous cast. Like pressing rewind, he thought.

"So what was it about CNN?"

Osborne breathed deeply and exhaled.

"Okay. So apparently there was this meteor that came down this morning right on the Zero. I only read about it in the paper. The Doctor, Suliman, he had this idea it wasn't really a meteor at all, but some sort of… What he called a time capsule. Nothing's ever what it seems with the Doctor. If something looks one way he'll tell you it's really some other way, and he always turns out to be right. I don't mean conspiracy stuff. It's just he's got a way of recognising the hidden aspect of things. Like the world's trying to peddle you a bum deal and he'll see the margin in it. It's what he does with people. He's a psychologist, sort of. He collects things, too. I suppose when you're rich enough, you collect whatever you like. Said he was already in touch with people on the salvage crew down in the Zero. The long and short of it is, he sent me to meet these people and do a trade. For a piece of the space rock, time capsule thing. Cash for scrap. No strings."

Fatima's gaze didn't leave him.

"There's always strings," she said, setting her coffee down. "Is that how you got the cracked ribs?"

"I ran into some crazies after I did the deal."

"I thought you said you fell down some stairs…"

"Stairs, crazies. It gets mixed up…"

Osborne watched Fatima reach across to the handset.

"I really wish you could hear yourself," she said. "I just can't believe you're getting involved in something like this. After what happened the last time?"

"It's not what you think. The Doctor helps me, I do odd jobs in return. No big deal."

"No big deal, you say. Why don't I call him?"

"Fay…"

Maybe it was the tablets she'd given him, but Osborne suddenly realised he couldn't feel his body anymore. He couldn't even feel his mouth. It was possible that he wasn't even speaking, that instead little thought bubbles were invisibly passing between them. He fixed his eyes on Fatima's mouth to see what would happen. Maybe, he thought, he shouldn't have come. He seemed to be upsetting her.

"I think you'd better tell me what else happened." Fatima's voice sounded strange. Heavy on the reverb. "Canal Street…?"

"Yeah," his thought bubble said. "There was a kind of loft.

Like one great big room. With a table in the middle of it. And lights. Lots of lights…"

Fatima picked up the handset. Her eyes didn't move.

"I couldn't see *them*," the thought bubble said.

Her fingers, working the keypad.

"But they were *watching* me."

"Watching you?"

"With *cameras*."

He blinked at her, but couldn't feel his eyelids move. Like the room had just blacked-out for a second.

"Listen, Fay, I'm serious. I don't know what the deal with these people was. I did what they told me. Then there was a blackout. But before that, there was this thing…"

"Thing?"

Osborne's thought bubble was silent for several moments while he bit his lip, unconsciously. He *was* conscious of an intention to bite his lip, but there was no way of knowing if he actually was. Suddenly afraid that anything could happen, he could be chewing right through his lip at that very moment and not even realise it. The way Fatima was looking at him, giving him the evil eye. He tried not to panic.

"It came alive…," his thought bubble faltered. He was sweating. "It…"

Osborne breathed hard. He heard Fatima's voice. Or maybe something else heard it. Some invisible third ear attached to his thought bubble. She was speaking into the handset, then stopped.

"This thing…" he tried to say. "It… got into my *head*…"

Fatima crossed over to him. She took the cup of coffee from his hands and set it down on the table. It was as full as when she'd given it to him. He hadn't even been aware he was holding it.

"You need some rest. Come on."

Fatima held his arm. When he stood up, he started shaking. She led him through the apartment to the studio at the back. The bonobo was sitting on a perch above a bookshelf in the hallway. It grinned at him, like it's grin was a permanent feature. Fatima pushed open a door. Street sounds through a window.

"Lie down here," she said.

There was a couch. Osborne sat, staring at his hands. Trying to get them into focus.

"Lie down," Fatima repeated.

Osborne did as he was told. He felt a blanket being pulled up over him. And then it was dark.

The view north was one of the most expensive in the city. The plume of the fountain caught in floodlights. Cruise boats on the river. The Sheraton like an argon filament lit up. And behind it, the Tower, cutting the night sky in two. The actual sky and not the dome's black silicon memory projected there. It bore no resemblance to anything Shinwah had ever seen. Palimpsests of futures that hadn't happened yet. That might never happen.

"Welcome to Cairo," Margarita said.

Shinwah caught the other woman's face reflected in the window. The line of her jaw intersecting with the line of the Tower, red light flashing atop its finial like a minaret primed to launch at the moon. Her own face dissolved into nothing. Like she wasn't really there.

The bellboy left their luggage in the adjoining room, a dozen suitcases packed with computing hardware. The penthouse suite was Margarita's idea. Momo had cracked de Laurentiis's credit line and as far as Margarita was concerned they'd earned it. The suite alone was three figures a night. Shinwah could see Momo through the archway already busy unpacking, brandishing what looked like a satellite dish and a bird's nest of insulated cables. He was right in his element, up in the information ether.

Their being there had something to do with a hack Momo was planning, to crash the Cairo grid long enough to write his name across the city with streetlights. The way he used to tag the New York downtown before the cops beat him up and deported his WOP ass. Only this time, instead of paint, it'd be strings of viral computer code scrawled through the information nexus in all-caps. They'd be able to read it from space. M-O-M-O a mile high. The ultimate tag.

Shinwah had watched him explain all this using signs and sketches. She'd got the drift. The tag was only the visible side of it, supposed to pull people's attention away from the real prize. But what the prize was, she didn't know. She thought it had something to do with the dead Russian's pendant. And what Margarita had told her about the crashed satellite, the protocols, de Laurentiis. And that word she didn't understand. *Cartouche.* Her ticket to freedom, so she'd said. But for the whole time they'd been on the yacht, Shinwah had been asking herself what Margarita's investment in all this was. Who she really was. How far she could be trusted. And if there was any choice.

She felt Margarita's hand on her shoulder.

"I'll order up some food."

Shinwah didn't feel hungry, but she nodded anyway, dazed from the long taxi ride down-river from Alexandria. The vast Delta conglomerate. Then underground, traffic tunnelling beneath the sprawl. Like time-shifting in excruciatingly slow motion. Something inside her eyes twitched, seeing still the after-image of the low-res video screen set in the partition dividing driver from passengers, New York style. An actual human driver and not some robot. Infomercials soundlessly flashing in the dark. Desert oases. Rolls Royce Silver Shadows. Roulette tables. Sheiks in Saville Rowe tweed. Sequined women flexing their abs. Pyramids in optic-fibre pre-dawn. Orange hazards blinked from the tunnel walls, six lanes, all one-way. Taillights. Enormous overhead ventilators like jet engines torquing the smog.

The penthouse suite had matching his-and-hers bathrooms. Mirrored walls divided by hologrammed stone columns with lotus designs, hieroglyphics, papyrus. Themed, according to the programme selection, as "Karnak." Some old Egyptian temple, supposedly, with a faint incense-of-sandalwood perfume. Shinwah flipped the settings. Immediately she was surrounded by a generic tropical landscape, redolent of warmth, vague sunlight, megahertz of thoughtless wellbeing cycled at camera-eye velocity. The type of scene you could find on just about any corporate wall-space from Baikal to Joburg, synced to background subliminals of de-periodised musak which to the naked ear are vaguely nature-sounding. Somebody's idea of an efficient paradise...

On their way up from reception – a peristyle hall with black marble columns – they'd run into a group of delegates from some environmental convention. Suits puffing on nicotine vaporisers, decals clipped to mid-width lapels identifying them as carbon traders for MISr Corp. Faces drawn. Wolfish. Haunted. The decal showed an X with a circle sticking up from it, like a balloon on a stick. Or a pirate's jack. Or the world possibly, about to be crossed-out. Whatever it was, it didn't seem to bode all that well for the big bright future.

MISr Corp wasn't a *gông sî* Shinwah had ever heard of. She had to remind herself that back in the day corporations were as common as baseball teams, like when the World Series went global and every backwater from Fukushima to Kalgoorlie was bidding on the Major League. Here one season, gone the next. Even the word *global* had an archaic ring to it. There were shops at Beijing airport that specialised in the whole retro scene: Luxor tshirts, Atari runners, Amstrad snapbacks, stuffed-animal mascots, fetish memorabilia of a gone-world.

But you could never be too sure. Maybe the world changed in the meantime. Everyone's idea of the future was just a form of resurrection anyway. Somewhere the old company wrecks were parked on a strip for history to ogle at, like those B52 graveyards the Americans kept out in the Nevada desert. The resurrection men need corpses.

All the original *gông sî* were like fallen gods, howling in the wilderness. Anachronisms of the embargo evoking old-world capitalist chic, long since appropriated as tribal insignia by the Beijing sub-proletariat – INC, LTD, LLC, IPS, LLP – like Galápagos iguanas adorning themselves in extinct DNA. The real powers were invisible, corporate ghosts in the system. Or they *were* the system, evolved out of step with any language that might've been used to describe them, warping the fabric of sense the way they'd learned to warp time.

Streetwise, *carbon trader* was just another name for the oldest con around, peddling bio-mass. It didn't matter if it was living or dead. Often enough the distinction didn't hold anyhow. The only way they'd ever be able to clean up the mess was turn back the clocks. Except the *gông sî* had *owned* the clocks...

Shinwah flipped the theme setting back to zero and the bathroom faded to white, seamless, the fixtures standing out like chromed oddments. Margarita was in the sitting room talking on the hotel phone. Shinwah could hear her through the open door. The place seemed suddenly ordinary. All you'd needed, she thought, were the minus settings, to get you down past street-level, see the glorified rat-hole for what it really was. And then it occurred to her, she couldn't remember what date it was. But what if the date didn't matter anymore? If someone back in the lab had simply dialled her into a kind of quarantine, while they debugged the system, flipped the settings? If all this, the penthouse suite, the MISr execs, Margarita, the scene back on the quay in Trieste, was just part of a programme...?

Shinwah screwed her eyes shut and forced them open again, told herself that this was all actually happening. That there was no going back now. Forced herself to believe. Thinking, if anything was out of place in this scenario, it was her. The bathroom concurred. Her shoulder bag floated beside the sink on a cloud of white. In the mirror, she too appeared to float. Her clothes had a faded, sea salt look to them, hazed-over in the glass. Without them, her body virtually dissolved into the backlight. Only her hair, eyes, pubic bush and the cinctured wound in her left shoulder stood out. She dialled down the contrast and her body's outline appeared to bleed, white on white. An alabaster Nefertiti. Her hand, when she reached out to touch the glass, seemed less real than its reflection did. Like her actual body was lacking a third dimension.

In the mirror, the rawness of her shoulder-wound was like a puckered knot. A second navel. It pulsed with backlighting. The eyes also pulsed. She could read in them a chemical ache, anticipating the rush of the ice that already in her mind she was scraping into I-Ching trigrams on the marble vanity. She reached into her shoulder bag, unhasping the jeweller's case, the dead Russian's face coming back to her in slow-motion replay.

Weird synchronicity. The black of her fingernail as it spooned the ice and the black of the dead man's pendant – the unspoken price of her still being there at all, it seemed. Some unconscious affiliation between the Prague job and this. Cairo. Margarita. The older woman's closeness in the back of the taxi, pressed beside her. The dark-eyed boy, Momo, in the far corner, watching without ever seeming to look at anything. The other one, Paladino, had remained with the yacht. So now it was just the three of them.

Shinwah bent her head to the jeweller's case, inhaling hard. The ice hit the back of her throat, burning her septum. And then she was falling. Through the whiteness of the room into a black hole. Blood pounding in her ears, a fatalistic drum. De Laurentiis's voice jolted her out of it. Only she couldn't make out where it was coming from. Kill time, the voice said, before it kills you. Her eyes searched, trapped in a confusion of lights. Slowly the lights dimmed, but de Laurentiis wasn't there, just the ice talking.

"You're dead," she said aloud.

Meaning de Laurentiis. Almost believing it.

Her reflection retreated into the glass cube of the shower, under fine needle-pricks of spray. A cloud of steam gradually erased her image in the mirror as if erasing the memory of a former-self. Everything that before now had been real, but that now... What was it now?

☾ SYRINGE

From the tannery to a room inside a house. Once the door closes behind them, the albino removes her hood. In the gloom, her face assumes an Asiatic cast. Pale. Luminous almost. Porcelain white. *Not from here, anyway,* he thinks. He tears his own hood off and gasps for air. Skin waxen. There's soot all over his hands, turned to a greyish sludge from the sweat. He can feel the back of his head begin to throb again now they've stopped moving, the cooler air stinging the wound. Gradually his eyes adjust to the gloom that's replaced the gauze grill. A residual pixellation invades his peripherals.

The albino takes his hood and does something with it, he can't see what, only that her hands are empty again. He wonders if she's still carrying the gun.

"Where are we?"

"One step at a time," she says.

The colour of her eyes seems to change while she's speaking, from pink to yellow and back again.

"First you need to have that cut looked at."

"This place belongs to a doctor?"

The stink of the vats hangs in the air. Sulphur. Ammonia. Untreated effluent.

"A kind of doctor."

"*What* kind of doctor?"

"You'll see."

"What about Momo? When do we see him?"

"Maybe never. It depends…"

From here, the door they've just come through looks like one of the hatches down in the Fustat subway tunnels. There are shapes moving around them in the shadows which his eyes can't make out. A shimmer in his visual field. A disturbance in the code. He half-expects the numerics to flicker back into life, for the Stranger to begin talking again, tell him what he's supposed to be doing here. But no. The albino steps past him and pulls back a curtain. There's an archway. She motions him through it. He can hear the shapes moving behind him.

Like the room before, this one's without any visible source of light. The gloom seems to emanate directly from the walls. Bare concrete, hung with tattered strips of curtain. A threadbare rug covers the floor with cushions strewn around on it. The air's even cooler in here.

A match strikes close to his left ear and he jerks around to see the albino lighting a cigarette. The matches and cigarette pack are then laid in a niche in the wall. The pack shimmers, gold with red oriental lettering. Tobacco smoke coils from her mouth. She inhales again and blows a stream of it in his face. A smell like childhood. And that's all, nothing else to hang the memory on. Perhaps it isn't even a memory. Or maybe she's the memory. That gesture. Lighting a cigarette. Smoking it. The sound of a match.

She's grinning at him. No. Not at him, past him. He turns his head. Someone, he realises, has been watching them. At first he thinks it's a boy, but it's a very small man with a boyish face. Slightly stooped in a grubby raincoat that ought to be out of place but somehow isn't. A squint in one eye.

He can hear the flare of the cigarette as the albino inhales, feel her breath as she exhales.

"He's the one," she says.

The midget holds a finger to his lips. Nods. They're both looking at him in a way that seems expectant.

"Who are you?" he begins to say.

But already the shapes are materialising around him. He can't move. Can barely breathe. Without knowing how he got there he's sitting in a chair with a light hovering above him. His entire body's immobilised. There are tears flowing down his face, but he can't blink his eyelids. He can just make out the small man peering intently at him through a telephoto lens, the albino standing behind him. The whir of the lens as it telescopes in and out. A door opening and shutting. The glint of a syringe as it clatters to the floor.

He struggles to move. Thinking it was a trap after all. And the albino's voice coming from a long way off now.

"Still here, baby, don't you worry."

Only she's not. Neither is the small man. The room's empty. Only the silhouette of something more machine than human drifting out from the shadows towards him.

☐ ELEPHANT'S EGG

Back during what used to be called The Troubles, old Uncle Hugo, ex-Sandhurst, had the good fortune to spend a tour of duty behind eight inches of plate glass in a pillbox in the fair city of Armagh. He'd been standing there one day watching the drizzle slowly mutating from bad to worse when some Fenian fucker, parked on a hillside a mile away, took a pot-shot at him with an elephant gun. He'd seen the shell embed itself three-quarters the way through the glass, big as his thumb. When he told the story afterwards, he'd always joke that if there'd been a tailwind the bullet would've caught him right between the eyes. And taken his whole bleeding head off.

Joblard had been thinking of Uncle Hugo's story while he watched the helicopters circle the Shard. It looked like the flattened head of an enormous glass prawn, sticking up above the Canada Square towers. Some Mujahideen types had tried to blow it up a week ago and now they had half the RAF up there every night at tax-payers expense, searchlights criss-crossing the rooftops. Every wisearse on the South Bank was probably laying bets on how long it'd be before some trigger-happy Afghan vet in a chopper went bezerk and did the job himself. Like the one that smacked into the crane over in Vauxhall. Maybe blame it this time on a meteorite.

What killed Uncle Hugo in the end was a brain tumour. "Size of an elephant's egg," he'd say, while the nurse prepared his bed-bath. "Elephants don't lay eggs, Captain Banks," the nurse would tell him. "This one did." And that, as they say, was the end of the matter. Joblard remembered the picture the doctor showed his mum. You could see the skull and what he supposed was brain tissue with a void right in the middle of it. Like that Fenian bullet had a bad karmic vibe that'd lodged in his uncle's head and grown there for forty years into a knot of dead cell tissue, invading whole swathes of cortex till his motor neurons finally packed it in.

Joblard had tried calling Bludhorn once more after leaving Nicky Cohn, but the proverbial Undertaker still wasn't picking up. *Piss-taker, more like*, Joblard thought. *If things keep the way they're going.* He decided to swing by the Hindu's hole-in-the-wall for a bucket of soy Vindaloo, papadums and sweet mango. Then back to the Fridge. When he got there, one of the regular parties was in full swing upstairs, sub-sonic bass shaking the windows in their frames. He killed the engine and wheeled around to the service lift, chained the BSA to the grill and hung a tarp over it. The basement lights weren't on, so he figured Bird Girl probably wasn't back yet. Decided to go in quietly anyhow, in case she was there asleep. Though how anyone could sleep with that Moby shit playing, he didn't know.

The basement wasn't exactly luxurious, but it was big. A single room, about ten yards wide, ran the length of the building, a kitchenette with garret windows at the back. It'd been used once-upon-a-time for storage. Upstairs was where the meat processing had gone on. Some of the residents practiced a type of voodoo to ward off bad spirits, appease the bovine gods. Joblard wasn't interested in animal karma. The place stank of rat bait. Every other morning he took a bag of dead rats out to the trash. He burned incense, told Bird Girl there must be some sort of rat disease going about. Had to be careful what he left the bait around in, though, in case one of the resident freaks from upstairs got to scrounging munchies on a comedown.

Joblard left the takeaway by the door, tiptoeing through the basement obstacle course in his boots and trying not to brain himself on any overhead fixtures. The sound of snoring was audible despite the thumping bass. Joblard peered into the bed – a king-size mattress on trestles high enough for a dwarf to camp under. On account of the rats. The bed, though, was empty. The snoring came from the other side of it. Joblard made out something moon-like wrapped in an overcoat, lying on the couch. It didn't look like Bird Girl. He went over and flipped on the lights. Ol' Pasty – head back, felt hat tipped forward, mouth open – was lying there snoring like a bullfrog. His coat was gathered at the neck in the ball of a skinny fist, blotchy like his face. His other hand was wrapped around the butt of a service issue .45.

By the time the scarecrow got his eyes open, Joblard already had an elasticated ocky strap round his wrists and was in the process of cocooning the bastard with an industrial roll of kitchen wrap. Ol' Pasty's eyes bugged. They bugged even more when Joblard shoved the .45 in his mouth and asked him very politely to sit still. Wearing about fifty feet of clingfilm, the scarecrow looked like a sick grub. He squirmed when Joblard pulled the gun out of his mouth. It made Joblard think of his first day in school.

"You're not going to piss on my couch, are you?"

Scarecrow shook his head. His grey felt hat had tipped to one side, revealing a serious case of eczema. It gave Joblard the creeps.

"Where's your mate?"

Scarecrow just looked at him.

"You're not fucking Polish, are you? *Czy rozumiesz po anglielsku, ty głupia pizda?*"

Scarecrow glared.

"Suit yourself."

Joblard tore off a strip of kitchen wrap and somehow got it around the scarecrow's head without making contact with the eczema.

"Since you've got nothing to say," Joblard pocketed the gun. "Any trouble with the old respiration, just remember to shout."

Joblard went to the kitchenette and grabbed a six-pack of Guinness from the fridge, then back to collect his vindaloo. He pulled up an armchair by the door and killed the lights, letting his eyes adjust to the gloom. Maybe, after he'd enjoyed a decent meal, he'd get the jumper leads out and see how the scarecrow responded to a little encouragement. Maybe the fucker was mute, hehe. That'd be a laugh. *Better him than me.*

Outside, the same Moby track was still echoing in the stairwell. There was the sound of the DLR rattling by. The usual peace and quiet. Joblard grinned to himself, spooned some rice into his curry, popped a can of stout and settled back, munching on a papadum, to see what the remainder of the evening might bring.

⊙ SPUD'S

Dix was sitting at a window table, stirring a cup of coffee with the mesmerising slowness of somebody who'd been repeating the same action intermittently for hours.

The roadhouse was set back off the B97 with a truck-park out front the size of a football pitch, though only a couple of Kenworths were taking up space when Lawson pulled in. The word RESTAURANT was spelled out above the petrol pumps in yellow letters four foot high and 24 HOURS in neon over the door. She idled the Range Rover back beside one of the rigs, lights dimmed, scoping the scene. That's when she saw him, second window from the left, glancing up from his coffee and turning his head to look out at the parking lot. It was only a brief look before turning back, but long enough for her to know it was him.

This is it then, she thought. You made it. Lawson closed her eyes, let the stinging subside. How many hours had it been now? Just a little bit longer, she promised herself. All she had to do was make it across the parking lot, leave the rest to Dix to figure out. She opened her eyes and stared at the blurred outline of the petrol pumps and the lighted squares of the windows behind them. She blinked. Very slowly things came back into focus. Time for that coffee, she told herself, reaching for the rucksack which lay propped on the passenger seat. I sure as shit hope you were worth it.

Just then a lorry steered into the lot, headlights sweeping the side of the roadhouse. A white Ford Transit, parked beside a corrugated iron fence off to one side, caught the glare. Above it a red-on-white signboard read SPUD'S ROADHOUSE HOTEL-MOTEL. Lawson could've sworn something behind the Transit's darkened windscreen moved. The lorry pulled up on the far side of the lot, carnival lights dimming, a hydraulic hiss and then the engine going quiet. A country music guitar twang wafted out into the night then got cut off by the cab door slamming shut. She listened for the sound of boots on gravel. Then the driver came out from behind his trailer in a skinny singlet and Hawaiian shorts, '80s mullet, crossing to the restaurant.

Something about the Ford Transit vibed government agency. It made her think of snatch teams sent out to the missions to abduct half-cast kids, like her. Only they didn't use Transits back then. Maybe it was the lack of sleep and a general sense of paranoia. Or maybe the situation was all wrong, like it wasn't supposed to turn out this way after everything that'd happened – just drive up and find Dix sitting there waiting. She sat and watched the Transit till her eyes started to burn. If she'd blinked she might've missed the telltale flare of someone lighting a cigarette in the driver's seat. Someone, like her, watching, waiting. *Stay calm*, she told herself. *If it's you they're waiting for, they still don't know you're here.*

Lawson put the Rover into gear and backed out of the lot, keeping to the lee-side of the trucks, then drove without lights down to the rail-crossing, turned left, cutting the engine behind the sidings. The branch-line terminated at Woomera, the main-line running west to east from the Indian Ocean to the Pacific like a meridian. If you were mad enough, you could follow the tracks all the way from Perth to Sydney. Walkabout. Rainbow serpent.

There was movement further along the tracks, a couple of freight cars being shunted under spotlights. The platforms were crowded with soldiers milling around. Lawson guessed an overnighter was scheduled to pass through to one of the cities. She shouldered her rucksack, leaving the keys in the ignition the way she'd found them, wiping for fingerprints. She scanned the far side of the perimeter fence for a back-way to the roadhouse. A dog barked. Some voices came and went.

Leaving the Rover, Lawson skirted the fence that ran past the sidings. There where holes in it wide enough to drive a trailer through. She kept to the shadows, between piles of breezeblock, concrete sleepers, busted palings, bundled wire, wooden spindles wound with communications cable stacked atop one another like some backblocks Babel. It wouldn't be good if any of the locals spotted her. Though she probably could've counted all the locals on both hands, it was that kind of town.

Behind the roadhouse was a row of bungalows with tin roofs still simmering in the night air, air-con units taking up most of the window space, working overtime. The bungalows, Lawson figured, were the pride of Spud's Hotel-Motel. There were no lights in any of the windows. But then, it was the middle of the night. Old Glory was parked in front of the last bungalow on the left. Somehow it made her sad to see it there. In the near distance a faint thrumming echoed off the walls.

Lawson tilted her head, alert. The echo came louder. A road-train ratchetting down through the gears. The hydraulic judder of it pulling to a stop. As soundlessly as she could, Lawson skirted the bungalows, keeping to the right of the ute. The window facing it had the curtains drawn. She scoped the back of the ute. The silhouette lying against the grill gave her an idea. She ducked down by the driver's door, slid her hand along the underside of the chassis to where she'd wired a spare key. *Gotcha.* Dissolving back into the shadows, towards the restaurant, past the kitchen entrance. Radio voiced behind a screen door.

In another minute, she'd taken up a vantage behind a blue-and-white icebox with a clear sightline of the restaurant interior. The Transit was about twenty metres away, the eye of a cigarette flaring and fading behind the windscreen. A newspaper headline was stuck up behind some wire mesh beside the shop entrance. Red serif above a mugshot of the Yunapingu man in shirt and tie. YELLOWCAKE PERIL! it said. Below, in smaller print: "JOINT ENERGY INITIATIVE" THREAT TO REGIONAL STABILITY. So they'd finally done it, Lawson thought. Sold-out to the Chinese.

Now whitey'd be more paranoid than ever. She felt the weight of the canister in her rucksack pressing against her spine. What if it belonged to a *nuclear* satellite? Did such things even exist? She could just imagine what Dix'd say. *They get their hands on you now, girlie, you'll make a pretty scapegoat alright.*

From where she was crouching, Lawson could make out the back of Dix's head, one window down. Closer to the service counter, four men in camouflage fatigues were drinking cans of VB. A couple of cross-country cyclists in matching his-and-her biking gear were sharing a table. The truckie with the mullet was nursing a hamburger by the cash register. Three non-descript types were sitting at the counter. Dix, when he wasn't stirring his coffee, had his eyes on the entrance. As she'd've expected him to, if he hadn't been sitting right out in plain sight. She glanced over at the Transit. If it belonged to the same people who murdered Kath, did Dix know they were out there? Was this all part of a set-up? They'd tracked him, and now they were just killing time, waiting for her to show?

This's crazy, Lawson told herself. *You need to get some sleep.* How long, she wondered, had Dix been waiting? The easiest thing would be to just walk in and sit down, order some of that roadhouse coffee. But something about the way Dix kept fidgeting with his spoon and not drinking, like it was a message. She still had one of the joyriders' cellphones. It gave her an idea. It was risky. If the whole thing was a set-up and she called Dix, they'd be able to trace it, know she was there. But what if they already knew? If the thing in the rucksack had a GPS tag, like a black box recorder, and they were just sitting tight, letting her bring it to them?

+ FORTUNE COOKIE

40°43'0.09"N
73°58'34.75"W

Later. The sound of traffic backed-up along the FDR. An orange light flashing in the window. The clock ticked, quarter-past-three. Osborne jerked upright. He'd been dreaming the thing with the meteor hadn't happened. Or hadn't yet happened. His body ached, even his eyes ached. Outside it was snowing now. Somewhere a horn was blaring.

Osborne groped his way to the window and stood there, naked in the orange glow. He wondered what'd happened to his clothes. They weren't anywhere he could see. Outside, the dark hulk of the Domino Sugar Refinery loomed across the river. Through the lattice of the fire escape he could just make out the exit ramp of the Williamsburg Bridge. Fragments of his dream swirled among the snow. Snow clung to the fire escape, blanketed the street below, black lines running along it in parallel.

Down by the parkway, a figure in a hooded duffel coat sat hunched on a bench clutching a paper bag. A bundle of newspapers lay on the bench beside him. A street-cleaning truck was stalled at the intersection, its revolving light making the snowflakes pulse in mid-air as they drifted down. Like static invading a picture. He couldn't tell if the snow was out there or in his head. Osborne wondered why the homeless guy hadn't found somewhere out of the weather. *Rio de Janeiro, Viajes Soul-Mate Tours.* Just thinking it made him shiver.

Osborne found the remote control and switched on the TV with the volume off. After a moment signal resolved into a giant Technicolor lizard. Then more giant lizards appeared, crawling out of caves onto a beach. Some people were pushing a raft towards the sea. One of them, a woman, tripped and fell. A giant lizard approached, teeth flashing. A man threw a spear at the lizard. The spear struck its leg. The man threw another spear, this time striking the lizard's mouth. Fake blood poured. The other lizards turned on the wounded lizard and began devouring it in a frenzy. The people meanwhile made their escape.

He'd seen the film before. He knew the raft was going to be sucked down into a whirlpool into the centre of the earth, but he couldn't remember if the people died or not. He flipped channels. A weather map came into view, replaced then by a live satellite feed of a tropical storm-front moving across the Gulf of Mexico. Footage of waves breaking against houses somewhere in Texas. Rescue workers evacuating residents. Wrecked oil derricks. Semi-trailers overturned. Nothing about a meteor strike at Ground Zero. He toggled the late-night news feed. Still nothing. He scrolled. There was something wrong with the date at the bottom of the screen. It said January 30. Was that what day it was? January 30…?

He thought: *I've got to call the Doctor.*

Osborne dropped the remote on the couch and hobbled over to the door. Fatima's bathrobe was hanging there. He somehow managed to get his arms into the sleeves without causing too much pain. He inched the door open. The apartment was quiet. Too quiet. He braced himself against the doorjamb and scoped the hall. The bonobo was on its perch above the bookshelf, asleep with its eyes half-open, framed in a halo of blue. As quietly as he could, Osborne edged out past the sleeping monkey to Fatima's bedroom. The glow of fish tanks faintly illuminated it. A crow turned its head and blinked at him from its perch. He turned on the lights. The crow shrieked. Wings flapping against bars. Fish hung suspended behind glass. No sign of Fatima.

The telephone beside her bed. Osborne reached for it. A china cup slid to the floor and broke into pieces that shone like millefiori. He keyed in Suliman's number into the cordless and hit dial, ogling the shattered porcelain. Nothing happened. He repeated. Still nothing. The crow flapped its wings, the porcelain glowed.

"What the fuck's wrong with you?" he hissed into the mouthpiece.

He tried again, dropped the area code, nothing happened. Try zero, he thought. This time he got a tone. The line clicked. Then he heard the pickup. It was a recording. A woman's voice. The same one as before. Secretary, brunette. She had a name, but Osborne couldn't remember what it was. He hung up mid-message, stared at the phone in his hands. It was shaking.

Not now, Osborne told himself. Just calm down. He tried to regulate his breathing, remember where he'd put the Doctor's private number. Not the time for a panic attack. But the number was in his coat pocket, and he wasn't wearing his coat. He glanced around for a phonebook, but there wasn't one. He felt ridiculous rummaging about in his ex-wife's bedroom naked in a bathrobe.

He dialled the office number again. This time he waited for the message to end. After the tone he said:

"This's Osborne. I'm at 212-923-4519."

He listened. He thought he heard breathing. He waited.

"Hello?" he said. "Hello?"

There was a click and the line went dead.

Osborne found his coat where he'd left it, draped over the rim of the bath. The copy of the Times he'd stuffed in the pocket was gone along with his improvised rolodex. D-for-Doom. So were the rest of his clothes. He looked into the medicine cabinet for more painkillers. Jars of Codeine, Zoloft, Nurofen. And behind those the unmistakable shape of a handgun. He took it down and stared at it. He was sure he'd never seen one there before.

"What d'you keep a gun in the bathroom for, Fay?" he whispered. "Killer roaches?"

Osborne took out the clip and cleared the chamber. And you keep it loaded, too, with that crazy monkey loose in the apartment. He made a wry attempt at imitating the bonobo's grin and raised the gun to his head. He made some monkey noises and pulled the trigger several times. Then he frowned, peered closely at himself in the mirror.

"What the fuck're you doing, Osborne?"

He lay the gun down on the edge of the sink and turned the tap on. Took some pills, one from each of the bottles just for good measure, and went over to the toilet to urinate. He eyeballed the gun. It gave him a bad feeling. He listened to the toilet flush. Voices in the airshaft. Spanish. A domestic going on in one of the downstairs apartments. He splashed water on his face. In the mirror, a shadow of something. He peered into it. His reflection peered back. There was bruising around his left eye. He untied the bathrobe and looked down at his body. Yellow and green bruises all up his left side. He dried his face and slipped the gun into the pocket of his bathrobe, just to be on the safe side.

His search of the cupboards in the hall turned up only an old pair of housepainter's overalls and a pullover. It'll do, Osborne thought. Maybe Fatima had taken his clothes to the laundry. But what laundry would be open in that neighbourhood in the middle of the night? His boots, at least, were by the front door, almost dry. He tried the door but it was locked from the outside with a deadbolt. He fumbled for keys. There were no keys.

From the other end of the hallway he heard the monkey shift about in its sleep. Osborne felt for the gun. It was still there in the pocket of the bathrobe. He yawned. He wondered if monkeys dreamt the way people dreamt or if there was some fundamental difference. The apartment grew quiet again. He stood in the kitchen doorway trying to think what to do. Had Fatima come back while he was asleep? Where'd she been all this time? The wall clock said half-past. Three. He glanced around the kitchen. Searched the breadbox where Fatima kept the spare set of keys, but they weren't there. She must've taken them with her. Why would you do that, Fay?

Sweeping the bowls and takeaway bags aside, Osborne sat

down at the table. The shattered remains of a fortune cookie lay to one side, a strip of folded paper sticking out of it. He pulled the paper out and unfolded it to see what it said, but both sides of it were blank. He turned it over under the light multiple times to be sure, but there wasn't so much as a mark. *Strange*, he thought, tossing the blank piece of paper aside. *A fortune cookie that doesn't tell your fortune.*

Time zeroed out. Waiting usually made Osborne nervous, but now he felt indifferent. He sucked on his lip. He felt parched. A carton of milk was sitting out on the counter beside the fridge. He reached for it. Fumbled. The pain killers making his hands feel slack. He sniffed at the milk, it smelled like the stale inside of a fridge. The way all milk smelled. He gulped thirstily from the carton. His head swam. It occurred to him he hadn't had anything since, how long? Little Joe's? *Meteor Strikes Ground Zero!* And before that? Osborne flipped the top of the carton back and blinked at the expiry date. *Shit. What they must use to preserve this stuff.* Then it hit him. He lurched to the sink and retched. A string of milky bile spiralled around the plughole. He wiped his mouth. He retched again, but nothing more came up.

At some point Shinwah turned over and looked at Margarita lying there beside her. Blond hair falling around her face, the geometry of her nakedness. A pain shot through Shinwah's left shoulder, reminding of where she was, awake suddenly in an unfamiliar city. As if all cities weren't unfamiliar. The clock on the table read 23:32. A vague sense of panic. That she wasn't supposed to be there, but somewhere else. Thinking how she'd have to live with that from now on, because there was no way back. Whatever that meant. She pictured herself in a building somewhere, waiting outside a door. The door opening. A man in a surgical mask. Then lying on a table, staring into a cold hard light. A needle. And the light going black. Thinking all the while of a laboratory mouse trying to find its way out of a maze, into another maze. Just one maze after another. Telling herself, *I'm not really here, am I? Any minute now, I'm going to wake up. Back there. In cold storage.*

"Time to go," a voice chimed in her head.

The transmitter's *bleep-bleep.* Waiting for the sub-routine to kick in. The room jarring back in a sudden focus. Margarita standing over her.

"Sweet dreams?"

Shinwah stared at the clock. The red digits still said 23:32. Shit. She was sitting with her back propped against a pillow, shoulder swathed in fresh gauze. The sheet beside her, unrumpled, cool beneath her hand. Margarita smirking, crossing the room, disappearing through the archway. Her clothes, Shinwah saw, were folded on an armchair beside the bed. Freshly laundered. Slacks, singlet, bomber jacket. *Did you do that? Or did she do that?*

Shinwah dragged upright, struggled into her clothes. Scanned the Hotel-complimentary toiletry set. Dior. What a five star penthouse suite at the Meridien buys. Sprayed perfume on her wrists, neck, trying to remember what'd actually just happened. Her face in the bathroom mirror. High-contrast. Dialing the settings to zero. Eyes, bloodshot. Dark crescents. *You look terrible.* A vague distant throbbing in her head. Reaching for the jeweller's case. Knowing it was a bad idea. Knowing not to would be worse.

Shinwah breathed deep, the afterglow of the drug radiating down the length of her spine. The warm air against damp skin. Just as it had when she'd first come out of the shower to find Margarita waiting on the balcony, champagne glass in hand. It felt like a dream somehow. A table with candles had been set for two, ice bucket to one side. The city was a shimmering menagerie.

"We might never get the chance to do this again," Margarita had said. "Tomorrow we make the connection. Everything's been arranged. Momo's preparing his show as we speak. Set for midnight. That gives us four hours. And we've booked the best seats in the house."

The lights of the Tower caught in the champagne flutes, each bubble a radiant sphere. As they drank, Shinwah had felt the other scrutinise every inch of her. Eyes made greener in the candlelight. Like an ironic cat. *Mão.* And her, the little mouse, *Xiâo lâo shû*, waiting to be dinner. She'd closed her eyes and drank till her glass was empty. Felt the glass being taken from her hand. And when she opened her eyes, Margarita's had been right there…

This time when she crossed the sitting room, Margarita was standing by the balcony doors, watching her with a tangible sense of curiosity. Her own face was reflected at a distance in the tinted glass, like someone looking in. A pair of existentially vacant eyes above angled cheekbones. The suite seemed to grow quiet around her. Quieter than it should have been. She tensed but there was no strength in it, as if the fight had gone out of her. Even the ice had no edge, but only an inward disintegration of light.

So what if they find you? she thought.

It made the palms of her hands itch. Like any second now de Laurentiis really might just step out from the shadows, with that Dirk Bogarde inscrutability of his, left hand in jacket pocket. And she knew if he did, she'd be powerless to do anything, other than submit. She wondered, if she'd had the chance back on the quay, if she'd've been able to pull the trigger. Or if somehow it was in her conditioning, not to.

She took the cup of coffee Margarita offered her. It had the bitterness of an astringent. Her head spun. Margarita's hand on the small of her back, guiding her out to the balustrade. Standing there, in a type of warp, as the drug surged again inside her head, peaking again, levelling out. Her hand holding the cup, no longer shaking. A stillness. She sipped the coffee. Stared at the city. Steel and glass ziggurats upside-down in the river.

"It won't be long now," Margarita said. "Are you ready?"

Shinwah nodded, wondering what it was exactly she was supposed to be ready for. The dead man's pendant, she saw, was hanging around Margarita's neck. Flashback to the Millennium Plaza in Prague. The dead Russian on the bed. A returning sense of déjà vu. Did they know what the pendant was? Margarita was smiling at her, like she could read her thoughts. Those eyes.

"The connection's agreed to meet just after midnight. Everything's been arranged. We each get what we want. Aren't you happy?"

"What about de Laurentiis?"

"What about him?"

"I can't help feeling he's here somewhere."

"You'll get over it."

Margarita's hand touched her face. Cold. A fingernail tracing the hollow under her eye.

"Take it easy with that stuff."

"I can't think otherwise."

The time sickness.

"You should eat something."

"I'm not hungry."

Margarita withdrew her hand. Turned back to the vista. Far below, a crowd was milling about on the hotel terrace. The convention, Shinwah supposed. She watched the crowd change shapes, the white-jacketted waiters weave in and out with trays. A spotlight played over the terrace. On the river-side, an electric billboard displayed the MISr logo above a bandstand with some empty chairs arranged on it. Behind it, the plume of the Nile fountain changing colours.

Something drifting down the river caught Shinwah's attention. It flickered, changed shapes. A burning funeral barque, paper lanterns on water, horses. Then she recognised it for what it was, a hologram, projected on the water. Its source, a floating discothèque rounding the tip of the island, pumping out raï. The music seemed very far away, drifting, like the river itself.

"They're celebrating," Margarita said.

"What about?"

"Our demise."

Shinwah glanced at her questioningly.

"They think it's the end of the Western World."

"What do you mean?"

"You'll see. While you've been asleep, stock markets have been crashing. The Dow, Nasdaq, FTSE, DAX, Nikkei. An unanticipated side-effect of a certain satellite going down. The little Egyptians would like to step in and fill the vacuum. But they'll have to beat the Chinese to it first."

Shinwah nodded as if the words meant something.

"A nice coincidence you turning up the way you did."

Yes, Shinwah thought, *a really pretty coincidence.*

Shinwah's eyes followed the disco boat till it passed from sight behind one of the adjacent hotel buildings. A circle of bright lights marked out a helipad on its rooftop. A Blackhawk sat there idling, its rotors cutting swathes through the humid air in slow motion. A couple of suits, like the MISr execs they'd run into in the elevator, were ushered across the tarmac.

Shinwah glanced across at Margarita, but the other woman's attention was fixed on something in the distance. It was almost midnight. She could hear the Blackhawk's engines begin to whine above the disco music as it slowly arced up into the air.

And right then, Momo must've flicked the switch on his little doomsday box. Like the shadow of a cloud passing over the landscape, darkness fell across the city. From east to west, the grids went down. And out of the sea of darkness, a single, continuous scrawl of light, spelled the letters M O M O. The name of some ancient trickster god. She wondered if anyone was up there, watching…

But the thought was unable to complete itself. As darkness swallowed the city, a scream came up from the river. Her eyes searched for its origin, finding the navigation lights of the Blackhawk as it swung out over the water. Pitched. Rose. Hung in suspended animation. Then veered suddenly into the black monolith of the Sheraton tower. There was an eruption, followed by another. A radiant nova against the blackout. Shinwah gazed at it, like it was some infinitely beautiful, impossibly delicate flower that would only ever bloom once. And very briefly.

"It's time," Margarita said.

☾ PROSTHESIS

A shadow crosses in front of the mirror. As the pupil in his eye dilates, he sees his own face gradually come into focus. It's grey, framed with a reddish halo like muted neon. He wipes the beads of perspiration from his forehead. The skin feels waxen. Somewhere, nearby, the sound of a fan chopping up the atmosphere. It's hot. A residue of steam clinging to the edges of the glass. A plastic curtain brushing his shoulder. The smell of blood turning cold. Something clotting in a plughole. He imagines dark strands of hair, bloodied hand-prints around the basin.

Inside the sound of the fan there's a ticking. It's time, he thinks. No, not ticking. A leaky faucet. A showerhead dripping. The reverberating echo. Surface tension, mass, a glistening sphere falling through space colliding with a foreign body. Something naked. Wet. Lying in the bath. Some viscous substance running slowly but inexorably out of it. Through a hole where the body's head ought to be. He tries to picture what's causing it. Some sort of analogue dial winding down inside. Systole and diastole. Pulsing but already dead.

In a practiced, unhurried motion, he pushes his fingers up into the socket of his left eye and draws out the glass prosthesis. Its weight in his hand. Not how he expected it to be at all. Something egg-like. Gelatinous. For a moment he loses his balance, gripping the sink one-handed, middle ear readjusting. His face grins sickly back at him. A red hole winking out of it.

He places the synthetic eyeball on the edge of the metal sink, in a moulded groove. Then takes from his coat pocket and patiently unwraps a nylon satchel on the narrow countertop. Within it, an array of steel instruments, glass ampoules, a syringe. He takes a small file and works the top off one of the ampoules. Something dark circulates within its amber liquid. A palpitation without form. From the ampoule he fills the syringe, the darkness slithering up inside it.

Into his one good eye he screws a black jeweller's loup, like a Cyclops with a telephoto lens. Leans forward, face close to the mirror. With the fingers of his left hand he spreads open the lids of the orbital cavity. He pauses. Inhales, then slowly exhales, raising his right hand in which the syringe glints in the reddish light. He carefully inserts the needle at the point where the nerve passes through the optic foramen into the brain. Slowly the plunger descends. The operation completed, he swiftly cleans the syringe and replaces the satchel inside his coat. Picking up the glass prosthesis, he regards it with a mix of fascination and distaste. Raises it to his mouth. Licks it. Then thumbs it into the flaccid orifice.

☐ SEA OF TRANQUILLITY

Nicky Cohn was standing in the middle of the room, toeing an orange-and-brown paisley rug Bird Girl had said *blended* with the couch. Joblard couldn't help thinking she was right. He spooned some instant into two give-away Wozzie Burger coffee mugs and snapped off the kettle. Poured. Doused the mix with soy milk.

"Sugar?"

Nicky Cohn pulled a face like the very idea appalled him.

"Nice place you've got here. Pity about the stiff."

Joblard brought over the coffee and stood beside Nicky Cohn. They both sipped their coffee, surveying the couch. The scarecrow's brains had made a complete mess of it. But there was no denying it had a certain affinity with the rug. Little fractalised blobules of red, black and grey floating in a type of Rorschach amber that continued half-way up the wall, punctured by bone shard. Bits of the scarecrow's brains were even stuck to the ceiling. Joblard thought he recognised a patch of eczematous scalp glued to the lightshade – a paper globe that'd once been white, but now looked like a sepia pock-marked moon. Sea of Tranquillity and all that.

At some point in the night Joblard had dozed off under a dusting of papadum crumbs and pilau rice. What woke him was a sound like rats trying to burrow out through the walls. He'd been dreaming of a boat, somewhere on a river. A sort of funeral barque. Egyptian. Head of a jackal at stern. Anorexis, or whatever it was called. Dog god. With a gold sarcophagus in the middle of it. Like Bludhorn's museum. Naked midgets at the oars. Ol' Pasty there, too, beating a big drum. A sail with billowing Rosicrucian eye. And Joblard himself, trapped inside the sarcophagus, gasping for breath, tangled in mummy wrappings, trying with all his considerable might to escape.

He spilled what was left of the vindaloo grabbing for the .45 wedged in his Bellstafs, lucky the safety catch had been on. At first he thought the scarecrow had gotten away. The place was quiet. The party upstairs must've ended. And then he saw it, a faint mock of paracelene from the back windows glinting on the kitchen wrap, casting a long shadow up the wall. Only it was no shadow...

"What d'you know," Nicky Cohn slurped his coffee. "Looks like your pal must've wore falsies."

"Eh?"

"Unless those are yours?"

He poked his mug towards a splotch on the back of the couch. Joblard squinted at it. A pair of dentures was embedded in the muck. They seemed to grin back at him.

"Yikes."

"Think someone's trying to finger you, old chum?"

Joblard pulled out the scarecrow's gun. Sniffed at it. Nicky Cohn glanced at him with a vague look of apprehension.

"Hasn't been fired. Beside," he held the gun out for Nicky Cohn to inspect, "no .45 on Earth could've done that."

Nicky Cohn demurred.

"Still, doesn't exactly look good, does it?"

Joblard stuffed the gun back in his pants.

"What're we going to do?"

Nicky Cohn held out his empty mug, Wozzie-the-Clown smirking sideways from it.

"I'll take another one of these, if you're offering."

It'd been just after four o'clock when Joblard called Nicky Cohn. Figured he slept in his office. Got the answering machine. Shouted something incomprehensible at it. Rang again. Third go, the answering machine cut-out mid-message and the real-life Nicky Cohn came on.

"D'you know what time it is?"

"Of course I know what fucking time it is!"

"This better be good, old chum."

"What if I told you there's a headless fucking corpse sitting on my couch?"

He'd made it there in fifteen minutes. The sort of thing possible in London only around four a.m.

"You weren't kidding," Nicky Cohn said, when he saw the scarecrow. "There's a corpse with no head sitting on your couch. What's he wrapped in plastic for?"

Joblard spieled it out while Nicky Cohn clicked his tongue, shook his head, toed the rug. Sniffed.

"Rat bait," Joblard explained.

His visitor appraised the room without moving from the spot, keeping an eye out for stray rodents.

"Nice place…"

Handing Nicky Cohn a fresh mug of coffee, Joblard pondered the situation. Nicky was right. If the cops got hold of this, they'd be all over him. Wouldn't matter what he said. Wasn't a single alibi he could think of that'd hold water. So to speak.

"In the films," Nicky Cohn offered, warming his hands around his coffee, "they always search the body first, get rid of any I.D., then put it − the body, that is − in a bin liner and dump it somewhere. Got any of those housewife gloves? You know, for washing dishes and stuff?"

⊙ CYCLOPS

The plan took shape all by itself. In an instant. The moment the truckie in the Hawaiian shorts started heading for the restaurant door. Lawson kept low, right along the parking lot perimeter, till she made the far side of the lorry. The cab was unlocked. She hoisted herself up, dug the oversized film cartridge out of her rucksack and stashed it under the passenger seat, pressed the door closed as quietly as she could, the sound of the truckie's boots on the gravel getting nearer. She stayed huddled in the shadow of the trailer while he smoked a cigarette, blew his nose, got in behind the wheel. By the time he'd backed up and pointed the lorry out onto the highway, Lawson was back behind the icebox, thumbing a message into the joyrider's phone. It was a long shot, she knew.

As soon as Dix got up from the table, things began to happen. The way the three non-descript types sitting at the counter all seemed to turn in unison, watching him walk towards the back of the restaurant. Dix said something, pointing to the toilets. One of the men got up as if to follow. Dix pushed through the swing doors before the man could get off his stool. And then she knew there wasn't a second to waste. Running now. Getting the key in the lock, into the ute, gunning the engine. Dix virtually diving out the back entrance to the kitchen. Her flinging the passenger-side door open, jerking the gearstick.

Then a crash from somewhere inside the kitchen. Tyres spinning on gravel. Dix gasping, barely in the seat. Old Glory fishtailing across the car park. Her shouting at Dix to wind his fucking window down as they spun out between the petrol pumps, straight at the Ford Transit. Its headlights coming on. Someone rushing out of the restaurant, clipping the front of the ute, going down. Lawson groping behind her, fast, for the shotgun, hoping to Christ it was still loaded. Swinging it past Dix's head. The look in his eyes as she pulled the trigger.

The blast almost deafened him. Lawson swerved hard right with the recoil, dropped the shotgun in Dix's lap. Floored it. Dix spun in his seat to look back through the window. The shot had taken out the Transit's front left tyre. A man was kneeling on the ground by the door, pointing something at them. It flashed. Metal thudded. The report barely sounded above the roar of Old Glory's V8, as they slalomed out onto the highway, pointing north.

Up ahead, past the signal-crossing, Lawson could just make out the lorry's taillights heading along the Woomera road. And off to the right, hovering above the faint crack of the horizon, the silhouette of something that looked like a black dragonfly.

"Get rid of your phone," she screamed. "Now. Anything electronic. Right now."

Dix groped in his pockets. Tossed things out the window. Lawson skidded into a handbrake turn at the signal-crossing, just shy of the tracks. Dix slammed against the door, groped for the dash, one hand clutching the shotgun. Lawson accelerated. The ute bounded across corrugations. Behind them, the boom gates at the crossing were coming down. A signal clanged. The ute swerved in a rut. Lawson was driving blind, trying to keep parallel to the tracks, the sidings somewhere up ahead, the Cyclops-eye of an approaching train flaring now in the rearview. The freight yard coming into view. Station lights. The tyres finding gravel, branches hitting the windscreen, Old Glory ploughing through the shadows of concrete silos, loading bays.

Then Lawson killed the engine. They came to a stop beneath a conveyor belt that once upon a time fed the rolling stock. Lawson took the shotgun from Dix's hands and tossed it behind the seats. Dix stared at her. It was the first time she'd ever seen him speechless. She left the key in the ignition and got out. *Twice in the same day*, she thought. She hated to leave Old Glory like this, but there was no other choice. This way, at least, there was a chance they'd make it. Slim. Extremely slim. But still a chance. Dix just sat there and watched her get out.

"Better get a move on," she called back to him. "We've got a train to catch."

+ VORTEX

Behind his eyelids everything was a collage of red and black. The pain wouldn't go away. Somewhere in the back of Osborne's mind the Doctor was telling him something. Words floated towards him through inner space as if he was an ear-eye detached within himself.

In ancient Egypt, the Doctor was saying, it was believed a person's individuality was preserved after death. By an alter-ego. A bâ. A man's bâ was a detachable part of himself, independent of the body. Capable of transporting itself through space and time...

Suddenly he was back in the loft on Canal Street. The darkness was reaching out towards him. He could hear Fatima's voice in the distance. She was speaking with someone. There was a long pause and then her voice again. He couldn't hear what she was saying. A silhouette was floating above. He struggled to open them. Fatima was looking down at him.

"You need rest," she said.

He felt something prick his arm, and then painlessness. Against his eyelids the Twin Towers flickered like time-lapse images in black and white, constantly disintegrating and reforming. Flash. Another room somewhere. White walls, white ceiling. He was lying on a cold slab with something turning overhead, clockwise. A flickering light. A voice.

Some say the eyes are windows into the soul.

He recognised that voice.

Do you believe in a soul?

The Doctor was leaning over him, two dark slits above a surgical mask, poking a hard finger into his left eye. The other hand held a syringe. He felt the cold steel enter. The needle seemed to coil into his flesh, probing for something. He tried to scream but nothing came out. Then another voice. He couldn't tell if it was a man's or a woman's. Questioning. Puzzled. *Fay?*

What is it?

Exactly what it looks like. The Doctor again.

"Fay!"

The Doctor smiled down at him. Took a small dark object in one of his gloved hands. Held it so he could see it, the surgical latex framing it against the light. An homunculus carved from black obsidian, smeared in blood as if it'd just been born. The more he looked at it, the more he felt himself being sucked into a black hole. A vortex of darkness. And then the hand was gone.

He was back in the white room. A flicker of red light from a source he couldn't locate. There was a fan hanging from the ceiling. Its blades radiating from a circle of chipped enamel. Reflected in the enamel he could see himself, his face, distorted, blurred at the edges. A head with no body attached. From somewhere outside the frame, Fatima was speaking to him.

"What else do you remember?"

And then his own voice. Coming from behind him. Far off. Like a projection. A ventriloquist's dummy. A recording. Slowing down. Speeding up.

"I saw something."

"What?"

"A… dream. Only real."

"…?"

"Like I was inside someone else's head."

"What do you mean?"

"Just that. Like I was inside someone else's head. Seeing things. Thinking their thoughts. Then the lights went out. I was in a strange place. I couldn't get out."

"Osborne?"

"Fay? You've got to help me. They did something to me, Fay. In my head."

Standing on the Al-Gami'ah Bridge watching the tower slowly go up in flames. It didn't look real somehow. Like a news replay. Or that floating hologram in the river. She envisaged a crew of engineers rigging projectors or some nanotech skein sheathing the tower's outer walls, generating urban camouflage-turned-spectacle on a monumental scale. And then she thought of Momo. The lightshow with the grid going down. As if the whole city wasn't already just a virtual skein. The way, in some essential sense, all cities were.

Standing at the end of the Bridge, where she'd stood before, in the future, traffic streaming as if in a far off peripheral vision. Only there hadn't been any flames, that time, only de Laurentiis levelling a gun at the face of someone she never had a chance to get a clear picture of. The Connection. *Double-agent*, he'd said. But the tower, had it been there? Rebuilt maybe. Or had the explosion come from some parallel universe to abolish whatever future she'd already witnessed there?

The scene behind the burning tower reminded her of those dome tinsel cities in Beijing junkshops when she was a kid. Only without the dome. Cities that didn't exist anymore, but had once. Data constructs you could log-in and tour. She'd even heard of die-hards who lived in them, wired 24-7, never logging out, plugged in at a terminal with intravenous drip, maybe. Or some weird cryogenic link-up. Ghosts in the machine. Perhaps this very scene existed in precisely such a construct, with a tower somewhere, just like this one, forever burning.

Margarita was in the taxi, speaking on her handset behind a black veil. The driver, stretched out in the front seat, smoking. Shinwah, too, wore the veil. It would be imprudent, Margarita had explained, to venture into the East City at night without it. She thought back to the nubile dancing girls painted on the walls in the hotel foyer. Naked, brown-skinned with black wigs and big eyes, from some pharaoh's tomb. The giftshop with ankhs, fake papyrus and figurines of long-extinct gods. Jackal, ibis, crocodile. Embalmed cats. Miniature sarcophagi. Canopic jars, where they kept the inner organs of the dead. There were pendants, too, identical to the dead trader's. With hieroglyphs engraved in black silicon like imitation circuitry. Horus eye. Crescent moon. Ankh. And something that looked like a death's head.

"It's called a labarum," Margarita had explained. "Coptic."

"What's it mean?"

"It was supposed to be the name of God."

"Isn't that the logo of the environmental guys?"

"MISr Corp. Not environmentalists. They just smell the money. Carbon credits. They're in the shit-conversion business. First you crap all over the planet, then you get someone to pay you to clean it up. Money in the bank…"

The tower burned, unabated, not a fire-boat in sight.

They'd stopped on the bridge because Shinwah had recognized the spot. With a little effort she conjured the dome against the night sky, reflected in the fiery light across the water. And the reason she'd been there, de Laurentiis at her side, as even now his ghost, haunting her, because it possessed her future the way it possessed her past. Though she'd never understood how de Laurentiis could've known their connection was a double-agent. Perhaps it was instinct. Perhaps something in the man's shambling gait had given him away.

She could feel other presences on the bridge, watching like her. Or perhaps it was her they were watching. She tried to remember what the connection had been for. Or who. It'd been an aborted run. But after Trieste, what'd seemed incidental then now took on significance. De Laurentiis's double-cross. Margarita.

Cairo. The cartouche...? Could it've been the same reason, the last time, in the future? She touched the bullet wound beneath the fabric of her scarf, just beside the collarbone. Saw uzi-boy's face when she pulled the trigger. The smirk on de Laurentiis's as she went down.

Something exploded inside the tower, the top half of it now obscured by smoke. She wondered if that'd been Momo too. Part of his plan. Whatever that was.

"We have to go," Margarita was saying through the taxi's open window.

Their shoulders touched in the narrow backseat of the taxi as it lurched out into the traffic.

"Everything okay?"

Shinwah nodded.

"You don't need to do this if you don't want to."

"Where's Momo?"

"Right now, he'll be somewhere inside the MISr mainframe."

Doing what exactly, Shinway wondered. She had an uneasy feeling. But her entire life had been one long uneasy feeling. Margarita's hand slid over hers, fingers entwining.

"This time tomorrow, you'll be free."

"Yes, free," she said, not knowing what it would mean. Or what it meant for Margarita. Right now she felt very far from being free.

☾ ANAESTHESIA

30°0'32.35"N
31°15'22.00"E

In his dream, if it is a dream, he's lying there on the slab staring up at the fan. But there's something wrong. The fan's only there when he looks with one eye but not with the other. If he concentrates very hard he can switch between them, fade in and out. Left eye, right eye. After a while, he can't remember which is which. And then he remembers the robot with the syringe. And the mirror. The glass eye. He jerks awake and immediately there's a sickening plunge, a descent into blackness, switching back into real time. Whatever that is. But it only seems that way. The dream-images are still there, residual, behind his eyes. And whatever he's lying on is moving. Going down. And down. And down.

It comes so suddenly to a stop the impact almost knocks him out. Then light pours in. Doors opening, sliding apart. He's lying, he discovers, on the floor of a narrow, coffin-shaped elevator. The sort of thing not designed for human cargo. Something beeps. A high-pitched, insistent beep. It takes all the strength he has just to drag himself into a sitting position. His head weighs a tonne. There's something plastered to the back of it. His clothes are gone. In place of them, a dirty green tunic. A piece of bloodied sticking plaster dangles from a welt on the back of his left hand. The beeping gets louder. He drags himself out through the lift doors onto bare concrete. The doors slam shut behind him, the lift whirs. Somewhere overhead a light flickers…

And then he wakes up. Head bandaged. Lying on a pallet with a camel rug. Faint shaft of light through a barred window high up near the ceiling. He can feel himself shivering though he's not consciously cold. There's an ache in his gut that reminds him he hasn't eaten in who-knows-how-long. Bit by bit the journey comes back to him. The dream also. He gropes at his eye. Feels nothing. A faint green glow that could be anything. A trick of light. He remembers the bridge. Starting out, blood on his shirt, on his hands. The details of the journey but not the reasons. Just a dead connection and a meaningless-sounding word. A name, barely. Momo. A ghost, is what the albino said. Perhaps this ghost can give his memory back. Tell him who he is. But what if it's something he doesn't want to know? What if it's better this way?

The wound at the back of his head doesn't feel like anything. Anaesthesia, he thinks. But is he supposed to be a prisoner now? He glances up at the window, the bars, then back around the room. There's barely anything in it. His clothes, folded on a crate. Something white hanging on the back of a door. The room's barely as wide as it is long, concrete floor with straw matting. An old storeroom, probably. In the faint shaft of light he looks down at his body, extending away like an object in perspective. He closes one eye and then the other. The perspective shifts, but that's all. He watches himself pulling his clothes back on, as if the actions belong to someone else. The Stranger, wherever he is now. Then he reaches for what's hanging on the back of the door. It's a white labcoat with a symbol embroidered on the breast pocket. A circle on a stick above a cross.

☐ WHORE

51°30'48.32"N
0°2'10.62"W

"What about his mate?"

And that's when Joblard knew he'd still have to find the dwarf. But even then, none of it made any sense. He'd spent half-an-hour scrubbing the wall and ceiling, scooping bits of brain matter off the floor, then bundling the stiff into a couple of bright yellow bin-liners – the ones they sold cheap at the local Sainsbury's. The couch was a goner. He tried getting the stains out with diluted bleach. It only made matters worse. Nicky Cohn sat over by the door and watched, throwing in the odd suggestion from time-to-time. Like why not just toss the carpet over the back of the couch and be done with it?

The only thing Joblard had been able to find on the scarecrow was a roll of tenners and a pawnshop ticket. Castle Square, Brighton. He could dump the stiff and get down there on the bike before the place opened. See what he could find out. But the first thing was where to do the dumping. He'd never been all that conscientious about recycling. And riding about with a couple of bright yellow bin-liners on the back of a vintage BSA wasn't exactly low-key. But then, nothing he ever did was. He figured the best thing to do was drop the lot into the canal, over by Tequila Warf. It was only a block away. Nicky Cohn didn't like the idea quite so much. It wasn't the headless corpse that bothered him. It was being a possible accessory that gave him the heebie-jeebies.

"Don't tell me you're suffering from a case of journalistic ethics?"

"Do I work for the *News of the World?*"

"Thought you type were all the same."

"Listen, chum, some of us have a future to think about."

"What about the poor fucker with his head blown off? You

reckon he didn't have a future to think about?"

"Not sure I get your point, chum."

"Nicky. There's a headless stiff on my couch. If we don't get it out of here, I'm screwed. You think I popped Johnny Fluoride? There were witnesses."

"I just want to be able to write the story without calling down any heat. My mate at the Yard already smells a rat. Like where I got the tip-off on the floater. This could end up ruining my expense account."

"Shut up and give me a hand, will you."

Joblard bundled the disposal job in Bird Girl's rug and left the stain on the couch to look after itself. Between the two of them they got the rug out into the yard, along the alley behind the Rajasthan Café. Nicky Cohn huffed and puffed at the back while Joblard shouldered most of the weight up front.

"For a skinny bastard, he sure weighs a bloody tonne."

Once they'd made it across the parking lot off Brunton Place, it was easy going. Trees lined the canal, shrouding it in shadow. Bits of concrete rubble lay piled hither and yon. Bricks. Steel piping. Coiled wire. A body-disposal paradise. Across the water, a billboard stood up from the wharf, facing the Commercial Road Bridge, as if the plan was to get your average out-bound commuter worked up for the homeward run, and the missus-and-three-veg. Miss Big Tits in the Wonder Bra ad. Hello Pikers! Some local vigilantes had sprayed out the offending bits, adding WHORE across Miss Big Tits's face. The marketing geniuses had really picked their demographic. It wasn't called the East End for nothing. Any further east, you'd be in fucking Cairo.

"I heard somewhere," Joblard said, hoisting the weighted bin-liners across the tow-path to the edge of the canal, "that if you cut the guts open, a body won't float. On account of the gas. When it decomposes."

"Not much good when it's wrapped in a plastic bag, is it?"

"Shit. He'll blow up like a fucking balloon."

"Forget it. Your man ever floats, he'll wash up in the locks. Maybe get pulled down to the river. Means they'll have company for Johnny boy. Give the fuzz something to think about."

"Shame about the rug."

It made less of a splash than either of them expected, swallowed by the dark water. Joblard tossed the gun in after it. There were lights coming on over at the wharf. The six o'clock shift. Time to get a move-on. It was going to be another long day.

☉ MOTION-CAPTURE

"We don't have tickets," Dix said, glancing nervously up the aisle of the second class dining car. A couple of early birds were hunched over the breakfast special, ignoring the sunrise.

"Pimba, Dix. Whoever checks tickets at Pimba?"

Dix shrugged. Wiped his hand across his brow for the umpteenth time.

"Where's it taking us?"

"Darwin, if that takes your fancy. Ever been to Darwin?"

Dix looked at her out of confused eyes.

"What's in Darwin?"

"Fuck all as far as I know. Japs bombed it during the war. Like Pearl Harbour, only worse. More planes, more bombs. Though officially it never happened."

Dix scratched his earlobe, eyes shifting nonstop.

"People thought the Japs would invade, so the government drew a line across the map. The Brisbane Line, they called it. 'Cause it started there and ran west. If the Japs did invade, everyone was supposed to evacuate south of the Line. Leave the Japs to starve in the bush of whatever. Everyone, that is, except the blackfellas. And to be sure blackie didn't give the Japs a helping hand, the government planned to shoot the lot of them. Just for good measure."

Dix's gaze stopped shifting and he stared at her.

"I didn't know any of that when I was a kid. No-one ever talked about it. They still don't. You ever get the feeling you're someone else's unfinished business?"

"All the time, *habibi.*"

Lawson reached across the table to touch Dix's hand.

"You look tired."

279

"I've been tireder. Funny, been sitting there for ten hours and all that time they weren't sure when you were coming. I hoped you wouldn't."

"You know better than that, Dix."

A waiter with a moustache and meticulously combed side-part came to take their orders, not looking at them but at some abstract remote distance, like his eyes didn't work properly.

"Coffee?"

Dix nodded.

"Make it two," said Lawson.

"Can I offer you breakfast? English, Continental…"

"Do you have eggs?"

"Poached, scrambled, fried, omelette…"

"Fried," Lawson said. "Two. On toast."

"Plain, wholegrain, rye…"

"Plain."

"Bacon, sausages, beans, tomato…"

"No."

The waiter swivelled his head, looking at the curtain this time. "And for you, sir?"

Dix shook his head. The waiter tore off a chit and set it on the table, then drifted away. Dix eyeballed his back.

"I haven't stopped since we flew out," Lawson said, letting go of Dix's hand. Her own hand was trembling. "I'm afraid that if I let myself relax, even a little bit, I won't be able to keep going."

Dix turned to her, but before he could say anything, she got up and lurched out of the dining car. The lavatory was in the adjoining carriage. She locked herself in, grabbed hold of the sink and screwed her eyes up, breathing hard. The air tasted of reconstituted drain cleaner. She tried not to vomit. Everything was coming back to her now in a kind of aftershock. Motion-capture silhouettes. Nothing seemed real. But it was all, she told herself, all very too-real.

Her eyes, when she opened them, were a mess of red. A mess, like the rest of what was reflected in the mirror. She washed her face, combed her hair out with her fingers, scraped the mud off her boots. She was still wearing what she'd gone out into the storm in. Jeans and a filthy singlet. *Times like these*, she thought, *you need Rexona*. A wry grin creased her lips. *Just don't let the bastards get you down, girlie.*

Dix was gazing morosely into a cup of grey coffee when she got back to the table. He looked like he'd aged in the time she'd been away. Face gaunt with unsleep, a five o'clock shadow. Outside, the landscape was shifting through the red-end of the colour spectrum. The train carriage cast a moving shadow against it. Below the window a ventilator matted with generations of dust-tendrils wafted cold air. Lawson shivered slightly as she sat down. The climate reminded her of Dix's office at the CSIRO. The whir of the hard-drives. It seemed so long ago already. Only a moment ago. As if she'd never left. As if it was all just one long ride. Dix looked up at her.

"Are you okay?"

Lawson nodded. She stirred some sugar into her coffee and sipped it. It tasted of luke-warm cardboard. She gulped it down anyway, undissolved sugar pasted to the bottom of the cup. She scooped the paste out with a spoon, let it dissolve in her mouth, setting in motion enzyme processes that stirred something in her brain. A faintly accelerated awareness. Things speeding up again. The time-lag phasing out.

"I'm sorry, *habibi*..."

"Kath's dead," she interrupted. "Did they tell you that? They killed her. Just like that. In cold blood."

She was aware of Dix scrutinising her now. During all the time, from the lake till she'd got to the roadhouse, she'd tried to picture this moment. What they'd say to each other. How she'd make sense of everything that'd happened, everything that'd brought them to this point. Both fugitives now. Dix remained silent. She looked into his eyes. As dark as hers were blue.

"And that's what they'll do to us, too."

"How'd it happen?"

"They shot her down, making a break for it. Helicopters."

"How did you…?"

"You mean, why didn't I die, too?"

But just then the waiter returned, gaze at one o'clock, with a plate of eggs and toast. The toast had gone limp. The eggs swam in a half-gelatinous state of undercooked. A yellow meniscus ringed the plate.

"Bon appétit," the waiter said. "More coffee?"

"May as well bring the whole pot," Lawson suggested.

Dix said nothing.

The waiter returned with the coffee and went back to his station at the end of the carriage, fiddling with something behind the counter. Lawson contemplating her meal. The eggs stared up at her from the plate. Faint shadows moved within them. All of a sudden she didn't feel hungry anymore. Dix coughed, looked out the window.

"How long will it take us?"

Lawson shrugged.

"We can get off whenever you like."

"They'll radio the train…"

Lawson picked up her fork and knife and wiped off the grease, in two minds as to whether it belonged to some previous meal or the waiter's Brill cream. *Baby chickens died for this*, she told herself. *So you'd better eat it.* She cut off a slice of egg white and soggy toast and forced herself to swallow. Repeated, this time with a runny yoke. Chewed redundantly. Poured coffee into her cup. Drank. Each action requiring a concerted mental effort. Fatigue was invading every part of her, she was afraid she was going to lose the struggle.

"I was on the lake when it happened," she said finally, smearing yolk on a napkin, orange as the sun now flooding the dining car. "When they killed Kath." Her head swam. She drank more coffee. "Now that I think about it, they must've let me go."

"Why?"

"Didn't they tell you?"

"No."

"Presumably because they wanted the recorder and knew I'd bring it to them. Exactly as planned."

"Recorder?"

"What it looked like. A flight recorder. Black box."

"You found it?"

"For what it's worth. But it's gone now."

"Gone?"

"I stowed it in a lorry headed to Woomera, back at the roadhouse, so they'd follow it instead of us. I figured there was a radio beacon in it. Isn't that what's in those things? How they knew I had it?"

"Maybe. But you realise you've probably just signed that truckie's death certificate?"

"I didn't know what else to do. It seemed worth the risk."

"Careful, habibi. You'll end up talking the way they do. Expedience can always be made to seem justified."

"I'm not a fucking expedience, Dix. You didn't have to fucking sit there the whole time and play along with those bastards."

"Easy now. Easy. I know. I was trying to figure a way out. At first they let me think I'd slipped away. But at the crossing, they were already waiting. They said if I didn't cooperate, they'd kill you. At that stage, it was hard to see what difference it would've made what I did. There was no way of warning you. Your phone went dead."

"They could track my phone."

"Wake up, girlie. They don't need to track your silly phone.

They can see us right now, *up there*." Dix pointed at the ceiling. "How many things move in this landscape? They have all the means of seeing whatever they want to see. We're right in the middle of a military exclusion zone, surrounded on just about every side by the most sophisticated tracking systems on the planet."

"Which you were stupid enough to hack into…"

"I know. It's all been my fault."

"And now we don't even have the thing that got us into this mess."

"They might believe otherwise."

"Do you think they'll come after us?"

"I have no doubt about it, *habibi*. At the very least, they'll find your car. Then they'll add two and two together and arrive at… Well, whatever the hell they arrive at."

"We can jump off the train."

"In the desert? With nothing? We're better off right where we are. If they arrest us, people will see. There'll be witnesses."

"Witnesses? What'll they see, Dix? An Arab and an Abo getting carted off by cops? Big fucking deal. D'you know how many Nungas die in custody each year? They don't need to hide it, Dix. It's public fucking knowledge. No-one does a bloody thing about it. *Abo found hanging in cell*. End of story. How about, *Palestinian terrorist shot resisting arrest?* All they have to do is say you're Al-Qaeda. Witnesses? Forget it. Besides, like you said, we don't even have *tickets*."

+ MANSONESQUE

Spirals of blackness turned inside his eyes. Then something collapsed. Something vast without dimension. There was a crash. Pain shot through his body. His eyes spasmed. It felt as if he'd been run over. The pain abated. Gradually a dark interlocking grid came into focus. Mystic geometries receding into a distance of TV static. He was lying face-down on Fatima's parquet. He'd fallen off the couch.

Osborne rolled slowly onto his back and tracked the luminous hands of the clock. Ten minutes past five. The night seemed unending. Osborne lay there in a cold sweat, listening to his own breathing and the beating of sleet against the window. He tried to do the arithmetic, how many hours, but already his eyes were drooping, pulling him back into the drift of sleep. Something in the tablets. He fought it. Gripped the edge of the couch. Pulled himself up. Swore.

When he got to his feet the dizziness returned. A high-pitched whine inside his ears. His hands searched for the remote-control among the cushions. They found it. He zapped the television off, the test-pattern folding in on itself like an after-images from a dream he couldn't remember, fading to black. The dizziness faded with it. Osborne shivered, drew the bathrobe he was still wearing closer around him. He'd fallen asleep in it. Something heavy in one of the pockets knocked against his hip. Inquiring fingers drew out a cold, metallic object. It was a gun.

Osborne blanked. Then frame-by-frame the memory of the medicine cabinet came back. It seemed fundamentally wrong. Fatima hated guns. Then the stairs at the subway station, the man with the gloves, the midget, the weirdness on the train. Did he dream all that? Or was it part of the scam with those assholes on

Canal Street? And before. What happened before?

Osborne stuffed the gun back in the pocket of the bathrobe. Just how deep had Suliman got him into this? *Sure, bright boy, and what if there is no Doctor? What if you just made it all up? One Zoloft too many?* His thought was interrupted by a muffled cry from somewhere in the apartment. *Fay?* He shuffled over to the door and thought he heard someone moving around at the end of the hallway.

"Fay?"

There was no answer. Osborne frowned, tugged the door open, staggered out into the gloom. Faint ripples patterned the hall ceiling from the aquarium in Fatima's bedroom. He groped around for a light-switch. A wall lamp came on. At first he wasn't sure he was seeing right. He stood there blinking. The hallway was strewn with books. Bird feathers. Parts of dead animals. Mice. Fish.

Jesus Christ. What the…?

Fatima's bedroom looked like it'd been torn apart by a maniac. An octopus lay on its back in a puddle of ooze at the bottom of a shattered aquarium, one bulging eye pressed to fissured glass. Its tentacles twitched, stirring the ooze. Light shimmered up from the detached base casting blue undulating against the walls. The crow hung from its perch by a chain around one foot, wings spread. The bed was soaked in what could only be blood. Dark stains spattered the walls. No sign of the monkey. He wondered where it was hiding.

Osborne navigated the debris, gripping the gun in his pocket. The trail of carnage continued down the hall to the bathroom, where something bloody and shapeless filled the bathtub. Insane symbols scrawled on the tiles. Bits of broken mirror were scattered on the floor. The scene vibed Mansonesque.

He found the bonobo sitting on the kitchen table, grinning its idiotic grin. Teeth chattering. Eyes wide. The floor was covered in trash and broken crockery. Somebody had made a real mess of the place. Then he saw what the monkey was clutching in its hands. The yell caught in his throat. He staggered backwards into the hallway.

From somewhere he could hear voices.

Footsteps approaching.

Then a fist pounding on the apartment door.

Osborne stared at the bonobo and then at Fatima's head. The pounding grew louder.

The city of a thousand and one nights drifting past the window, a flickering ghost under the blackout. Grey smoke and orange haze. The fortress of El-Gezirah, the burning tower, the Al-Fisqiyyah fountain in the Nile. The taxi passed through one checkpoint after another, dark figures waving them on. Like some game of deferral, Shinwah thought, as if the whole thing was a set-up. The whole fantastic city, looking like a mainframe that'd short-circuited, but in which some secret programme waited and watched, hidden, camouflaged, to catch them when they least expected it. De Laurentiis, she thought. It could only be him. She was being sent as bait. The whole thing from the start had been planned and she'd fallen for it.

Shinwah kept her eyes fixed on the side window, telling herself to stay calm. The dead Russian's ice was making the backs of her hands itch. Somewhere across the river she saw lights beginning to flicker back on. She wondered where Momo was. And if everything was the way Margarita said it was, what part were they playing right now? The crowd-control barriers outside the Manyal Palace compound, eerily silent. The Rawdah canal, a train swaying above it, windows blacked-out, in suspended animation. Faces in the windows. Then turning south through unlit crowded streets towards the Maydan al-Khalig. Margarita's voice fading in and out of understanding, repeating the strange names, giving the driver directions, checking her handset for coordinates, issuing new directions.

Their destination seemed to have no fixity. They were approaching it in a general way, reducing the variables, till eventually there'd only be one. Or nothing. Some sort of quantum indeterminacy at work. The word they used in the Beijing lab.

Guâng pû. Meaning *spectrum*. Everything, she knew, existed within a band of probabilities. What they were doing now was reducing that band. Zoning-in. Some unconscious navigation of interlinked virtuals. Complex topology of code, as real as anything was real.

"God's still hand but shaking eye."

Something de Laurentiis had said once. Though he, of course, believed in no human gods, but only that god-in-the-machine, the eye in the sky, blind now, which had forsaken him. Or so she'd been led to think. Forsaken them both. What would it mean, to be free of it? Meaning, trapped in time. Time or a cryogenic vat.

Shinwah had a nagging feeling all of these things were connected: the reason she was here now, the reason she'd been here before, the one event somehow destined, programmed in advance to complete the other. Overlapping contingencies. A fail-safe built into the fabric of events. The feeling only got worse the longer she thought about it, watching the city pass by through the taxi window. The dark hulking walls of Fustat. Transiting the Tilal Ayn Al-Sirah in the direction of the City of the Dead.

Flashback to the burning tower, its apex shrouded in the Dome's empyrean haze. Another tower, at another time. Not burning, but lit-up by searchlights. Searching for what? For them? Scenes leaked out of one another like a watery film projection, planes of celluloid dissolving and reforming within the time of an optical flicker. As unconsciously as someone tracing ripples on water.

As if, somewhere inside, she'd known all along that she'd be here, at this time and place, seeing it the way she was seeing it now. Half-expecting the night sky to dissolve onto an array of geodesics. The burning tower collapsing one pixel at a time, to expose the hidden substructure beneath. The armature of an illusion. And all the while Margarita's voice directing the driver in a language Shinwah didn't understand. Building in her mind a sense of disjunction that, the more she became aware of it, seemed to invade everything. From the city itself right down to the atomic substructure: imperceptible, unverifiable, yet indisputably *there*. A ghost inhabiting the world the way a mind inhabits a body...

Shinwah stared out at the recession of lights studding the black like time crystallised, facetted by all the anti-MOMOs that instant-by-instant their present scenario was already generating, as if to render it the most unlikely of all. The anti-selves of all their possible selves. Of this body she inhabited but barely believed in. *Stuck here.* Implying a limit she knew didn't operate. There *was* no fixed terrain, no singular, chartable entity. She, all of them, were no less forms in flux than the city was. This city or any other city. It didn't matter what the protocols were. They could switch off the lights *here*, like in a fairy tale, on the stroke of midnight, but they'd never switch off the lights in all the *other* Cairos existing in dimensions beyond this one.

She knew.

She'd been there.

☾ SKINS

"What's it mean?"

"What?"

"That. It was in the tunnels. The ruins."

He points at the embroidery on the labcoat he's holding. The albino glances at it. Shrugs. She'd opened the door to his cell just as he himself had been about to try the handle. The shadow of the bars across the window made a pattern on her face. He half-expected to've been locked in. A stranger in their midst.

"It belonged to one of the corporations," she says, "who built the Dome. Before the intifada. Then it became theirs, the intifada's. Spoils of war. Now it doesn't belong to anyone."

"Why not?"

"Just because."

"What about the coat?"

"What about it?"

"It's what scientists wear?"

"Maybe."

"You're not one of them, then?"

"One of who?"

"This intifada you keep talking about."

"There's no intifada anymore."

Something about her eyes, he thinks. The way she's always looking just past him, like he's not really there. Evasive. But he has not choice but to trust her, right? She saved him, after all. But then, he was half-dead. *I'm better now. I can think for myself.* But think what? What's he supposed to think? He doesn't even know where he is. The City of the Dead seems a long way behind him already. He remembers the coloured vats. Is that where they are now? He sniffs the air, but there's only a smell of sweat, walls, a commingling of effluents.

"Leather factory," he says.

"Skins."

"What?"

"They use the skins. The meat's processed somewhere else. How they feed the Dome. Organs get put on ice. Whoever can't afford a clone. The rest's boiled down into a type of DNA soup they use in the labs. Used to be they'd just collect the scraps left by the Eugenics squads, but now it's a home-grown industry. Too dangerous for the Eugenics boys out here now. And the industry's too valuable to fuck-up sending in the drones. You want to know what happened to the intifada? That's what happened. They feed off each other. Dead eating the dead. You don't belong here."

"What about you?"

"Who says I am?"

He can't help staring at her. *What the hell's that supposed to mean?* Involuntarily he raises his hand to touch the bandages on the back of his head. They feel the way he expects them to feel, though beneath them there may as well be nothing. Just numb. He thinks back to the dream and the dream within the dream. *Cannibals? Human skins?* But he's sure he's not dreaming now. What the albino just said makes no sense, but he's sure she said it.

"Come on. Someone wants to see you."

"Who?" he asks

The albino turns without saying anything and begins walking off down the corridor. Bare concrete, like his cell. Some sort of compound, he thinks, glancing back then following her, hurrying to keep up. And because he's still shivering he drags the labcoat on over his *jilabîya*.

☐ PUSSY GALORE'S

50°49'15.87"N
0°8'12.20"W

Garvey's Money Shop was a whitewashed Georgian affair only a couple of hundred yards up the A23 from the old Brighton Pier. The sign in the shop window said WE BUY. It was surrounded by nightclubs, neon strip-lit, blacked-out windows, meathook-in-the-anus joints for ambi-gendered speed freaks down from London on the prowl. The pavements were littered with last night's dross. Drunks puking in the gutter. Vampires blinking into North Atlantic gloom. Tracksuits and white-soled brothel creepers and Crisco-slathered hairdos.

Joblard left the bike on its side-stand and took a butcher's into Garvey's shop-front. There was a light on over the counter and a turbaned Sikh polishing the display cases. Joblard tapped on the glass. The Sikh looked up, shook his finger and pointed at a sign with the trading hours written in type large enough even for an idiot to be able to read. Joblard waved the pawn ticket. Held up the scarecrow's roll of tenners. Smiled. The Sikh looked unhappy. Muttered something. Joblard made a pleading face. The Sikh relented. Came to the door. Squinted through the glass at the scarecrow's ticket. Did the arithmetic on the roll of tenners. Stalked back behind the counter and rummaged.

Joblard waited, keeping one eye on where the BSA was parked. A couple of clubbers had decided to start an argument. Out came the bouncers. A bottle got thrown. Then one of the clubbers got thrown. Joblard heard the door of Garvey's Money Shop open on a chain. The Sikh peered through the gap. Beckoned without saying a word. Joblard handed him the ticket and the cash. The Sikh held up two fingers. Joblard found a twenty and handed it over. The Sikh stalked away, returned with a package wrapped in butcher's paper. Sellotaped. Joblard threw the Sikh a questioning look. The Sikh shrugged. *Like fucking charades, this.* He took the parcel and the Sikh made to shut the door. Joblard wedged the toe of his boot in.

"What's the address?"

The Sikh shrugged again. Joblard pulled out another twenty. The Sikh put his hand out. Pocketed the note.

"Dalton's," the Sikh said in perfect BBC English.

"How do I find it?"

The Sikh pointed past Joblard's shoulder.

"Sea."

Joblard turned and heard the door slam behind him. He looked at the package then back in the direction the Sikh had indicated. *See?* What the fuck was that supposed to mean? The clubbers had moved across the street, loitering among the parked cars. The bouncers had withdrawn just inside the club entrance. *Pussy Galore's* was the name on the sign. It sounded like a misnomer. Joblard stuffed the package inside his jacket and kicked the bike into action. One of the clubbers made to launch a bottle at him, just for the heck of it. He was out of there before the glass hit the pavement, aiming for the Pier.

What was in the package looked like an anti-tank grenade. The sort of thing Uncle Hugo might've kept under his bed as a souvenir. Joblard regarded it with a degree of scepticism while he sipped his coffee at the Madeira Coffee stand overlooking Brighton Beach. Though it really wasn't much of a beach. More like a lot of red brick from a demolition site dumped for landfill. He couldn't imagine why anyone would ever want to come down here for a holiday when they could fly to the real Madeira ten quid return. The coffee, at least, could've been worse.

When he asked the girl at the espresso machine where Dalton's was, she pointed behind him, just like the Sikh had.

"Under the wheel."

And there *was* a wheel, too, ferris type thing, right beside the sea. Big, like London's Eye was big. The type of big you don't even see unless you're looking straight at it. It was sitting there not doing anything, gondolas rocking in the breeze. Joblard thought of Orson Welles in that film, something about a cuckoo clock. West of the wheel, the charred pilings of the old Pier stood up from the grey water like the skeleton of a giant sea monster.

Joblard returned the grenade to its wrapping and stuffed it back inside his coat, wondering what he'd find at Dalton's to make the trip worthwhile. It looked like a medium-security remand centre, though he figured it was supposed to be an amusement arcade, shuttered for the season, like everything else along the parade. The Madeira Coffee stand was about the only thing open. A couple of early bird Jap tourists were wandering about with cameras, snapping the seagulls. The sky looked like it couldn't decide whether to piss down or just rain. Out past the waves, some mad bastard in a wetsuit was ploughing with slow determination, arm-over-arm, through the freezing water.

☉ WHITE MAN'S HOLE

30°42'37.72"S
134°34'4.68"E

The sign on the platform said TARCOOLA. Lawson opened her eyes just in time to see it slip away and the same dusty red landscape flicker between telegraph poles. She glanced across the table to where Dix had been sitting. An empty coffee cup. The pot in the middle of the table still half-full. Something like panic began to creep into her. *You idiot*, she thought.

The waiter at his station at the far end of the dining car was regarding the space behind her abstractly. Moustache like a bit of black bootlace glued to his upper hip. Hair greased down. Company tie Windsor-knotted, tucked slightly sideways into a burgundy waistcoat. Great Southern Rail embroidered above the breast pocket. The only thing missing was the gold braid. Lawson approached, more conscious than ever of her appearance.

"Um, excuse me?" she said, trying to sound polite. "Did you see where my friend went?"

The waiter brought his index finger to his chin, as if to think about it. Eyes swivelled to nine o'clock

"I believe," he said, "it was *that* way," pointing past Lawson towards the rear of the train.

She started off, then stopped, groping for her wallet.

"Your friend already paid," the waiter said, expressionless.

Jesus, Dix, what've you done? Lawson rushed to the window, but the town was long gone. On the off-chance Dix was still on board, she tried the next carriage. It was mostly full of locals travelling between stations, backpackers, soldiers on R&R. Further down she found the second class sleeping carriages for the long-haul north, to Alice and Darwin. Compartments with curtains drawn. No sign of Dix. Why would he've left her like that? She continued all the way to the end of the train. There was an engine coupled on the back.

Lawson leant against the connecting door that led nowhere and stared out the window at the diesel. Dusty and red like the land, with black slits for eyes. Nothing behind them. Why she hadn't noticed the scrunched napkin in her left hand before, she couldn't say. It was simply there. It'd been there when she woke up and in her panic she hadn't even registered it. She went to toss it away, but something stopped her. She uncrumpled it. It was half-soaked with sweat from her palm but Dix's handwriting was still legible. *You stand a better chance alone, habibi. Take care. xx Dix.*

Lawson gritted her teeth so as not to scream.

It'd be two hours before the train reached Manguri Siding. Which was a stretch of track out in the desert 40 clicks from Coober Pedy. White man's hole. Where the opals came from. Lawson huddled down by the connecting door, staring at the scuffed linoleum, trying to think. The look in Dix's eyes when she'd told him about Kath. The reality of the situation coming home to him. Had he gotten off the train on her account, thinking he'd draw fire while she made good her escape?

It sounded too much like a bad movie. One of those midnight Chuck Norris double-features they used to play on the box when she was a kid. Maybe they had the same sort of thing in Palestine when Dix was a kid, too. She tried to picture him, eating falafel or whatever, watching dubbed American B-films on a black-market TV. Maybe he didn't need Chuck Norris to fake the moves for him, just the cunning of a tunnel rat who'd grown up smuggling contraband into the Gaza Strip.

But whatever Dix had gotten them into sure as shit wasn't bags of rice or refrigerators. The thing he'd picked up on the Gap's computer had to be worth killing for. The sort of thing they'd hunt you down in helicopters just for knowing about. White man's secrets.

One thing she *was* certain about, the first opportunity, she'd be off that train. Go bush. Vanish.

+ EAST BROADWAY

Then something took hold of him and he was running, adrenaline shutting down the pain. By the time he reached the bottom of the fire escape the snow was coming down so thick he could barely see. The bum in the duffel coat called out from across the street. *Run whiteboy, run!* Footsteps above, on steel rungs. He staggered through the projects out onto Delancey. Traffic. A taxi slammed on the breaks. Squeal of rubber on wet tarmac. Headlights and voices. *Crazy asshole!* He kept running until he couldn't get his breath anymore and his legs went out from under him. Something clattered to the ground. He groped for the gun. Picked himself up. There really was blood on his hands this time. Cop sirens on the Williamsburg exit ramp. He kept moving. South. Spectral in white bathrobe camouflaged against the snow.

East Broadway ran south-west under the blacked-out hulk at the foot of the island. It was like the entire financial district had crash landed, *Planet of the Apes*-like, in a tundra formerly inhabited by Lower Eastside freaks. Osborne blinked through the snow, aware that behind him somewhere others were in pursuit. Signs stood out from darkened store-fronts. Miss Behave's Tattoo Parlour. A billboard advert for a Taishu-Izakay Kenka samurai film. A blue arrow pointing directions to Manhattan Bridge. Bleak snowdrifts spilled from the basketball out onto the street. A twisted bike frame chained to a post stood out from the quagmire like an archaeological artefact. Scorched-out project towers, sheet-plastic fluttering high up where once were windows, might've been the Stonehenge of the ancients of the canyons.

Osborne pushed on. Mounds of bin bags poked up from the snow-bound sidewalk. Huddled figures in cardboard boxes, wedged beneath service entrance overhangs and hydrant bays, watching with slitted yellow eyes. The walls said POST NO BILLS. Up ahead a light was coming from a subway entrance. Emergency generator. Osborne waded down the steps, found a payphone by the turnstiles, fed it some quarters and punched the Doctor's number. He dialled up the volume and heard ring tone. Click. The same voice on the answering machine. He pictured the Doctor's secretary. Bloodless. Brunette. Lacquered fingernails tapping the desk. Bored. The signal beeped.

"What the fuck's happening to me, Suliman, you sonofabitch?"

The phone crackled. He smashed the receiver against the coin slot. A handful of change spilled onto the ground and spun away. Osborne grimaced, let the phone drop, clutching his side. He glanced around to see who was watching. Bored transit cop maybe with an itch in his holster. No such pleasure. Except for the homeless types camped on the platforms, the place was deserted. Somewhere far off perhaps a train blasting its horn, light flickering between uprights, shaking the ground. Ghost trains running on ghost tracks, from the Cloisters to Atlantic Avenue. Like a parallel universe home to rats, wild dogs, alligators and lunatics. Midgets with flapping feet.

Osborne stared down at his hands. Grazed, covered in blood he wasn't sure was his. The image of the monkey with Fatima's severed head flared behind his eyes. Grinning. Smacking its lips. The head in a Mr Chow's noodle box. Fortune cookie wrappers everywhere. *What the fuck's happening to me?*

Then he was running again. Up the stairs, street-side, skidding on wet pavement, colliding with a street sign. He had no idea where he was going. An old Hassid in grey beard with black plastic shopping bag shuffling by in the opposite direction. It was suddenly as if he'd stepped out of a time machine, transported to an entirely different place. Shop fronts stencilled in Hebrew. Mural-covered walls. The Jewish Forward. The House of Sages. Ezras Torah. Adath Israel.

Then *zap!* Dumpling Town. Lucky Bloop Inc. One Long Hing Market. Oriental faces staring at him from the other side of windows. Sidewalk noodle stands. Umbrellas crowding the street, like swimming through a tide of black nylon. Voices in singsong Chinese. The snow coming down thicker and faster, blowing head-on. Hunching into it. Almost a blizzard now. He can't see for the white. Finding his way by pure luck under the shelter of the Manhattan Bridge, a mass of dark steel behind a high wire fence, echoing with sounds of distant seas. The flicker of headlights. Traffic Eastbound. No incoming.

An M22 bus had been abandoned out on the street, snow banked halfway up the door. It acted as a windbreak. An old negro on a busted sofa had taken shelter under the bridge in the lee of the bus beside a trashcan set on a wooden crate. The embers of a fire glowed through rust holes in the trashcan, sending up faint vapours of smoke and steam into the falling snow. The old negro seemed to be playing chess with himself on a tiny plastic board.

Osborne stopped to get his breath and warm his hands. From across the street came the sound of an alarm clock ringing, like an oriental wind-chime. From an apartment window, a drunk swearing at a radio. The negro coughed. The chessboard, Osborne noticed, had only one piece on it, a white pawn, which the old man shifted around the board with apparent aimlessness. The negro looked up, eye-white glinting in the firelight. The irises glazed over. Dead.

"You won't find it," the blind man croaked. "Whatever you're looking for, you'll never find it."

He chuckled, exposing the black stumps of teeth, made hideous by the flames. Osborne backed away, out into the blizzard again, gripping Fatima's bathrobe tight around his neck, the cold and wetness seeping through. Without having noticed, he'd begun to shiver. Coming in spasms now. Head down, struggling to make progress against the wind. The snow coming in a continuous gust, almost horizontal.

At the next intersection, the sign above the button told him to CROSS WITH CARE. The signal flashed red. While somewhere in the back of his mind, he sensed his pursuers closing in.

≈ SNAKE MEAT

The place they arrived at was set back from the street in an alleyway littered with packing crates. In the taxi's headlights, a sliding freight door, corrugated iron, Arabic scrawled across it in broad faded strokes, white on grey. Razor wire topped the walls. Margarita paid the driver and they stepped out into the dark. Nearby someone coughed. Shinwah watched the taillights of the taxi recede along the alley till it turned into the next street down. Margarita's handset flashed. Behind the freight door, locks were being turned. A moment later a crack of light showed at one end and a shape beckoned them through.

Something about the location made Shinwah tense. It wasn't what she'd expected, though she couldn't say what she *had* expected. A travel bureau, maybe, with a clinic hidden in the back with dentist's chair and laughing gas and drill-gun for excavating brain implants. *Kill two birds with one stone.* Or whatever Confucian crap might suit the occasion. Instead they were being led through a loading bay into a maze of whitewashed breezeblock. Echo of a generator thumping nearby. *Which would explain the lights at least,* she thought wryly.

Shinwah had to remind herself that, technically speaking, they were now in the City of the Dead. She'd expected something like Hell, but it was more like a shanty town. Breezeblock gave way to an amalgam of plastic, mudbrick, concrete, scavenged steel. They'd entered a kind of factory. She couldn't imagine what a factory would be doing in the middle of a graveyard. Dead snakes lay in heaps on the floor. Their guide, head swathed in a red and white *keffiyeh*, wended his way between row after row of stretched snake skins hung from the ceiling like ancient strips of celluloid. Everywhere the stench of raw snake meat. She could see it being fed through grinders into white styrofoam boxes. A dozen women moved around the machinery in soiled green surgical masks, gloves, caps, with eyes that never looked up.

Margarita stayed ahead of her, saying nothing. They passed through a low corridor into another room, with tanning vats, the air almost too thick to breathe. A man with blue skin was standing astride one of the vats in a loincloth, stirring the black broth beneath him with a wooden oar. Gas lamps flared along the walls. The figure in the keffiyeh glided through a door hung with strip-plastic and when they followed Shinwah found herself descending a steep narrow staircase, bracing one hand on either wall. Overhead a light flickered behind a grill. The stairs telescoped. The ice playing its tricks again.

By the time they reached the bottom, Shinwah was panting beneath the black veil. Her shoulder ached. The two figures ahead of her blurred then came back into a skewed focus. Her thoughts, even, seemed to've come unwired. She could almost smell de Laurentiis. Like the smell of a snake playing dead. If anything was to happen now, she'd be helpless. Everything depended on Margarita, just as it had since she'd pulled the trigger back on the quay. The chain of cause and effect. Which could be broken, she told herself, before either of them would know.

The stairs ended in front of a steel door. Rust-red. A concrete ceiling hung low overhead. Tiny grey and white stalactites. The man in the keffiyeh stood aside while Margarita typed a code into a lock. The man's eyes were blank. Dark holes above the scarf that obscured the lower half of his face. Something about the skin around his eyes. A wrong déjà vu. The keypad over the lock flashed green, the door clicked open. Margarita pushed through into the darkness beyond. Shinwah followed, the nape of her neck turning suddenly very cold, hands folding into an involuntary clench. The man in the keffiyeh remained exactly where he was as the door swung shut behind them.

☾ RATS

The first thing he notices is the place's full of rats. Thousands of them. White, pink, brown, black. Each in its own glass cage, stacked floor-to-high-ceiling in rows a city block long, sniffing, scratching, hissing, silent behind a vague background hum of fluorescents. Rat canyons towering overhead. Each cage with its own monitor, coloured decals and dials, victual dispensers, as if they belonged to some Tokyo coffin hotel in miniature. At irregular intervals between the stacks, rusty pincers dangle from hydraulic cabling like mechanical luckydips.

To get there, the albino had led him down into a basement full of tannery chemicals in steel drums. A single low-watt bulb hung from a wire overhead. Vague shapes stalked the periphery. A guard, face veiled by red and white *keffiyeh*, leaned against a wall, an old carbine slung over one shoulder. Though what he was guarding it was impossible to say. An elevator cage opened between piles of steel junk.

The albino slammed back the door. *Don't ask questions,* she'd said. And for the time being he hadn't. The elevator whined through further levels of subterranean darkness like déjà vu. Eventually it brought them down to the canyons. The transition vibed weird. Like stepping from a manger into a space station. Out of the elevator a couple of orderlies in green smocks materialised as if out of nowhere, keeping one pace behind...

"What is this place?"

The albino is once again walking in front, leading him through the canyons, the orderlies keeping pace behind. When she speaks, he can't see her face, just the dirty blonde cut of her hair.

"Used to be where the Dome outsourced some of its less technical experiments."

"What experiments?"

"Stuff. Pharmaco. Genotech. Behaviour stuff."

"Is that what the rats are for?"

"Maybe. Slimane calls it the nerve centre. He says the rats know things people don't."

"What stuff?"

"You'll have to ask him. He talks a lot of shit about planes of consciousness. He thinks the rats control the universe. Reason they're so happy to live in cages. Like us."

He wonders if she's laughing at him, or if she's serious. It's the first time the idea's occurred to him, that something might be funny about all this. The orderlies' footsteps dispel any sense of humour from the situation. Reflexively he reaches up and massages around his eye. Residual images flare. The journey. His dream. The Stranger.

"Who's Slimane?"

"You'll see."

"They still do the experiments?"

"That's what you're here for, isn't't?"

He has no opportunity to make sense of what the albino's just said. All of a sudden they're standing in front of a mirrored glass wall in whose reflections the canyons appear to recede indefinitely. If the albino hadn't brought him to a stop he'd've walked straight into it. She punches numbers into a panel and a section of the wall slides open. He follows her through into what immediately appears to be a laboratory. Consoles, wallscreens, centrifuges, test-tube incubators, a vista of white formica. He can sense the presence of the green smocks still behind him. The mechanical wheeze of the door sliding shut.

The albino steps off to one side and he finds himself facing a vivisectionist's slab, a dozen headless rats pinned-out beside a tiny guillotine. A glass vat, wires coiling out of it, sits on the left of the slab with rat heads suspended in formalin. *Death to rats...*

"When the skulls soften," a voice says, more machine than human, "it's a simple matter of popping out the brains, which can then be examined for mutations."

The synthed voice comes from the other side of the slab, from behind a mesh of technical apparatuses. Retort stands with tubes and flasks, beakers of dry ice, the inner organs of vivisected rodents suspended in jars. It's then he becomes aware of the slides laid out beside an oversized microscope, each garnished with a fine sliver of something reminiscent of bonsaied cauliflower.

"In certain parts of the world," the voice rasps, "the brain of the common rat is considered something of a delicacy. Would you care to sample one?"

"Spare us your fucking humour, Slimane," the albino says, fingering a switch on the vat. Bubbles rise. The rat heads begin to tumble about.

"Those are delicate, my dear," the voice says. "Would you kindly refrain from doing that?"

The albino flicks the switch back. Heads bob, drift down, settle into a slow oscillation. Forlorn rat eyes seeming to swivel about, fix him with their dead stare. He turns to the man sitting on the other side of the slab, propped in some antique piece of ergonomics that turns out to be a wheelchair, arms crossed over de rigueur labcoat with a mechanical tracheo-implant above his collar.

"Welcome to Necropolis…"

"Momo," he says, not sure why.

"I'm sorry?" the scientist looks at him amused.

"Where's Momo?" he turns to the albino, his recent guide through the labyrinth, who's leaning now with her back against a glass cabinet, reshaping the cuticle around her fingernails.

"Didn't she tell you?"

This time the voice comes from behind him. He half turns. A very short man shuffles between the two attendants in smocks. Their mask-like faces are identical. They could be twins. Clones.

He recognises the very short man as he shuffles around to the far side of the vivisectionist's slab to where the scientist, the one called Slimane, sits quietly grinning to himself. A sudden recollection of a room and a syringe. The very short man is still wearing the same grubby raincoat, three-day growth and teeth that look like they've never been cleaned.

"The Connection," he glances back at the albino, who's attention remains focused on her fingernails. "She said there was no Connection. Only ghosts…"

"Sadly, yes." The mechanical voice makes disappointed sounds. "In a manner of speaking."

The scientist gives him a disappointed look. Shorty, too, assumes an air of disappointment.

"I told him what he needs to know," the albino hisses.

"You did a commendable job, my dear," the scientist smiling benevolently at him, at the albino, at his audience in general, "bringing him here alive."

Despite the implant, the scientist appears in no way discomforted by the demands of speech. Quite the contrary. There's the sense that talking gives him distinct pleasure.

"Why don't we just get on with it?" says the very short man, one rat-like eye swivelling in its socket.

"Doesn't our friend deserve an explanation before we begin?" rasps Slimane.

"Maybe," shorty huffs.

Then he does something strange. He turns and climbs up onto the scientist's knee, arranging himself there like a ventriloquist's dummy. That face. He can hear the attendants behind him turn and shuffle away. The sliding doors open and close. Silence. From across the vivisection's slab, Slimane and the very short man are both grinning at him now.

"Well?" says the albino, arms crossed, leaning with her hip against the slab. "Out with it," giving the one called Slimane a withering stare. "I'm curious to hear this myself."

"All in good time," the scientist chuckles.

The smell of formalin is starting to burn his sinuses. Rat brains bobbing in delayed action. He shakes his head. *Human meat? Rats in vats? What the fuck is this?*

"You've been down here with rats so long, Slimane, you're becoming just like them."

"How do you mean, my dear?"

"You know exactly what I mean. Besides, where the fuck *is* Momo? He was supposed to *be* here."

"Tut-tut. Now really, my dear..." The scientist pats the very short man on the head. "Shall we tell her?"

Shorty's grin spreads a little wider. Slimane drops his left hand and does something to the back of shorty's raincoat. Then the hand disappears inside the body. The scientist works his entire forearm in, up to the elbow. The very short man does nothing but sit there and grin. The albino taps her fingernails on the edge of the slab impatiently. Slimane is staring hard at her. Something not right here.

"Time for you to go back in your box..."

Then all of a sudden the albino stiffens, edging back from the slab, fear or disgust written on her face. While the mannequin on Slimane's knee starts laughing, flapping its jaw, bouncing, its eyes gone blank.

"Sonofabitch!" the albino says, very quietly.

So quietly he can barely hear it over the laughter. And then he sees the barrel of the gun protruding from shorty's mouth. Laughter becoming a fizzing sound. And then...

☐ AWOL

Dalton's Bastion was like a sideshow at a circus that'd set up in a concrete blockhouse half-a-mile long with a giant ferris wheel stuck in the middle of it. A scaled-up version of Canvey. From the top of the wheel, there would've been a really priceless view of the approaching weather. Joblard shivered in his jacket. Brighton, he figured, was one of the reasons they built the British Empire. Kingston. Sydney. Jo-burg. Places where sunshine was known to exist. And beaches where the name wasn't just some smart-aleck euphemism. What it must've been like back in Roman days, drawing a short straw to be sent over here. He could just imagine some poor African bastard standing right where he was now, shivering in his lace-ups, a faint bronchial wheeze and soon-to-be crippling nostalgia for the sands of Tobruk. Despairing at the unbroken vista of grey they called Britannia and wondering what he'd ever done to deserve such punishment.

Joblard gave Bludhorn another call, to let him know he might be late for the scheduled ten o'clock at the Red Lion caff. It wasn't nine yet, but he had a feeling. And it was about time, he decided, that Bludhorn came clean about the geezer in the photo. And what the fuck was it the man had with little people anyway? Joblard was never able to fathom what anyone found kinky about midgets and stuff. But then, Joblard was sensitive when it came to size. And if he was obliged to go in and buttonhole anyone under four foot, he wanted to be satisfied it was for the right reasons. Besides, no-one had tried to blow his head off. So far as he knew. And there was still that business about the rug.

But Bludhorn wasn't picking up. Funny. He tried Nicky Cohn. Nicky's answering machine wasn't quite awake. It yawned. Suggested in a combination of quaint Anglo-Saxon that Joblard should go and perform unmentionable acts upon himself and not call back. He persisted.

"Do me a favour, Nicky?"

"Bugger off!"

"Ask around if anyone's seen the Undertaker since yesterday afternoon. Still no word. He's got those pictures. It's the only connection."

"For cough, chum."

"Come on, Nicky. You're in this up to your neck already."

"Bastard."

"What if he's next?"

"Good bloody riddance."

"Thought you wanted the story, Nicky?"

"Blackmail never pays, chum."

"Want to know what I found?"

"Where?"

"A pawn shop. In Brighton."

"Go on."

"You'll do me that favour I mentioned?"

"God, why'd I ever get involved in this?"

"Nicky?"

"Yes, I'll find out if the dirty old bastard hasn't died in his sleep. Or having his arse ridden off by one of his pet monkeys. So what gives?"

"Looks like a tank grenade. Antique. I reckon our mate the stiff was part of some racket. And I reckon that's what the punter in the photo must've been into as well. Bludhorn was on about antiques just the other day. That Soane character, turned his gaff into a museum? Bludhorn wanted to go over and shoot some film."

"John Soane?"

"Yeah, him. Maybe there's a link. Know anything about antiques?"

"No. But someone knocked over the British Museum last night, while we were busy dumping corpses."

"Only one corpse, Nicky."

"I've only just got back from the Commissioner's briefing. Haven't had a wink, you realise, in two days."

"What'd they get?"

"Eh?"

"From the Museum."

"That's the funny bit. Only thing they found missing's a one-inch figurine. Old Kingdom something-or-other. The Black Osiris it's called."

"Black virus? You mean, apartheid anthrax stuff? What's that got to do with the British Museum?"

"O-si-ris. Ancient Egypt. God of something. Had a thing for his sister. Cause of which, got his balls cut off in a blood feud. Sister had to sew 'em back on again. Something like that."

"Black sheep of the family, was he?"

"They're kicking up a right royal stink about it. Hard to believe, but the little chap's supposed to be the main attraction in a big exhibit due to open tomorrow. Egypt gallery. Which is where the break-in happened, incidentally. One of the upper windows. They reckon whoever it was got disturbed in the act."

"Coitus interruptus, eh? Well, you didn't exactly miss much then, did you?"

"You're all heart. By the way…"

"What?"

"Seems the curator's gone AWOL."

"Curator?"

"At the museum."

"Maybe he got abducted when they nicked the golliwog, ransom note in the mail."

"Went AWOL two nights ago, apparently."

"Did they phone his mum?"

"Had a taste for the birch, apparently."

"You don't say."

"Old Mate at the Yard says apparently his regular slag's gone AWOL too."

"Regular what?"

"Whip lady, ol' chum. Punters've been ringing the agency to complain about her not showing up. Apparently."

"You got a name for me, Nicky?"

"Smyth-Jones. Supposed to have a bent for underage boys, but when he eats leather prefers a woman's touch. Some doxy with pierced tits, calls herself Mistress Doreen. Day job at Barclays. City Branch."

"Apparently?"

"Apparently."

"What comes from all them bonuses, Nicky. Not in the natural order of things. Honest wage for honest work, I always say."

"Too true, ol' chum. World's gone to the dogs."

"Well give me a bell if you hear anything more, eh? Got to see a man about a grenade..."

Joblard rang off, slipped his phone in the side pocket of his Bellstafs.

Over at Dalton's, two men in boiler suits appeared on the roof with sledgehammers, engaged in a brief discussion, then set about taking chunks out of whatever they were standing on. There was a hoarding around one side of the building. Some type of reconstruction in progress. It looked like a shower-block you'd find by a body of water in which sane people might actually choose to swim. Here, it was just the sort of place you'd go to watch the great unwashed bend over to pick up the soap. A rusty sign said there were public baths inside. Adjoining it, across an arcade of peeling whitewash, was the fun fair and the Playful Possum burlesque gallery. PRIZES FOR ALL THE FAMILY! A ratty banner fluttered in the breeze. THOR EQUITIES PRESENTS: FESTIVAL BY THE SEA.

Seeing no-one about, Joblard ducked his head and swung his legs over a turnstile, thinking to poke around the arcade. It opened onto a courtyard. The ferris wheel stood up out of the middle of it creaking in the wind, weirdly foreshortened like a great big oval eye. Four or five trailers were parked around the bottom of it, painted in circus colours. The nearest advertised an old-school freak show, the type Joblard hadn't thought still existed. Equal opportunity and all that. It reminded him of one of those late night TV programmes, like *The A-Team*, only with these weird looking women in underwear instead of George Peppard and Mr T. First you got Lizard Woman. Then the Woman with the Extraordinarily Long Neck. The Woman with Two Heads. Duck-Billed Woman. Snake Woman. And a woman in a frilly cocktail skirt with three legs. JOHN STRONG'S, it said. THE STRANGEST SHOW ON EARTH.

Propped against the side of the trailer, beneath the picture of the Woman with Two Heads, was a mannequin wrapped in bandages like Tutankhamen's mummy. A character in a grey overcoat was kneeling in front of it, winding a length of additional bandage around its torso. Probably the sort of thing they did in a circus during the off-season. Bit of housecleaning. Repairing the props. Laundering the linen for the mummies from the House of Horrors. Joblard had been in the House of Horrors as a kid. The scariest thing about it'd been the girl beside him on the ride, puking bright pink candyfloss in his lap. He could've sworn there were eyes in it. But right now, watching the grey character at work with the bandages, the one thing that struck Joblard as kind of odd was the mannequin didn't have a head.

☉ FLYWIRE

Mid-summer the mercury tipped fifty centigrade in the day and not a stick of shade anywhere. At night, it froze. Unless you were dead, crazy or black, you stayed down a hole. White man's lore. Lawson stood by the tracks watching the train shimmer and slowly melt into the heat-haze. A wall of liquid glass she could almost have reached out and touched, if it wasn't an illusion. The Manguri Siding was nothing but a stretch of doubled track with some busted sleepers piled to one side like a cairn. All around was a desolate expanse of red the sun had leached to a dull taint, like something the blood had been washed out of. The only thing moving was the black speck in the sky.

It was coming from the north. The Gap. Dix had been right. They'd ended up stuck plum in the middle. The last place you'd expect. She could've almost laughed. Except she was sprinting already. Across the scrub. Away from the sun. Telling herself if she could just make it as far as Coober Pedy, they'd never find her down the shafts. If she could get there.

Lawson fixed her eyes on a lump of rock in the distance, standing out of the shimmer. Concentrated on her breathing. Kept her mouth closed, to preserve body water. The sound of the chopper crept up slowly until the beating seemed to be coming from inside her head. She hit hard to keep the fear at bay. The animal panic. Pumping harder. Focusing on the rock.

A vague memory coming out of nowhere, old fella at the Mission back when she was a kid, pointing a stick off into a remote but somehow too proximate distance. *Only thing that'll keep running in a straight line's a white man.* But the old fella never said anything about how to outfox a helicopter. No way to feint, nothing to blend into, the soles of her feet chafing in the RMs.

Just keep moving, she told herself. And barely felt the jolt in her back. The sting. Only the whiteness invading her vision. The rock blurring. Her legs finally going out from under her as she plunged head-first into a black hole that went down and down and down. When she finally hit bottom, it was made of hot vibrating steel. Her throat burned. Something black covered her head. She was lying on her side, blood throbbing in her ears. The gyro's whine. *Nigger bitch*, a voice said. She could hear them around her. Smell them almost. A dog-smell. The people who'd murdered Kath. Dix too, by now. Trying to keep the panic at bay. Wondering why she wasn't dead yet.

Vague memories of running, pain between her shoulder blades, the fall into blackness. Tranquilizer gun, she thought. Sniper in the helicopter. One shot. Like a safari animal. They'd tag her, put her in a game reserve for wealthy Gunyas to hunt, then stuff her in a trophy room collecting dust. Green baize, cigars and port by the fireplace. Shadows in the firelight. The glass-eyed menagerie watching through the gloom. The way in days-of-yore they'd collected Aboriginal heads. Exotic curios of a soon-to-become-extinct race. The missing link. So they'd thought.

But she was still here, she told herself. Meaning something would have to come next. Something they'd do to her to tell them things. So when they killed her, it'd be in the certainty that nothing would ever get out. No loose threads. Just her and Dix and Kath, on a fool's errand. No-one anybody was ever going to miss. And she thought about her mother, the green caravan by the blockhouse, the longnecks, the radio, the flywire. They'd buried her in an unmarked grave, under a tree, so the Mission Man wouldn't find her, sell her body to the labcoats. Somewhere in her mind, a meat truck with gibbets, skeletons with strips of black skin hanging off. Sirens. Blue lights.

Whatever the drug they'd used in the dart was turning her thoughts to nightmares now. A man with a rocket-shaped head was grinning down at her. A Minute-Man nosecone. Tickticktick, he said. Then blew up. Like a fireworks in the sky. Rotors whirring and thrumming. Sweat pouring down her face, in her eyes, soaking the sackcloth against her cheek. Her throat was swollen. There was a raw metallic taste in her mouth, paralyzing her tongue. Like a giant grub in her mouth. A wave of nausea wrenched at her guts and she was heaving into the dark. Gagging. Suffocating in the stench of her own vomit. Before the drug plunged her back into the hole.

And plunged.

And plunged.

+ MANEKINEKO

73°59'48.69"W
73°59'48.69"W

The store window was the only source of light at the foot of the incline before East Broadway changed its name and petered out onto the Brooklyn interchange, like a dark tunnel onto some Cro-Magnon vision of flaring red-eyed bison ploughing through snowdrifts. *Double Happiness* it said over the window in chipped gold. A pair of oriental stick-figures side-by-side, like a two-headed Siamese twin. *Better than one...*

In a window display cabinet, an oversize manekineko waved its paw back and forth, rictis grin, bidding eternal greeting and farewell. Beside it a monitor glowed, flashing CNN sports coverage. Bad news for Little Joe. It was Pittsburgh 4-0 with the final away-game already in the third quarter and not going the Yankees' way. Tomorrow's news looked like calling it a whitewash. Then over to the weather: a blonde in pleated spandex was pointing vaguely at dubbed satellite pics with more cloud-cover than landmass. The inset showed downtown blizzard scenes, abandoned traffic, airport runways snowed in. Like living in science fiction, the entire planet stuck in near-death experience watching the whole spiel on remote with the volume switched off for entertainment.

Osborne found himself thinking about the Blizzard Ball King on 181st street. Where was the old man now? Somewhere like the blind guy huddled under a bridge? Then up came the Zero, a black scar in a white landscape. Something out of a dream only real. All he had to do was get to the end of the street, then onto Chambers and he was almost there. Wondering if the tribes were still gathered or had sought refuge from the snow. The TV flickered. No sign of riot cops, religious nuts, disaster junkies, just the wounded city street grid-plan. A face staring out of the screen with the zero for a

317

mouth, telling him something he couldn't hear. Ghost harmonics echoing up from subway gratings. Then back to the news of the hour. Text stream zapping across the frame at high speed: Lower East Side homicide. Crime scene wreckage. Flash up on the victim: a woman, mid-thirties, brunette. Smiling. Suspect identikit, eyes too far apart, or maybe that's just how he looked objectively and not the way he saw himself. But he wasn't sure anymore exactly how he did see himself.

Osborne watched Fatima's murder on the TV till it rotated to the next news item, a tainted milk scare in Idaho. All he could think was how it wasn't fair, Fatima hadn't deserved that. But how would he ever convince anyone it hadn't happened the way they'd showed it on TV? And suddenly somewhere in the back of his head was Suliman's voice, saying: "Fate's as arbitrary as a name." But what'd that have to do with anything? It wasn't fate that his ex-wife was dead. Flashback to the bloodied mess in the bathroom, the monkey in the kitchen playing with her head. Suliman would know. That it wasn't true. That it wasn't me. But a horrible feeling began to overcome him. What if there was no Suliman? The wrong number he'd dialed. And the Kinezology Institute. But the headline in the Times? No, it was too much. They couldn't just make all that up, then zap it out of existence afterwards. There'd be traces. Clues. Like at a crime scene. Something they would've overlooked. Evidence.

Osborne huddled against the window, eyes screwed shut, trying to remember, detail-by-detail, the precise order of events. For Fay's sake. You've got to figure it out. If not the HOW, at least the WHY. But it was no good, he didn't even know where to begin. All was vague, darkness, with no line this time to lead him through the labyrinth. What'd he done to deserve this? The Doctor. Where the fuck was he? "As a great writer once said, We're all under sentence of death, but with a sort of indefinite reprieve. But some of us discover opportunities to live out that sentence many

318

times over." Suliman had said that, just before handing him the address on Canal Street.

Osborne dug through his pockets, but there was only a piece of scrap paper. *Cedar St.* 10:00. D-for-Doom. Right back where he'd started. Something twitched inside his left eye. A rustling sound in his ears. *Dry leaves.* And there he was, staring back at himself through the window, driver's license mugshot on TV screen. Hair parted, blue Census Bureau uniform. And the dark shape of someone reflected in the glass behind him. A dark shape clutching its head in its hands. Now groping down its side. Hand closing around the butt of something. The deafening report and ringing in his ears as the screen exploded and the head with it. Shattered glass strewn around him on the snow. Wind howling through the black hole of the window. The manekineko waving after him as he dropped the gun and ran.

≈ CYCLIC REDUNDANCY ERROR

The faint popping sound barely registered. Like the sound of ice cracking along the synapses, pressure building in the ears…

And then a light came on. A single desk-lamp over a grey steel office desk. Blotting pad. Typewriter. Ashtray with a thread of smoke trailing up into the glare. A red and gold packet of cigarettes lying to one side. Handgun with silencer. A stark cone of light spilling down the front of the desk and everything else in shadow.

Margarita was lying on the bare concrete floor, a black hole the size of a fist where her left eye should've been. The other, nothing but a sliver of white between the eyelids. The muscles around her mouth were twitching, like a robot with a cyclic redundancy error trying to smile. She was lying with both arms flung out, legs folded beneath her. The slipped veil across her throat made her head appear to float by itself in a glistening pool, separated from the body.

Shinwah tried to connect the gun on the table to the corpse on the floor, but somehow the causality escaped her. This wasn't one of the eventualities she'd anticipated. Her eyes strained to see beyond the cone of light at whoever was on the other side. The fact it was Margarita lying there and not her meant something. What it meant, she'd soon find out. The situation didn't allow for too many variations on that particular theme. She waited for de Laurentiis to say something. He took his time. Drew a cigarette from the pack on the desk. Lit it. Flame cupped behind a hand. Smoke eddying around the lampshade obscuring his face.

Shinwah made a rapid calculation. Barely three metres separated her from the cone of light. Four from the gun. She watched for the telltale glow of the cigarette. De Laurentiis was right-handed and the gun was lying to his right. She guessed he was watching her directly over the top of the lamp, the place most in darkness. Sitting. If she went directly at the light, he'd still be able to see her, but there'd be no clear firing line. If she stayed low. The lampshade would obstruct, he'd have to shift off-centre. It'd be split-second. Perhaps enough. Enough to take him where he didn't expect it…

But right then everything came undone. De Laurentiis's hand closed around the butt of the gun as he stepped around the desk. But it wasn't de Laurentiis. And he hadn't been sitting. The man who motioned at her to move away from the door was barely five feet tall and dressed in black. Flashback to the Millennium Plaza, Prague. Two men, one carrying a briefcase. He looked straight at her long enough for her to know it was him. *The opposition*, she thought. *They followed us.* She'd always wondered what this moment would be like, meeting face-to-face, so to speak.

The dwarf crossed the room quickly then bent down over the corpse, the gun all the while pointed at her. Shinwah watched him remove the pendant from around Margarita's neck. So far the dwarf hadn't said a thing. Pocketing the pendant, he tapped on the door with the end of the silencer. The door opened. The man with the keffiyeh stood there. The dwarf fished something from his coat, tossed it at Shinwah's feet, then went out through the doorway. Bloody footprints trailed behind. At the last possible moment he turned.

"Nothing personal, you understand," he said, in a voice that sounded very much like a child's.

Shinwah watched the dwarf climb the stairs and then the man in the keffiyeh follow. When they were both out of sight she removed the black veil from her face and knelt down to retrieve what was lying on the ground. It was a handset. Hers. She'd been missing it since Trieste. *So how'd it end up here?*

She touched the keypad and the screen glowed, but there was

no signal. She dialled through the sub-menus. The scan of the dead Russian's pendant had been erased. She scrolled to the GPS settings. They were set to transmit, if and when a signal ever came up. How long would it be, she wondered, before someone was sent to bring her in? Or maybe Margarita *had* been right. Maybe the protocols weren't in operation any more and they'd got caught up in something none of them even suspected. But what'd it matter? She'd never know for sure, till it was too late.

☾ POLYHEDRON

The albino's face does something strange. A type of pixellated vagueness turns it into a blur that begins, by increments, to spread outwards into the laboratory.

He glances down at the slab, which has also begun to assume a certain vagueness. The microscope, the slides with sectioned rats' brains. He tries to blink-away the mist in his head. Only it isn't in his head. The formalin jar with rat-heads dissolves into a mosaic of course- and fine-grained pixels. He glances at his hands. They look normal. He glances at the scientist, the one called Slimane. He, too, appears unchanged, minus the laughing dummy. Of which, no sign. The scientist's right hand is doing something strange, poking at thin air.

"You see," Slimane is saying. "I had to be sure you'd come. It seems you're the Connection."

He tries to make sense of Slimane's words, but can't. Like he's walked in on the middle of a joke, and suddenly he's the punchline. Ghost numerics hover for an instant behind his left eye and are as suddenly gone again. He feels extremely hazy. He notes the albino's disappearance with a sense of detachment. As if she'd never been there in the first place. He knows he should be doing something, but the knowledge remains abstract, detached from any action. No inner voice to tell him what to do. A vague sense of panic seeps in as if from the edges of a picture that dissolves faster than he can see it.

He tells himself this shouldn't be happening, but he doesn't know what should. Slimane's hand ceases its weird convulsions and returns to the armrest of his chair. The pixels have gone but the panic remains formless. He feels something has changed but isn't sure what. Something fundamental, behind the appearance of things. As he thinks this, he realises Slimane's machine-voice is addressing him.

"Long, long ago," it's saying, "a Traveller arrived in this city seeking the wisdom of the ancients. The ancients of the ancients. It was believed, in those times, that the secret of absolute knowledge had been hidden here. That the priests of the old religions knew where it was to be found. That the geometry of the place held the key. Have you seen the pyramids at dawn?"

He struggles to find the words.

"What's a pyramid?"

Slimane looks at him from far away and at the same time very close-up, with a practiced, scrutinising look. As if, he thinks, through a microscope.

"A triangular-sided polyhedron," the voice rasps, like dead leaves, "formed by connecting a polygonal base and an apex."

"...?"

"Never mind."

While the scientist has been speaking, the laboratory has transformed. Instead of a wheelchair, the scientist is sitting in a padded leather recliner. Enormous stone columns rise from a stone floor, towering against a metallic-blue sky. Something snickers from behind his shoulder. He turns. A pink-eyed rat is grinning at him from atop of cracked pedestal. He looks down. A rat's tail disappears between the flagstones at his feet. The more he looks, the more he sees. Rats everywhere. Slimane swivels in his chair. Rats scuttle up the length of the columns, perching on high Broken stone columns and rats as far as the eye can see, like a trick with mirrors.

"Rats are highly intelligent creatures. Unlike humans, they're acutely sensitive to fluctuations in the chronosphere. Time-shift idiolects. These fluctuations produce a pattern of lesions in the rat cortex. By analysing the lesions, we can map when and for how long these fluctuations have occurred. Like tree rings. All we need to know is how old the rat is. And some rats are very old indeed..."

The scientist's giving him that look again. He can feel the pain in his head returning. A sound, like static, at the back of his head. Faint green shadows cast inside his eye. He blinks. Glances at the slides, the sectioned bits of rat cortex. Like canapés. He tries to make sense of what Slimane is saying. *Time-travelling rats? Mutant brains?* First the Dome, the eugenics squads, then the tunnels, abandoned subway stations, bunkers with wrecked meme machines, now this. If those things were real, why do they seem so strange? Like something gone wrong. A crashed programme.

The scientist's smirking at him. The smirk spreads across his entire face...

"Now where were we? Ah yes. The wisdom of the ancients. Our Traveller journeyed a great distance to see what he could learn. He arrived in Cairo, feverish and sick, but he pressed on with his mission. By-and-by he was led to the temple of Ammon-Ra, god-of-gods. The temple lay in ruins. But within the innermost sanctuary the Traveller discovered an old blind one-eyed man in rags that were once priest's robes, sitting at the base of a pyramid made of glass spheres. The old priest looked like a bum. And he stank. All skin and bones. Our man asked him why he was sitting there... Are the lights bothering you?"

Out of the flagstones, a mountain of crystal balls rises up between the columns, glittering with light. *A triangular-sided polyhedron.*

But the scientist isn't there any more. The armchair's gone. There's only the glass pyramid. Yet still the voice. It's begun to sound familiar. Like the Stranger. He turns to look over his shoulder, but there's no-one there. Shadow of a rat slinking behind a column. The mirror maze of repeating geometries which, he assumes, are part of some complex optical illusion. An uneasy feeling is coming over him, that from the very start none of it's been real. The bridge. The blood on his shirt. The journey underground. Necropolis. This.

"Get on with it," says a rat perched mid-way up the pyramid, the words floating out of its mouth like a speech bubble. *Still here, baby, don't you worry*, a voice echoes in his heads. He imagines, or thinks he imagines, an albino rat with arms crossed, pink eyes luminous, watching him. Like something from an extra dimension given arbitrary form. A rat. A person. A machine. In this place, the difference might just be in the way you look at things.

Before he can begin to explore this theory, night seems to've fallen. The rat-eyes, unblinking, seem to multiply. Each of them inside a glass sphere, a whole mountain's worth. The spheres themselves begin to glow. And there's Slimane again, white labcoat, corporation logo stitched on right breast pocket, reclining in a black padded armchair.

"I see you're becoming curious?"

Slimane is grinning out at him now from the wall of glass spheres as if from countless synchronised video monitors, eyes pinholing rat-like. Crystal-ball stuff. King Rat. The image jolts, shimmers. Zigzags of static crisscross and swirl about. Then the picture goes out, comes on again. This time the entire pyramid is one giant face.

"That's better. Now, where were we? Oh yes, the priest in the temple. Well, to cut a long story short, the old man in whatever strange language they spoke back then, or by sign language, charades – it really doesn't matter which – communicated to the foreign traveller the meaning of his vigil. At which point the raggedy old bum croaked. Ah! Perhaps, for the sake of our little tale, we'll call him Momo. What do you think? And you, my dear friend. Who are you in this tale? The Traveller, perhaps? Avid for knowledge. Only you don't know what of. Don't know anything at all, really, do you?"

Rats snickering in the dark. Peripheral rat haloes. Slimane's mechanical voice booms.

"And what did Momo the Magician say to our weary traveller before he so unceremoniously turned his toes up?"

The giant face vanishes and now there's just a mountain of glass balls illuminated from above by a shaft of blue light.

"Each sphere of the pyramid, he said, represents a possible future. While the one at the very apex represents the most perfect of all possible futures…"

□ KING TUT'S CURSE

51°31'1.05" N
0°8'5.82"W

"Well if it ain't Ol' Pasty, back from the dead. How'd you manage that, then, eh? Pulled a little switcheroo, did we? Got a whole store of headless stiffs around here, I s'pose, on hand just for the right occasion? Whose corpse you leave on my couch, then? It better not've been anyone I know."

The character in the grey overcoat glared up at Joblard from under the brim of his fedora and snarled. Joblard took a few steps forward, flexing his fingers, then stopped. Ol' Pasty grinned, turned back to his work and took his time tucking the loose end of the bandage somewhere up the mummy's backside, exhibiting all the confidence of someone who knew, really knew, that Joblard wasn't going anywhere.

It was just about then Joblard felt the blunt end of something hard being pushed against his back. The voice behind him said the usual thing people say in such circumstances, about not moving etc., and Joblard decided it'd probably be a good idea for the time being to do just that. That's when he saw the dwarf holding a sawn-off shotgun half his size come around in front of him. Joblard looked at the dwarf with open curiosity. The dwarf gestured with the shotgun and Joblard raised his hands. Funny, but he had a feeling this wasn't the same dwarf as the one in the smartcar. This one looked older somehow. Or maybe it was the face. The fact he could see the bottom half as well as the top. But then a second dwarf stepped around from his left, also pointing a sawn-off. They were both wearing yellow plastic raincoats and blue suede two-inch crepe soled shoes, like they were planning to knock-over a retail outlet on King's Road.

"Well fuck me," Joblard said. "If you ain't twins, I'm a monkey's uncle."

The two dwarfs said nothing. When he'd finished with the bandage, Ol' Pasty came over and stood between them, grinning still. Joblard tried to figure what was so damned funny.

"You're not bloody Polish as well, are you?"

"Polish?" the dwarf on the left said. "That supposed to be a fucking joke?"

"*We* come all the way from Manchester, shithead," chimed in the twin. "Which fucking planet did *you* come from?"

"Hey, don't take it personally. I'm sure they have midgets in Poland, too."

"Who you calling a midget, cuntface?"

Dwarf number one pointed his sawn-off at Joblard's knees.

"Try saying that with your fucking legs chopped off."

"Gentlemen, *gentlemen*," Ol' Pasty interrupted. "I do believe we have here an associate of Mr Undertaker."

That worked a charm. Dwarf two jabbed his shotgun at Joblard's bollocks.

"Lucky for you, bright boy. Next time, you'll be singing soprano."

Bludhorn was sitting at a fold-down table in a trailer behind the ferris. This one was painted with desert scenery, pyramids, the Great Sphinx. The sign above the door said BEWARE TUTANKHAMEN'S CURSE! Bludhorn barely glanced up when Joblard came ducking under it. He was busy with a jeweller's loup, closely inspecting a tiny black figurine. Behind him, propped upright inside a pair of those Egyptian sarcophagus things were two more mummies, likewise headless. It gave Joblard a nasty feeling. King Tut, as far as he could remember, was never decapitated, unless they'd kept the fact secret from the public all these years. Like in those forensic cop TV programmes, withholding some key bit of evidence from the press to sort the fake confession artists from the psycho killer with a pedant's eye to detail and a lust for the limelight. Joblard doubted it. Whoever snuffed King Tut did it a long time ago.

But then, it was always possible someone had nicked it, the head, slipped it in a complimentary tote-bag while the corpse was lying in one of those museum display cases. Just kind of screwed it off while the guard was out on a fag break, bandages and all. Maybe couldn't tell his Tut from his elbow, so hedged his bets and lopped every mummy he could get his hands on before the proverbial window of opportunity came clattering shut. Which would've meant three tote bags. Getting on the conspicuous side. Especially, come to think of it, if it was dwarves with tote bags. What'd they do, disguise themselves as a junior football team on their way to a kick-around at Bethnal Green, just happened to stop in for a bit of culture? But Nicky Cohn hadn't said anything about stolen heads at the British Museum. Let alone exploding ones.

Ol' Pasty pushed past him and plonked a bundle of sellotape and butcher's paper on the table. Something inside the bundle made a loud thunk. It was the anti-tank grenade from Garvey's Money Shop.

"He had this on him," Ol' Pasty said.

Bludhorn sighed, unscrewed the loup and folded it inside a jeweller's cloth which he slipped in his coat pocket. The figurine seemed to've vanished into thin air. A magician's sleight of hand.

"Well, my son, couldn't it've waited till breakfast?"

Joblard yawned, fanned his mouth.

"Seeing as I was in the neighbourhood."

Behind him, one of the dwarf's snorted. Bludhorn waved Ol' Pasty out of the trailer. Joblard heard the door slam shut, figuring it was okay to put his hands down now.

"Take a seat," Bludhorn indicated a wooden chest by the door. Joblard sat. "What's this then?" pointing at the bundle.

"Anti-tank grenade."

Bludhorn peered at the bundle with increased curiosity.

"Not your usual modus operandi, my son."

"I got it from a pawn shop up the road. In return for a ticket I found in the pocket of a stiff that just happened to turn up on my couch with its head blown off. Funny thing about that, is the stiff was the spitting image of your mate Ol' Pasty out there."

"Old who?"

"Felt hat. Complexion issues."

"Ronald."

"Ronald?"

"The caretaker. I have a majority stake in the arcade."

"You run a circus act as well?"

"Pays to diversify," Bludhorn said, extracting the grenade from its wrapping. "My, my."

"You got a majority stake in a headless mummy business, too, by any chance?"

Bludhorn turned the grenade over, inspecting it from the other side, then placed it carefully back down on top of the butcher's paper.

"Unfortunate, that." Bludhorn sighed. "There've been some developments. I've been *contacted*. Certain *demands* have been made. *Threats*. I need your help."

"If I recall correctly, yesterday you wanted me to find a dwarf."

"Dwarf, yes."

"Don't you have enough of them already?"

"This may seem funny to you, my son, but believe me it isn't. The, err, individual I asked you to find is extremely dangerous. As has already been demonstrated."

"Did you know Johnny Fluoride turned up with his head missing last night? East Ham Mortuary, in case you're inclined to pay him a visit. Quite a body-count your dwarf's been tallying up. What I want to know, is why Ol' Ronnie was waiting at my flat last night with a .45."

"Ronald was here last night. That was probably Alfred.

331

Ronald's half-brother."

"You're sure about that?"

"Sadly, Alfred seems to've fallen in with a rather unsavoury character who's currently involved in an effort to blackmail me."

"Not any more he isn't."

"Oh?"

"Like I said. Someone blew his head off. On my couch. Your Alfie's presently residing at the bottom of the canal by Tequila Wharf."

"Blew his head off, eh?"

"Just like in Johnny Fluoride's pics. Only they did it while I was asleep in the same room. Or else his head just went splat all by itself. Which do you reckon it was?"

It bothered Joblard, how they'd gotten into his place, done the scarecrow with a bazooka, or so it looked like, and he never heard a thing.

"Very mysterious. And the receipt for this, you say, was in Alfred's possession when he died?" Bludhorn ogled the grenade. "You sure this's safe?"

"Well," Joblard leant forward with his elbows on his knees, "you could always take a peek inside and see."

"Mmm."

"Listen Bludhorn, someone pulled a stunt at the British Museum last night. What'd be the odds you know something about that?"

Bludhorn raised his eyebrows.

"Do go on."

"And what'd be the odds that mummy in the box over there is a geezer named Smyth-Jones? Same geezer Johnny Fluoride caught with his pants down before his head got blown off. Same geezer happens to work at the British Museum. Or did, till two days ago. I suppose the other one's Doreen…?"

"Doreen?"

"The tart with the whip. Which leaves the mummy out on the steps. Anyone I know?"

"Doubtful."

"Why not just dump 'em in the sea?"

Bludhorn shook his head.

"My son, this is a very *delicate* matter, it wouldn't do…"

"Don't tell me. I reckon I've almost got it figured. Nicky Cohn said someone made a grab at the British Museum. Part of some big-note show supposed to open to the public tomorrow. Egyptian stuff. Only they got caught in the act. Or almost. Made off with just some itsy-bitsy statue or something. Except they *didn't*, did they? Because the statue was never there, was it? Old boy in the box had it. Nice coincidence, you keeping a sideline in antiques. Put it up to him, did you? Slip the goods out on the sly and instead of stumping up the cash, you figured on framing the bastard instead. *News of the World* stuff. Only it didn't turn out that way. A couple of rogue circus freaks pulled a swift one and beat you to it. What was the snatch job at the museum for? To cover-up for the missing statue? Is that what you've got there in your pocket? I'm curious. I mean, how'd you get it back?"

"Get it back?"

"From the dwarf."

"Who said he had it in the first place?"

"So why the fuck did you want me to find him?"

"As I might've told you already, I've been contacted. Demands have been issued. Threats implied. The dwarf, one suspects, is simply an intermediary. Emissary of higher powers."

"Higher powers? Don't tell me. I got it all backwards. It was you who walked in on someone else's deal?"

"You know, my son, I've always had great faith in you. You're much smarter than people give you credit for. But right now, this whole business is bigger than the both of us. Far too complicated to be resolved by brute force. Events have not yet begun to clarify.

The situation remains extremely fluid. We're in what some might call the flux. Still, when you get down to it, when all the apples in the cart are counted, it's principles that matter. *Principles*. You know what I always say, business is business. And if you can't trust your partners, who can you trust?"

"That's a wonderful sentiment, Bludhorn. I sympathise. But I still don't see what any of this's got to do with a headless corpse messing up my fucking couch."

"Trust, my son," Bludhorn stabbed his finger emphatically at the grenade. "Trust."

☉ SCHEHERAZADE

Lawson stared at the watch on the man's wrist. She could barely lift her eyes. Just an inch, two inches, from the point of scuffed light directly in front of her. From where she sat. Head tipped forward, torso against the edge of a steel-topped table, hands plasticuffed behind her back. She was vaguely aware of the man scrutinising her. The way a camera scrutinises you. Objectively. Mechanically. She could just make out the edges of a ring-binder, pushed to the side. Perhaps he was waiting for her to look up. Or not.

Her eyelids drooped. She blinked. The watch blurred, sharpened again. Stainless steel with a brown leather band. Hands on the dial, radium-green. The type that glow in the dark, like they used to have when she was a kid. Found one once, on the side of a road. Cracked glass, the hands motionless but the mechanism still ticking. Something inside that kept going round even though the parts on the outside were dead. Thinking back to when she'd got Dix's message, driving overnight from Broken Hill, where they used to mine the stuff. Radium. Back before they knew it could kill you.

"Soviet watches," a man's voice, heavily accented, "are the best, most accurate and fastest in the world."

Laughter. Turning to a cough.

"So they say."

The hand with the watch withdrew from Lawson's field of vision. She heard a faint rustle, a match strike. A cloud of tobacco smoke wafted towards her. The hand with the watch came back into view, holding a cigarette.

"A joke. The man who gave this to me was a major in the KGB. That was a long time ago, when politics meant something. Now it's whoever pays. Today Americans, tomorrow, who knows.

Chinese maybe."

The hand withdrew again. More smoke.

"Do you like it?"

The hand reappeared, turned over, then back.

"Thirty years of loyal service and this is all I have to show. And a state pension. In the old days, a man had to be satisfied with little things. For example, we might come to a little arrangement to make your stay more pleasant. But now, how can I afford for my daughters to get married? And for my wife to have her hair done at Ahmed and Abdou? It's not the steady work it used to be. So, we must rely now on the Americans. Whatever about them on TV, they pay good money. And for you, my gazelle, they have promised to pay very good money. Let me offer you my thanks."

Lawson struggled to raise her head. She pushed back, almost righted herself. Slumped. Pushed again, shoulders stiff, arching to accommodate her hands. The man sitting opposite seemed pleased. He reminded her faintly of Dix. The same complexion, the same shaped mouth, same coloured eyes. His eyes smiled at her.

"Also, it will be my first time," he said, with obvious gratification, "with an American woman."

"I'm not a fucking American." Lawson's throat was so dry her voice barely sounded at all in the closed confines of the room. More a cubicle, as far as she could see. Her, the desk, and the man grinning at her. "And you touch me, I'll kill you."

"Yes, yes, yes. Very good. Very spirited. A wild gazelle. I am truly blessed. Perhaps, afterwards, who knows. I have only one wife. A man, as he grows older, seeks the comfort of a woman who can understand him. There are a great many things we will have shared, when it is over…"

On the side of the table stood a jug of water and two glasses. Lawson's eyes fixed on it though she tried to avert them, to focus on the man's stupid watch instead, or the packet of *Cleopatra* cigarettes. Already he knew he had her.

"You would like a drink?" Voice all milk and honey. "You have very blue eyes."

The jug blurred and the room blurred with it. She could hear the man with the watch speaking, but not what he was saying. She blinked and the room collapsed. It was gone, just like that. A mirage. The hot desert dissolving into sky. If only she could move. A jug of water hovering just out of reach. Ice clinking against the glass. Her arm, hand, fingers. And something like a scorpion scuttling across the sand, coming towards her. If only... The scorpion getting closer. Grinning, she thought, with Dix's face. Coming up her arm, tail arched above its head. *What blue eyes you have.* No, not Dix, the man with the watch. Tickticktick. Then a stinging in the crook of her arm. Her chest thumped so hard she gasped, eyes wide, unseeing...

The room she was lying in was a different room from the one before. A light shone directly from above. She couldn't move her arms. Tongue sticking in her throat, mouth gummed up. Voices in a language she couldn't understand. *Agnabi!* Then everything was suddenly cold and wet and black. Gulping, unable to breathe. Lungs heaving. Retching. A breath of air. But almost straightaway she was under again, gulping for the surface, knowing this wasn't a dream now, that it was something else, that she had to stay alive. The sound of a watch ticking close to her ear. Counting the seconds, focusing on that. Struggling to keep track of time as once more the darkness closed in.

She woke in a cell the size of a kennel, her body a knot of pain. The cell pressed in around her in the blackness. She lay there, the starkness of her body and the vagueness of her mind. The drowning. The fire and ice. The pain inside from where they'd burned her with electrified steel. The smell of her own flesh cooking. Shit and vomit. Too exhausted to sleep. Wanting only for it to end. And all the while the sound of that watch. Ticking. Like a kind of mockery. And the implacable silence of her tormentor.

She'd expected questions. But after that first interview no-one had said a word to her she'd understood. First, she tried to reason, they break you, and after they break you the questions come. But it'd gone on, with no sign of ending. The fear had given way to fatigue, ritualised into something graspable, with a shape of its own, that if only she kept focused in her mind she knew she could survive. Though it never seemed like that when the real pain kicked in. Just the opposite. If somewhere inside the pain there existed a type of serenity, she never found it. Only ever greater degrees of desperation, despair, resignation. At times she thought of Dix, but the thoughts were always incoherent. Accusation vied with supplication, terror, hope, even love.

"Do you know the story of Scheherazade?" her interrogator finally asked.

The voice of the man with the watch. She must've been dreaming it. Thinking of Dix, the Sinai tunnels, escape. But the voice didn't go away. She was sitting in a chair, she realised. Tied. Blindfolded. She could smell the residue of her own fear. Some type of tunic they'd put over her, sodden, clinging to her in the erratic draft. Lawson pictured the cubicle with the desk. The man smiling at her. A ceiling fan chopping up the atmosphere.

"There was a Sultan, once upon a time," the voice returned. "Who believed all women were unfaithful. So he decreed that every evening he'd take a new bride, and in the morning strangle her. The dead, at least, cannot submit to temptation."

Lawson felt her stomach turn, but mindful of the gag in her mouth stifled the urge to throw up. The voice went on.

"One day the Sultan proposed to take for his wife the virgin Scheherazade. Scheherazade knew the fate in store for her, but wasn't afraid. As the fatal hour approached she began to tell an intriguing story, but broke off as soon as it became dawn. The Sultan, enthralled, issued a temporary reprieve. Until the next night, when again he became captivated by the girl's story, but was once more denied the gratification of an ending. He issued yet another reprieve. And then another. After one-thousand-and-one-nights, the Sultan rescinded his original decree and became Scheherazade's slave for life."

+ BRODIE

The bridge towers stood out against the slanting snow. Faint constellations of ferry lights flickered below. The intermittent outbound traffic. Wind thrumming the suspension cables. Osborne climbed the barricade onto the entrance ramp, teeth gritted, weaving between snowdrifts. The inbound lanes were deserted. He found the railing, hauled himself blind into the wind, stopping from time to time to catch his breath. Behind him, the city faded into silhouette, like an old cut-out in a snow globe.

He wondered when his pursuers would catch up with him. It couldn't be long now. He pushed on, under the stone arch made invisible against the gloom, the blacked-out cables making weird evanescent geometries. The East River cut a dark swathe between grey massifs. Grey on grey. Then south, past the islands, out into the big expanse. Go for a Brodie and float off out into the grey Atlantic waters. Grey being the general condition of all things now. Like static closing in.

Leaning against the guard rail, heaving for breath, unable to go on. Osborne, face in hands, strangled a howl of desperation. There was nowhere left to run, he'd never make it to the other side. His body ached. His mind ached. He let his hands slip from his face and gripped the cold rail. It felt more real to his touch than anything had ever felt before. Straightaway he felt a numbness begin to creep into his hands and resisted it. *How do you wake*, he thought, *from a dream in which you're already awake?*

Something was taking hold of him, something more powerful than fear. His grip tightened. His hands, he could see, were covered in blood. The wind blew his bathrobe open. There was blood all down the front of his shirt. *Jesus, Fay. I'm sorry. I'm so sorry.* He braced himself, struggling against a nausea that was rising within him. Stared down at the water. If he faltered now, they'd have him, whoever they were. It was essential to keep focused, try not to think. Think and he'd go mad. He was already mad. At least, this way, whatever they had in mind for him... Whatever he had inside his head for them...

Better off this way, he thought.

It was as if, after all this time, he'd finally received his mission. And he knew exactly what to do. Hauling himself up on the guard rail, balanced against the overhead girders. Down below, the faint navigation lights on the river, blinking in the snow. And it seemed there was something out there, hidden behind the grey veil of the water, of the sky, of the city's hulk on either side. Something operating all of this. It was the same feeling he'd had back in the loft on Canal Street, at the moment the darkness reached out towards him. The vertigo of déjà vu.

For a long while he stood there, unable to move. A sound like a clock ticking through the sound of the outbound traffic in the far lanes, on the opposite side of the bridge, behind him, infinitely far away. Then it passed. Bracing himself against the wind, he stripped off the bathrobe. Hurled it over the railing. It fluttered in the air like a Halloween ghost before wrapping itself around a girder. The whole bridge rocked beneath him.

Then a voice in his ear.

"You want a good breeze behind you, Jack, when you jump off a bridge. Sucker tried jumping into the wind off George Washington last weekend. Got blown back onto the lower deck, run flat over by a meat truck. Trailer load of hogs from North Carolina. Had to scrape the son-of-a-bitch off the tarmac with snow shovels. Besides, you jump from here, it's fifty-fifty you'll just make a mess on the FDR. Spare a thought for the poor motherfuckers have to clean you up. Now if you were to jump a hundred yards thataway, it's a surer bet you'd hit water."

At first thought, an hallucination. Then Osborne saw him, the pockmarked face from the subway. He was crouching against a pylon wearing a dark raincoat, collar pulled up around his ears. A pair of yellow eyes regarded him with a vague look of amusement.

"You didn't think we were going to abandon you, did you Jack?"

In the corner of his eye Osborne caught a movement. He turned his head. A black van drifted out of the sleet. Black tinted windows. He wondered what Little Joe'd make of all this, picking his nose behind the counter, wise to the world. Or how different everything would've turned out if he'd ordered the breakfast special instead. Two eggs over-easy. Everything on the side. No piña colada. No Doctor Doom. Shit.

"I hope you haven't forgotten about our little conversation, Jack? The people upstairs have been waiting for a progress report. Personally, I think they might've overestimated you."

Osborne glanced back at the crouched figure now busy lighting a cigarette, gloved hand cupping the flame. Smoke gusted. Something about the glowing ember made him sad. Like a falling star. And if right now he had a wish, what'd it be?

Pockmarked face stood up, stomped his feet.

"Well, it's been nice talking, Jack. But it seems your time's up. Had your chance. Like they say in the movies, *game over*."

Osborne stared down at the white ghost of Fatima's bathrobe flapping from the steel girder twenty feet down. It was like that thing in nightmares, always just out of reach. The unobtainable object. He pictured himself leaping into the void, only to rebound, the air elastic, like gelatine.

"Time," a voice said, "to re-set to zero."

But what if there was no opposition? If the whole thing was a frame-up from the start? You got snuffed by your own team to cover the tracks. Expendable. After all, who'd miss an ex-junkie with time at Daxing hanging over their head? But if Margarita had been in on it, where was de Laurentiis? And who the fuck were the dead Russian's associates? The black Audi at the marina in Trieste? Was there a connection? All the *what ifs*. Like trying to tell the difference between a plot and a conspiracy.

She looked down at Margarita's dead body on the floor. The body that'd made love to hers only hours ago. Or had she dreamt that, too? Face still twitching. The smell of ozone, solder, burnt silicon pervading the room, blotting out the stench of snake meat. Shinwah came closer. There was something about Margarita's face. A mesh of wire and fibre optic piercing the hole where the eye used to be. Shinwah blinked, but the image stayed the same. She blinked harder. There had to be something wrong in her brain. *I've been fucking a machine?* The words came to her with the shock of realisation. *I've been... But if... if I'm still there, in that room, with the dead man, the pendant, how can I be here? Or...?*

But there was no point thinking it. There was no point thinking anything.

Shinwah left the corpse where it was and sat down behind the desk. Where the dwarf had left them, a gold pack of cigarettes with red printing. *Shuāngxî. Double Happiness.* They used to make them in Shanghai, back in the old days. Maybe it meant something. Maybe it didn't. *Maybe you need to straighten your head out.* She fished the jeweller's case from her hip pocket and laid out some lines on the grey steel. Hit three before it kicked in, low down, the rush spiralling through a cone of light and then the still

343

point. *And what if you're a machine?* Thinking, chipset in the cortex. Just that much. What she'd always suspected of de Laurentiis, that *he* wasn't human. But what *did* it take, anyhow, *not* to be a machine??

She glanced at the cigarette pack. A gold halo with ideograms floating in it. *Double Happiness.* Like happiness itself wouldn't be enough, you had to always keep doubling the stakes...

Flashback to Beijing. The lab. The first time she'd met de Laurentiis. An old woman wearing a man's pin-stripe suit, who she'd understood was a type of procuress. De Laurentiis had been standing with his back to her, cigarette in hand, the old woman telling him something all the while watching *her* over his shoulder. A face more ancient than a museum sculpture. Voice like dead leaves. *Something about those eyes.* The way they watched her.

Shinwah had immediately known that in some specific way she *belonged* to that old woman. And that now she was being sold-on. Like in the story of *Wu Shi.* The sorceress. From before her memory had been erased. Or almost. Leaving only the fragments of something former. Pictures. Voices. Someone who might've been her mother, telling her folktales, children's stories, in a place underground. Before the rats. Before they took her away. Before the lab.

Something that happened, a long time ago.

A very long time ago...

Senseless at a threshold of forgotten things.

Knowing it, Shinwah sat. And waited.

The scientist's voice was coming from nowhere in particular now, surrounding him in a general resonance. Could what was happening now be the thing he came here for? But what *was* happening now? The rats. *Death to rats.* What'd it mean? And the albino. *Still here baby.* Still *where*? He feels the questions disabling him. He wants to stay focused. The purpose at hand, what he knows of it. Groping inside for some clue to actions yet to be performed. The programme. *Is this a game? A test? Do I kill him? Do I try to escape? Tell me what I'm supposed to be fucking doing.*

"She said the Connection was dead."

The scientist's mechanical voice relayed from a dozen points on all sides of him at once.

"Yes. In a manner of speaking. Like the old man in the story. Dead as a Dodo. Or perhaps I should say, *dead as a Momo.*"

"But..."

"Things that are joined can't necessarily be separated."

"..."

"Each dimension is the horizon of another dimension. Let's say that your Momo is no longer of this dimension. But you are. While you've been searching for him, he's been waiting for you. And now you're here and it's all been to no avail."

The portentous voice stutters into a laughter that peters out as soon as it begins.

"How?"

"Perhaps the Traveller killed him. Perhaps he was just sick and tired of sitting around. Perhaps his purpose in life had already been served and death was the final act, the completion."

The spheres are starting to make him dizzy. Like being in two places at the same time. He looks away. Flashback to the bridge.

Drizzle. A geodesic sky. The Stranger speaking. Telling him something. The Dome... Memory traces in the machine... Brains in vats... *And if the Machine also evolved?* Cannibalising itself. *Intifada.* Unaware the disease was *theirs* and not an error in the system. Like him?

"How'd he die?"

"What does it matter, how a man dies? It's enough that he does. Death's no great accomplishment."

"How?"

Slimane's voice made a mechanical yawning sound.

"Consider the weary Traveller. How will he know if he's reached his destination. At the end, he can't even be sure the destination exists. It seems like such an anticlimax, merely a point in time, a point in space. The true character of his journey's been kept from him. If he ever knew it, it's long been erased from his memory. Like you, he's in search of something, but how will he know when he's found it? Or what it is? A way out, he thinks, but of what? A place? A predicament? A *probability?* Perhaps *he's* the thing he seeks and he's only had to find himself, to connect the missing elements in a puzzle he alone constitutes. To stand at the point where all the maps converge. The hidden pole. As if his journey has been to make a constellation of the coordinates. Provide the missing link. The imaginary thread. One question leads to another. Yet are his questions adequate to what he seeks?"

"Who are you?"

"Not *who*..."

"What then."

"What am I? Or what's happening? For example, right now. To you. What it all means. Why you're here. Your role in this allegory. This *hypothesis.*"

"...?"

"Perhaps we wouldn't be having this conversation if things had turned out differently. If you'd arrived a little sooner. Or a hundred years sooner. Or not at all. If instead of me sitting here, it was your precious Momo. Perhaps you might've been him. Perhaps, though you don't realise it, you've been here already, before, many times. But each time the clock was re-set, the game begun anew."

Something about that voice beginning to sound familiar. He grimaces. The pain in his head's getting worse. Behind his eye a pinprick is gradually opening outwards, radiating an inner light. He blinks, stares into the middle of the pyramid. His own face staring out, the mirror of him, now contorted, now blank.

"Perhaps, all the previous times," the voice drones, "it was you who arrived first, and I who was late. Perhaps you're a messenger and it's been my task to prevent the message you carry inside you from ever being delivered."

That laughter again.

"And now I have. After all this time replaying the same scenes, advancing the frame instant-by-instant. Till now, when the tables have been turned. And for the last time, the game's over. And the only thing left to you is to climb to the top of that pyramid, to discover that none of those futures includes you. That they never did. That you've been – how shall I say – forsaken. That in fact, in the final analysis, you're not even here. Not even dead. That you never even existed."

While Slimane speaks, he sees, or thinks he sees, a hand reach up into the frame and begin clawing at the edges of the scientist's face. Strings of latex and silicon detach themselves, pealing back from a moiré of fractured light. Where his face was, something moves behind the glass. Impossible to tell what. He feels himself being drawn closer, against his will. Inside the pyramid there's something black. A shape warped by the spheres. Hovering. Twisting. A sound like dead leaves...

And then he sees it. As he does, the mocking voice of the scientist echoes in his ears. Not even here. Not even dead... Out of the shadows of the glass, enlarging into close-up, a bruised iris. The hole of a pupil, dilating, vertiginous. Like an eye at the end of a microscope.

He feels himself spiraling into its vortex. And as he spirals it multiplies. Like a cell dividing and multiplying. Like a fly's multicellular eye. In each cell, a figure is falling. The shape of a man, falling backwards into a river. The further he spirals the faster the man falls. Muzzle-flash. Bloodied face. A hole blossoming from the falling man's head like a kaleidoscope rose repeating and repeating.

"Time, my friend," the voice echoes, "was never on your side."

The screen flickers, dissolves to red. And he's suddenly very cold, grasping at the glass spheres as they slip away from him like bubbles of air. The falling man's still there in their reflections. His face all too familiar now…

He gasps, unable to breath. Somewhere in the distance, far above him already, the voice has become an indecipherable reverberation. His body convulses. He's like an unconscious swimmer, struggling to reach a surface he'll never find.

☐ SUPERSIZED

Something about the antique grenade seemed wrong. For example, the way it was beginning to glow. Joblard wondered if it really was a grenade after all or something far worse. Like those Himalayan crystal rock-salt lamps they sold in lifestyle shops.

They'd retreated to a tea room across the strand. *Val's*. Val herself was busy whisking trays of tea and scones between the clutter of unoccupied tables, in anticipation of the nine o'clock rush. So far it hadn't come, but Val bustled about nonetheless while Joblard and Bludhorn settled themselves in an extravagant window seat, with paper flowers and doilies, a British Bulldog sugar bowl and a milk-jug clotted with yesterday's cream.

An incongruous TV set with bunting on its aerial sat propped behind the counter, tuned to the 24-hour news. A lady presenter with a Maggie Thatcher blow-dry was running through the day's essentials, ending with the cricket round-up. England had been forced to follow-on, trailing heavily. The rest was the usual gab about the latest government austerity plan, ministerial expense accounts, tabloid phone hacking. The talking heads rotated. Some earnest-looking ponce in wire-frames spieled the human interest segment, about a couple of chavs left battered and bruised after bungling a hold-up at a Wozzie Burger joint in Bethnal Green. The chavs' barrister alleged grievous assault by angry diners wielding food trays and supersized ketchup bottles. His clients intended to sue the fast-food chain for damages. You could see the barrister's toupee was slipping, it looked like a job for someone handy with a staple-gun. The segment closed on an up-note, with an interview of Bruce Wellie, dressed in pink sunglasses and daggy sheepskin.

Joblard sighed and turned from the tellie to gaze into his hands. The glow from the tank grenade was a faint orange, which might just've been the low-wattage of Val's mood-lighting reflected in the antique metal's oxidised sheen. Or not, as the case may've been. Gingerly he handed the grenade back to Bludhorn who equally gingerly slipped it inside a leather briefcase, where it bulged.

"What if it's radioactive?"

"A bit late to start worrying about that now, my son."

Bludhorn's trilby had slipped forward so the brim was almost touching his nose, casting the upper half of his face in shadow. Only his mouth and jaw were clearly visible.

"There's a bloke at Marble Arch, name of Standish. Ex-Falklands. Logistics man, all that stuff."

Bludhorn slipped Joblard a grubby piece of notepaper with an address pencilled on it.

"You take this over and let him have a pole at it, see what he says."

Bludhorn pushed the briefcase across the table. Joblard stared at the bulge. Slid the briefcase onto the chair beside him, where his helmet lay.

But the grenade inside the briefcase wasn't the only thing to give Joblard pause for thought just at that moment. There was Ol' Pasty's twin, for one. Hadn't been too impressed when Bludhorn and Joblard left the Bastion together without him. He'd had the distinct look, to Joblard's discerning eye, of someone with something weighing on his mind. A brother's murder? Revenge most foul? Blood libel? The buck would have to stop somewhere. *Him or me?* Joblard thought. *Or the rogue dwarf? Or the higher powers? Who'd it be?*

From where he was sitting, Joblard had a prime view of the ferris wheel creaking in the wind. He pictured the movement around the trailers. The gathering posse. Dwarves with sawn-offs. Ol' Pasty's doppelgänger with a pair of .45s stuffed down his trouser-fronts. The whole circus fraternity worming out of the woodwork and armed to the teeth with throwing knives, lion whips, human cannonballs. All ready to ride out at the first smoke signal. *When the shit goes down,* Joblard thought, *it's gonna really go down.* The whole Sergio Leone extravaganza. And of course there'd be the Undertaker, last man standing, hunched over his breakfast at the Red Lion Saloon, twirling the end of his golf club. Another day, another of life's little challenges to overcome.

As for himself, he'd already decided the best move would just be to ride off into the sunrise. Let the freaks take care of themselves, deposit the briefcase in the nearest available recycling bin, point his trusty BSA up the M1 and keep going till the tarmac ran out. He wondered vaguely what Bludhorn had in mind for the dead curator and the whip-lady and the odd-man-out, but he didn't really want to know. You could only get in so deep, he reckoned, before it all got way too far over your head. And that couldn't be a good thing.

Right then Val bustled up to their table with a pot of tea and scones and jam and double cream. Bone china rattled. Cutlery.

"There you go loves. Anything else, just shout."

Joblard watched her bustle back out into the other room, noticing for the first time a heart with a dagger stuck through it tattooed on her left calf, below a hem of floral-print gabardine. The sort of tattoo you made with a needle and ballpoint when you had a two-year stretch of time to kill. Bludhorn busied himself smearing raspberry jam over half a scone, dolloping on the cream. Joblard felt woozie at the sight of yellow ridges of congealed dairy-fat. He gulped unsweetened tea, felt the tannins settle his gut. Poured a second cup and knocked that back too. Bludhorn stuffed the scone in his mouth and chomped. Pavement traffic ambled past the window.

"Mmm," the Undertaker mumbled between bites.

The Adelaide Oval flickered on the TV, playing back through the day's highlights before stumps. The England batsmen going out in a blaze of glory, then ignominiously sent back to the crease to start all over again. Seventy-nine at the follow-on, trailing by three hundred and thirty-three. Bludhorn had savaged another two scones by the time the replays ended. It was all over for England, in more ways than one.

"Ever thought of packing it in, calling it quits?"

"Eh?" Bludhorn wiping clotted cream from his chin.

"You know, head off some place the sun shines once in a while, sip cocktails in the afternoon, forget about the rat race. Bruges maybe."

"Not ready to be pensioned off just yet, my son. In the prime of me bleedin' life, I am. Besides, job's not half done. Never start something, my old dad used to say, that you can't finish. Well, that's life, init? No good upping stumps and buggering off to fecking Bruges 'cause a couple of muppets start losing their heads. Stay focused. Bat out the innings. Not like those fairies," waving his nine iron at the TV. "Bloody disgrace that is."

Joblard couldn't bring himself to disagree.

"*Avdi vide tace.* Know what that means?"

Joblard shook his head, pondering a third cup but deciding against.

"Latin. Masonic Lodge stuff. *Hear, see, be silent.* Words to live by."

"Anything particular you had in mind?"

"I like to keep a clean shop, you know me. None of the messy stuff. I'm gonna find this joker, whoever he is, and put him to bloody rights. Now once you've run by Marble Arch, I want you to meet me on Queen Street at twelve o'clock. Tonight. There's that job I mentioned before. John Soanes. We'll be paying a little visit. In the meantime, let me know what Standish makes of your package there. And Joblard," tapping the side of his nose, "maybe find yourself new digs, eh? Keep your head down for a bit."

"Sure, I'll do that."

Bludhorn tipped the brim of his trilby and went to work with gusto on the rest of the scones. Val would've been pleased.

Outside the day was shaping up. Lighter shades of grey here and there holding out the prospect that it wouldn't rain at least till afternoon. The big wheel looked forlorn down there by the sea.

The girl at the Madeira Coffee stand was absorbed with painting her fingernails, turquoise it looked like. Joblard wiped the salt-spray from the seat of the BSA and figured a visit to the Ace for a grease-and-oil before heading on to destinations unspecified, just to keep the old girl running smooth. He eyeballed the briefcase. Was poised to stow it when he caught sight of Ol' Pasty's brother loitering by the esplanade. It vibed trouble. He tied down the briefcase with a pair of ockey-straps to the pillion seat, got astride, checked the brakes just to be sure. Then kicked her over. The engine's low growl. Stomped her into first. Two-finger salute to Ol' Pasty's doppelgänger as he wheeled out onto the road, heading north-east.

First thing, he thought, he'd call Nicky Cohn, soon as he put some miles between himself and the Undertaker's freakshow act. Give Nicky the low-down on the latest caper. *Hear, see, be silent.* Right. It hadn't even bothered the old queer that a stiff had made a mess on his couch. He thought of Bird Girl. What if she'd come back? Hell. Maybe he'd try calling later in the day. Or leave a message with the cook at the Rajasthani café. His life mightn't have amounted to much, but what it did amount to had just been shitcanned by the mess Bludhorn had got him involved in. Straightening out woolly Greenwich types was one thing, headless corpse disposal was another. And now the bastard expected him to ride across London with a depleted uranium anti-tank grenade, or whatever, for some ex-Falklands nut at Marble Arch to take a gander at. With the half the fucking city on terrorist alert.

The whole thing was giving him a headache. He tried to figure what Bludhorn had in mind for him. That crap about John Soane and some midnight porno guerrilla raid. He could just see it. Dwarves in stocking-masks. Night-porter, kosh to the back of the head. Creeping down into the basement crypt. Lights in the eyes. *Surprise!* Bludhorn in his Director's chair, camera's rolling. Four-foot nymphos grinning. Ol' Pasty's ghost with a sledgehammer ready to tap him between the eyes. A real orgy. Sending him, Joblard, off in a style to which he was unacustomed, in a stone sarcophagus. *Only good secret's a dead one, my son.* Locked rooms no-one would ever enter again. The sheeted furniture of the mind. What'd Nicky Cohn make of that, he wondered?

Too much imagination, his old mum would've said.

☉ STICKMAN

The stickman looked as if chemical bleach had burned away most of the skin below his hairline. He was speaking into a phone, but the way he talked sounded fake. It reminded Lawson of TV. The way her father might've talked, with his Yank accent. Though whenever she tried to picture him, her father, he was always silent, more effigy than man. The story of how they met changed every time Lawson's mum had told it, but what she'd never told was the story about him leaving. As if behind all the retellings, he'd never really been there at all. As if he'd come to her like a voice out of the wireless, while she sat there in her caravan nursing a bottle, watching her own existence bit by bit disappear.

Now the stickman had put down the phone and was saying something to her. He made those TV jaw-flapping sounds, but they didn't mean anything. Yabber yabber. If she concentrated hard enough, she could probably tune the sounds out altogether. She'd lost count of the days, waiting for the questions to begin. Waiting for the madness to begin making some sort of sense. Though by now she knew it never would. It was just what it was. The realisation made her feel strangely whole, as if a destiny had been revealed to her. As long ago it'd been revealed to her mother's people. Her people.

Lawson was sitting with her hands cuffed behind her back, in a chair, facing a steel desk, in a narrow room. There could've been hundreds of identical rooms for all she knew, but she was sure it was the same room she'd been in before. She recognized the scratches on the desktop, where she'd first seen the watch on the man's wrist. The man who reminded her of Dix. Arab, she'd guessed. Egyptian. There'd been clues. The man's cigarettes. *Cleopatra.* A gold packet with red lettering. *Special Filter Tip.*

355

This time, instead of the Egyptian, there were two other men in the room, which would've made it crowded except that the one whose face wasn't deformed was very small. The stickman and his squat little turd of a sidekick. They were both wearing overcoats, like a couple of stooges in a TV rerun. The *Kuinyo and Kudna Show*. Lawson kept them in her peripheral vision, blinking away the sweat that kept stinging her eyes. The clowns seemed immune to the heat.

Dix had told her once about how he'd been arrested as a student in Cairo. They never told him what he was supposed to've done. He'd spent two weeks in an underground cell with thirty others. It'd been mid-summer. The sewer had flooded. A man had died and they'd left him in there on the floor. Then they'd let him out, with no explanation.

"Chaos, *habibi*, is the only explanation you can always rely on."

She thought about the windsock on the airstrip at Maralinga. How they would've taken his office apart, trying to find out what he knew. Finding all that random data. Had they made it mean something? Evidence of a non-existent conspiracy? His last unwitting act of sabotage. *Dix, you crazy bastard...*

Now it was the turd's go. Yabber, yabber, yabber. Then the stickman again. The turd meanwhile began unfolding something from a bag. Like surgical instruments on a square of black cloth. The plastic bit into her wrists. The one without the face was leaning towards her over the desk, teeth barred, trying to force her to meet his eyes. Lawson stared right through him at the whitewashed wall. A fly was crawling up it, following an invisible line it kept deviating from and yet always returning to. She tried betting herself which way it'd turn next. Left or right. If the odds held, the worst that could happen was she'd break even. It was as close as you'd get, under the circumstances, to a sure thing.

+ ATAVISM

The room was just the way he remembered it. Ceiling fan strobing through red light. Like the anteroom of a meat locker. Something cold, hard, pressed against his back. He was lying face-up, staring into the vortex of a spinning fan, trying to remember what he was doing there. He could feel the cold working its way into him, from the extremities, hands and feet, slowly towards the centre.

The fan turned. The strobe flickered.

As time passed, Osborne began to wonder if he was dead. If he'd jumped from the bridge and this was where he'd ended up. Or if the bridge was only a dream and he'd been here all along. And then Doctor Doom appeared. He was suddenly just there, stern-faced, scrutinising Osborne from on-high. And beside the Doctor, the pockmarked visage of the man from the bridge. A pair of sardonic yellow eyes. Suliman brushed away a fly.

"Is your boss satisfied?" said the Doctor.

"For the time being."

"What about the woman, was that entirely necessary?"

"A glitch in the software," the other one said. "It's been fixed now. Won't happen again."

The voices jarred. Osborne struggled to replay them in his head. The Doctor's face came closer. Screwed into one of his eyes was a jeweller's loup. Flashback to the midget in the subway. Canal Street. The lights in the loft. Too real, to've been dreaming. Unless he was dreaming right now.

Fay? What've they done to me...?

But Fatima was dead. It was them. They'd killed her. He knew that now.

Suliman held up a pencil flashlight and something flared behind Osborne's left eye. From the end of a long dark tunnel a grossly dilated pupil blinked at him. He felt himself being stretched, like a taut wire. As if he was standing on the edge of a black-hole. Falling. Or not falling, but *distending* across the event horizon. From a point into infinity. And a sound, like the wind through the suspension cables of a bridge. Or the stressed cables of a freight elevator. Or a mechanical umbilicus...

The blackness of the pupil reached out towards the blackness of Osborne's mind as it closed-in on him. And through the blackness, something falling, turning through space in slow-motion. A bright disk. Growing larger and larger. Like an enormous penny about to drop on him.

The Doctor straightened up, unscrewed the loup from his eye, looked thoughtful. The one with the pockmarked face stuck a toothpick in the corner of his mouth and chewed. The ceiling fan hummed.

"When will it be ready?" asked the Doctor.

"All depends." Pockmarked face extracted the toothpick from his mouth between gloved thumb and index finger. Using the unchewed end, he commenced to scratch above his ear. Adjusted the grey fedora on his head. Inspected both ends of the toothpick, as if weighing something up.

"We're still missing some of the components," he said. "A hold-up with delivery. One or two *unexpected developments* that're being taken care of by our friends abroad."

"I hope so. I've done everything to uphold my end of the bargain."

Pockmarked face grinned.

"You've got nothing to worry about, *Doctor*. No-one's putting the blame on you..."

"Just as long as well all understand each other."

"We all understand."

"I only want what was promised to me."

"No fear, *Doctor*. The Boss never forgets..."

It seemed to Osborne that Suliman shuddered. Something in the other's voice. He wanted to call out, tell the Doctor he was in there, that he could hear them, that he wasn't dead. Warn him, even. But his interior darkness was growing more and more profound. The voices, the faces, more distant. The fan turning above him was far off already. He felt himself sinking. A shrunken effigy of himself pulled down into a cold undersea current. And the invading sound of static, dead leaves...

"Where'd you find him, by the way?"

Suliman straightened his tie, turning his back to the body laid out on the mortician's slab. Pockmarked face grunted, stuck the toothpick in the breast-pocket of his gabardine.

"The usual place. They always go for the bridges, for some reason. Kind of atavism. This one's no different."

He gave the corpse's face a light slap on the cheek.

"Are you, Jack? Eh?"

Osborne lay there, dead-eyed, in cryogenic stasis. An array of electrodes, tubes and wires, trailed onto the floor, where a complicated-looking machine was faintly humming. Suliman's back shivered.

"It's cold in here."

Pockmarked face shrugged.

"Dead don't feel the cold. Dead don't feel anything. Could have its up-side. What d'you think, Doctor? Who gets the better deal, them or us?"

Suliman shook his head and began slouching across the room towards the door. Pockmarked face turned to follow him, laughing softly to himself.

"Maybe next time I'll ask. Hey Jack, which way's best...? Pity he's such a lame duck with the dames. That could've been interesting."

The Doctor stopped at the door, half-turned. Pockmarked face came up beside him, grinned. Then, also turning, looked back at the slab. A fly had settled on Osborne's nose and was slowly making its way up his face.

"Does he know?" Suliman asked.

"Know what?"

"What it's for."

"Tell me," pockmarked face said, turning to the Doctor, "do you know what it's for?"

"Only what I've been told."

"Well, then."

Suliman watched the fly crawl down the side of Osborne's nose onto the corner of his eye. An involuntary reflex caused his own eye to twitch in sympathy. He sniffed. A faint chemical aftertaste in his throat.

"You're sure it'll work?"

Pockmarked face pushed a button beside the door and the door slid soundlessly open. A scent of Alpine air-freshener wafted in, cut through with formaldehyde.

"Who can be sure about anything, *Doctor?*" he said, allowing Suliman to pass. "They should do something about those flies... *So long, Jack.*"

The voices trailed off into static. Time passed. Osborne floated through the blackness. After a while, another voice emerged from the static. A childish singing voice. It sang only one line, without variation or modulation. Osborne couldn't get it out of his head. *The egg that laid the chicken*, it sang. *The egg that laid the chicken...* Over and over again.

And as the voice droned on, Osborne pictured Fatima's monkey poking its face out of the blackness and grinning at him. The way a mirror grins at an idiot.

♒ TIME-LAPSE

The ice was the closest thing to time-shifting she knew. Slamming you into fast-forward. Then freezing the frame. Dustmotes in the air, molecule by molecule, telescoping to sudden deep-focus, mind rastered in the conflux. But however long it lasted, it'd never be long enough. A hundred years compressed into an instant, irretrievably lost, edited-out in the cosmic time-lapse.

Face it, you're never going back. You don't even want to go back. It's just you're afraid. That some essential part of you's been cut off. Not the physical part you thought you'd left behind in that lab, but the other part. Like a vessel in which all the hidden memories are contained, adrift in time. Unreachable now...

Shinwah stared at the pack of cigarettes on the desk. *Double Happiness.* Like a message from a parallel universe. She reached across and turned the gold box between fingers blanched in the glare of the light. On impulse she flipped the box open. Inside the foil was torn. She took a cigarette and put it between her lips. But there was nothing to light it with, so she put it back, lipstick smearing the filter. For lack of anything better to do, she began counting the scratches on the desktop. Anything, not to have to think about Margarita's corpse lying there on the floor. Knowing she'd died because of her. *Not a machine*, she told herself. *Not a machine.*

Perhaps, one day, there'd be no way of telling the difference. The future beyond the one she'd been permitted to see. The one she suspected de Laurentiis belonged to. And beyond that even, from where the old woman came. *Wu Shi.* A future more ancient than anything in the past. More than all the dynasties. More ancient than myth. Forced, it occurred to her, to forever-more watch over their shoulders, like gods afraid the stupidity and greed of mortals would one day undo them, cast them into oblivion. That something as incidental as death in a Prague hotel room, or a Cairo snake factory, might change the entire course of Time. Prefigure untold genocides. Apocalypse. Interstellar migrations of corporate death and greed. MISr.

The desk-lamp flickered. Rewind to the Blackhawk ploughing into the side of the tower, erupting into flame. Fastforward to searchlights flaring across the Dome substructure. Two images cancelling each other out. Was it decreed that she be present to bear witness to them both? What did a circuit concealed in a fake Egyptian pendant have to do with the future of carbon credits and environmental extinction? Or was it Cairo itself that was the key? The way out of the loop? What Margarita had said. Was the *cartouche* real, then? Would she be able to find it on her own? And the doctor? What kind of doctor could untangle Time?

Something stirred out on the stairs. Reflexively Shinwah reached for the lamp to kill the light. But it was only a rat. She watched it come out of the shadows, crossing the threshold into the room. A fat, ugly pink rat, with almost no hair, sniffing around the pool of blood on the floor. The rat stretched its head towards Margarita's face, whiskers erect, rising on its hind legs but unable to reach her.

Shinwah clutched her throat in pain. Seeing not Margarita but someone else, from the past, face eaten away by rats illuminated in the firelight. An underground prison in a half-collapsed subway station. Beijing. She remembered how she'd fallen asleep holding her storybook and when she'd woken they were already eating her dead mother...

The footsteps were so faint she didn't hear them at all. But the rat heard. Sniffing the air, teeth barred. A pair of dark eyes peered around the door. Shinwah stared at them, still clutching her throat. The rat hissed. Wordlessly, Momo stepped out from behind the door. He looked at Margarita, dead, then across at

Shinwah sitting behind the desk, face cut in half by the lampshade's chiaroscuro. The rat trembled. Shinwah looked back at Momo, then down at the rat.

The tableau they formed might've gone on indefinitely, if the handset hadn't suddenly begun to vibrate with a low-frequency chime. The rat shot off into the shadows. The corpse lay still. Shinwah glanced after the rat then back at Momo who'd come forward into the middle of the room. Grey-green anorak done up half-way. A bag slung over one shoulder. His eyes were fixed on her, scrutinising.

The handset chimed again. Shinwah's fingers slid away from her throat. She glanced down at the handset's lit screen, then back.

Momo nodded.

She picked it up.

BREAKFAST AT MIDNIGHT
Louis Armand

"Armand has written a perfect modern noir, presenting Kafka's Prague as a bleak, monochrome singularity of darkness, despair and edgy, dry existentialist hardboil." (Richard Marshall, *3:AM*)

"Armand has done to Prague what Genet achieves in *Our Lady of the Flowers*. *Breakfast at Midnight* is the most savage book I've read in years." (Jim Ruland, *San Diego City Beat*)

"A pinball fever dream, sopping with sweat, booze, and sex, that bathes its confines in an unsettling atmosphere of grime." (Benjamin Woodard, *Rain Taxi*)

"*Breakfast at Midnight* is a wonderfully executed nod to Kafka's special brand of disorienting surrealism." (Michelle Bailat-Jones, *Necessary Fiction*)

"A debauched, hallucinogenic noir... If Georges Simenon had smoked angel dust he might have come up with a style like this." (*Prague Post*)

"When you finish reading this book you want to take a shower for a very long long time." (*Reads by the Beach*)

"The sort of thing Iain Sinclair might write if he'd morphed with Chris Petit..." (Stewart Home, author of *Red London*)

"An impressionistic noir which teeters on the edge of being a thriller... Pitch-perfect." (Robert Kiely, *London Student*)

Kafkaville. Blake is a pornographer who photographs corpses. Ten years ago, a young man becomes a fugitive when a redhead disappears on a bridge in the rain. Now, at the turn of the millennium, another redhead has turned up in the morgue, and the fugitive can't get the dead girl's image out of his head. For Blake, it's all a game — a funhouse where denial is the currency, deceit is the grand prize, and all doors lead to one destination: murder. In the psychological noir-scape of Kafkaville, the rain never stops, and redemption is just another betrayal away...

978-0-9571213-0-0   WWW.EQUUSPRESS.COM

Louis Armand is the author of seven collections of poetry and five novels, most recently *Breakfast at Midnight* (2012), described by *3AM* magazine's Richard Marshall as "a perfect modern noir," and *Canicule* (2013), both from Equus. His screenplay, *Clair Obscur*, received honourable mention at the 2009 Alpe Adria Trieste International Film Festival. He is an editor of *VLAK* magazine and lives in Prague. www.louis-armand.com